Seeds of the Guardian

Seeds of the Guardian

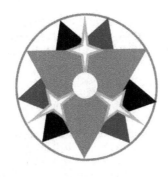

Book 1 of

Heirs to the Taxiarch

Terry Lee Martin

SILVER GOBLET *Press*

SILVER GOBLET *Press*

1251 Briarcliff Ct.
Gallatin, Tennessee, 37066
USA
www.silvergobletpress.com

For Luke

Seeds of the Guardian

Chapter 1—Choices.. 1

Chapter 2—Conspiracy.. 17

Chapter 3—Slave and Sorceress............................. 30

Chapter 4—Curdoz Travels North 40

Chapter 5—Idamé 56

Chapter 6—Twins 73

Chapter 7—Explanations....................................... 91

Chapter 8—Surprises 113

Chapter 9—Leaving Home.....................................125

Chapter 10—Wisdom Exchanged 139

Chapter 11—The Principality of Hesk...................157

Chapter 12—Kodi's Adventures 184

Chapter 13—Secrets Revealed................................208

Chapter 14—Independent Moves............................227

Chapter 15—Royal Greetings, Royal Gifts.............244

Chapter 16—Farewell to Solanto............................263

Chapter 17—Conflict in the South 288

Chapter 18—Battle at Eye-Tower Fifty-Five 307

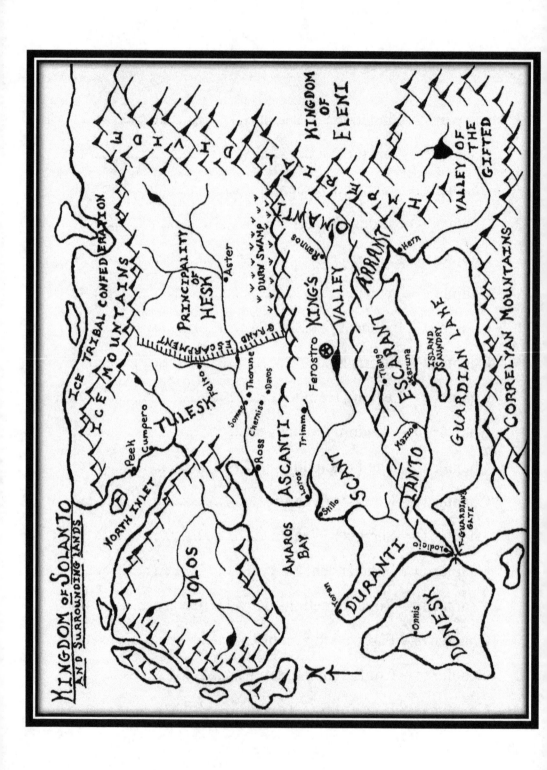

Chapter 1—Choices

Trunks of oaks and evergreens passed him by, dark columns in a golden twilight. Having raced to a split in the path, Kodi paused here as he often did. The trail to the left climbed upward to the old cliff overhang, a once-favored camping spot. Nowadays, he preferred hiking a longer trek and nights with friends atop the Escarpment beyond the river. It was a place of stunning views and sunsets, and a whole lot of Fifty-twos playing, storytelling, and cheap rum. And so he'd abandoned the earlier site he'd used so much as a boy.

It wasn't the only reason he'd given up camping at the old overhang. For Kodi it held the rather acute recollection of an old mistake—one he didn't particularly like revisiting. That was where he led Jonell one memorable morning some three years back.

He had become much more self-disciplined since then.

Yet, recalling the details, he grinned in spite of himself. It began of course when she pounced on him from the hayloft in her father's stables. He'd gone early to saddle his horse for a day of hunting, but Kodi, just fifteen at the time, instead found himself overcome with the thrill offered by the rather forward local beauty. He then rode her out here for a few secret hours of follow-up activity.

With a last look up the hill, he shook his head and prepared to run again. The right-hand path led to his destination. Since that day with Jonell it was the only choice for him. This was the trail leading to a series of swimming holes on the Wolf where he would regularly wash away his troubles. He looked forward to a late evening plunge. Musca was some way ahead, probably already cooling off in the water—that dog loved to swim as much as Kodi.

He looked back, wondering where his friends had got to. Kodi was fast, but had he outpaced them by that much? Maybe Tanksen had convinced them to go back for a barrel and a horse to strap it to, or to acquire a couple rum bottles. Kodi hoped so. He was in the mood for it.

Continuing on the river trail, almost at once the light around him seemed to increase, the muted gold turning to bright silver. A strange feeling stole over him causing him to stop again. He wondered, as there was no sign of bright Solvermoon. It seemed oddly darker above the trees than it was here below. He shivered as a brisk wind blew across his bared torso. Forcing his body to relax to the coolness, he looked more closely at his surroundings and puckered. He discerned now the vestiges of snow drifts anchoring the tree trunks.

It was the tail end of winter, he remembered. It would be a couple more months before the men and boys of Felto reclaimed late evening baths and their occasional ale-drinking fun by the river waters.

Unwittingly his thoughts shifted back.

"Come, Kodi! Let's go back to your hideout."

He had chosen the right-hand path. So why did he hear *her* voice? He turned reluctantly, and now he could see Jonell's nude figure through the trees up the left-hand trail. He wondered she wasn't cold. What perfect round breasts she had. Remembering keenly from long ago their coolness against his hot chest, his body began to respond. His throat went dry and he swallowed.

With firm resolve he squelched it. *"No, Jonell. I admit it was all great fun. And we sure lucked out that day, you know? But I'm not for you. The right man will come along, and I wish for you and him every good thing."*

He watched as clothes appeared, covering her body. She pouted a little, turned and walked away up the path, disappointed…and alone.

"Sorry, Jonell. I really am sorry," he called out.

Kodi could not altogether forget that day, despite how hard he might have tried. He chuckled at the juxtaposition of his thoughts— sorry for his rash immaturity at the time, but not sorry for what he called 'a really useful body lesson.' All things taken into account he was more sorry than not. He knew what pure luck it was there had been no 'consequences.' Yet the good luck wasn't enough; he wished for a clearer separation from that past.

He looked down his chosen path. All else was still, though the rapids were audible at the bottom of the slope. Yet the Wolf River, his favorite haunt in the world, no longer seemed sufficient to ease his cares. He needed to leave Felto. For the first time he now realized that another level of his guilt had been in the way he treated Jonell afterward. He never did say such words to her. Explaining himself was too awkward back then. After that one wild day he ignored her completely—barely spoke another word to her—until eventually, in her confusion, she left him alone. She finally Bonded Esseth about a year ago, a very good man; they had a baby boy now, and lived on a farm two miles west of town. By all accounts they were a happy family.

But there were probably another two dozen young, un-Bonded women who still pursued him (and three or four Bonded who still flirted with him rather outrageously), and none were what Kodi wanted for himself. He knew this piece of his overall angst was not really about Jonell, at least not wholly. Rather, she represented for him the young women in the town. Though he had disciplined himself and been chaste since that day, he feared a reckless mood would take hold and he might give in again soon—turn into some cad, rather like Tanksen or Bluuter. Despite the trouble they caused, Kodi often found himself envying those two lads and the stories they told of their female escapades.

What he really wished for was a shift in focus and new worlds to explore. Kodi was becoming increasingly restless, a capable young man in a state of what was really an imposed sort of confinement.

Thoughts of Jonell and the rest vanished. Anger washed over him—anger at his father who withheld the required Familial Blessing allowing Kodi to leave home freely and make the life changes he so desperately needed. Count Hess had gone yet again on one of his expeditions to the Tolosian Peninsula.

When his father stood suddenly on the trail before him, Kodi spoke first.

"At least take me with you this time, Father. I can hold my own on the journey and help you out. I'm tougher than most of the other men going, and you know it. And I'm a better shot with the bow than anybody."

Infuriatingly, his father laughed. *"What are you going to shoot at, Kodi? Songbirds? The Dragons died out because they ate every game animal on the peninsula and starved."*

"The point is I'm a grown man, Father!"

"Maybe so. But you'll do what I tell you. Your job on the manor work site will start up again in a couple weeks as it gets warmer. It's good work for you, and you're always telling me you like engineering and design. I think you've got a real knack for it. You'll stay here and watch after your mother and Lyndz and your grandfather. You mean the world to your grandfather, you know."

"I know it, but they don't need me. You can hire more servants. You swore to me you'd send me to cousin Amerro to train for a knighthood. You promised years ago. You promise me every

time you come back, and then Amerro asks you to do something for him and you keep changing your mind! I'm nearly nineteen, Father. Most men leave at sixteen or younger. You were fourteen when you left home and started up the old farm and sixteen when you Bonded Mother. Why are you making me stay here?"

For a moment his father did look guilty. But then the look was gone.

"I'm not arguing with you anymore about it. I swear when I come home in the fall, you can go to Amerro then. You must do this for me one last time. One last time, I swear it, Kodi! You know I don't like leaving your mother without good, solid help she can depend on. Besides, you're still young…"

Kodi's anger crossed over into powerful resentment. If it were not for all the other good in his life it would have been very easy for the resentment to turn into hate. But he could never hate his father. Even so, he had sworn to himself the other day if his father returned and put off the Blessing once more, he would leave anyway and disavow his inheritance. He hardly cared anymore what bad luck he might incur by such a decision. He looked into his father's eyes, matching the sternness there with his own. In spite of the chill air he felt steam rise from a hot face.

Then he caught himself. Why was he thinking like this? Why was all this anxiety and cheerlessness taking hold? He didn't feel this way when he went to bed…

"Oh!"

The apparition of his father faded, replaced again by the branches of trees. In his new-found lucidity he breathed, forced his heart to settle and allowed his mind to clear. When he did so, Kodi half imagined he heard a Voice—a whisper on the wind. It was a turning point, and for some reason it helped calm him. For now he was able to cast off his latent guilt, his angst, and his anger.

Sighing deeply, the air felt suddenly warmer. A new third trail appeared, veering off southward down the river valley. He raised an eyebrow. With innate curiosity he strode forward. Yet he had hardly taken three steps when he sensed movement, though he quickly realized the deception. Changes on the otherwise stoic landscape gave the impression of movement. The remaining snow melted away, and a nearby brook began its rushing course towards the Wolf. In a moment, the blue-gray of the nighttime snow drifts was replaced by springtime green, and a light more like the morning supplanted the moonless silver light. He did not know where this new path led, but it felt right. The whisper on the breeze tickled his mind. As he took in the warm air, he felt refreshed.

In the distance, an odd darkness among the trees drew Kodi's eye. As he pondered what it might be, he felt himself lifted above the path, drifting towards it. Unlike most lucid dreams he felt he had very little control over this one.

Except on his own attitude.

"I can face this. Whatever is coming, I'll deal with it."

Upon approach, the darkness turned to gray mist and grew greater, replacing the lofty hemlocks. It moved toward him now at a rapid rate, faster than he knew he could run. Swirls of mist. Suddenly he was engulfed by them and cast upon clouds. The earlier parts of his dream surrounding the stablemaster's daughter and of his father were gone beyond recall.

The forest vanished and the fog withdrew, revealing a somber scene. The agreeable air of the Tulescian Woods was replaced by a brisk hot wind. Upon it he detected an odor—a saltwater breeze off the ocean—a smell he had experienced before when Hess took him once on a short expedition to the port city of Ross on Amaros Bay as part of the family lumber trade. Kodi liked it then, the sight and smell of the sea and the seagulls crying. But this was different, with a hint of decay—rather like dead fish. Yet he only thought on it a moment as sight overcame odor and became the primary sense. The scape became distinct and harsh. His mind wandered to the stories his grandfather Yugan used to read to him when he was a boy—of the ancient Ralsheen Slave Empire with its dark towers and carved reliefs of battle scenes on monumental walls.

Yet this was no storybook tale.

He drifted among stone buildings in a large city, shades stone gray in mute competition. Maybe in the distance beyond the confines of its walls did Kodi glimpse hints of brown and green, cultivated fields perhaps, but it was too limited a palette to suggest a sense of hominess or comfort.

Instead of seagulls, crows swirled like black flies around towers. This dream, Kodi realized, was very different than any he had ever experienced before. He understood that the Gifted had Visions from Meical the Guardian.

Is that what was happening here?

Below him innumerable people prowled the streets and alleyways. Most wore drab clothes, blending almost with the stonework. As his dream body weaved around and about the city, he saw also thousands of men in black wearing steel breastplates and with weapons at their sides. These soldiers were everywhere: at street corners, doorways, on the tops of towers, and on the walls of the city.

"Where in Dumhoni is this place?" Kodi asked himself. *"Or is it some awful time in the past?"*

Since boyhood Kodi loved hearing old stories, but the emotions attached to the telling were very different than actually being in the story itself. That was what he was feeling now. Some of his angst had returned. He was part of a story, a story bigger than he, yet, with great significance, including him. And it was 'now'. It was not the past.

On a stony height—Kodi could even sense directions and somehow knew this standout was 'northward' of the city—stood a tall, forbidding fortress of the same colorless stone he had seen in the city itself. It raised itself high in an iron-gray sky to overlook the nearby city and the vast lands about. He turned in the direction of the tainted wind and in the distance saw what he knew to be the sea, pale gray, reflecting the sky, not at all like the brilliant blues and greens off Amaros Bay. He knew he was very far from his home in Solanto. To the south of the old kingdom of Lintiri, he knew there existed a Southern Continent, lands beyond the old Anterianhi Empire.

His gaze was drawn to the fortress. It was not a happy place, not like the inserted wood-cut art in books he had seen of the proud castle of the kings in Ferostro, for here the crenellations on the battlements and towers were not in the typical style. Rather, they were spiked like Dragon teeth, and on the towers were hideous shapes carved in the likeness of monsters: contorted animal faces and grasping tongues protruding several feet beyond the walls into the air. Far below were great gates of muted bronze with what Kodi supposed were hateful battle scenes molded or carved in the metal, and the gates had huge iron fittings and studs.

Just like the Ralsheen stories.

These gates were not closed. Traffic could be seen moving to and fro, mostly soldiers, some on horseback, some not, on a massive bridge over a shallow ravine and then down a pale road which led from the fortress to the gray city.

As he observed these things, he detected a presence, though for a minute he did not know where it was coming from. For some reason he could never properly explain in words, he knew in the depths of his soul the presence was 'female'. But it was a hideous, unnatural femininity in horrible contrast to the emotions he experienced around his kind mother, or his twin sister with whom he was close, or the physical attraction he felt for certain young women in Felto, that which he carefully reined in since his encounter with Jonell.

What he was feeling now was the opposite of that—repulsive, rather, as on the edge of sickness. Some domineering magic infused the air. He allowed his eyes to drift upwards to the tallest of the fortress towers. Here, on a balcony of black stone, he saw what he knew to be the source of this pervasive and sinister will.

Tall and forbidding, she was the only object of vivid color he had seen so far. Kodi drew closer. He saw that the brilliant yellow garments she wore were embroidered with black and red images of intertwined beasts. Wolves, he realized. Totally covered, her face was masked in painted metal of the same colors as her robes. A short helm stood on her head. Her arms and hands were covered in black leather. Never had Kodi imagined a woman so hideous and evil. Just her costume was enough to inspire fear.

Beneath her helm coarse hair fell, white and fearsome, bristling in the strong wind. Yet her face was so well-concealed, Kodi could otherwise tell nothing of her features.

As she perused her domain—there could be no doubt she was the ruler of this city and these lands—she spoke softly to the skies in a language Kodi did not understand. Was she some magical enchantress, uttering spells of domination? He had heard parts of the Southern Continent were ruled by enemies of the Anterianhi domains. There had been wars in which his Escarantine ancestors fought. His grandfather's books did not explore those. The Kingdom of Solanto was far away from such places, and the Anterianhi Empire dissolved into its constituent realms some hundred years ago. In his own country, tales of enemies and war centered upon the northern Ice Tribes.

He moved even closer in his nighttime flight towards this witch woman. With effort he squelched the negative emotions she engendered in order to focus only on what he was seeing and hearing. Through slits in the mask Kodi perceived her eyes were as yellow as her robes but with cat-like pupils. He could not even tell what her skin tone was, as her mask and gloves concealed her so perfectly. Perhaps at the lips she was pale; they seemed rather gray and colorless.

She did not seem quite human. Or if she was, she was altered somehow. Ancient and cold. As he floated in the space before her he felt confident she was in no way aware of him. Her garments flapped in the uneasy wind, but she herself was as still as stone, her lips no longer moving. She was looking through or perhaps beyond him, intent upon some far off point. He turned to see what it might be.

He had not noticed before, but looking beyond the water, he saw on the edge of sight high cliffs or snowless mountains. Maybe it was not the sea after all. Or if it was the sea—he still smelled the salt—perhaps it was a bay or strait. The vision was not clear enough to get a firm grasp of the geography. He imagined a dark point on the distant heights. He turned back and looked at the woman.

Doing so he caught his breath, as he was presented with a new and disturbing site. Above the witch's head, as if floating in a mirror frame was a clear image of the face of Lyndz.

His own twin sister.

"What does Lyndz have to do with this?" Kodi felt both fear and a sense of protective anger.

In the frame, Lyndz appeared perhaps not much older, but certainly with a serious, determined expression. Only her face was revealed. Seeing this image of his sister temporarily unnerved Kodi. If this dream were indeed a special Vision for his benefit, he was no longer enamored by it.

After a few moments the image faded leaving only the strange woman, who continued to gaze at the far cliffs and again chanted incomprehensible words. Kodi turned, and as fast as the wind—in fact much faster than any wind—his body was propelled far from the woman and the city, high across the water, towards those distant cliffs. He took a moment to look down. Far below on the gray water were tiny black ships with sails the same shade as the witch woman's robes. He was correct about the water; it was a strait, though very wide, yet with wider waters opening out in the distances north and south. However, he had no time to consider it, for he was now over another gray land, mountainous, and looking up he saw he was headed straight for that dark point he had wondered about. It was a great many miles from the water, and far higher, but before he could think much about it he had arrived.

He could hardly believe what he saw, for here was another city, and its fortress was very like to the one he had just left, with its hideous gargoyles, pointed battlements, gates of similar make, and many towers. The two fortresses were as twins, he thought.

With that realization he found himself stationary in front of its tallest tower and another high black stone balcony. Here, a second figure stood. Very much like the great queen, though with black robes, but this was a large being in masculine form, masked and with a helm taller and even more sinister. No hair escaped the confines of his helm. He too had yellow cat-like eyes, perhaps less calculating than his female counterpart across the strait. More mad, Kodi thought.

And Kodi hated him. It was an upsurge of emotion stronger than any he had felt so far in this night journey, but for reasons unknown he felt beyond a doubt this mad king was his mortal enemy. He felt fear but he also felt anger. A desire to strike the king before the king struck him. A combat. A fight until one of them was vanquished. Kodi felt his muscles tighten. His heart beat in his ears.

The mad sorcerer king was also gazing, and like the woman he stared across the distance—westward. Could it be an invisible line connected the eyes of the sorcerer and those of the witch all those miles away? Surely, they could not see each other across the vastness. Yet Kodi wondered if between the countless miles they were somehow in commune, and he knew that though they were perhaps not talking, the two were certainly aware of each other.

Kodi recalled news his father had brought the last time he came home that there was war in the distant east and that it had been going on for perhaps a year now, though it did not involve the Kingdom of Solanto. Was this figure the one referred to as 'the Alkhan,' the warlock ruler from the Southern Continent? Kodi tried to picture a map in one of his grandfather's books, the name of the kingdom of the Alkhan sorcerer. After a moment's reflection it came to him: Eastrealm Khestadon. The Alkhan was the one being held at bay by the navies of Nant and the armies of the eastern kingdoms. Which would mean his female counterpart was the Alkhaness of Westrealm. It made perfect sense to him, now. In his heart he knew he was now staring into the masked face of the Alkhan himself.

The wild expression in his eyes was difficult to endure, yet Kodi fought it. For some reason he kept thinking of the old Ralsheen tales. He looked below and could see that, whereas the witch-woman's fortress was apart from the city, here the citadel of the sorcerer-king was upon a pinnacle of rock in the middle of the city on the edge of an otherwise isolated mountain valley. Kodi wondered much at this. There were soldiers here, too, and they were also in black, and there were no others in sight besides soldiers. Maybe there were other towns or cities hidden nearer the coast or in other valleys that Kodi could not see from this vantage. If there was anything to see eastward, it was all dim and hazy.

Just as the idea of exploring further entered his mind, he was unwittingly transported from the presence of the mad sorcerer king, in a direction he knew was 'northwestward'. All was a jumbled blur, and he could make nothing of the geography. Clouds shot past like arrows. Barely a few moments passed before he arrived at his new destination, and what he saw amazed him.

He was again flying over a great city, but there could hardly have been a more remarkable contrast with the anemic abodes of the sorcerer and witch. This city was vast, with enormous palaces of white and rose-colored stone topped by pointed domes and spires of gold or of turquoise. There were many of these grand and colorful buildings, particularly in its central part, and it was larger than any city Kodi had imagined. Hundreds of thousands could live here. As he looked below he could see countless people and carts moving about the wide streets, and they wore good clothes of a variety of colors, prosperous and friendly.

In the center on a large hill was a palace, larger and grander than the others, and in the near distance shown a blue-green sea, more reminiscent of the coast off the city of Ross in County Ascanti. Yet here, due to the great height from which he was experiencing this, the ocean appeared as a carpet of sparkling emeralds and sapphires. In an inlet seemingly carved into the heart of the city by vast hands, hundreds of ships with white sails sat at anchor in two ports, some small and others with great masts and many sails. Where the inlet cut inward from the sea, a high wall began, which, with impeccably straight lines, formed an octagon around the massive city to a point opposite the other side of the bay. This impregnable wall was interspersed with many towers, though with much taller and grander ones at its several corners. There was another, even taller wall of white stone in the middle part of the city. Like a vast crown on a headpiece of jewels, it surrounding the base of a broad hill upon which stood the finest manors and the great palace.

"Tirilorin!" Kodi thought he could identify this place, for he had seen colored drawings of it in a book his grandfather possessed. This was the old imperial capital of the Anterianhi Empire, south of Solanto on the southwestern shores of old Lorinth, the Domain of the Emperors. Since the Abdication, Tirilorin and its surrounding lands were now ruled as a 'republic' with an Assembly, although Kodi did not really know what that meant. All he knew was there hadn't been an emperor for almost a hundred years. Yet the city was still one of the wonders of the world. He had for years longed to go there, and the splendor of the scene before him only increased his desire.

A full minute he viewed this stunning site but was finally drawn to the central palace. He knew it had to be the old imperial palace, for apart from its size and its central location on the hill, it had a tower of bright white stone attached to it, which stood glittering in contrast to the blue of the sky and the sea, and on top of the tower a great bird, an eagle of gold, stood with outstretched wings. It clutched a silver sphere like Solvermoon, and peered into the distance, westward over the bay. This statue was huge, and as Kodi descended to it, he wondered how it could possibly have been placed on its lofty perch, for it must have weighed many tons.

Under the eagle's gaze he drifted downward into a vast array of gardens, green with trees of great height, fountains, and flowers in manicured beds which he knew his green-thumbed sister Lyndz would covet. He settled his two feet upon an emerald lawn looking towards the front of the magnificent palace. He never imagined so much gold in all his life. The walls were of pink and white marble, but every feature of its trim was gilded: the accoutrements around the windows and doors, the statuary and reliefs, and the great entrance doors themselves. Kodi was struck by the amount of labor that must have gone into it all, and the mind-boggling wealth of the emperors to afford such splendor. His eyes were then drawn to the massive statue adjacent to him, also gilt, of a warrior on a rearing horse set amidst a bubbling pool. In his left hand he held a sword, and in the right a staff, thus unencumbered by reins, horse and rider so in tune with one another as to render such unnecessary.

Kodi felt a surge of warrior-like inspiration as he peered at the likeness of the first Emperor, Terianh the Great. Terianh had been Chosen by the Guardian Meical five hundred years ago to lead the armies which overthrew the evil Ralsheen Empire, ushering in an era of freedom and of greatness beyond anything the Ralsheen could have achieved with all its enslaved populace. Terianh was a War Wizard who carried a magic war-staff, and easily Kodi's favorite hero. He stared at the staff again. He felt himself drawn to it, topped with its eagle likeness and sphere not unlike the great tower behind. It held his interest for a while.

At the base of this magnificent representation, near the low stone wall enclosing the pool he soon became aware of the approaching figure of a young man. Kodi deduced he must be about the same age as himself—three years or so into traditional manhood—tall, slightly thinner than the muscular Kodi, and wearing remarkably rich clothes. The young man sat himself on the stone wall of the pool, grinned caddishly, pulled an apple from his pocket and began to munch away, looking off in the distance.

Walking around the pool for a closer look, Kodi perceived a cocksure face framed by curly blond locks. Chuckling to himself, he felt he was looking at a friend. Though his rich, gold-embroidered finery was of a sort Kodi would never allow himself to be seen in, he could not help but think the young man was familiar. The other was perhaps as adventurous and easy-going as himself, and he believed if he could engage the other in conversation he would find they shared similar ideas, experiences and goals. Kodi had many friends among the other fellows in the town of Felto, but they also looked up to him as a leader and respected him as the son of the count and countess. As for his twin sister, Lyndz, the two were bound together heart and soul. Yet for all that, she was a woman, and there was much about either the other could never understand. Men and women were different. But here before him was the truest sort of friend, a *comrade-in-arms*, so to speak. Despite the young man's obvious wealth, Kodi knew the two of them were equals in other ways, and he heartily looked forward to meeting him.

Because for some reason, Kodi felt the two of them would indeed meet soon. It was as though they were wrapped together in some shared adventure. Yet he couldn't imagine what they were expected to do. As he contemplated this, the young man stood and sauntered toward the low marble wall surrounding this level of green lawn. Having finished his apple, he tossed it without a care over the wall and walked away.

As he drifted upwards again, the gardens and palace sank below him, and Kodi found himself among wispy clouds far above Tirilorin, moving with increasing speed 'eastward' across grassy plains. Before he could think to look down again, he was among thick clouds and could see nothing. He only wondered a moment how far he would go this time. It seemed a shorter trip than the previous. When he came to a stop—it was so sudden it was dizzying—he found himself above a forest of deep green. It was a shocking contrast to the gray lands of the sorcerer and the witch, or the blue and white and gold of Tirilorin and the sea. Before him, rusty red cliff walls rose like an island in a deep green leafy sea, and atop the cliffs were trees of great height with many birds circling in and about carrying on an airborne dance. In the far distance beyond this carven plateau was a mountain range of great height, peaks topped with white. It was a lovely and wild land appealing strongly to Kodi and more reminiscent of his home in the Duchy of Tulesk, though lusher, warmer, and the size of the trees made it feel 'older.'

Most strangely, the dark night closed in as if by magic. Stars by the multitude expanded in a black sky. A three-quarter Solvermoon shone, and the land, beautiful in the light, was just as beautiful in the night. Shadows were alive and fanciful. On an outcrop, the forest trees ended a hundred feet or so from the outer edge, and standing in this open space, close to the cliff, was a human-like figure. Kodi settled himself before her.

She was different from any human he had ever seen. Even in the moonlight it was plain hers was a face serene, yet troubled. She wore loose white linen that shone in the night light and was very tall for a woman. She was queenly. Dignified and beautiful. No blemish or wrinkle could be seen on her skin—a rich brown with maybe a tinge of red. Though her features were flawless, her stance and demeanor implied a mature woman. His mind raced, but he could not come up with a name for the type of creature he was looking at, for though she was very human-like, her differences implied otherwise. She was lovely in a way difficult to describe, for her hair was dark and long, her eyebrows traced out and slightly upwards, and her eyes, even in the dark, shone a sapphire blue more vivid than the ordinary; she was more graceful and noble than any human. The figure looked up, and Kodi was startled when a rather large bird, white in the moonlight, streaked past him and then carefully landed on the woman's shoulder. He had never seen such a bird before, for though it was crow-like, it was definitely white. Perhaps it was a crow or raven of a variety he had never heard.

Oddly, the bird was speaking in the woman's ear, and it was clear she was listening intently. The proud countenance she bore was affected by its message, her shoulders fell slightly, and she appeared sad. He wondered if she might cry for she seemed so desperate, and then, very oddly, Kodi realized he was actually sensing the woman's feelings. He 'felt' her sadness and wondered how it could be so. He had not experienced the emotions of the others in his dream. She exhibited an element of defeat—and he wondered what could possibly have happened, or what message the white raven had brought that could cause such a sense of hopelessness in the otherwise proud woman. The bird then flew off into the darkness and the woman turned and began to walk away.

Abruptly she stopped and turned around. Kodi sensed the woman's sadness shift into startled curiosity. He hesitated. But after a moment's reflection he knew. He drew himself close and looked into her face. She sensed him! He could not imagine how, but beyond any doubt he realized the two of them were somehow connected in the dream.

Maybe they could communicate, he thought. And with this idea he felt as if the strange woman had indeed now entered his mind. It was the oddest experience, as if she were magically probing for answers, trying to discover who he was and if he were of good intent. And though he did not have the capacity to explore her mind in the same way, through the connection itself he was able to determine she was of noble heart with high motives, though mingled with sorrow and worry. He then wondered if this strange person could speak his language. He was just opening his mouth to test this theory with a simple greeting when all of a sudden, she faded into the background and disappeared. It was strange, for Kodi could still sense her presence for another few moments: the anticipation and curiosity. He looked everywhere to see which way she went, to no avail. As his connection to her faded, Kodi discerned one final thought coming from her: hope.

As with the young man in Tirilorin, he knew too he was meant to find this person. He felt strangely connected to her in some way. He half imagined some Voice in the background of his dream telling him to seek her out.

Unlike before, when this last encounter ended, Kodi was not immediately propelled in a new direction or to a new scene. The dream seemed to have come to a standstill. He had not moved from the cliff edge where he first sighted the strange woman. She was gone, and there were no birds, nor any sound of night creatures.

But there was a sound: a quiet whisper and deep rumbling on the wind which seemed to mean nothing at first and was easily ignored. It was as a Voice continual in the background, in competition with—or maybe it was complementing—all the thoughts and emotions since the beginning of his dream. He found himself intensely curious about it all of a sudden. He concentrated, trying hard not to breathe. Yes, there were words in that Voice, though they were so very quiet he could not quite make them out. Maybe, just maybe they were calling for him? He turned this way and that to see if he could sense a direction from which the Voice might be coming, if it even had a source. He wondered. Was it a bit more audible when he turned his face to the right? Northward.

To this point the dream had largely been out of his own control except for certain movements he made in order to peer more closely at the four persons. Now it changed. It was with the realization there really was a Voice that this freedom came. He felt he was being given a choice, and making up his mind, he leapt skyward and soared northwards, beyond the green plateau. The darkness gave way again to startling daylight. He brushed the mountaintops, white with snow, gleaming in a blinding sky. Here the air was golden and fresher than any spring breeze he could remember. It ought to have been too cold.

Without warning, a bright valley opened below marked with vivid spring colors and silver rushing streams. All was outlined by the various greens of trees and grasses studded with wildflowers. About this vast garden were scattered beautiful temples and monuments of white stone. It was an incredible place. He later described it as "spiritual," a word the meaning of which he had never before contemplated very much, let alone used. He flew joyfully among the temples and explored the whole of the valley. Most of the streams spilled towards a central huge lake of deepest sapphire, darker than the sky it reflected. Out if it a breathtaking waterfall plummeted and a river rushed off through a narrow gorge southward.

He moved closer to the ground. The Voice had disappeared, and yet he was certain it had originated in this magnificent place. He wondered where the people were, for surely there had to be many who lived in such a land and who built the beautiful temples, yet silence continued to reign. It was not, though, a silence of sadness, but rather one of anticipation—of waiting for something unexpected to happen. Kodi then placed himself on a tall green hill somewhat in the center of the valley nigh to the blue lake. No temple was located on the hill, yet it seemed an important place nonetheless. Contemplative, he looked all about. It was beautiful here, more beautiful than any place he had ever before seen or imagined, a holy place, and he felt as though he could dwell here the rest of his life, drinking in the poetry of the setting. In the distance he could see lines of silver, waterfalls dropping from precipices all around, creating the little rivers which all meandered toward the lake. Here and there were scattered groves of tall evergreens.

He began to hear sounds—the silence was broken. From the distance he could hear the roar of the falls at the outflow of the lake, and there were now birds of all kinds flying to and fro, singing each their joyful songs. Kodi felt the enchantment of the place grow in his heart, the image of it branding itself upon his mind for all time. He began to believe his body was actually here rather than lying on his bed; he felt solid and whole, and he began to breathe steadily, drawing into himself the fragrances on the wind.

In broad strides he walked down the slopes of the hill, which ended in a low cliff beside the water. The sapphire lake was inviting, compelling beyond all else. He had a sudden inexplicable desire to dive into its depths and drink in the crystal blue water.

As he stood at the edge he felt permission had been granted him to do exactly that, and so with all hesitation removed, he cast aside the phantom night pant he wore. Standing bare now, he felt more alive than in waking life. He felt his very body was bigger, even giant-sized, and immeasurably strong.

Godlike, he dove. The seconds afterward were long, full of a kind of ecstatic anticipation. When he hit the water it was more glorious even than he had hoped, as warmth enveloped him. Returning to the surface he took some water into his mouth and swallowed. He had never tasted anything so wonderful. It was as though he were experiencing joy for the very first time. He could taste it. His skin was penetrated by it. With powerful strokes he broke back into the air. Golden sunlight greeted him. And so again did the Voice.

"Kodi."

It was clear, the vocal quality of a powerful young warrior. Yet it was filled with the gentle warmth and confident wisdom of a wise and ancient lord. In and of itself the Voice felt giant-like to Kodi, though it did not diminish him, not by any means. In fact, he felt as though it were the source of the godlike strength and powerful emotion he was experiencing.

Maybe, had he been a few years younger, Kodi would have maintained his silence, but growth both physical and emotional over the last few years had created within him a level of assured maturity. He had no hesitation now and answered, *"Yes, I am here."*

"Go."

"But where, m'Lord?"

"You will not be alone. Someone will come to you soon to guide you. You will know him when you see him. Follow and seek."

"Follow and seek? Yes, m'Lord, but what? I don't understand."

"Remember what I have shown you. I need you, Kodi."

"I… yes, of course, m'Lord."

"And then lead."

"Me? But…"

"The wisdom to do so will come. You must learn to trust yourself. And Kodi…"

"Yes, m'Lord?"

"I am with you…My Brother."

With this filial connection proclaimed, emotion more powerful than any so far flooded Kodi's whole being, and mixed with the warmth of the blue water he felt tremendous chills, as if he had stepped off onto clouds from the highest mountaintop.

It was more than he could hold onto. Hot tears erupted unbidden. The moment was debilitating while it lasted, and yet a part of him wished he could experience it forever. He lay back afloat the waters of the lake, absorbing strength and purpose from the light and from the water and closed his eyes.

When he opened them again, his face was wet and he was shaking all over. Not from fear, but rather it was as if he had run a great race or had moved some massive barrow load of stone, taxing the fullest extent of his strength. All his muscles seemed to ache as he leaned up on an arm and looked around the room. A bit of moonlight seeped through the closed and shuttered window. Kodi had no fireplace in his room, but rather kept his bedroom door open to allow in the heat from downstairs. Musca had risen from his spot near the door and, cocking his head, looked curiously at his master.

Without any hint of unbelief or need for confirmation, Kodi knew what he had experienced in the last moments of his Vision. For Vision he now knew it was, and no mere dream. With stumbling effort he sat up on the edge of the bed. Despite the coolness of the air, he was dripping and his bedclothes were wet from a heavy sweat. His heart raced as the reality of it all sank in.

"Meical the Guardian!" he announced, although Musca was the only one to hear. "Musca, can you believe it? And…and He called me 'Brother.'"

Oddly, Musca seemed pleased by this news and wagged his tail.

Chapter 2—Conspiracy

As the three Ice Tribesmen stood by, Filiddor, Prince of Hesk studied the old parchment. He was one of the few in the Principality, along with a few of his cousins, and of course Theneri at the Asterian Library, who could read Ralsheen. This was one old document, however, he would never allow old Theneri to read—he was a Monastic, a member of the Orders, and would disapprove of its contents. It could bring war.

Indeed it could. Filiddor read greedily. The document was everything the Tribesmen had promised.

"What do you think of it, Your Highness?" asked K'trek, leader of the Tribal delegation.

Turning to them again, the prince almost winced. Being 'Of the White' yet wearing their dark furs high on their shoulders, the three recalled the appearance of white-headed vultures. Most of the ancient Ralsheen imperial family along with much of the nobility had these physical traits, ones they deliberately interbred: all-white skin, close-cropped white hair, and almost colorless eyes. It was said the world goddess Siriné preferred these features, and they were favored in the ancient imperial court. Five-hundred years later, their descendants the Tribesmen had deliberately carried them on by way of arranged couplings through the centuries. Perhaps, the prince thought, they believed it connected them to a proud, ancient past.

Filiddor did not much care to look directly at them for long. He had grown up thinking them barbaric. That was the common understanding among most Hescians and Solantines, though he knew the Sages of Meical preached that those born albino should not be discriminated against. Perhaps so, when it was natural. But to deliberately interbreed the trait was not.

He made some attempt to squelch his distaste. "I am most pleased, Ambassador K'trek. It is exactly as you say. The question is, why was it never delivered to my ancestor T'vani, the first Prince of Hesk? It has Terianh's Great Seal. How did your people come across it? Clearly it was stolen. Do not deny it."

"It was intercepted," the Tribesman coolly replied.

"Same difference."

K'trek seemed unwilling to argue the point. "It is yours now. So, you agree to its authenticity? Terianh as you know used Ralsheen writing before the Anterianhi script became standard in his empire later."

"Oh, yes. It is authentic," the prince stated firmly. He did not notice the corners of K'trek's mouth as they traced imperceptibly upwards.

"Then you agree to…"

"Don't press me, Ambassador! I agree to nothing until we discuss it with my counselors."

The albino man nodded. "Certainly, Your Highness."

The prince looked back at the document. After a time he turned to face K'trek once more. Despite all, the oddness of the man's bright eyes with their black pupils were mesmerizing. "All right, Ambassador. It proves your good intentions. You must wait in your chambers while I call them together. We will meet again tomorrow morning. Lord Ultrech will arrive sometime this afternoon from his estate in the country. I especially want him to be here."

K'trek and the other two Tribesmen all dipped their heads. They were pleased. From their perspective this was going well. Very well indeed.

The three were led away by a servant and a contingent of several guards who then stationed themselves in the hallway outside their bedchambers.

The Tribesmen had arrived the previous night and found the palace and their chambers sumptuous. Certainly the cold gray buildings in their own land beyond the mountains were nothing to this. The grandiosity of classic Ralsheen architecture, its spectacular domed ceilings and wide arches appealed to K'trek. They had worn their furs in their audience with the prince, for these denoted their status on the other side of the mountains. They removed them again now, as the roaring fireplaces made their adjoining rooms quite warm. They then relaxed on heavily stuffed furniture. As their presence would arouse suspicion, they knew they would not be allowed out of the palace in daytime. Perhaps, K'trek thought, he could arrange for a walk around the city in the dark of night. There was the city curfew, so none of the common folk would mark their presence.

He noticed P'nar looking at him. In the guttural Tribal tongue descended from the Ralsheen language, he spoke. "Yes, P'nar?"

"Congratulations on your handwriting skills."

"Thank you, P'nar," K'trek replied. "And yet without her magic through the cube the document would not have appeared so perfectly aged. And the seal engraving was excellent. All the magic seemed to work, did it not?"

The third man spoke. "You gained the proper eye contact, just as she directed. You could sense the change in his demeanor; he was much more receptive afterwards. You have been given a powerful gift, Your Grace! You will have to do the same tomorrow with each of the Prince's counselors. If we succeed, she will reward us."

K'trek smiled. "Quite right, P'lental. She will."

In the audience chamber, after he had sent servants to deliver his messages, Prince Filiddor stood gazing out upon the morning through the triple-arched westward-facing window. It was bright, and his city, Aster, on the edge of the North River Gorge, stretched before him.

The Principality of Hesk had been established over four-and-a-half centuries ago during the earliest days of the Anterianhi Empire. The Hescian Highlands had been granted to Filiddor's ancestor, and the hereditary title of Prince arranged at that time. Yet its capital, Aster, was much older than the Principality. It had been a small city of the Ralsheen Empire. It had a different name then: R'magdelos, "Star City," though it was forgotten by most. In fact, it was the only Ralsheen city to survive the Conquest, for all its people had fled to Tolos at the advance of the army of Terianh the Great. Abandoned therefore, the city was spared, though its old temple to wicked Siriné was destroyed by the Sages. Filiddor's ancestor, T'vani, a Ralsheen minor nobleman, not *Of the White*, switched allegiance to Terianh, and was granted the city and the lands around as a gift by the new emperor for his timely help in a critical battle.

Under the princes, the city grew again. In theory, they were subject to the Kings of Solanto and were expected to guard the borders from Tribal incursions. Remnants of the Ralsheen, the Ice Tribes were a continual if diminished threat. But it was a critical point that the Principality was chartered by Terianh himself and not by the King of Solanto. In reality the princes, no longer attuned to the worst evils of the Ralsheen, nevertheless could not wholly forget their former pride, and they made successful attempts to guard their political independence, often refusing to conform to the wishes of the Solantine kings and queens. There had been animosity off and on over those centuries, though never open violence between the

Principality and the rest of Solanto. In trade there was tremendous coming and going, and the Highlands contained a number of important resources the Kingdom traded for. These resources created great wealth for the princes, making Aster into one of the great cities of the north.

The Orders of the Guardian, too, had a Monastery on the outskirts of the city. They would pilgrimage here in order to study in Aster's fine library. This had been built upon the site of the old Siriné temple. Only in Tirilorin, the former imperial capital of the Anterianhi Empire, was there maintained a collection greater than the one in Aster. Monastics and the Gifted would come in order to continue their learning among the books, manuscripts, maps, scrolls and letters, to increase their knowledge of the world at large. There were even a number of ancient tomes in the Ralsheen language, though few could now read them.

Filiddor's princely ancestors, in the generations after T'vani, were vain and consumed with acquiring wealth and embellishing their palace and their city. Forty years ago when the young Solantine man Duganri conquered neighboring Stavenland from the Ice Tribes, Filiddor's father, Prince Lanwi, had sent an army to assist, and took the opportunity of their weakened position to rid the mountain passes on his northern border of all presence of the Ice Tribes. Lanwi was infuriated when Duganri was awarded Stavenland, renamed Tulesk, as a new duchy. He believed the land should have been added to his own, but too many of the noblemen in the rest of the kingdom opposed this. He continued to be at odds with Duganri, and these attitudes had not changed with the accession of their sons. Prince Filiddor and Duke Amerro maintained a deep mutual distrust.

The lords of the Kingdom had said that the Princes of Hesk had sufficient wealth and land, and did not need more. Certainly the Hescian Highlands were rich in resources, as the land itself was well-suited to grain production and cattle farming, but there were mines as well. Silver mines, and iron ore aplenty, and these were traded for textiles, wines and other commodities from the south, ambernut and other precious hardwoods, and of course exotics from the sea trade as came through the ducal ports westward.

Yet the princes always considered it a limitation that they did not have direct access to the sea. The Grand Escarpment defined its western border. Falling four hundred feet at its base in the southwest on the border with the Duchy of Ascanti, and over which plunged the North River and its mighty falls, the wall continued in a line northward creating the border with Tulesk, on its way to the Ice Mountains. This great range ran west to east for many hundreds of miles and formed the northern boundary of Hesk, and beyond which lived the Ice Tribes. On the eastern boundary, and proceeding southwards as the border of the Kingdom, marched the Imperial Divide, beyond which lay the Kingdom of Eleni. A tough people, and being in an almost constant state of warfare with the Ice Tribes, and with bad relations with the Barantines on their eastern flank, traditional ways worked well for the Elenites to maintain their place in upholding the old values of the Anterianhi Empire. The Durn Swamp, and beyond them a set of chunky hills running east to west, formed the southern boundary of the Principality. The Swamp was a wild place where few lived except on the edges where peat was cut as a major heat source for those living outside the marsh, but the southern hills and the Imperial Mountains were the location of the many rich mines of Hesk. Beyond those hills lay King's Valley and the personal domain of Carlomen, King of Solanto.

Through the middle of the prince's domain, beginning in the Ice Mountains, cutting through the sandstone and exposing the softer limestone beneath, were two rivers, the Eastern and Western Forks of the North River. As the shallow canyon spread apart, the rivers themselves adjoined, and at the juncture stood Aster, gleaming city of the northern lands, and the Grand Palace of the Princes. It was very different from other cities in the former Anterianhi Empire, for construction was required to adhere to ancient Ralsheen notions of design and scale. And though many in Solanto proper were not inclined to think this a good thing, it was imposing nevertheless.

The Palace of the Princes was over six hundred years old, for during the Ralsheen era it was the seat of the regional satrap. Most impressive was its central dome with gold tracery overhead, and below this was the audience chamber where Filiddor now stood, containing the Throne of the Princes, draped in golden yellow hangings.

Filiddor turned from the window and read through the document yet again.

This would change everything, he thought. It was better than any Prophecy expounded by Meicalian Seers and legitimized all his ancestors' claims. If he could get Ultrech, Funeas, and the rest to agree to it, an alliance with the Ice Tribes would give him the support he would need to press his claims. He would go to war for them if he had to. And obviously the Ice Tribes were very willing.

They wanted Stavenland back.

A new morning came. The private council chamber of the prince, though smaller than the audience chamber, was sumptuously decorated with tapestries and rich Barantine carpets of fantastical design. An oversized fireplace made the room warm, and none felt the need to retain their cloaks. Behind where the councilors sat in a semicircle at a round oak table, tall, leaded windows faced northwestwards towards the shallow canyon of the East Fork of the North River.

In all there were six lords who lived in the vicinity of the city and came at the summons, although there were seats for as many more. All men, of course. In the earliest days of the Principality, women served on the Prince's Council, but those kinder days were long gone as the male egotism of T'vani's successors reasserted itself. Unlike Solanto proper, women had few rights in Hesk.

The Ice Tribesmen had not yet been invited to the chamber, for Filiddor needed to confer with his lords first. It took some time for all of them to process the document, for only two of them, Counts Ultrech and Funeas, could read the ancient script, and so, along with the Prince, they had to translate.

They were all of them pleased, but wary.

"This would have replaced the original boundary agreement!" stated Ultrech. He was the prince's cousin and closest confidante. In fact, all the counselors were to varying degrees related to the prince, and all shared common descent from Prince T'vani, the first Prince of Hesk.

"So, the Tolosian Peninsula and Tulesk, old Stavenland, were meant to be a part of the Principality!" exclaimed Funeas. "This is news! What do you propose to do with this, Your Highness?"

"I will call a Council of the Kingdom, and press my father's claims."

They all shuffled in their seats and looked at one another.

"If you were to take this and present it in Council, it could lead to war, Your Highness. Amerro has had control of the peninsula for nearly three years, and Tulesk has been established for forty. He will give up none of it, I tell you!"

"Why should we agree to an alliance with the Tribesmen, Your Highness?" asked a third counselor. "They are barbaric!"

"They are our...cousins," said Filiddor, carefully. Everyone shifted uncomfortably at this. "Those of us sitting around this table are as much connected to the Tribesmen as we are to Solantines, whether we look like them or not."

Uncomfortable, but true. The lordly families of Hesk were heavily intermarried, and though certainly there was Solantine blood, the old Ralsheen bloodlines were well preserved, not so unlike in the land of the Ice Tribes. Though none were *Of the White*. That was absolutely not a desired trait in Hesk.

Yet the fact, stated aloud by the prince, meant more.

"So, are you implying they know about..." Ultrech paused. He did not wish to say it aloud—the great secret of their house. It was presumed should the Solantines ever find it out, they might disclaim the alliance.

Filiddor hesitated for a moment, but finally he nodded. "Yes. They know about T'vani's mother, Shandira."

Funeas and the others drew in a collective breath.

Filiddor continued. He was oddly unconcerned. "They know her true Ralsheen name was Ch'ndra, that she was the last Ralsheen emperor's sister, and so the daughter of the previous emperor. She was *Of the White*, of course, although N'belli, T'vani's father was not. They know all of this, yes. They claim to have discovered T'vani's bloodline through ancient records."

"I didn't know they had *ancient records*," said Ultrech, skeptically.

Filiddor pounded the table, stood, and paced by the window. "You must understand," he said almost angrily, "That this is an opportunity for our advancement! Don't you see? As the last of the imperial house with living descendants, they wish to swear homage to the heir of Ch'ndra!"

They all raised their eyebrows. They were silent for a long moment as Filiddor allowed the information to process.

After a time, Funeas spoke. "They...they wish to bring back the Ralsheen empire? Under your leadership? The Solantines will never agree to anything of the kind! Consider the implications, Your Highness!"

"I don't care anymore what the Solantines agree to!" said Filiddor in a dark tone. "What have we gained in nearly five centuries of alliance with Solanto? Nothing! Not a square foot of land, and yet they have gained greatly from our help over the years. Do you deny it?"

They all shook their heads. "No, Your Highness," offered Ultrech. "It cannot be denied. You are correct."

"I say it is time to turn the tide. Even so, and I want it to be made clear here and now, I have no desire to return us to the hateful days of the Ralsheen era. I care little for Meical the Guardian and the Orders as you well know, but I care even less about returning to the slave-like worship of the old goddess Siriné. It was an abominable time. The Ralsheen name was discarded for good reason long ago, and it is not to be resurrected."

"But the Ice Tribes are nearly as barbarous, Your Highness," said Ultrech carefully. "It is said they still worship Siriné. You think they will...change?"

"They are willing to swear homage. Once they do, the Chieftains understand much will change. They are desperate as we are for expansion. They need farmland, and we want the treasures of Tolos! And we need to find them before Amerro's men do. The Tribesmen claim to know where the old capital is on the peninsula and how to find the hidden vaults, presuming the Dragons did not, and they will help us. And think of the new order! Hesk, Tolos, Stavenland, the land of the Ice Tribes!"

"It is greater than the Kingdom of Solanto," said one of the lords who had not yet said very much. He was impressed by the idea.

"It is," admitted Ultrech. "I am willing to hear them out then, Your Highness. This *ambassador* and his aides."

All nodded agreement.

It may have been that the counselors did not like looking at the strange albino as he stood with his white, cropped hair. However, he spoke so effectively, they found him more compelling even than the prince. Like the prince they found themselves intrigued by his eyes, though of course none offered aloud this observation.

"...and we of the Ice Tribes will help you recover what should rightfully be yours. The document gives you legitimacy in this cause, and it might gain you some allies on the King's Council, might it not? We believe this document coming from Terianh himself gives you what you need to take Tolos and Stavenland, what you call Tulesk. Even if King Carlomen opposes you, we are willing at once to come to your aid."

"In what way?" asked one of the lords.

"Most importantly we will put our forces at your disposal. In alliance with your own, we will be equal to any force put together by the king. Together, we will take Stavenland and Tolos. After that has taken place, we will openly declare His Highness King over a new northern kingdom which will include the Principality, Tolos and Stavenland, and the lands of the Ice Tribes north of the mountains. In size and power and wealth your kingdom will be greater than what will remain of Solanto."

"So you really do espouse war? Are you certain you understand what you're saying, K'trek?" asked Funeas. "Solanto is not alone. You forget the Elenites. And what of your current fighting with them? How do you expect to manage two conflicts?"

"If you ally with us, we will immediately withdraw beyond the Ice Mountains from Eleni. Our conflict with them will be over, for the Elenites will not cross the Mountains to engage us. Your own pass into their kingdom is easily defended even if they should then choose to side with King Carlomen. But we believe they will be so grateful for an end to the war they will shun further conflict. The Barantines will keep the Elenites always alert to their eastern border."

The prince's counselors could not help but to be conscious of the possibilities. There were unspoken flaws in this plan, and yet, as they looked into the ambassador's eyes, none of the flaws seemed to present themselves in their minds. After a long pause, Ultrech looked in Filiddor's direction and spoke. "I despise Duke Amerro as much as any man, and the influence he has with the king, not to mention the fact his father was given Tulesk in the first place which has always set badly with me. Tulesk should have been ours, and the king openly spurned your father, Your Highness, with his broken promises in the last war. Some scattered gold from Tolos has already gone to enrich Amerro and his own. If old vaults or Dragon hoards are discovered, he will be able to buy all influence and pay armies to assist him in holding Tolos. If we want Tolos for ourselves, and it is our right to have it, proven by this document, then we cannot wait long to make a decision. They have a foothold there and we understand they are building a town and fort already at the mouth of the Tolos River. Hess, the Count Fothemry, has been sent on another exploration, this time of the deep interior, according to my sources. Amerro is hoping he will find the old capital city. I will adhere fully to your wishes, my Prince, even if it means war with Amerro, or even King Carlomen. But I will say this, you can attempt a peaceful way in the King's Council, and you should try it. Call for a Council of the Kingdom, just as you suggest, and take the document to Ferostro. It would be sinister to dispel a nearly five-century alliance without first attempting peaceful methods."

"I agree with Lord Ultrech. However, and quite frankly, Your Highness, I have many a problem with an alliance with the Ice Tribes." Funeas looked then at K'trek and the two Tribesmen standing with him. "Your methods in war are barbaric!"

One of the other lords spoke, "I concur with Lord Funeas. Kidnapping women and children, butchering them when ransom was not prompt in coming!"

At that point K'trek bowed respectfully. He knew he had to be careful. The debate was going well, but it could fall apart. His gift through the magic of his eyes was not foolproof, just as she had warned him. Persuading with well-chosen words was his best option. "We admit our error. However, you must also admit you burned the homes of our farm families in Stavenland and left them to flee in terror to the mountain passes to escape the wrath of your armies. But times have…progressed. You are aware we do not use such tactics in our skirmishes with the Elenites?"

"You may no longer butcher your captives, but you sell them into slavery, do you not?"

The fact could not be denied. "I am authorized by the Conclave of the Chieftains to say that once they pledge allegiance to His Highness as King, they will follow his dictates, including one calling for the elimination of...slavery. The system of serfdom as it functions in the Principality of Hesk will serve in all of His Highness's lands easily enough, and if His Highness commands it, all those taken in the Elentine war will go free. In fact, such a course of action might very well ensure that kingdom will not aid King Carlomen against you."

It was certainly a short term possibility, though K'trek knew in the long run it was an irrelevancy. In the long run, *she* would dictate.

Even Filiddor blinked. "Brilliant, Ambassador! They might see me as a deliverer! Hmm. Lord Ultrech, how do you see the situation now?"

Ultrech spoke directly to K'trek. "Your goal is a compelling one, but in my opinion, you seem too assured, far too assured of success in this game. For it is a game, a risky one that if we choose it, it will have to be slowly and carefully played out. The irony! You bring an *Anterianhi* legal document to further the goal of a *Ralsheen* cause. What gives? Why do you act now, and why do you believe this will work?"

The prince nodded. "Lord Ultrech has a very good point, K'trek. In our previous messages, this was a point never touched upon, for I have myself only looked at the worthiness of the goal itself. I do hope you can convince my lords. This is your chance."

From K'trek's angle, he believed all had gone very well so far. He had expected this could go on for days. Clearly, the lords of Hesk had been operating under much resentment towards the Kingdom of Solanto.

She would be pleased. She had said she was transferring to him some of her powers of persuasion, though at the time he felt only a mild pain under a yellow light when she secretly cast her spell through the cube. In combination with the resentment of the Hescian lords, it seemed to be working. He had done his part well. The prince was sold already, which was something, but these gathered lords were the key, it seemed. It was time to convince them, as well.

He began again. "I see the irony, but make no mistake. In the opinion of the Chieftains, it would be an error in judgment for us to re-claim the Ralsheen name. It should be abandoned. This is why we are willing to keep your descent from Imperial Ch'ndra secret. It can remain hidden until some distant future, perhaps, when your rule is better established, and the world begins to envy you and your rule. The House of Hesk, the *Kingdom* of Hesk, these are names which should not derive any fear among the remnants of Anterianhi. Besides, there were indeed excesses upon the part of Ch'ndra's brother and father, and neither you nor we wish to return to their ways, do we? Rather, let us together reach back years before those Dark Times, when Ralsheen rule was considered enlightened and the height of all civilization! With the riches on Tolos, it can happen."

He looked at Prince Filiddor and continued. "The Dragons are gone from Tolos, you have assured me, an event foretold. Also, to claim you as our sovereign is critical. Our civilization beyond the Mountains is at a critical juncture. There is no more room for our people. We need land to grow food again, and Tolos can provide it. Or Stavenland. But we need a king, and only one from the Ralsheen Imperial House will suffice for the Chieftains to agree to submit in homage. We look to you, Your Highness, for you are a man worthy, indeed the *only* worthy, for your claim to the imperial legacy is best. Lord Ultrech asks how we believe this goal of ours will succeed. The reason we believe this 'game' will play out well for us is due to a recently decoded Prophecy."

All the lords at the table looked around at one another.

"Really!" replied Ultrech, skeptically. "It is hard to believe Meicalian Prophecy would lend itself to a Ralsheen resurgence."

"It is not Meicalian Prophecy, m'lord, it..."

Funeas interrupted. "Not Meicalian Prophecy? I don't follow. What other sort of Prophecy is there? I have heard of ancient Dark Prophecy, but surely you don't mean that!"

"No, m'lord, it is indeed not very old at all. But for it to be called Meicalian Prophecy, they say, the Seer or Seeress must study in the Valley of the Gifted and submit to their High Synod."

Funeas nodded. "True, go on. Where did you acquire this Prophecy?"

"We only just decoded it before we traveled here, and we have not even shared it yet with His Highness. It came to us in the last war from a Seeress who lived in your very own land who refused to go to the Valley of the Gifted."

Prince Filiddor stiffened. "What? Pray tell us her name, Ambassador!"

"She went by the name *Kalemna Deroge.* She died during the war. Have you heard of her, Your Highness?"

For Filiddor's part, he hesitated, and he and Ultrech eyed each other. They had no memory of her, for she disappeared when they were children. But their grandfather, Lanwi's father, the former Prince Muldone, did.

She was both a cousin and one of his lovers. And there was no denying she was a Seeress; she correctly predicted the day of Muldone's death. When Lanwi, Filiddor's father inherited the throne of Hesk, he made Deroge leave, hoping to be rid of anymore unsavory predictions. Unfortunately for Lanwi, on her way out the palace doors, she predicted correctly his death date as well.

"She disappeared during the last war," said Filiddor cautiously. "It has been suggested Tribesmen captured her, K'trek. Is that how you know she died?"

"The Chieftains might know more of her story, Your Highness. But yes, she was captured. Apparently, in a fit of despair she managed to acquire a dagger and took her own life."

"Yes, I can imagine one such as she might do such a thing," replied Filiddor. "I presume she proclaimed this Prophecy while in your capture?"

"It was on her person, Your Highness, on a tiny scroll."

"And did you bring it with you?"

"I was to make it clear to you, Your Highness, the Chieftains felt it unwise to send it with us this time. However, if all went well this visit, I am to assure you it will be presented upon our return. But I know the Prophecy, for I was required to commit it to memory and to repeat it for you.

The Door is shut, the Dragons sleep
Their last sleep. Their prey is dead. They famish.
Meical's Scourge ends.
One claims Tolos. The Usurper, his child will defeat.

The Door is shut, though look deep.
Look very deep. The child, a scion of Ch'ndra. No blemish.
Time bends.
Old Empire renewed? When New and Old meet.

From the North they will come to set it aright.
With alliance of Princes they will fight.
South will bend to the will of the North.
New kingdom will now spring forth.

The councilors sat listening carefully. Filiddor considered. He might not have cared much for the person of Kalemna Deroge. As far as he was concerned, she was nothing better than a whore and troublemaker, the source of much animosity in the family. But he liked what he was hearing.

"So, as you see, m'lords," concluded K'trek, "all is in order! The door is shut to the past. The Dragons on Tolos, Meical's Scourge, have died out, starved of prey. Your father the former Prince lay claim to Tolos but was denied it. His Highness, Prince Filiddor, the scion of Ch'ndra will defeat the usurper's child, Duke Amerro of Tulesk. The Chieftains and Prince Filiddor unite to form a new northern kingdom. The South, that is what is left of Solanto, will accept the new order."

The ambassador's eyes seemed to capture each of them as he spoke. Not one person in the room appeared remotely skeptical as to this interpretation, and all nodded appreciatively in his direction.

"Seems simple enough. Deroge's Gift was never called into question, not even by the Sages." Filiddor said, looking around at the others. K'trek noticed Ultrech and Funeas wink at the prince.

That was too easy, said the Tribesman to himself. *She will control them readily.*

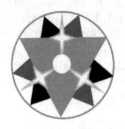

Chapter 3—Slave and Sorceress

Silently he stood, guarding the entrance to her private chamber. He was a giant of a man, black skin of eastern origin, and with massive musculature, obviously trained over many years for physical combat. His garb was black with the yellow wolf insignia emblazoned on his breastplate. A long and heavy sword hung at his side. Seeing him for the first time, a stranger might perceive a proud and fierce face, a professional soldier in his prime.

Dru the Topslayer was famous in his division, a skilled weapons master. Yet despite the aloof pride demonstrated among his peers, he was still a slave. He was both a Citadel Guard and combat champion in servitude to the Alkhaness of Westrealm Khestadon. His life was not his own. Bound by mindspells to serve her wishes and hers alone, Dru had no means to escape and choose a different path.

She had been away for some time, an expedition to the lands westward, on the borders of the land of Berug and the Etoppsi menace. He had not been ordered to attend her this time, and so it was not his concern. Yet he realized it was the longest she had been away from the Citadel in all the years he had served her.

"Dru."

He did not know why, but he found he didn't mind she was gone. He was loyal, but somewhere within himself, in a deep place he rarely visited, he had a hint of remorse his life couldn't have been different. Simpler, more free. A farmer in a distant village far from this dark castle and this bleak city, or even a fisherman in one of the coastal villages. However, it was only when she was away such thoughts took shape. Distance from her opened his mind to independent observation, minutely anyway. Yet when near, the spells of compulsion she wove around her guards and officials assumed greater intensity, and all those internal thoughts Dru occasionally had were abandoned. He feared her, and above all feared failure in her presence. As did everyone. Few who failed her lived long. He had watched comrades die in torture for their failure. From her hand yellow lightning would burst forth in torturous pulses. In agony they crumpled. Those were the ones for which she showed mercy. When she was in the mood to teach a lesson, it was worse.

"Dru. I Call you to Me."

Suddenly, unexpectedly, and surely for the first time, Dru realized something strange had captured his thoughts. He hated her! The emotion startled him, for it came unbidden. He wondered, reaching into his mind. He kept imagining there was a Voice calling him, calling him to open himself to a truth. Perhaps he had always hated her; why had he never really considered it before?

A dangerous emotion it was. He shook his head as if to clear his mind. It really was as if there was Someone Else competing for control of his mind—some Voice not quite his. And certainly not hers.

True, his nightly dreams had been troubled of late, as if memories were being pulled from him while he slept. In waking life all he could remember was that he was a slave to the Alkhaness and that it was his purpose in life—he was *chosen*, they had said—to be a palace guard, and since boyhood he had been trained for this purpose. Later he understood only certain boys with particular traits were chosen, those biggest and tallest for their age, and it was always presented to him as a privilege to serve in this way.

But these recent dreams suggested something different, and Dru couldn't be sure if they reflected memory or fancy. In one dream there was a young but care-worn woman next to a small fireplace in a tiny shack and the smell of fish cooking. In another, the same woman was there with a large bearded man, a laborer in a slave's tunic. Yet always the man wore a happy expression as he tossed a young boy playfully into the air and with confident strength catch him again. The two would laugh and enjoy the play, and the woman, too, smiled.

There were many dreams of this sort and then finally a dream occurred of a day when the door opened, and men in black garb and armed with swords took the boy and carried him away as the woman cried and the man pleaded.

"Dru. You are light in the darkness."

Were they his parents? Western white and eastern black ethnicities were equally common in the Khestadone realms, and much mixing, for that matter. The father and mother and little boy in these new dreams were notably black-skinned like himself, of purest eastern blood. If the dreams reflected the reality of Dru's past, he certainly never saw them again. All he could remember in his waking life as a boy were tough, brutal, strong men, and other boys like himself living in stone barracks, being flogged with whips for their indiscretions, trained to fight one another under supervision, and regular bouts of prostrated prayer to a strange goddess he had never heard of before.

Over time he grew exceedingly tall and strong, a giant among men. There were quite a number of these giants like himself in the bodyguard units, yet even among these he was the tallest. He stood proudly in skirmishes in the north against the Nantians and had even encountered and slain an Etoppsi spy once upon a time, for which he had won renown and his nickname 'Topslayer.' Their males were as colossi and not easily killed. Finally, he was chosen as one of the elite few. The Citadel Guard had great renown throughout Khestadon. At least in the army it did, and in the Khestadone realms it was only the army that mattered. He clearly remembered the great ceremony in the presence of the Alkhaness herself, where he and the others prostrated themselves before her, and the temple priests sang dirges. One by one she laid her black-leathered hands upon them and spoke strange words in a language only she and the priests seemed to understand. He remembered a physical pain under a yellow light, as her words were those of power and contained spells of enchantment. Through them there would be no question he would always be loyal to her, and he would give his life to protect her.

It had been ten years now since that ceremony. He wasn't sure his age now, but he believed he was perhaps in his early thirties. He continued to serve her and was one of her champions in the tournaments against chosen ones from the lands of her cohort beyond the Strait, the Alkhan of Eastrealm. Dru had even slain one of the great bears the Alkhan had championed, a remarkable feat. The impressed Alkhan offered to buy Dru, but the Alkhaness refused.

Dru often guarded this chamber door. She might have favored him. Yet he could never quite tell. He never saw behind her mask. Only her yellow eyes. And those cat-like pupils only and always contained one message, and they were the same for everyone: *Fear me.*

"Dru. Come to Me. You are needed."

As he thought on these things, however, he felt strange. Empty. It was as if these great deeds and honors had lost their value. What good was it serving a wicked sorceress as she attempted to expand her hateful dominion across the lands? Perhaps it would have been better had he died long ago in one of those skirmishes with the Nantians. He admired the enemy northerners, for their faces were noble and proud. Was that the mark of a freeman? The Etoppsi

Feather whom he had slain came unexpectedly to mind. Proud, strong, with his great, dark wings—why did Dru now feel regret? Was it that the Nantians and the Berugians had something to fight for? He despised himself for having no control over his own life. But a slave he was and always would be.

Shaking his head again in puzzlement, he saw that his counterpart on the other side of the door was glancing sidelong at him. The other guard was surely wondering why he appeared out of sorts. Dru ignored him.

"She comes now. Yet I will not leave you, Dru. I will be Calling you for as long as you live. I claim all Light for Myself."

The last of the morning slipped away. A sense of dread began slowly and with inevitability to overtake his faculties, and Dru knew from experience what it meant. The Alkhaness had returned to her city and was approaching the citadel. He swallowed hard. Maybe he did hate her, but he was also enthralled. Try as he might he would never be able to separate himself from her, and escape was impossible, not because he wasn't capable of running and hiding, but rather because he was not in control. Invisible threads of magic bound him to her. She would find him.

One short moment again of wondering why he was thinking like this in the first place. But then it was gone.

His dread and anticipation increased as another hour went by. She was very near now. Dru looked to his left at his cohort. Their eyes met briefly, for it was clear he too sensed her approach, but neither spoke. More minutes passed...a quarter hour, maybe longer. He had become oblivious to the time, for time was irrelevant for a slave. Finally, the distant clanging of great doors, and at the end of the long, dark hall a flash of yellow robes appeared in his line of sight. He now lost all control of his own thinking and stood straight. He was now only a body trained for protecting the Alkhaness, guarding her chamber and serving her needs. He lost his individuality.

Torches lining the wall flickered, bowing to her masked presence. As her yellow robes swirled past, Dru the slave also bowed.

In a harsh language a word was spoken. Slowly, but by no visible means, heavy doors swung silently inward. Red light immediately welled within, displacing the darkness. When she entered, she raised her hand, and the doors closed silently behind her.

Dru's mind opened again oh so slightly, but the sense of dread did not dissipate. He looked at his cohort who stood resolute and unflinching. Making an attempt to recapture his earlier thoughts, Dru could no longer remember any of it. Except for one thing.

He remembered he hated her.

Inside, the chamber was unnaturally cold for this southern clime, but the Alkhaness preferred it that way. The chill reminded her of the past...of a long ago time when she dwelt in the far north as a young child nearly five centuries ago. She approached a large, white, columnar pedestal, atop which stood a strange cube—the facets of which were perhaps twelve inches across and made of black glass, or perhaps it was a massive onyx crystal sculpted and polished.

She bent her thought upon it causing a yellow light to flicker within. *Was he there?* Another minute she waited, patiently, and then a voice emanated from the crystal, and a pale white, sharp face appeared in each of the cube's various facets.

"YOU HAVE RETURNED," said the voice. It was drear. Conniving. She was used to that voice, but it had no power over her, although she knew he liked to pretend it did.

She removed her helm and mask, revealing a severe feminine face in complexion like to that of the one in the Cube. She responded, "Yes, Ch'ain, I have."

He waited a few moments, expecting her to say something more, but when she did not he inserted, "YOU DID NOT FIND IT."

His displeasure did not particularly bother her, and she looked directly at one side of the cube, the one which showed his face looking forward, so she could peer into his eyes and make it clear she was not intimidated. "You have made an error. I have wasted two months trusting your word."

"THAT DOORWAY IS THERE. THE MAP IS WITHOUT DECEIPT."

"I have many still searching, but they will not find anything. The location you have declared appears to be in the Infested Jungle itself, near to the southern end of the Wall of the Etoppsi menace. Many died from the dangers under the canopy, and wild Dragons are likely to find the rest and kill them." Not that she showed remorse at this. These could be spared. She had thousands at her disposal and could later send more if she felt the need. But she doubted it would be necessary. He had been wrong before. Yet she had to admit she too wanted that Doorway to be there. "Send me the map, Ch'ain. Perhaps I can determine something from it."

She doubted he would do this. They shared a common goal, but he did not trust her. He left her realm years ago in order to rule his own in the mountain lands and desert across the Strait. He was impatient for conquest. Without her advice he had begun a war with the eastern kingdoms of the old Anterianhi, a war for which she wished him well, but for which she believed he should have waited. He should have delayed and waited for her plans to bear fruition. Of course she could not tell him her plans. She did not trust him either.

"IT IS THERE. GO BACK AND SEARCH AGAIN," he said in a commanding voice.

She would not take orders from Him. She had only gone this time as a favor, for the opportunity seemed too great to let pass. But those two months had proven nothing. The place he had pinpointed was perilously close to the Berugian border, and in addition to Dragons there was risk of war with the Berugians, something she had prepared long for, but for which she was still not quite ready.

"Go yourself. I will not stop you. You may travel through my lands if you please." She thought for a moment, and then had an idea. "Ch'ain, perhaps we should search together. However, I will only do so if you bring the map you say you found. I wish to study it for myself. The land itself may have changed since the map was made. Perhaps I can determine something from it. I refuse to bother about it again until I see the evidence for myself."

He was silent for a while, frowning. His yellow eyes shifted in his blanched face, looking fully into those of his counterpart. He forced a smile although it was not pleasant.

She returned her own. It had been a very long time since they had hunted together. She continued, "Since you are so certain the Doorway is there, then the chances of our success would be much greater. Together we may discover something."

There was silence between them for a long minute. Finally, "YES, CH'YAD, PERHAPS YOU ARE RIGHT. I WILL BRING THE MAP AND I WILL COME. YOU SAY THERE ARE DRAGONS NEAR THE LOCATION? I MAY HAVE A SOLUTION FOR THAT PROBLEM. AND ANOTHER TOURNAMENT, PERHAPS?"

"No, Ch'ain. I have no more time for frivolity, and neither do you. Soon we must act in concert. You have yet to tell me of your preparations for a second front."

"WHEN I AM READY TO SHARE THEM, I WILL."

His face instantly vanished from the crystal, replaced again by the eerie yellow light which faded slowly until finally snuffing itself out. Ch'yad was annoyed by the abrupt dismissal. She knew he intended it as a subtle means of control. Annoyed or not, she told herself she did not care. Once he crossed the Strait, her powers would be as great as his, and he could not dominate her. Despite her distaste for Ch'ain's methods, they nevertheless shared a common goal.

"The time is near," Ch'yad said aloud to no one but herself.

Which reminded her: she had another task at hand. Ch'ain kept his secrets, but she too had hers.

She returned to the black crystalline cube. This was one of her secrets. The two cubes came with them on the last ship, and she allowed her counterpart to take one when he relocated across the Strait. They were of an ancient pre-Ralsheen magic, and as far as she knew no record existed of their creation. They used them to communicate with one another; they were very useful.

Only two years ago Ch'yad became curious again about the cubes, wondering if she could make others. As her realm expanded, a faster method of communication with the satraps and temple priests would have been very useful. She had not succeeded in making new ones, and it appeared the secret to their making was lost. Still, it was upon her exploration of its magic that she discovered a critical difference.

This cube was not the same as Ch'ain's.

Yes, one of her own secrets. Oh, how jealous Ch'ain would be if he only knew! But she had no intention of telling him. Yet in addition to its other attributes, she had discovered there was yet another cube.

With her long, black-gloved fingers she touched a particular point of the facet on the right side. The yellow light that kindled within was soon replaced by natural white light. There was a brief glimpse of clouds, snow, and mountains. It had been close to five centuries since Ch'yad had last felt snow on her face, but she cast the thought aside. There it was: a quick sight of a stone citadel built in a hillside next to an ice-filled bay. After another moment of concentration the cube responded as it was intended.

For this she would not wear her mask.

She touched the cube and closed her eyes and found herself 'inside' the other prism looking out onto a somewhat dark, circular, stone room, lit with many torches. One large fire—its smoke rising to an oculus in the dome far above—crackled only a few feet away from where she knew the cube in which she appeared rested on a block of granite. She had visited here many times in the last two years, directing the affairs of the Ice Chieftains of the far north, maintaining her commanding presence over them. The Ice Tribes were descendants of the last holdouts of the Ralsheen, driven out by the rebel Anterianhi in the last battles. They did not know exactly who Ch'yad was, for she had not told them yet. Nevertheless, they rightly understood she was connected to their past, for she was clearly Of the White, and she understood their language.

This was the chamber where the Conclave of the Chieftains gathered in the cold north beyond the Ice Mountains. In this chamber, directed outward from their own cube—a relic from the time of the Anterianhi Rebellion which their ancestors had saved, though its purpose until recently forgotten—she had other powers over them through it. She had not long ago transferred a tiny portion of her magic to the one called K'trek. He had a mind that worked like hers. And he was Of the White. It was a trait common to all the Chieftains and their families, but K'trek was young and handsome. She liked the way he looked at her. One day she hoped to meet him in person. She would touch him, and he would be hers.

There they sat in a large circle all around, some thirty, all in seal fur capes. In a moment she had their fullest attention. It had been over two months. One of the Chieftains, K'lent by name, spoke. "Yes, Mistress, we are your servants. How may we serve you?"

She looked long and hard at his cunning face. These were a proud people, and she had developed some pride in them, but at this moment she was not happy. Perhaps it was her annoyance with Ch'ain. Perhaps it was something else.

Ah! Now she realized. "How did you address me, just now, K'lent?"

Through the cube she felt the fear abruptly build in him as he lowered his eyes. "Your Exalted Majesty!"

He bowed low.

That was better, but if this one made one more error he would have to be taught a lesson. He had learned to fear her, although he hated himself for it. She did not care as long as he did as he was told. He had been somewhat useful in the past. But there were other chieftains. They had no single leader, which had so far been convenient.

"I want to know if there has been any progress on our plan, K'lent. Why else would I have contacted you?"

The others shifted in their seats as they looked uneasily from the cube to K'lent. "Yes, Your Exalted Majesty, of course. Yes! Yes, there has been great progress!" He stepped closer. "The ambassador returned only yesterday, though he is not here at the moment. We were about to contact you again, since we are now all gathered. It took time for all to travel here. We have been holding conference."

"It is a good thing, then," she said. She looked around the circle. Nearly all were present, she believed, as she scanned their faces. None dared look into her eyes for long. "Pray, continue. So you have good news, K'lent?"

"I do, Your Exalted Majesty! I do, indeed! The Prince has accepted our offer of allegiance...and an alliance!"

Yes! K'trek managed it. That was exactly as she had wished. Oh, how she now wanted to contact the prince herself. The Ice Tribes had been a key. A key to a greater plan.

"The ambassador brought us further news, Your Exalted Majesty! We have firm confirmation there are no more Dragons on Tolos! In fact, some of the Solantines have attempted to settle there.

We have always believed when the Dragons disappeared out of the northlands, it would be a sign of the Restoration!"

Remarkable, she thought. A Prophecy fulfilled! Yet she was taken aback at the idea of settlement. There were secrets on Tolos which must be protected. She might have to advance her plans more swiftly. Finding that Doorway would be providential. She would have to devote more resources to it and wondered if Ch'ain's offer of assistance might really prove useful.

"Send this cube to the prince," she abruptly exclaimed.

K'lent appeared stunned. In fact, they all did. There were shifting movements and many whispers in the chamber.

"Not wise. The prism has been here for over four hundred years! It has been a symbol of our connection with our ancestral past! Surely, Your Exalted Majesty, you must understand!"

They appeared even more shocked than before as they stared with open mouths at K'lent. Secretly they may have agreed with him, but their fear of her kept them wisely silent.

It was unfortunate K'lent's own wisdom had failed.

With a sudden fire in her yellow eyes she pierced him with a deadly chill, and she sensed the terror now gripping him. Yes, he had been useful in the past. But there were plenty of Chieftains present who would be willing to do her bidding without question.

"A symbol of your past? I am in the present, you fool, and I will determine events! From this point forward you no longer need mere *symbols!*"

Assuredly, she thought, a *master* cube. They needed to learn. K'trek knew. Now they would all know.

She watched as they all gasped, and many had risen from their seats in the circle, though they dared not approach the man. K'lent appeared frozen in place, looking at his own legs. Blue-white ice traveled rapidly up his body and he cried out in pain. He looked at her in horror. She smiled maliciously.

"Your Exalted Majesty!" He could barely choke out the words. "P…please forgive…!"

But it was too late for that. She had to teach him a lesson. Yes. Teach them all a lesson they would not soon forget. She would not use the mind control spells on them that she wove upon her southern slaves and armies, for the Tribesmen were her own people and devoutly worshipped Siriné. Nevertheless, they would obey her unchallenged or suffer the consequences.

The poisoned ice was now at K'lent's chest, and he was constricted and losing consciousness. He looked pleadingly into her face, but he could no longer speak. None in the chamber dared to move.

Suddenly, his head froze so hard it cracked, followed by an explosive fracturing as his body in a hundred pieces scattered grotesquely across the floor and across the feet of those gathered. Shards that fell near to the fire began to steam and hiss. The other Chieftains stood aghast at the carnage.

She repeated calmly, "Send this prism to the prince immediately."

Another Chieftain, however, with some boldness but with greater tact, stepped forward. "Yes, Your Exalted Majesty, immediately! But how shall we communicate with you? You have led us for so long, now!" and he bowed low.

"The Prince of Hesk." she stated flatly. "I will now hold conference with the Prince of Hesk, and you shall now follow him. And if things work as I expect them to, it will not be long before he is your king."

They all bowed low. "Yes, Your Exalted Majesty!" they said in one voice.

"That is better," she said. "I prefer one mutual voice! But soon the Prince of Hesk will be your one voice. Choose one of your number to represent the Conclave as he offers homage to the Prince for all of you. Have the ambassador explain to the Prince how to contact me through the prism."

And when this cousin of mine looks into my eyes, he will know me, and I will have him as my own. She looked all around to ensure no more was to be said. All were silent. Her own was to be the last voice in any of her communications with those she ruled. They had learned this well.

Task completed, she disengaged from the cube.

She considered the new information. It was mostly good. However, there was a problem if the Solantines were already settling Tolos. She thought of Ch'ain again and the Doorway. If it could be found, it would indeed make many things easier. He had better bring that map with him, she thought to herself. She wondered where he obtained it.

Ch'yad had much to think about as she stood silently now in her red chamber. Despite the problems, her plans were progressing well.

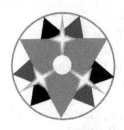

Chapter 4—Curdoz Travels North

The muslin swirled softly at the window of a bedroom at the Laughing Dog, a small inn just off the Northern Road in the important crossroad town of Trimm. Cool air fell across the face of the occupant in the bed causing him to stir. In length below his ears lay brown hair, full, flecked with gray. Thin lines at his temples spoke of a man in late middle age. It was still early when High Lord Curdoz, Sage of Solanto, awakened refreshed from his slumber.

A pair of blue-gray eyes noted first the movement of the curtain, and the morning light around its edges. He shuddered. Perhaps it was a mistake, he thought, to have cracked opened the window the night before, but it had been warmer than was comfortable when he dropped into bed. He stood, rubbed his scruff, pulled back the curtain and secured the window. Then he made his short way to the grate, grabbed a poker and stirred the ashes to uncover the remnants of glowing embers, and tossed in some leaves and pine needles from a nearby wooden box. After adding some of the kindling and logs stacked near the door it wasn't long before bright flames reflected upon his face. Looking out the window again, he noted the morning was mostly clear, and he guessed what little snow remained in Trimm would be gone by the end of the day. He thought of dressing immediately, changed his mind, filled his pipe for a smoke, and then leaned back in the chair near the fire in order to consider his plan for the day.

He pondered the idea of borrowing a horse in the town. It would have been easy for the asking. Many would have appreciated a chance to assist the important man any way they could. Count Ferono, whose estate bordered Trimm on the west side, would have loaned him one without a second thought. Or he could borrow at the local Kingsmen barracks. Maybe it was time to proceed with more speed. Curdoz had brought no horse of his own, for he had thought the extra time taken on foot would be of value in several ways. First he knew it would give him more time to work out the meaning of the Vision that Meical the Guardian had incorporated into his dreams those weeks ago. Too, it was bound to build up his strength after a winter spent mostly indoors at his home, Villa Saundry. There was assuredly a longer journey to come once he found the twins in his Vision, and then begin the quest the Guardian had appointed them. Finally, he thought, he had no idea who the twins were and whether they themselves were up to a long journey, and they, too, would benefit from a walk through peaceful Solanto to toughen them before departing the country southwards. Curdoz knew there would likely be times when they would have the use of horses. He expected much of the journey would be by ship and foot, although he was yet uncertain of their first destination once they left the country. Upon meeting the twins he hoped there would be some clarity. Had Meical sent them Visions as well? The Sage certainly hoped and even expected so. It would make it much easier to explain to them why they would have to leave their home, although the picture in his mind indicated they were of age and were perhaps ready to make their way in the world.

After this quarter hour mental debate, Curdoz thought it best to stick with his original plan. Some of his notions he knew did not make sense on the issue, for ultimately horseback was really no hindrance to anything. It was more as if he were making excuses not to borrow a horse. Yet, speed did not seem to be of sufficient value for now. He almost felt he was being told by an inner voice not to rush. Patience, rather, was a virtue, a lesson taught to all those who studied in the Valley of the Gifted, and nothing in the Vision he had received indicated there was need for speed, at least not yet. He believed if the twins had been presented with Visions, there would be more clarity on this point as well. So much depended on whether they had. It bothered Curdoz, because there were just too many pieces missing to the puzzle. If they had not had a Vision, he expected he would just have to wait until the Guardian offered more clarity somehow. Yes, he thought again, patience was a virtue. Finding the twins was the most he could ask for at this point.

He looked at his now smokeless pipe. Carved of ambernut and given to him by his friend, Grand Duke Mannago, he turned it to look at the detail. It was a beautiful piece, of intricate pattern with tiny frolicking dogs and cats winding around it, and he wondered what skilled craftsman made it. The Sage stood up and stretched, putting it away in his pack. He then took the opportunity of the basin of water and soap to wash up as best he could, which he proceeded to do close to the fire in order to stay warm. He blustered, for he had become accustomed to hot water being brought to him by the Monastic servants at Villa Saundry. He skipped shaving again. He didn't like shaving, and only did so when he knew he was to attend some function or to meet important persons such as the king. Besides, the water was cold for shaving.

After he dressed, it did not take him long to finish his packing. He made his way to the kitchen. His friends, the innkeepers Leskin and Anni, would by now have prepared more food for his travels.

There he found a plump, graying woman, cheerfully humming a tune. "Good morning, Curdoz!"

She was in her checkered apron bustling about in front of the fireplace. Her face was bright as she began to dish the food she had prepared. At the end of a large deal table cut from one enormous oak log were three place settings, for as it turned out the Sage was their only guest.

Leskin, her equally plump and nearly bald husband, burst in the rear door, humming the same tune as his wife. He unloaded firewood near the hearth, and then they all settled to consume their meal. Their conversation was for the most part light and friendly. Breakfast was divine, thought Curdoz: ham hash, fried diced potatoes, flat cakes and butter, and a crispy, honeyed apple dish, made from some of the last of the winter store.

"You'll go through County Ostin of course on your way to Tulesk. Are you stopping at your old homestead?" inquired Leskin.

The three of them shared Ascantian heritage. Anni and Leskin had grown up in the village of Cerocco not far from the Hescian border. After their betrothal and the traditional Matrimonial Bonding they removed to Trimm to take over the management of the inn which had once belonged to Anni's great uncle.

"No," Curdoz replied. "I'll travel through Davos, of course, as it is on the road, but I don't really have a reason to go over to the farm. I realize now I never told you my father died. Last year."

"Is that so?" asked Leskin, looking up from his meal and setting down his fork. "I'm sorry to hear it, my friend. No, it wasn't in your last letter."

"His name was Normene, wasn't it?" asked Anni for clarification.

"No, you're confusing him with my uncle. He is Normene. My father's name was Luvin. I'm sure I've talked about my uncle more often, for I am close to him. Uncle Normene was the one who helped me understand what was happening when I began having Meicalian Visions in my youth. He's very old now, and he lives on Island Saundry with me. I have plenty of Monastics on hand to watch after him."

"I guess we've not heard you talk of your father, Curdoz. I presume you communicated with him?"

"Oh, yes. He never wanted me to go off to the Valley of the Gifted, and it caused strain between us, but in the end he didn't stop me. But yes, I would go see him when I traveled through Davos." He took a swig from his mug of chicory coffee, looked out the kitchen window as a memory was stirred. After a minute he added. "Anyhow, the farm has changed hands, now, and I don't know who owns it. I doubt I will ever go back."

There was a minute of silence following this bit of finality. Curdoz sensed Leskin and Anni weren't quite sure how to respond. Maybe he'd been too plain in showing his true feelings for his father.

"I've packed some food for your journey," said Anni finally. "You should have plenty for a few days."

"Thank you. I was running short. People will happily feed me wherever I go, you know, but I, oh…"

"Everyone wants you to solve their problems, don't they?" offered Leskin, smiling.

"Exactly so," Curdoz said with a chuckle. "I don't mind proclaiming the Guardian's Affirmation on anyone. But it's the other. The king's justices are very fair, but the people often want to pull me into their legal arguments. I should have more patience of course, but it gets to be a bother, and I don't usually have time for it. What you've packed will keep me from having to feel obligated in the daytime as I travel."

"We're glad to help you. You may be the Sage of Solanto, but we just hold you as a dear friend."

"Which is why I stay here when I come! It has been great seeing you," and he meant it.

"Count Ferono would not like…"

"Ah, yes, but what he doesn't know won't hurt him." It was somewhat customary of the local lords to entertain the Sage when he traveled the country carrying out his duties. Though it was good to maintain cordial relations with the powerful, Curdoz often felt the need to be apart from such people. Besides, he thought the lavishness of many of them was absurd (except, of course, for the fine wines they served) for it was all a pretense as they competed for favors. He was happy to sacrifice his wine for a chance to light his pipe by a warm fire, a habit considered uncouth by noblemen, and for pleasant common folk to talk to.

With breakfast complete, Anni and Leskin walked Curdoz to the end of their street where it connected to the Northern Road. Only a few other travelers were present this early. The Sage shook Leskin's hands and then took both of Anni's and held them together to kiss them. "The Guardian Affirms you, dear ones."

"Thank you, my friend! From what you were telling us of your journey, you will come back through here, certainly?" asked Leskin.

"Two or three weeks at the least, though. I don't know how long until I find the twins I spoke of from the Vision. They could be anywhere in Tulesk, perhaps as far as Cumpero or even Peek for all I know. The Guardian didn't give me much to go on, I'm afraid. Which reminds me. Keep our conversation from last night to yourselves. I haven't had a Vision in many years. It wouldn't do to have people questioning me."

"No worries there. Since no one else stayed with us last night, we don't even need to share the fact you were here. We were lucky to have such a quiet night!" said Leskin. "Anyway, we wish you peaceful travels. We hope you find what and whom you seek."

"Thank you again. I'm sure I will. Goodbye for now." He walked briskly down the road, but turned one last time. They waved, as did he. He felt as close to them as he did only a handful of others. There was Grand Duke Mannago, Father Marco, and his uncle, but Normene was losing his memory and could no longer provide helpful company. Too, there was cheery Theneri in Aster, and most of all, Idamé, his close companion from their days together in the Valley. As he considered her he wondered where in Solanto she might be. He hadn't heard from her in some time. He had thought much of her lately and hoped he'd see her once more before he had to leave the country. There was no knowing how long he would be away. He knew he would miss her more than anyone.

He broadened his pace. He reckoned if all went well and the weather stayed fine, he would manage all the way to Thorune sometime on the fourth night.

The day proved itself warmer than expected, and the Sage was obliged late in the morning to lower his hood and remove his gloves. The remnants of the last winter snow were rapidly melting in the bright sun. Three nights he stayed with farm families whose homes were near to the road and who felt immensely honored to host such a guest. On the fourth morning out from Trimm, the prevailing westerly wind dropped away, explained by the fact the land was less open now. Creating a border between counties Nees and Ostin, a series of woodlands, low quiet hills and intermittent small homesteads marked a change of scenery from the snow-patched plains he'd traversed the last few days. He knew it would not last long, just another day's journey until the lands opened out again a few miles beyond Davos. Curdoz was familiar with all the landscapes throughout Solanto due to his extensive travels, but more so with Ascanti and especially the land of his old home in County Ostin. Indeed as a boy he often romped among these very hills. That is, when he felt he could escape from his father for a half day.

As he walked, the memories inevitably returned. So much had happened in the years since he had left this place to go and study in the Valley. His earliest years were not unhappy, but his mother had died young, and his father refused to find another Bondmate. Because there were only the two of them at home, there was a tremendous amount of labor to keep the farm operating smoothly. They had a couple of hired hands, for his father Luvin was a freeman farmer. The land was his own, one of the few such holdings in this part of the country before the Reforms, and so they were better off than some. They sold a good deal of produce and thus made a decent living, but it was nevertheless a tough life for the two of them. Without his mother's intermediation, conflict increased between son and father. Luvin was infuriated when Curdoz claimed he was having Visions and had to follow the Calling. Only with the aid of his father's brother, his Uncle Normene, did Luvin relent, though he refused to offer his Blessing. That was hurtful.

So, it was Normene who escorted his young nephew to Island Saundry to see Galin the Sage. He confirmed they were Meicalian Visions and sent Curdoz on to the Valley for the required seven years of study. The years there were the most enjoyable and carefree Curdoz had ever experienced, though the last war with the Ice Tribes, which had begun before he'd left home, was still taking place between those peoples and Solanto. The Valley was untouched by it. It was a land of powerful beauty that inspired the soul.

It turned out his magical powers in the Gift were significant, though not at the level of Healers. Yet he gained knowledge rapidly through devoted study and was accounted wise, a good orator, and demonstrated administrative skills. It soon became clear that Curdoz was destined to the Order of the Sages, those Gifted few who were charged with administering the Orders within the various kingdoms and acting as advisors to the rulers. Galin, now aged and tired, was pleased when Curdoz was sent back. After long conversations in which the older man imparted upon Curdoz his knowledge of Solantine politics, he resigned his office to Curdoz and retired to the Valley.

Curdoz returned just as the war ended, and it was a busy time. He was still quite young, but he approached the recently anointed King Carlomen with a view to changing many things. With the help of the old Grand Duke of Escarant, Mannago's father, the king agreed to use his power and influence to make these changes. The Sage, the king and the grand duke together made a formidable trio. There were many of these Reforms, but the most important as far as Curdoz was concerned was the re-appropriation of vast tracts of land from the nobles to the peasants and the freeing of the towns from their control. It was perhaps Curdoz' greatest achievement when he used his skill for oratory, and with the Book of Histories and Prophecies in hand, he convinced them at the King's Council that their subtle oppression of the masses was leading them down a path similar to that of the old Ralsheen Empire, and the same trouble lay ahead for Solanto if change did not come soon.

He would always deny the accolade, but most claimed Curdoz was the greatest Sage Solanto had ever known. Certainly the common folk revered him. Even so, he had his few detractors, and he now grimly thought on these. The former Prince Lanwi of Hesk, and his young son Filiddor after him, attempted to block the Reforms whenever possible and refused to implement any of the changes in their Principality, continuing to rule sternly through a system based on serfdom. Due to their special circumstance in the kingdom—they were essentially independent—the king could not demand submission from them on the Reforms. The Principality was a key ally in the wars with the Ice Tribes, and the king could not afford to alienate its lords. There was enough lingering tension due to the recent war, for the princes did not gain any of the lands they wished for. Nevertheless, Curdoz tried. He personally met with the Hescian barons on many occasions when he needed to consult the Asterian Library, but though they always showed him the proper courtesies, they never budged on any of his suggestions. And whenever the prince deigned to attend the King's Council, his presence created tension, particularly with Duganri, Duke of Tulesk. Duganri had been granted most of the conquered lands following the war.

The tension continued when the sons inherited their father's offices. Prince Filiddor despised Duke Amerro, Duganri's son. It bothered Curdoz greatly, for he had great admiration for Amerro, whom he thought a generous, though admittedly ambitious, nobleman. Amerro's support actually hurt the cause of the Reforms with regards to the Principality of Hesk. Curdoz shook his head as he considered Prince Filiddor's obstinacy.

Thinking of Amerro caused Curdoz' thoughts to circle back to his current task. The Sage realized it was just as likely the twins from his Vision were provincials and did not even live near Cumpero, Amerro's ducal capital. The Vision was too vague. Tulesk was all that was made clear to him, and the faces of the twins were imprinted on his mind as well—he knew he'd recognize them instantly. They were handsome, strikingly so, and possibly of Escarantine ancestry for they were dark-complexioned. But Tulesk was a big territory, and he reckoned he might walk for days seeing barely anyone on the road to Cumpero. All he could do was force himself to have trust. Would another Vision present itself after he arrived in Tulesk? He could not think of any other means by which the task could be made simpler. Maybe he did not feel the need for a horse now. Yet he now decided if he were in Tulesk three or four days without success, he would then borrow if he could. He knew there was the new County Fothemry and the seat of Felto not too far from the border with Ascanti. Maybe he could acquire a horse there if need be.

It was mid-day when he approached the small town of Davos in County Ostin on the Northern Road, the nearest town to his family's old farmstead. Being the tail end of winter, his travel so far had been relatively quiet. Perhaps three dozen wagons each day had passed him going in one or the other direction laden with trade goods, and there was once a small south-bound contingent of Kingsmen foot soldiers who recognized the Sage with the green stole he wore, easily seen when his cloak was open. They stopped and saluted. After he pronounced a customary Meicalian Affirmation, they continued on their way. He knew in a few short weeks the road would be busy with spring traffic, yet he did not mind the relative quiet, for it allowed for good thinking.

Being hungry, he stepped off the road and climbed a nearby hill and sat down to eat some of the remaining provisions Anni had provided. He looked to the northwest and far off he thought he could make out the castle-estate of Count Ostin on a distant hill. Curdoz appreciated Ostin, or more particularly his father who was no-nonsense when it came to implementing the Reforms. He knew his neighbors to the northeast, Counts Mere and Nees, on the border with Hesk, had more conservative views and had been opposed to change, implementing them only reluctantly. They were certainly not the only ones of the noblemen of Ascanti to resist the Reforms, and Curdoz knew it had as much to do with proximity to and influence of the Prince of Hesk as anything else. Snoffit, Duke of Ascanti, was the only high lord on the King's Council who would occasionally speak in the prince's favor, but nevertheless his loyalty was to the king and he ultimately agreed to the Reforms, his barons following suit.

After his solitary lunch, the Sage returned to the Road and made his way toward the town. He strongly considered taking across fields on the west side skirting the village and speaking to no one. However, it dawned on him all his long thinking was causing him some low-level anxiety, and this in turn was leading him to want more solitude. This happened to him a great deal, for in his deepest nature Curdoz preferred quiet and sometimes had to force himself to communicate with the people. Sighing, he changed his mind and continued on the road. Besides, he did very much like Arturo the tavern keeper, a good man, close to Curdoz' age, and one of the few remaining in the village Curdoz remembered well, having grown up near him. But he told himself if anyone called upon him to judge in a dispute, he would just refer them to the king's justices.

He entered a village somewhat larger than the one he remembered as a boy. In his youth there was barely more than the inn Arturo's folks ran, a blacksmith shop, two or three other businesses and a handful of houses. There was very little his father could acquire in Davos to meet even the few extra needs they had as a family, and they nearly always had to travel to Chernis, the county seat, to get supplies. It was only after the Reforms that Davos bustled with an influx of craftspeople with their accompanying shops and houses. Yet the inn was still there, an ever present reminder of his childhood. His father Luvin would often stop in for an ale and to chat with the locals and hear what news he could, as the tiny town and its inn were on the Northern Road, and there were Kingsmen and others who would travel through to the fortresses that were at that time along the border just prior to the war. The socialization always seemed to lift Luvin's spirits from the drudgery of the farm. It was only at the inn Curdoz remembered his father occasionally laughing at jokes and the stories of the locals, whereas on the farm he was gloomy and severe, elements of his personality which only increased after Curdoz' mother died.

There was more traffic, for there were several lanes connecting with nearby farms that attached themselves to the Northern Road. He noted the very trek leading off westwards to a series of farms which included the one formerly his father's. Curdoz paused here for a moment looking down the lane then turned his face towards the inn. It was in the middle of the village, somewhat larger than the Dog, but nevertheless it had a cozy appearance with a high-pitched roof, typical this far north where snow could be heavy. Some riding ponies tied to a tree and a couple of mule carts stationed outside indicated the presence of several people inside. Curdoz resigned himself to the inevitable greetings, opened the simple lever latch and stepped across the threshold.

Several patrons looked in his direction. Upon opening his heavy cloak Curdoz' green stole stood out, and two men at one table recognized him immediately. They at once rose and bowed. "Your lordship!" proclaimed one of the two.

Some intake of breath and whispers aside, and the rest of the patrons rose and bowed, too, as the landlord, wiping dry a freshly washed tankard, stepped out from his kitchen at the sound of so many chairs scratching the wooden floor. He looked at Curdoz and beamed in recognition. "Sage Curdoz!" he bowed. "Bless us! Welcome home, m'lord. It has been too long!"

"Two years, actually, Arturo!" the Sage addressed the innkeeper. Curdoz turned to the hopeful crowd, and raised his right hand above his head and forward, thumb against palm. He then lowered his head an inch or two and pronounced the expected Affirmation, first in formal Anterianhi, "Ela mor Tunan Meical Enamoros Ien Olloray!" and then, "For you I offer the Affirmation of Meical the Guardian!" Again they bowed and came forward as one to welcome him and shake his hand, and his desire for solitude seemed to vanish as they gathered warmly about.

It was an enjoyable hour and word traveled the town quickly, for Arturo sent his stable boy around the village to inform everyone that the Sage of Solanto had come. Forty or so additional villagers came to the tavern—some crowded the doorway—to greet him and listen to his news. Some asked for and received a personal Affirmation. "Tunan Meical" was a phrase Curdoz had proclaimed perhaps tens of thousands of times over the years. Or "The Affirmation of Meical!" depending upon where he was and who he was with, but these townsfolk and farmers were more traditional in their expectations than the high lords and city dwellers, and Curdoz himself preferred the older form and language.

There were some surnames that seemed familiar to the Sage, but for the most part the few whom he knew something about were much younger than he or not even born when he left his farm long ago. Most were relative newcomers who had moved here in the prosperous times after the Reforms. Nevertheless, he experienced a sense of comfort. Every one of them knew Curdoz had lived nearby as a boy, for it was the main claim to fame the town had. They welcomed him both as a high lord of the kingdom and also as a local son.

Two whom he recognized, however, had just left the confines of a small house and crossed the road to greet him, but these were not from Davos. Like him they were Gifted—Brothers from the Order of the Healers, who traveled an assigned area in the kingdom tending the sick. "Lord Curdoz!" they exclaimed together as they came up to him nodding in respect.

He took their hands, "Brother Xeno and Brother Danly! It is good to see you!" Xeno was very large, taller by a foot than the stocky Danly, though it was Danly who had the outgoing personality and cheery expression. Both wore heavy, brown woolen travel robes common among their order. "How are your travels? Were you tending to someone in that home?" Curdoz pointed.

"Two young girls with fevers, but they should recover well now," replied Danly.

The Sage looked at Xeno. "Your Gift?"

"Yes, m'Lord," he replied in a rotund yet quiet voice. Xeno, despite his almost intimidating size, was reserved.

Brother Danly felt the need to expand on his friend. "Yes, we used it. We don't always have to, of course. Often we find there are needs such as hunger, or the consequences of neglect which we have to somehow accommodate, or other troubles we can only provide guidance for, but this time the Gift proved most useful."

"You do your job well, I hear," said the Sage. "Father Marco mentioned you to me recently when I traveled through Ferostro. He said that together you make a formidable pair with the Gift of Healing."

"It is good to hear kind words said of us!" said Danly, expressing surprise. He looked at Xeno who also raised an eyebrow.

"Yes, Father Marco can be rather dour, can he not?" replied the Sage, knowingly.

"Indeed, m'Lord!" said Danly.

They were surprised the Sage would say something like this about the Head of their Order. Of course, the Sage administered all the Orders, and Father Marco was answerable to him, so he could say what he liked. Father Marco was a friend, though, and Curdoz chuckled at the pair's sense of shock.

"You take him too seriously, I see," said the Sage.

"We obey his wishes, Lord Sage. We really do not try to engage him very much."

"I understand fully, Brothers. But he truly is pleased with you two. When I was there, he and I went over his recent accountings, and though he had a number of problems to discuss with me, he had only positive things to say about you."

"We appreciate it very much," replied Danly.

But then Xeno put a hand on Danly's shoulder and looked intently at his Healer Brother. Danly nodded in return and spoke again. "Lord Curdoz, it's opportune you are here. We need to talk to you about something. We thought of sending word to Father Marco, but feared he would insist the situation was none of our business. You are traveling north? We could talk and walk at the same time. We were about to gather our packs and walk over to Chernis ourselves."

The Sage saw no reason why they could not travel together for the next hour anyway. "I intended to pass by Chernis. I suppose we will part at the first Chernis Road?" he asked to see if this suited them.

"That is well," Brother Danly replied, nodding.

Yet it was at least another quarter hour before Curdoz could get away. There were a few newcomers who wished to receive the Affirmation, and he wanted to properly take leave of the innkeeper Arturo, who expressed the common wish the Sage return and stay at the inn in the near future. Finally, the first hour past noon found the Sage and the two Brothers leaving the town of Davos behind.

Out of earshot of the last houses, Brother Danly deemed it private enough to begin. "Lord Sage, Brother Xeno and I spent a month this winter in Aster studying at the Library. Father Marco had ordered us to rest at the Monastery and suggested we further our studies."

"Sounds pleasant enough, except for the weather. Marco tells me the two of you are superior scholars as well as Healers. I have been to the Library a few times. And the Monastery is a beautiful place, at least in summer."

"And can be in winter, too, though it was bitterly cold of course traveling to and from the central part of the city where the Library is. But the Library itself was warm enough, and the fires and the company at the Monastery were very pleasant. In general our time there was good."

"But I'm assuming you encountered a problem?"

Danly looked at Xeno, "Brother Xeno, tell Lord Curdoz what you saw."

Xeno usually let Danly do the talking, but he now gathered himself and spoke softly but clearly in his deep voice. "Yes, m'Lord. I could not believe my eyes, and I had a difficult time making Father Jarom believe me, but finally Brother Danly here also happened to see them leaving the Palace of the Princes only a few days before we left the city." He paused.

This was curious. "What did you see, Brother Xeno?" asked the Sage.

"Several nights we remained very late at the Library, and one night after dark as I left it on my way back to the Monastery I saw three of the barbarian Ice Tribesmen walking together through the city. They were being escorted by the Prince's soldiers."

"Prisoners?"

"That's just it, m'Lord. They could not possibly have been prisoners. They were being treated far too well and were not bound. They were moving about the city as if sightseeing, and yet oddly enough at night, unwilling to be seen by others. If they had not passed so closely I would not have realized it, but as it was, with a torch one of the soldiers was carrying I clearly discerned the pale white skin on the faces of the three, and their speech. They did not see me."

Curdoz thought it curious, but not out of the realm of possibilities. He decided the Brothers could be trusted with some information. "Well, Brothers, it is not widely known, but I know more about the doings in the Principality than Prince Filiddor thinks I do. The Hescians engage in a lucrative fur trade with the Tribesmen. It makes me think they are no more than traders."

"The fur trade?" questioned Danly. "I thought the trade was with Eleni across the mountain passes!"

"Well, some of it is," Curdoz admitted. "Just enough to cover the fact of the other. You see, they trade for furs from Eleni, but they get far more from the Ice Tribesmen, but knowing most Solantines would not be pleased, the Hescians tell everyone the furs come from Eleni."

"The king knows this?"

"King Carlomen ignores much of what goes on in Hesk. He has almost no authority there as you know."

Xeno looked at Curdoz. He did not seem too happy with this.

"I understand your dilemma, Brother Xeno, but I don't think you need to worry," added Curdoz.

"No, m'Lord, I suppose when I think about what you're telling me about the fur trade that doesn't really bother me, but frankly I just do not think these three were traders, because I have reason to believe they were staying inside the Prince's palace as guests and had been there some days. Their clothing was fine, even rich, and they carried themselves with great pride, not to mention being Of the White and obviously high officials. Why would soldiers show them around the city if they were mere traders?"

"A secret delegation of some kind?" asked the Sage. In retrospect, Curdoz could see the strangeness of it. It was odd that Ice Tribe traders would be Of the White.

"Yes, exactly, m'Lord. The war ended long ago, but at the same time we've always known they are not trustworthy. It makes no sense Prince Filiddor should receive them so cordially. To date he's always been their sworn enemy."

"True, Brother Xeno. I must admit, you've piqued my curiosity. And you, Brother Danly, what were they about when you saw them? What time of day was it?"

"Again, sir, it was late at night for the very same reason as Brother Xeno. I was leaving the Library after a long evening of research. I am certain they were leaving Aster, for they were packed for traveling, and I tried following them out of the city, though the gate guards held me back for several minutes, for they plainly did not wish anyone to see the Tribesmen. However, after they let me through I ran and secretly caught up with them. This time their hoods were up, but now that they were outside the gates they spoke to one another. They were unaware I was near. They have that distinct brash dialect that descends from the Ralsheen. I can read Ralsheen, but I cannot speak it, of course. They passed on by the Monastery. There were at least a dozen Hescian soldiers accompanying them and they were headed northward."

"Did you have any communication with the palace people?"

"No, m'Lord! Of course not!"

"Good. The Prince can be a tyrant to those he perceives might want to interfere in his business. Theneri the librarian as you know is a Monastic, and very trustworthy. I rely on him for...information. Did you say anything to him about what you saw?"

"No, m'Lord. Only Father Jarom, who did not really seem especially interested. Pardon me, Lord Curdoz, does Brother Theneri spy for you?"

"Spy?" Curdoz laughed. Just the question itself was rather bold. Maybe he could make use of these two. He liked them. "All right. Since you have guessed. I do rely upon certain individuals in the Orders to provide me with, like I said, information."

"If you don't mind me asking, did Brother Theneri inform you of the Ice Tribesmen already?" asked Danly.

"Admittedly he hasn't, but there could be reasons. If he had sent messages in the past few weeks to me on Island Saundry I would not have been there to receive them, of course. Or it could be he doesn't think it important enough to inform me. Yet it is all very curious. It could be Theneri was aware of them, too, but believes them to be traders. That is what I suspect. But what you've described is admittedly odd."

"M'Lord, if you wish it, we could go back to Aster to see if we could discover more."

Curdoz was intrigued by their eagerness. These two were young, having only arrived from their training in the Valley two years previously. They seemed to have adventurous personalities, even the quiet Xeno, and were evidently fascinated by Curdoz' use of Theneri for gathering information. Deeply perceptive, Curdoz understood most people after a few minutes of conversation. With them he could sense their sincere intent, and their reverence for him, or he would not have told them about Theneri's position.

He likely could use more eyes and ears in Aster, and these two were willing. "Let me think on it for a while. My last communication with Theneri is his Gift was failing him. As Healers, you two could..."

"Gift? I thought he was a Monastic? They only have occasional Visions."

Curdoz laughed again. "You are incorrigible. Though I don't mind your boldness. It is refreshing. But I see you are discontent without information. You two are sworn to me as Order Members, and I am ordering you to keep the information to yourself."

They both nodded, and even Xeno spoke, "Yes, sir, Lord Curdoz."

"Theneri is a Moment Master."

"A Moment Master!" replied Danly, flabbergasted. "I…I didn't even know they existed anymore!"

"Well, as far as I know, Theneri is the only one. He has been of immense value and service to me in Aster, and for Galen before me. But he is very old now, and I am beginning to worry for him."

"If you command us to go to Aster and work for you, we will do it, my Lord," said Danly, and Xeno mirrored his willingness.

Curdoz looked at Xeno and puckered his brows. "Brother Xeno, if I determine it is needed, can you offer the Gift of Mind Support to Theneri? It might allow him fuller use of his Gift."

He nodded, "Yes, m'Lord, I am capable…"

"Capable?" interrupted Danly. "Xeno is expert at it, Lord Curdoz. His magic is very powerful."

Curdoz knew this from Father Marco, of course. The Healer Father was of the belief that Xeno was the most powerful Healer in Solanto and with the most focused mind. "You two will be here for how long?"

"We're traveling mostly between Chernis and Nees for the next month."

"How many of you serve these two counties?"

"There are twelve of us altogether. Six pairs."

Curdoz thought for a moment. "Very good. I plan to be back through here in a few weeks. I have business in Tulesk. I will consider the idea. If I think it necessary I'll find some way to inform you. If I don't find you on my way back through, I'll leave a message in Davos with the innkeeper."

Their conversation moved on to other things, and Curdoz grew to like the two men even more. They were intelligent, even studious, for their scholarship was apparent. Xeno, Meicalian Healer aside, was a war historian. Danly liked to study the ancient myths of the world pertaining to the world gods, the Making of the Three Peoples of the Mold, and the First and Second Appearances of Meical the Guardian. He had learned the rare specialties of written Ralsheen and also much of the Ancient Language used by the gods and the earliest of the Three Peoples. This intrigued Curdoz immensely. Scholarship aside, if they were not in brown Monastic travel garb, Curdoz could have pictured them in Solantine armor and carrying swords. There was a hard quality about the two that spoke of warriors almost, especially the extra-large Xeno.

It wasn't long before they came to the fork where the first of two side roads to Chernis veered westward and the main Road continued northward. Here the two Brothers parted from Curdoz and went on their way.

The Sage was left alone to consider the two Healer Brothers and all they had to say. Could he manage a side trip to the Principality? Perhaps he should look in personally on Brother Theneri, the librarian.

He hoisted his pack higher on his back and walked more briskly. It would be long after dark before he reached Thorune.

Chapter 5—Idamé

Taking advantage of the double moonlight, Curdoz did not stop. It was some hours after dark when he finally arrived at the southern edge of Thorune, an important town on the main route between the port of Ross on the Bay and the Principality of Hesk to the east. The Hescian Road crossed the Northern Road he had been traveling, and he knew there were several inns near this crossroads. Nevertheless, he was tired and stopped at the first one he came to. The facade seemed familiar; maybe he had stayed here before, he wasn't sure. Interestingly, his heart experienced a surge of emotion. He wondered. He always found he should trust these sorts of instincts. So he directed his steps towards the door and went inside.

He didn't know if he would find anyone awake as it was hours past bedtime for most, but surprisingly there were still several people in the common room. In one corner were two Kingsmen. They were sipping ales, and eating bread and cheese, and were a bit reserved in their demeanor, not loud or boisterous as was typical of soldiers at taverns late at night. Then he saw the explanation. High-pitched female laughter came from a small crowd of women seated around three or four tables in the center of the room. Curdoz' arrival was not immediately noticed, for his cloak was still fastened, thus hiding his stole, so he had several moments to survey them. Clearly it was a Troupe of Matrimonials, those women charged to travel the country and proclaim nuptial Blessings on betrothed couples throughout the kingdom.

"What a lark!" he thought, as he looked at them. He hardly expected to meet them this time of year as it was still cold, and yet he always enjoyed the company of Matrimonials, for they were full of humor and goodwill. The two soldiers must be their guards and servants, for Matrimonials were, except under rarest circumstance, un-Bonded women, and though Solanto was generally safe and at peace, it was considered wise to provide them protection when they traveled. But his breath caught when after a moment his eyes rested on someone he knew.

Someone he knew very well, as a matter of fact.

It was Idamé, his friend whom he had known for thirty-five years. They had both been in the Valley of the Gifted together, and still corresponded regularly, but being as busy as they were in their designated offices—he the Sage of Solanto, and she a traveling Matrimonial Sister—returning to Solanto they only occasionally saw one another. In another world, in another time, Curdoz believed he and she might have settled together and formed a family. He knew she felt the same and had even said as much in her letters, but they were both called to two Orders which typically denied relationships of that sort. Since the two were equally devoted to their chosen paths, they never went to the High Priest of the Synod to request the rare Dispensation.

Nevertheless, the two remained close, and aside from his uncle, the Sage probably had no greater trust in any other living person. Without moving he observed her, and all his concerns seemed to drain away. He then attempted to reach her with his mind. Some of the Gifted could communicate emotion with one another. It was quite common among Healer pairs, and yet he and Idamé were also adept at this intimate form of magic.

He targeted her with a deliberate emotion that spoke of happy recognition. She apparently sensed it, for she turned and sat up abruptly. The other Sisters were too much into their own conversations and laughter to notice the sudden movement, but Idamé beamed as she then stood and walked towards him. She too sent forth similar sentiments to Curdoz' mind, though with a curious twist—relief. Seeing her now, Curdoz now knew in the depths of his heart he was exactly in the right place at the right time with regard to the mission the Guardian had set him on weeks ago. He realized his friendship with Idamé had been intruding upon his mind the last few weeks for a reason; he wanted, no, needed, to see her. Forgoing the use of a horse, the walking pace he had set, the asides at the towns where he lingered or stopped, all choices were immediately justified in his mind as a rush of connective spirituality embraced him through the Presence in his mind. As the two friends met and embraced, he immediately realized she felt the same. He felt it through their connection. Whatever situations and events had been directing her steps, he could feel the same sense of mystical destiny permeating her thoughts.

"By the Guardian, Curdoz! What brings you here?"

"Funny you should say it that way, Ida!"

She had light brown hair surrounding a round and kind face. Her eyes were a bright blue. Her smile was as beautiful and kind as always. Nevertheless, in addition to the smile she bore, a wrinkle in her brow and a new emotion issuing through the connection spoke of concern, even anxiety. It was definitely not the typical look of a jovial Matrimonial. "You are troubled by something, Ida," he said. "What is it?"

At that moment a delighted cry went up among the Sisters at one of the tables. "Look! Look who Mother is talking with! It is the Sage! High Lord Curdoz!"

"Later," Idamé whispered to him, and in an instant she broke off the emotional connection and turned around beaming as the other Sisters gathered around them. They all greeted the Sage with delight.

For now he had to set aside his curiosity, and for the first time noticed the multi-colored shawl his friend wore, and it hit him how the other white-shawled Sisters had just now referred to her. "Why, Ida! You're a Mother in the Order, now? When did that come about? It was not in your last letter! Of course, it has been several months…"

One of the Sisters, a middle-aged woman by the name of Lucchenda, interrupted. "Why, m' Lord, it was at the Winter Solstice that Mother Idamé was appointed the title in Convocation." Her tone was formal like a grandmother at a dinner table, though she beamed like a girl.

"I had not received a communication from the Mother Superior regarding Convocation and presumed there was no news of import," responded the Sage in the same tone, looking at the diminutive woman and suppressing a laugh. She was the sort, he knew, that would make for a good Mother Superior someday. And certainly friendlier than the current one residing at the Convent in Ferostro. He would have to keep an eye on her career.

"Well, it wasn't! It was about as dull a Convocation as I have ever attended. Bunch of silly nonsense." Idamé stated flatly. Idamé, though sometimes serious, was rarely formal in the way she talked.

"But you were made a Mother of the Order!" responded Curdoz.

"What is that? It isn't any great news when a Mother is chosen, Lord Curdoz!"

Curdoz replied, "But it is to me, and I'm delighted! You are most deserving, Ida. It should have happened years ago."

Idamé smiled, but it was again tempered by the same wrinkle in her brow and the look of frustration, and Curdoz felt it again through their connection she had now reestablished. *She didn't want to be appointed a Mother!* He said to himself. *But why not?*

His own brow wrinkled.

Idamé then turned to the sisters and said, "It is late, Sisters. It's time to retire to your rooms. We leave after breakfast for Tulesk." Curdoz looked at her and raised an eyebrow in wonder, but chose not to say anything just yet.

"Yes, Mother!" the Sisters replied as one. Some returned to the tables to retrieve capes and gloves, but after a minute they were off to their rooms.

As they were leaving the common room, the landlord bustled in. He was surprisingly young, probably in his early twenties. When he saw the Sage, his jaw dropped.

Curdoz was used to this sort of reaction, but he noticed then that the man's eyebrow went up, and he hesitated before speaking, as if he were recalling something. Oddly, he put on a face that the Sage thought was less friendly than it was shrewd. It made Curdoz feel disconcerted. The man recognized him even though his stole was still hidden under his cloak.

"Why, High Lord Curdoz!" the man said in a rather nervous voice. All his words seemed forced, the manner of a deeply introverted man, Curdoz supposed. "I am truly blessed this evening! A Troupe of Sisters and now the Sage of Solanto!" He bowed to the Sage. "Onri is my name. The last time you stayed here was about fifteen years ago. My father was the keeper then."

"I wondered if I had stopped here before. Fifteen years is a long time."

"Yes, m'Lord. I was quite a young boy." He hesitated again and was obviously very curious. "But I remember you very well. What brings you to Thorune, m'Lord?"

It was rare that Curdoz would take an almost instant dislike to anyone. He had always been intentional not to judge—certainly not by first impressions—and he had always chided those who did. Nor was 'dislike' the right word for what he was feeling, he realized. The man was not wicked of heart; Curdoz could at least sense that much. Nevertheless, he felt wary. He looked at Onri and smiled. "Well, Onri, as you say, it has been a long time since I traveled this way."

"I see," Onri replied. It seemed as though he wanted to ask more questions, but decided otherwise. "It is late; I will find you a room straight away! Your mount needs to be stabled?"

"No, but thank you. Just myself, and please—just a cozy room with a fire is all I wish for." He looked at Idamé and then back at the innkeeper. "Onri, the Mother and I would like to sit up and talk. We are old friends."

"Oh really? Fascinating. How long have you known one another?"

Curdoz frowned, "A good long time. Now what about a place where the Mother and I can talk?"

The man hesitated for a moment, surprised perhaps by the abrupt reply. But then he said, "Oh, please. I have a small parlor down the hall; I'll just go add some more wood to the fire. Come right this way."

Onri led them a short way to a comfortable room containing a center table around which were four chairs and two rocking chairs on either side of a small fireplace. The fire had burned low, but the room was still warm. As the landlord stooped to add more wood, he said, "Anything to eat, m'Lord?"

Curdoz admitted he was hungry, so within a few minutes Onri returned with cheese, apple pie, and a loaf, along with, Curdoz thought surprisingly, a decanter of wine. "I presumed you might appreciate some wine instead of an ale?"

Curdoz nodded. He tried to believe that perhaps the man wasn't so bad after all.

While he ate, he and Idamé shared the news, each commenting politely on the doings of the other. Onri returned two or three times, checking on the needs of the Sage, but Curdoz halted the conversation every time the man entered the room. Finally, Onri returned one last time with another decanter, for Curdoz had happily shared the first with his friend. "Is there anything else you will be wanting m'Lord?"

"No, this should do it. Thank you. You won't need to interrupt us again now." Curdoz said firmly, hoping this last would allow him and Idamé the privacy they wanted.

Onri blinked, uncertain how to respond to the dismissal, but he finally cleared his throat and said, "Your room, m'Lord, is up the stairs, down the hall, last door on the right. It is our best room! Please let me know if you need anything."

He bowed and was about to walk out when Curdoz called after him, "Was that meant for us I hope?" Obviously the man had forgotten himself for he still held the decanter in his hand. *What is on his mind?* Curdoz wondered.

"Oh certainly," said the innkeeper. "How mindless of me." He set it down on the table, gathered the remains of the Sage's supper and closed the door behind him.

Curdoz refilled his goblet and went to sit in the other rocking chair close to Idamé by the fire. It was burning cheerily now.

She said, "You don't like the innkeeper?"

"Was I too obvious?"

"No, I don't think so. He'll simply presume that is your manner."

"Yes, I don't know. He doesn't seem a bad sort, just nosy."

"I must admit, he strikes me as odd."

They both laughed. "Oh, Ida! Oh well, maybe I should put up a voice ward, so he can't hear us, especially if we both have doubts about him."

Idamé nodded. The Sage drew his chair close to hers, then used practical Gifting by placing his hand on Idamé's head and speaking a few quiet words. An unusual green light seemed to emanate from Curdoz' hands. It surrounded their upper torsos and heads and then dissipated. "There, that should do."

It would allow the two of them to speak to one another in a small space, the confines of which the sound of their voices could not escape. The only way someone could hear their conversation was if they placed their ears between the speakers. If someone had the skill, they could perhaps read lips, but even if the odd-acting innkeeper had such ability, he of course would have to be in the room watching them.

"One of your best Gifts, I'd say. Reminds me of a thousand conversations we had together back in the Valley," said Idamé, pleased.

It did bring back memories. "Ida, I know there is more to this meeting than mere chance."

"Yes, I feel it too!" she replied, looking intently into the Sage's intuitive blue-gray eyes.

"It has been a very long time since I felt that sense of destiny like I did when I saw your face tonight."

"Yes, I believe you. Really, Curdoz, I do not think I ever experienced it in the past. Although it was talked about in the Valley. That sense of 'clear purpose' or whatever it was you all called it. I just didn't fully understand what they meant then. But I do now." She looked at the fire. "I do now."

His friend appeared deep in thought. She was obviously very disturbed about something. He could sense it in the bond between them.

Then it hit him like a rock, and he leaned forward, and put a hand on her knee.

"Ida! You had a Vision!" he exclaimed. "That's it, isn't it? You had a Vision from the Guardian!"

Before she could respond the tears started to flow. The emotions she sent to his mind were so mixed that he had some difficulty categorizing them, but above all there was one emotion which stood out—intensity. It was almost more than she could handle. With one hand he took both of hers, and with the other he lifted her chin and looked into her kind face. With all the tenderness he could muster he said, "My dear friend, Ida! Idamé, you are not alone."

He applied a healing touch. This was nothing on the level of what Healers were capable of, for it was a minimal application of the Gift meant primarily to ease exhaustion. Yet it could sometimes achieve the desired result.

Idamé felt a sense of relief and it seemed to show in her face. "Curdoz, I have wanted to see you so badly since it happened! It was just before the Convocation, but I have been so busy, and there was no way I could come all the way to Island Saundry. And it seemed really stupid of me to describe it in a letter, and something told me not to. Drat this being a Mother in the Order! I always thought I wanted it—dreamed of it most of my life—but now the responsibility is weighing on me. I *do* want it, really, but it is interfering with what I think the Guardian wants me to do, now! At least I think so, anyway."

"Ida, let me tell you something," he said. "Meical spoke to me, too! I had a Vision only a few weeks ago."

"Really? Tell me about it, Curdoz!"

"I will, Ida. But as children say, 'you go first!'"

She started hesitantly, allowing him first to pour more wine into her goblet. After a couple more swallows, she was expounding in great detail what she had seen and heard in her Vision. Among the images of clouds and flying and time spans and distances, she painted a picture that in some ways mirrored Curdoz' own Vision, and in other ways it was very different and contained images he did not experience in his. She told of a small ship sailing along the coast stopping at a vast city set by a large bay and port, then a different and larger ship was docked in another bay where on great cliffs stood many white, stone buildings and palaces. Then there was a further journey of three ships along a coastline, whereupon laying anchor, passengers boarded with serene facial appearances and brown complexion, some with birds resting on their shoulders and more birds flying in and out among the sails.

The people were unmistakably Qeteral, as odd as it sounded, for no one had report of the elusive people in a hundred years. Much of this Curdoz had also seen in his Vision, including the Qeteral, and he nodded several times while Idamé spoke. However, though she knew she herself was 'traveling' on the ship, she had no sense of who else was with her, and could identify no faces until the ship took on the people with the birds. Finally, there were great dark cliffs and she spoke many details to Curdoz of a gray and wicked fortress and the lands about.

The dream ended there. She did not know where any of the places were, except she strongly suspected the first vast city to be the great city of Tirilorin, the old imperial capital.

"But I only believe it because of the descriptions and the paintings we saw of it in the Valley, Curdoz, so I'm not sure."

"It was in my Vision, too. I have been there before, as you may remember. Once you've seen Tirilorin, you will never forget it."

"What about the other places?"

"I can guess at a couple, though the coastline you mentioned is vague. But I believe the second port you described with the cliffs and white stone buildings may be Sevarr on the island Kingdom of Nant."

"What about the evil city and fortress?"

"I doubt it's anywhere in the northern world. The Twin Realms of the Khestadone, deep in the south, on the Southern Continent. Considering the lands you describe, it is likely Westrealm of the Alkhaness. Eastrealm is mostly mountains and desert."

"The Twin Kingdoms! And I've never been so fearful of anything in all my life! There is rumor of war, but the Mother Superior doesn't usually discuss news of that sort with the Sisters. What do you know, Curdoz?"

"The eastern kingdoms of Hralindi and Essemar are at war with the Alkhan of East Khestadon. Westrealm Khestadon has not engaged. The Nantians have kept them hemmed in with their navy. But based on my Vision I think Westrealm will involve themselves soon."

He then proceeded to tell Idamé about his own Vision. Curdoz had remained passive when she related her story to him, but Idamé's expressions and constant interruptions were marked. The Sage did not mind, because the questions she raised at each point— some were very discerning, not to mention the parallels in her own vision—really helped him to get a somewhat clearer picture of what they were facing.

They. There was no question on either's part they would, from that point forward, remain together. This was why they were brought together, why the Guardian Himself directed their steps to this inn on the Northern Road in Thorune.

One of the most intriguing aspects that Curdoz had not thought about before, but one Idamé had immediately remarked upon, was a possible parallel between the rulers of the Khestadone and the young twins the Sage was seeking on his journey to Tulesk. "...and they are male and female, too, are they not?"

At this, Curdoz raised his eyebrows and drew a breath. "Ida! Incredible point! Why had I not made the connection before?"

"But what could it mean, do you think?"

Curdoz pondered for a moment, but realized it would require a good deal more thought. "I do not know, and frankly it could be a very long time before we know."

"And the strange people with the birds on their shoulders…nobody's seen the Qeteral in how long?"

"A hundred years. They withdrew from doings with Humans after the abdication of the last Anterianhi Emperor, Zarelio. As far as I know, nobody has seen them since. And even before then, very few ordinary humans actually traveled to Ulakel. One of the Gifted, on occasion, would be politely received because of their connection to Meical. The Qeteral were always very reclusive."

"Why, do you think? I know you've read the histories, Curdoz. I never cared for them."

"Different philosophies, different understanding of our connection to nature, different way of looking at Meical, whom they call Myghal the Master. They believe Myghal is the actual Hand of the Creator, whereas of course we look at Him more as a Messenger and Guide operating on the Creator's behalf. They give Him more divinity and believe Him to be incapable of error which gives them more a sense of the fateful. They are more likely to stand back and watch the history of the world unfold, whereas we Humans prefer to be the makers of history. They did not want to be a part of the Anterianhi Empire, but Meical told them He wanted them to ally with Humans and acknowledge the overlordship of the new emperor as their protector. So, after the last emperor abdicated, we presume they no longer felt the need to connect with Humans any longer. What minimal trade there was before between Ulakel and the rest of the Empire—what remains of the old Empire rather—ended then, and it is said they have reconstituted their magical wall on the border of their land atop the Great Plateau near the Corellyan Mountains.

"Then there is the implication in my Vision that there are other Qeteral in the South of the World, an idea I had never imagined nor read of anywhere. I cannot see why there would be Qeteral on the Southern Continent. Maybe some traveled there before the rise of the Khestadone. The Qeteral are a different people. I say that, but some of the Human accounts I have read do whiff of prejudiced attitudes. There's a good likelihood if Humans had the opportunity to engage them more, we'd find them less different from us than we may think. They are, of course, magical by nature with unique perspective. I don't know how they connect to this or what purpose they could play, or would be willing to play." Then he laughed and concluded, "Of course we really don't yet know what our own purpose is or what part we play."

There was a long pause as each pondered the future. Finally, Idamé spoke again. "Curdoz, we can only presume the paths you and I have so far chosen to get to this point *together* are the right ones. You were headed to Tulesk to find the two young people in your dream. We still have to find them."

"Yes, I just hope when we find them that somehow more of our questions will be answered. We'll head out tomorrow."

Idamé's countenance fell, and she seemed on the verge of tears again. Her emotions through the connection were intense. "I don't know what to do, Curdoz! I lead the Troupe! I'm the Mother!"

There it was, of course. Curdoz in his position could move about freely. He was the Sage. Idamé, on the other hand...

"Ah, now I see why you didn't want to become a Mother." He took her hand and held it.

"I should have been honored and happy at the Solstice ceremony when they elected me. I've always wanted to preside over more of the Bondings, and of course over all of the Aura Bonding Ceremonies, in our Troupe assignments. But I had just had the Vision, you see, so it was weighing on my mind throughout Convocation. But now what am I going to do, Curdoz? I can't just abruptly leave them!"

Curdoz already had his answer. "It is not a difficult dilemma, Ida. I will write a letter to the Mother Superior."

Idamé blinked at him. "She'll never agree."

"She won't countermand a direct order of the Sage of Solanto."

"Curdoz! She will not appreciate you interfering in her affairs! There are already too few Troupes to cover the Kingdom. Solanto has grown so fast the last ten years or so. As you see, she made us start our routes much earlier this season."

"Yes, it has, and no, you're right. She won't. But the 'affairs' of the Guardian supersede any excuses she may think of. And the affairs of the Guardian are my responsibility as Sage. I know her well. She won't like it, but she'll come around. She will not go against me on this."

Idamé's mood lightened somewhat; Curdoz could sense it. Yes, he knew as she did the Mother Superior was a bull-headed woman with a hot temper. Though Curdoz happily sought out Father Marco of the Healing Orders on his recent trek through Ferostro, he deliberately avoided seeing the Mother Superior. But she would do as Curdoz required.

Idamé's mood returned to the cheerfulness Curdoz knew was the basis of her personality. They discussed their Visions further.

After a quarter hour of this they considered their next steps.

"Curdoz, I don't think it's wise to tell the Sisters much about the Visions. We'll seal our letters to the Mother Superior, and she will be the only other person who knows."

"A good point. What will you tell your Sisters, especially if you don't want them asking questions?"

"I think we can tell them some parts of the truth. I'll tell them that you were actually looking for me, which is partly true based on what you've said, that you need me to help you with something involving the Orders, that Lucchenda is to take charge of the Troupe after we get to Tulesk, and that I've sent a message to the Mother Superior. Lucchenda will be allowed to preside over Aura Bondings if you give her direct permission in a written document, Curdoz. She'll be thrilled! I'll tell them we are still all going to Tulesk, but that in a few days you and I will have to leave them."

Early the next morning, Curdoz packed quickly. He approached the innkeeper to pay, who seemed disconcerted for some reason. He began again to ask the Sage leading questions, but Curdoz dodged each one, growing more suspicious than ever of the innkeeper's motives and his nervous ways. The Sage was as polite as he could be, but was determined to give the man no information about his current business or destination.

There is something not right about him, Curdoz concluded. He left the inn.

He made his way to the Kingsmen's barracks. These were enclosed in a stone fort in the middle of the town. It was a stronghold left over from the wars, for before the last war Thorune was not far from the frontier with the Ice Tribe presence in Tulesk, old Stavenland before it was taken by the Solantine army. Since the threat had been removed, so too were the gates, and there were no guards in the old gatehouse. The fort remained the King's property, however, and the keep within was used as an office for the commanding captain of a large contingent of Kingsmen soldiers, and a barracks for those stationed in and around Thorune to keep the peace and to monitor and protect travelers on the roads. On the east-west Hescian Road there was a tremendous amount of travel particularly spring through fall when ships could safely navigate the currents to and from the port city of Ross. As the North River was rocky and unnavigable, the road was the primary route of trade between Ross and the Principality of Hesk, whose border was only thirty miles east of Thorune.

It was still early in the season, and it would be one or two more weeks before the traffic would flow with more regularity, and for now most of the soldiers had few duties and remained close to the town and barracks. Those present in the office stood and saluted the Sage with his green stole as soon as he stepped inside. He was delighted when he recognized the captain, for he had once been in service in Escarant to the grand duke, and the man greeted him warmly.

"How good o' ye to remember me, Lord Curdoz! I be so honored! Are ye well? How can we be o' service to ye?" asked the captain. Santher was his surname.

After pronouncing the Affirmation and politely dismissing the other soldiers, Curdoz turned to the captain, "Thank you, Captain Santher. I am very well, thank you! I did not know you had left Escarant."

"Aye, as to that, m'Lord, I do be missing it; the winters be long here! But ye see, I have a wife and two little 'uns now, and this be where m'lady's family hails from. 'Twas a 'fittin' to remove here, for since I must on occasion be away from home, at least she has her folks near to help her with the young 'uns. The grand duke arranged the transfer, which be very good o' him."

"Mannago is good and kind," agreed the Sage. There were few of such high rank that would even bother to listen to the requests of a simple captain in the Kingsman Army. It was this sort of character, however, that allowed the Sage and Mannago to develop such a close relationship. "Listen, Captain Santher, I need to hire a carriage and driver, and I need you to assign a trusty man, a soldier who is happily Bonded, mind you, to accompany two Sisters of the Matrimonial Order with messages for the Mother Superior in Ferostro. Will you arrange it for me?"

"Surely, m'Lord. 'Tis an honor to serve. I can have it all arranged within an hour. I know just the man to accompany Sisters of the Order, yes. Be there anything else?"

"The Sisters should be here by the time you have the carriage ready. I do, however, wish to make an inquiry." He then proceeded to ask the captain if he knew anything about the innkeeper Onri at the sign of the Gray Fox.

"Hmm, only a little, m'Lord. Comes in here, he does, from time to time, and talks with the men, asks lots of questions, he does, though citizens they come in here all the time. What might be a bit strange, since you asks it however, is he closes down the Fox from time to time, disappears for a week or more, and then returns. It be odd that he appears to have sufficient income not to have to remain open like others in similar capacity, and yet he seems to have no more business than any of the others, mind ye, in fact I would think less since he closes down sometimes. From what I understand he inherited the Fox from his father. I am certain he be not Bonded, a bit of a loner. But beyond that, m'Lord, I know of nothing else. He causes no trouble and is respectable enough from what I can tell."

"Where does he go at the times he closes the Fox?"

"I must apologize, m'Lord, I have never noticed nor heard anyone say anything on that. If ye be wishing it, however, I can set someone to observe his movements if ye deem it important."

"I do not want him followed far. He is a freeman, of course, but if it is not too much to ask of you, Captain, perhaps you can find out which direction he heads: north, south, east or west."

Only one answer would be sufficient to make the Sage suspicious enough to have Onri's movements further scrutinized, but he would find oath-sworn Order members for such a task if it proved necessary.

"I can do it easily enough, m'Lord, yes. Does that mean ye will be here again soon to have my report on it?"

"I will. I am traveling to Tulesk with a Troupe of Matrimonial Sisters. If my business goes as well as I am hoping, I shall return this way, and I will check back with you then. Of course it may be the innkeeper will not choose to close the inn and depart within that time, but…"

"I can ask around, m'Lord, discretely o' course, and have an answer for ye in any regard."

"Thank you, Captain Santher. Excellent."

Curdoz believed he was probably over-reacting, and if it hadn't been for Mother Idamé confirming her own wariness around the man, he would have ignored it. And yet, the one interesting fact Captain Santher was able to add was curious. Why would Onri have a need to close his doors and disappear? Even if the man was wholly innocent, he nevertheless had an odd demeanor and strange habits.

The Matrimonial Troupe met the Sage at the old fort around the third hour. It was cool and breezy. The two Sisters Idamé had chosen to deliver the letters to the Mother Superior were packed away in the carriage provided by Captain Santher. Sitting by the driver was the proud soldier who had been assigned to accompany them. The two men were pleased when Mother Idamé delivered into each of their hands a gold coin, and they made effusive promises to watch after the Sisters and deliver them safely to the Convent in Ferostro. With that, the carriage left the confines of the walls. Idamé, the remaining Sisters, their two Kingsmen guards, and their baggage ponies joined the Sage on the trek northward out of Thorune.

"It doesn't hurt, Curdoz, that you wish to get a bit more information on the man," offered Idamé when the Sage brought up the subject later in the morning and told her about his inquiry at the barracks. The two of them were walking some distance behind the rest of the Troupe and were from time to time discussing their Visions, their tasks, and recent events. It continued to be breezy and chilly, though the sun was bright. There were still patches of snow, yet they crossed numerous small bridges over little streams, these rushing coolly northwestward on their way to the North River. "You worry he may relay information of some sort? But I don't think the innkeeper really learned anything."

"He should know nothing about our Visions, true. Which is what we should really be most wary of. I rather wish I had been more discreet in my travels here, for there are others who know, though I trust them all or I wouldn't have shared. Onri seems to have made me anxious. He does know I was traveling through Thorune. He knows I haven't been this direction in a long time. He knows I am not on horseback, which is rather odd for me. He knows I met a Troupe of Matrimonial Sisters at his inn, that I had long conversation with the Mother of the Troupe, whom he knows now is my long-time friend. He could possibly know our conversation was deliberately secretive for there was the voice block, and that would be rather curious to someone seeking information. He knows I refused to answer even simple questions about my business. Which makes me almost wish I had lied deliberately in order to throw him off the track. And there of course is the possibility that he has learned we are now traveling together and our direction if he was watching or had someone else watch."

"When you put it in that way, Curdoz, it does seem like a lot of information he could share with an antagonist." She was silent for a moment. "Well, from now on, we will just have to help each other guard these secrets. We'll have to come up with alibis, and answers to possible questions. It should be simple enough. Nothing we've done can't be justified with some tale."

They continued to chat, and eventually they came up with a story as to why they were traveling together. If anyone asked, Curdoz in his role as Head of the Orders wished to learn more directly how the Matrimonial Troupe system was functioning in the kingdom. He wanted to learn if the system was efficient, or if the long tradition of the Sisters traveling on foot needed to be changed in favor of horseback travel. In reality, the debate on the tradition was a fact, and there had indeed been many complaints that Matrimonial Blessings were not taking place as rapidly as needed since the kingdom had been growing in population. Curdoz had for years been urging the Mother Superior to consider such a change, but was unwilling to dictate it. He'd been presuming she knew best, and he had no facts other than his own logic that it should be better. This was his opportunity to see for himself how the current system worked.

The idea appealed to Idamé especially, because she was one of the few who were actually in favor of changing the tradition, although she admitted she hated riding horseback, and had a fear of horses any larger than their baggage ponies. She knew if push came to shove, she would force herself to learn.

"We're just pretending, though, Ida," he said, laughing.

"I know, but who's to say that you can't indeed use this to challenge the Mother Superior's system? You really could, you know."

"I'm not challenging her tradition now, because I don't want her using it as an excuse to be even angrier with me for taking one of her Matrimonial Mothers out of the country."

"It's when we get back to Ferostro that I'm expecting you simply to tell her the way things are to be!" She laughed, and so did he.

It was a light moment which they needed, and at least for a while they stopped talking about serious matters. For many hours they reminisced about their time together in the Valley of the Gifted.

The landscape opened out again. Curdoz had reentered the coastal plain now and the wind picked up. There was still snow here and there, but there were also budding trees and snow crocuses. In some locations were earliest daffodils, too, and the Sisters would go and pluck them whenever they could, building up bouquets to use for Bonding Ceremonies. These and branches of winter honeysuckle were the first really useful blossoms of the season, and flowers were nearly a requirement at any Bonding Ceremony.

At noon they stopped in another roadside village by the name of Somme, only a mile from the North River, which they would have to cross by ferry into Tulesk. They rested for a while and ate a lunch at a roadside inn. A young couple approached Mother Idamé requesting to be Bonded. This happened in most towns, and Idamé and the Sisters were quite used to it. Idamé had to inform them their own assignment for this season was in Tulesk, and that they were not allowed to perform Bondings outside their assigned region. Curdoz thought to use his authority to allow them to perform it anyway, but again he remembered it was best not to interfere with the Mother Superior's strict policies. Giving permission to Lucchenda to perform Aura Bondings, though necessary, was pushing it.

Idamé reassured the couple, however, that in late spring another Matrimonial Troupe would be in this part of the country, and they could proceed with the nuptials then. The couple was disappointed, but Curdoz gave them a very formal Guardian's Affirmation and some words of wisdom which cheered them.

When they walked away, Curdoz ventured to say to Idamé, "They were very young! They were no more than fifteen and sixteen."

"Times are good, and early Bondings are becoming more common these days, especially in the countryside."

"And no Aura over them, I presume."

Curdoz was referring to the Gift common only to Matrimonials. On rare occasions, a mystical light would appear over a couple if they were in close proximity to one another, and Matrimonials were the only ones who could see it. Not all couples were the subject of such magic, only those it was understood that the Guardian Meical absolutely meant it for. An Aura was uncommon, yet when it occurred, it meant plainly that this one woman and this one man were meant to match and that no other coupling that either might engage in was Affirmed by the Guardian. It had a further ramification, too, very unusual. The woman who was the subject of an Aura was not capable of bearing a child to any other man, nor could he father a child through another woman after the Aura occurred. It connected the two at a magical level. The Aura was more ancient than any other known magic. Such couples were usually held to be lucky in their communities.

Idamé chuckled. "No. If there had been, I would have performed the rite regardless of my assignment. Aura Bondings are allowed regardless of the circumstance."

"I knew it. I was just curious about this couple, because they are so young."

"Yes. Probably wouldn't hurt them to wait a few more weeks anyway. Their commitment to one another might change by then. I doubt it, though. They had that particular look in their eyes. Aw! To be young again, Curdoz!"

She looked at her friend, and he looked at her. An objective observer might possibly have seen the same look Idamé was speaking of in the eyes of the Sage and the Matrimonial Mother. Though bodies might age, eyes do not.

If Curdoz were forty years younger he might have blushed at this point. Idamé did anyway.

She ventured, "Curdoz, being together like this will not be easy."

"No. Seeing you again, Ida, creates much emotion for me, as well. Let me tell you something, though." He lowered his voice to a whisper. "It is important that we were brought together! Let us take joy in one another's company, shall we? No need to worry about the might-have-been's. Let us enjoy being friends! It can be like our times together in the Valley!"

Idamé sighed and smiled. "It is a special gift from Meical, isn't it?"

"In part, Ida, we are meant to rely upon one another. He understands the trust we have."

"Yes. It is very good to be together." She looked around at the bright day. "I admit I am happier than I have been in a long time, Curdoz!"

Curdoz looked at her with a bright expression on his own face.

They stood and joined the Troupe who had packed up after their lunch, and they all made their way down the shallow slope to the ferry at North River.

Chapter 6—Twins

It had been a cool day, although the bitterest of the north winds were long gone. The skies, instead of harboring snow-laden clouds as they might have been a mere fortnight ago, were today a welcome blue. With the change in the weather work had resumed on the new baronial manor of Lord Hess, Count Fothemry, and of the Lady Elisa. Farther south in the kingdom, particularly in the duchies of Scant and Escarant, the snows were gone, spring demonstrated its charm, and farmers were planting leafy greens, peas and a number of early harvest crops between spring rains. In a few more weeks, in those climes anyway, they would be harvesting beets, onions, and other root vegetables sown back in the fall. It would be some weeks yet before farmers in this northern duchy could consider planting. The warmer spring breezes off Amaros Bay were slowed by the eastern flank of the Dragon Mountains on the Tolosian Peninsula. It was only the melting snow and the buds of early daffodils appearing in some of the sunnier open glades that signaled spring's initial arrival. Though the brooks and streams were running more freely, the snow was still piled in drifts in the forests near the foot of the Grand Escarpment east of the Wolf River.

Lord Hess had been gone a month on his third expedition to the peninsula, yet here in the town of Felto in southeastern Tulesk, his wife and their twin son and daughter dwelt in the home of Elisa's aging father, Yugan. Their new manor was being built west of the town, and it was to be the seat of the baron over the new county Duke Amerro had created with the King's approval. Yet it would be many months still before it would achieve a livable state. Elisa hoped by then that Hess would have returned from Tolos, and they would all be able to make the move together.

Returning to their grandfather's home after a long day's work at the manor site, the twins, Kodi and Lyndz, spoke together of their efforts, remarking upon their productive day. They noted the glad sunshine, but admitted they would be even gladder after they had their evening meal. The stews brewed by the women in massive kettles for the working men could not remotely compare to the culinary creations of Ansy, their grandfather's live-in housekeeper and cook. They anticipated a virtual feast tonight, as it was Yugan's birthday, and it promised to be an enjoyable time for the family.

Though the manor was being built for the Fothemrys, it was important to Elisa to demonstrate they were not sitting idly by while others did all the work for them. The men were paid well for their labor, but even so, with the exception of a handful of the artisans sent by Duke Amerro to lend their expertise, the workers were neighbors for the most part, nearby country folk and villagers from Felto. They honored the new count and happily recognized his leadership. But before he had been elevated to his new estate by his cousin the duke, Hess had been one of them. Elisa felt it unwise to alter those neighborly relations, to act with airs of superiority, something too common elsewhere in the kingdom. For these reasons and others, Kodi was on the building site every day when the weather was good enough for any work to take place, and Lyndz was out there many days, too, when her mother didn't need her for other chores.

At eighteen, Lyndz had mastered all of her mother's skills, and Kodi was tall and powerful of build like his father with plenty of confidence to match. These last several days he had been involved in helping set more of the stone blocks of the manor, making use of levers and weighted lifts, though intense muscle work was involved even in that, and his body ached. Lyndz too went around much of the day carrying buckets of water and ladles to the many men at work and helping tend the large fires where the men would gather at intervals to break and eat. She also assisted the other women at the cooking.

Sometimes, she would pause from these tasks and take time to walk in and around the site, making sure as to not get in the way of the construction. She would daydream of what her life would be after the place was completed and the family moved in. She had reached the traditional minimum Bonding age nearly three years before, but Lyndz was in no hurry and intended to push that event off for at least two more years. Knowing she would be attractive to a man of noble birth, she was determined to learn somewhat the operation of a large household. Even now, as she and her brother were walking home together, she was reviewing in her mind the formal garden plans. Having admired those at the duke's castle in Cumpero on an excursion there with her father last summer, Lyndz hoped to recreate something like it here. Gardens were one of her passions, and her mother and father had already promised to have her well-drawn plans executed where practical.

The sun slowly settled beyond high hills to the west, and at the top of a low rise, the two turned to gaze at it. Unseen on the far side of those forested hills was an inlet of Amaros Bay, and across the inlet was Tolos, an extensive peninsula. Until recently it had been a land of fierce wingless Dragons. It was their own brave father who determined that these had at last died out and disappeared. On the edge of sight, especially on this clear day, Kodi and Lyndz could imagine a line, the Dragon Mountains, demarking the craggy connection to the peninsula.

Unlike his sister, though, Kodi was not daydreaming. Watching the sun dip below the distant peaks, he had grown rather quiet.

Lyndz now noticed her brother's troubled face. "You're worrying about the dreams aren't you, Ko? Did you have another one last night? Was it like the long one from two weeks back?"

From gazing at the sunset he turned to her. "Pieces of it. I guess they're like reminders. Although there's no chance I'm going to forget any of it. While I'm working I don't think much about it. But after, it all starts to run around in my mind."

"You're still convinced they're some sort of *Vision* from the Guardian, like they say the Gifted have?"

"Well, what else would explain it? I reckon I've told you everything, Lyndz. You believe me, don't you?"

Lyndz knew her tone had not meant to imply doubt. It seemed her brother was becoming more frustrated when discussing these recent dreams. She thought to lighten the exchange without changing the subject altogether. "Yes, I do. But I've said it before, I thought the Gifted have other powers, too, which you certainly don't have," she laughed. "You don't have any Healing magic or mind magic or anything."

Kodi looked at her appreciatively, familiar as he was with his sister's logical approach to most things. He made the attempt to try to dismiss his self-brooding. For the moment at least, he came back to his typical self.

"You've not noticed, but I've been using my 'mind powers' lately to block away all the women," he joked. "Because they won't leave me alone and I need my rest."

Lyndz chortled and Kodi grinned. He was not the cad as some he knew, though he could pretend it sometime. But usually that layer of his humor was reserved for male friends only, such jokes being common among the lumbermen his father employed and among the laborers at the manor site, and of course among his own set when they would drink ale and camp at the river or up on the highland beyond. His willingness to add his sister to the list of recipients of this demonstrated their closeness. They readily shared with one another many of their concerns and joys. Kodi refused to talk crudely around other women, and even at the worksite his own participation in the man-to-man banter would stop the instant he believed the ears of any of the cooks approached too closely.

Though absent much of the time the last few years while Kodi matured into manhood, Hess when he was at home did his best to teach his son how to behave with proper decorum in the presence of women. Kodi by now took strongly after his father, not only in looks and character, but also in his manner and humor, and this made him greatly popular among those in Felto. The young admired him, and there was hardly an un-Bonded girl between the ages of twelve and twenty-five who didn't try to catch his eye. More mature men for the most part forgot he was as young as he was and treated him as an equal in their circles. This was surely due to an expressive self-confidence, but also to an innate generosity exhibited in his willingness to go out of his way to be helpful. In other words, people were readily attracted to Kodi: the women for his looks and pedigree, the men for his humor, the old for his genial politeness and generous, helpful nature, and the young because he made them all feel good about themselves when he was present.

This nature led him often to overlook his duties closer to home, but his mother rarely complained. Elisa knew it only improved the reputation of the family in the eyes of the locals. She took immense pride in her son. For the most part Kodi followed the rules of the house and the family, and though he was adventurous and high-spirited, he almost never got into any sort of serious trouble.

It must be said that Kodi was not immune to the admiration shown him, and on occasion it could bolster his self-assurance to the point of being cocky. Lyndz would tease him for this, always trying to deflate what she thought was a bit of overblown self-importance. However, there could be no doubt she admired her brother.

"Right, Ko. If nobody else, the only one you've blocked lately is J'neen, and she's the only one in this whole town who is remotely good enough for you."

"Maybe," he replied with a bit of a knowing smirk. *And what is it with women whose names start with 'J'?*

He knew his only attraction for the daughter of the general store owner was a tightening in his groin when, allowing his mind to wander, he would lower his eyes from her rather plain face to her remarkably conspicuous and curvaceous figure. Kodi knew better than to act on these itches. He had been in a similar position before with Jonell, the stablemaster's daughter, and in that situation events transpired in such a way that he was left in secret fear of consequences and of a possible Bonding void of real love. He was lucky that time, and neither of their families ever found out about it. It was one of the few secrets Kodi had not revealed to anyone, having learned his lesson. He might from time to time let the young women flirt with him, as it boosted his ego, but he had never since that incident allowed such flirtations to go anywhere.

With regard to Lyndz' friend J'neen, he had simply changed his pattern of entering her father's store at the times he knew she was manning the counter. On the occasions she would appear at their house to pursue friendly activities with her friend his sister, he would abruptly leave and find something busy to do in his grandfather's woodshop in order not to allow lust a foothold on his mind. He'd developed in himself a powerful self-discipline lacking in many young men.

"She's in love with me, I'm pretty sure," he added. "But I'm not interested in her."

"She is. But I swear I'm not encouraging her, and I'm certainly not pressing you. J'neen's a sweet girl and a good friend of mine, but you're young."

Kodi was weary of that phrase, *you're young,* used too often by his father. Almost three years ago now he turned sixteen and entered manhood according to all tradition, and when his father returned then, Kodi expected to receive the customary Blessing guaranteeing his inheritance, and leave home. The warrior archetype was powerful in Kodi, inspired as he was by his grandfather's tales of the last war with the Ice Tribes, and he aimed to train as a knight with their cousin the duke. It was common for those younger than Kodi, of his same social status anyway, to leave home for this purpose, and he felt he was missing out.

His father kept delaying, an odd situation to be sure. Kodi was not rebellious. In fact, he was generally very obedient and responsible. Yet as much as he begged, his father's stance remained the same. It created much strain between the two, for otherwise father and son got along well.

Again Hess went to Tolos, leaving Kodi to watch after the family, and again he returned. This time it seemed Kodi's desire was about to be fulfilled, for Hess believed he would be able to remain home and at peace in Felto, to focus on the administration of his new county and his lucrative lumber trade. However, even as plans were being made for Kodi's future, messages came requesting Hess return once more on another expedition to Tolos.

This time Kodi made it plain his father should at least take him along, but Hess, dealing with the pressures of fulfilling the requests of his overlord and cousin the duke and his sense of guilt for leaving his wife and home again, required his son to promise to remain and watch after the family yet one more time. It angered Kodi, who would in fact soon be nineteen, to make such a promise, and he hotly resented it. The argument between them seriously tested Kodi's resolve to remain connected to his father. Yet in the end, he had too much respect for him to refuse. Leaving home without the full consent and Blessing of one's parents was considered inauspicious and out of keeping with the Disciplines of the Guardian. Kodi forced himself to submit and wait.

Despite his lingering bitterness, Kodi refused to take it out on his well-meaning twin. He attempted to steer the exchange. "Young. I suppose that's how I think of you when I hear Haral talk about you. Talk about 'in love'. But to me, J'neen's just another, er, pretty face. You need to watch Haral, though."

"Yes, but he's not going anywhere with me. I've thrown him off pretty well. Don't you think?"

If Kodi was considered by the young women in the town to be the top catch, in the minds of the other gender the same was true for his twin. Lyndz blossomed late, but when she did all noted she had transformed into a remarkably beautiful, even stunning young woman. Like her twin she had the dark hair and dark olive complexion common to their father's Escarantine forbears, exotic in this region where fair complexions were the norm. She had deep brown eyes and a perfect feminine figure.

But her beauty was only an added bonus. Lyndz was both intelligent and perceptive beyond what was typical of the town folk. She read books voraciously, for her grandfather kept a personal library, always buying new books with his income as a master woodcarver. Lyndz knew more about the world than probably anyone in the county aside from her own parents and grandfather. But more importantly was the uncanny ability she had in discerning the motives of others within a few minutes of shared conversation. She was attuned to subtleties and had both a very logical and perceptive mind. She was the very opposite of flirtatious, and a sense of perceived aloofness seemed to set her apart. Yet many of the young men looked at this as a sort of challenge and found her desirable.

"Yeah, maybe temporarily," replied her brother. Kodi thought Haral a clever opportunist, attracted to his sister less for her good looks and high intelligence and more for the fact she was the daughter of the local baron with presumably a nice dowry attached.

"Mother doesn't like him very much either. I'll be glad to teach him a lesson if you need me to."

He grinned menacingly and cracked his knuckles indicating the sort of lesson he meant.

She laughed at her self-appointed protector. "I don't think so. I wouldn't want anything to happen to that pretty face of yours. He's bigger than you."

Her brother cracked. "Right! He's a chunky bastard if that's what you mean."

Lyndz was savvy to the ways of these typical men her age, the ones still searching for their Bondmate, and so she was no pushover. She had an odd way, which Kodi admired, in which every flirtation aimed in her direction she was able to somehow deflect, turning it into a completely innocent exchange. Without their realizing it, this baffled most of her would-be suitors to the point they never found the urge to flirt with her again. Yet even more than acting on her own common sense, it was simply impossible for Lyndz to promote herself in a way as to remotely bring embarrassment to her mother.

Finally, like Kodi, she aimed high, though in a different way. Much like his father, Kodi was almost immune to class distinctions. Though Lyndz was too at a certain level, when it came to a Bondmate, however, she had no intentions of Bonding someone who was not well-to-do and highly intelligent. She wanted someone who appreciated her own agile mind and her goals of maintaining fine gardens and an extensive library. Perhaps it limited her, but she was the duke's cousin, after all, and thus good connections were likely. She had met a number of possible suitors at his court only the summer before. Local sons like Haral had no more chance with her than the resident young women had with her brother.

In the clear darkening skies above, Kodi heard a sound that caused him to look up, the cry of a hawk—a Bluetail. He loved hawks. He admired their freedom and gracefulness in flight, and so his keen eyes followed it for a short while.

A pang of longing hit him. Every time he saw the raptor, he wished he too could sprout wings and fly...away from home. His anger at his father flared, but he allowed it to subside as the sapphire lake in his dream came to mind. He became thoughtful again and no longer seemed interested in talking and laughing about such trivial things as which women loved him too much and which of his twin's hopeless suitors he was ready to pounce upon.

But the momentary joking served the purpose Lyndz intended—ensuring he still trusted her on this matter.

Seeing how his face had become solemn again, she pressed him. "No, but really, Ko, about the dream. You know I believe you. But I'm telling you, you should tell Mother."

They walked along, but his eyes continued to follow the distant Bluetail. "I think it would just upset her."

"Well, tell Grandpa, then. He's been around a long time and maybe he can give you some advice."

"I've thought about that too, but I just don't know." The Bluetail was far away now. Kodi looked down again. "If Father hadn't gone..."

"Yes, but it'll probably be next fall before he's back, and you just can't wait that long keeping it to yourself. Grandpa, though. He won't tell Mother if you ask him not to. He has sure kept a lot of secrets of ours, hasn't he?"

Kodi had actually pondered telling his grandfather several times the last few days, but something kept him from it. "It's just that he's getting old. What can he really do?"

"Well, you're so experienced in comparison? Grandpa knows a lot. He's been around. He's smart and he's read about a hundred books. And don't think you can act on this dream, this Vision, on your own. You've got to get advice from someone." She suddenly had a thought. "Besides, didn't you say the Guardian said in the dream that someone would advise you? Who knows! Maybe Grandpa is the one who is supposed to do that. You remember the stories he told of the old Seeress he knew when he lived in Hesk? He really knows a lot about these things. You know. About the Gifted."

"Maybe, but it was a long time ago." He thought on it more. "No. It's absolutely not Grandpa. Remember me telling you the Guardian said I would *know* who it was when I saw him? It's not Grandpa."

"Yes, hmm, I forgot that part. But I think you should still talk to him about it." She continued pushing because she felt her brother was at least responsive to the idea. "And eventually you're going to have to talk to Mother, too, especially if you think you will have to leave Felto. I know you've been ready to leave home, to go train with Cousin Amerro, but you can't just run off. You promised Father you'd stay till he got back, and only Mother can let you out of that promise."

Kodi considered this as their footsteps brought them to the edge of the village of Felto. "Father obliged me to promise. So no, I won't just run off. All right, then, I'll talk to Grandpa first. After his birthday dinner, though. When I help him get ready for bed." He seemed to ease up slightly. There was a good deal of hope in that Vision especially near the end, and he wanted to latch onto it. Mostly his hesitations centered on how to go about getting the Familial Blessing and not breaking the promise he made to his father. He knew his mother would not want to go against his father's wishes. He had to approach her in just the right way. "But I don't know about Mother, yet."

They entered the village proper and were approaching the house of their grandfather near the center of town. This had been the home of the Fothemrys, too, for several years since the death of their grandmother and Hess's shift from farmer to lumber tradesman. With the strong income from that business, Hess decided to honor his wife's wish and move into the home of her father in town, so that as a widower Yugan would not be lonely.

It proved a good choice, too, when Hess began his series of expeditions to Tolos, for the family was no longer saddled with the hard and constant work of a farm. In town it was easy to operate the lumber business, and Yugan had the help of his grandson in his woodshop as needed. The house was larger than nearly all of the others, for Yugan's income was sizeable, and so it functioned reasonably well as a place for administering the new county when Hess was later ennobled and given jurisdiction over it. Of course in his many absences it was Elisa who was unquestionably in charge. The home was built of local timbers, attractive, with a high-pitched roof and many windows.

As soon as the twins came in sight of the house, they heard a familiar bark.

"Musca!" called Kodi and then whistled. A large silver blur raced towards them.

Musca was of an unusual breed known as the Elentine Noble from beyond the Imperial Mountains. It was said they were bred by that country's armies centuries ago as fighting dogs in their wars with the Ice Tribes and the Barantines. They were huge, fierce, fighting animals prized for their intense, protective loyalty.

Around familiar faces, however, they were unabashedly friendly creatures. On this side of the Divide, they were rare, recognized sometimes by older Kingsmen who had fought in the wars, and indeed there were none known in the duchy besides Musca. But upon a time only three years before, Hess had the luck of acquiring one from a merchant who had come to County Fothemry to acquire several loads of valuable ambernut lumber. The man himself was an Elenite, having established himself in the lucrative trade over King's Pass.

Hess was captivated by the rarity of the animal, a pup at the time, with its sleek silver coat, square face and pointed ears. He noticed that this one, unlike all the others in the litter, had green eyes.

The merchant admitted it was odd, but didn't think anything of it, saying they would probably change to brown given time. Hess provided a large wagon load of precious ambernut in exchange for the rare animal and promptly gave him to Kodi and Lyndz to raise. Not surprisingly, considering the sorts of outdoor activities Kodi engaged in, boy and dog naturally gravitated to each other. Even Lyndz acknowledged Musca as 'Kodi's dog,' and yet the animal would often pay extra attention to Lyndz, sometimes sleeping beside her bed or going with her on walks. It was almost as if he were saying to her, *Kodi's my buddy, but I love you, too, and I want you to know it. I'm going to watch after you.*

It grew within a few months to its current huge size and might have proven a burden to keep fed if one of its qualities had not been its instinct for hunting on its own. Wolf-like, he would disappear into the nearby fields and woods to find his dinner, but strangely ignored the chickens and other stock belonging to the villagers and farmers. Nor did his green eyes ever change, becoming even more distinctive as he grew. He was treated well by Kodi, and in return Musca was intensely loyal to the family, protective and obedient. Kodi, and sometimes even the neighbor men, took him on excursions into the country. As it turned out he had uncanny senses beyond what was typical of any of the shepherding and retrieving breeds common in the region, and proved a great asset on the hunt. The neighbor men continually raved about him. *He has a sixth sense, that one does,* they would proclaim animatedly.

In a moment, Musca was by their side accompanying the twins on the last street to their home. Without fail he could always improve their mood, so even though Kodi in particular was dealing with deep thoughts, by the time they were at the threshold of the front door, he couldn't help taking upon himself some of the joviality of the dog's greetings.

Entering the hall, they realized their mother Elisa was not present—her cape which typically hung on one of the many pegs was missing. They could tell supper was being prepared by the smell of potatoes and herbs mingled with roasted chicken, all coming from the kitchen in the back of the house. Ansy, the cook and housekeeper who was brought into the family years before, was obviously hard at work. The aromas promised a hearty dinner for their grandfather's celebration.

Yugan was as usual sitting by the fire in the front parlor, working diligently with his carving tools on a magnificent walking staff he had made from heartwood ambernut.

He stopped his work for a moment, turned the object, and studied it closely. Beside him on a table was a sizeable book, opened wide to an artistic woodcut insertion of a Winged Dragon. Yugan was using the picture as his model. He carried an expression on his face the twins knew meant he was pleased with himself.

"Elisa should be back soon. She's over at the inn. The town runner came by a short while ago to say that Lord Curdoz the Sage and a group of Matrimonial Sisters had arrived."

The twins looked at one another in amazement.

"Lord Curdoz, here?" Kodi was wide-eyed at the thought of the Sage of Solanto in Felto. What could it mean? It was definitely odd that the great Sage would come to Felto; it was not on the main road to Cumpero. Did it mean anything? "Mother went to meet him?"

"Yes, of course, it is her duty to welcome important guests."

"Grandpa, nobody important ever comes to Felto, except Duke Amerro, but he's a cousin anyway."

Yugan reciprocated Lyndz' laugh. "That may have been true in the past, but as a new county seat, and once your parents' manor is finished, Felto will only become more important as the years go by."

Lyndz looked at the staff. "Grandpa, it's really coming along."

He turned it over again and again. "I've never used a Dragon theme in anything I've made before."

Having a plentiful supply of the finest wood available to him, Lyndz' grandfather created beautiful walking staffs, trinket and jewelry boxes, smoking pipes, and also many carvings of animals and birds, and sold them in the markets. Two years ago after a severe fall, he switched over to making these smaller objects, for he could no longer manage heavy lumber for the making of fine furniture—once his forte. He was considered a master craftsman, though he had never apprenticed with anyone, and he would receive orders from distant places.

Now in his sixties, Yugan still received significant income from this work, enough to hire Ansy and to run the household. Perhaps it wasn't necessary, not since his son-in-law Hess was in the ambernut trade and had also acquired some gold from his exploration of Tolos, but it made Yugan feel important to do what he could, as long as he could, and as long as his daughter and her children dwelt under his roof. He was insistent his own income be used to support the workings of the household; it was still his house, he would remind them. He did not want to sit idle and content on the wealth of his son-in-law. Though his feet had become unsteady, he could still do much with his hands.

Kodi, too, came over to see it. Yugan handed it to him. "What do you think, Son?"

Kodi looked steadily at it. "It's incredible, Grandpa," he said. "When you're done that Dragon will crawl right off the shaft and fly away!"

Kodi and Lyndz loved their grandfather. He could do much with his hands, but since his fall he could not get about well and often needed assistance with otherwise simple tasks. Elisa was completely devoted to him, and as his only child she did all she could to help her father feel important and loved. He doted on her in return and was very fond of his twin grandchildren. An avid reader and storyteller, he did much to teach them reading and writing as children, and he surely had more books on hand than anyone else in County Fothemry. His collection was now up to ninety volumes, and he had read them all, many of them several times over.

"Thank you, Son." Yugan looked at his grandson appreciatively. "That's exactly what I expect it to do when I get done with it!"

Musca walked over and licked the man's strong but wrinkled left hand. Yugan patted the dog on the head.

Lyndz took the staff from her brother. "It's amazingly intricate! You've never made one like this, have you?"

It wasn't just the head, but rather the entire body of a Winged Dragon. The figure was perhaps a total of thirty inches and began about three feet up from the bottom end of the staff, and wound itself sinuously around the main shaft, wings folded tightly behind, and its fierce face topping the end. It was neither bulky nor clunky, but a fine piece of art. The whole staff was of solid ambernut, stunning with its lustrous golden hues, but Yugan had installed in its head a pair of black sapphire eyes each on close inspection donning a star pattern in its center. There was still much work to go on it, however. Every hand-carved scale would have to be perfect before Yugan was satisfied.

"No," said Yugan. "I don't know why, but a little voice in my sleep told me to make a Dragon staff. So, I did. Just a bit of inspiration."

Lyndz caught Kodi's eye, yet the two didn't have any time to ponder this revelation, for Ansy abruptly appeared from the kitchen where she had been busy in the final preparations of the birthday dinner. In her bustling manner she transformed the mood of the room. She looked around. "Look at the shavings all over the floor. What a mess! Musca will track it everywhere! Lyndz, you sweep that up later, please. You're going to have to come to the table tonight, old man. We will not wait for Madam any longer. Get off your duff and come."

"Impertinent creature." Yugan said with a chuckle. "Yes, of course I will come to the table, but no, we will not begin before my daughter returns. Now run along and do your best to keep it warm until she gets here. What kind of birthday pie did you make me, old woman?"

"Ha! Nobody is as old as you! What makes you think I baked a pie for you anyway?"

This brief interchange was met with much laughter, for Yugan and Ansy had really a very excellent one-on-one, despite her station as a servant. She had been with the family for perhaps ten years now, not too long after the Fothemrys themselves moved in, and since then she and Yugan had become quite attached to one another. There had even been a time when Lyndz as a young girl would tease her grandfather and tell him he should Bond the servant woman. He would always smile at her and say, *Yes, Ansy is a fine lady, but I have no desire to Bond again.*

Ansy retreated to the kitchen, and the twins settled in to await their mother's return, already having forgotten Yugan's odd reference to the staff. Musca lay close to the fire at Yugan's feet and began to doze; he'd been gone from the house hunting most of the day.

"Mother will never finish this," Lyndz said, picking up a half-knitted shawl from a wicker basket at Elisa's elaborate chair, another ambernut piece Yugan had long ago made for his only daughter. Lyndz promptly began adding to her mother's stitches. Kodi decided he needed to wash up, but hardly had Lyndz picked up the needles and Kodi entered the hall before Musca let out a fantastic woof, and charged towards the door wagging his tail. There were voices outside, and then Elisa their mother opened the latch and walked in, as always with a cheerful expression on her still young and very beautiful face.

She was not alone. Immediately behind her entered two other people, a tall, fairly thin man with rather long dark hair sprinkled with gray, and a woman of similar age, though rather short and dumpy with shoulder-length light brown hair.

Lord Curdoz, the Sage of Solanto, was a figure almost of myth to the twins. There was no doubt as to his identity. He had discarded his gray traveling cloak and now donned a plain green stole over finer clothes, and of course there was the news Yugan had expounded which settled any doubts they might have had. As they had been taught, the twins bowed out of respect for a high lord. Even Yugan managed with effort to rise from his chair and nod. "Welcome to our home, Lord Curdoz! What a great honor to have you here! I was hoping my daughter would bring you so I could meet you. I don't get out as often as I once did!"

The Sage was quick to realize Yugan's difficulties and himself walked over to the old man with his hands out. "The honor is mine, good sir. Your daughter the countess is very kind to invite us for dinner. She tells me it is your birthday?"

"Yes, Lord Curdoz. As you can see," he joked, "they continue to come each year on this date whether I want them to or not."

"May Meical the Guardian Affirm you as you celebrate it, and may you celebrate many more to come!" Curdoz then turned around, "Let me introduce you to someone else, Master Yugan."

The woman had the most cheerful round face Lyndz had ever seen, and over her shoulders was draped a shawl of various hues, decorous, and with what appeared to be gold-threaded tassels. This, without any other garb denoted her office, a Mother in the Order of the Matrimonials.

Lyndz looked over to see what her brother thought of these important persons. She saw Kodi, oddly enough, standing rigidly with the most startled expression. He was staring at the Sage as though he couldn't believe in his existence, let alone his presence. By the fire and the lantern on the mantle, Curdoz' face was now well-lit, and Kodi could see it clearly. No one else in the room seemed to notice this, as the Sage introduced Yugan to Mother Idamé. Yugan was extravagant in his greeting of the Mother Matrimonial.

Finally, the Sage himself began to take in his surroundings and to see who these others were, bowing respectfully to him. He first looked at Lyndz who was closest to him, and he started, and then he turned quickly to look over at Kodi standing inside the second doorway to the back hall. There was an audible intake of breath as their eyes met, for Curdoz now appeared almost as stunned as Kodi did.

Before Kodi could stop himself, and without thought as to the sort of reaction his statement might garner, in a voice just above a whisper he proclaimed, "It's…it's you! You're the one!"

For a moment, no one moved or spoke. Lyndz noticed that the Sage was as intent on her as he was on Kodi, for he kept looking back and forth between them. Elisa's cheerful expression changed to one of confusion, whereas Yugan looked back and forth between the twins and the Sage, wondering. Finally, Lyndz realized how disconcerted her brother's face had become, and in another second it dawned on her exactly what her brother must have meant by his whispered exclamation, and she caught her own breath.

The Matrimonial Mother looked too at all the faces and had her own moment of revelation. She was the first to speak. "Why, Lord Curdoz, have you found the very ones you've been looking for? And you've only just begun!"

"Yes, Mother Idamé," said Sage Curdoz slowly and in a quiet voice, as he continued to look from one twin to the other. "By the Guardian, I have!"

Again silence reigned except for the hiss and crackle of the fire. Yugan's creased face was contemplative as if he were working out a puzzle in his mind. His daughter the countess was obviously bewildered. Oddly, Musca the dog now walked over to the Sage, and looked up into Curdoz' face. He then sat on his haunches and whimpered, nosing the man's hand and drawing his attention. Curdoz seemed to notice the animal for the first time.

"An Elentine Noble!" he said, breaking the silence. "And silver-coated at that! It has been at least twenty years I know since I've seen one." He reached over and scratched the huge dog behind its large pointed ears. "Interesting. Green eyes? Fascinating! I don't know whether I've heard of such." Then he looked up again at the twins.

Elisa spoke now for the first time since entering the house. Hers was a voice melodic and warm, yet she was mystified by this apparent recognition between her children and the Sage.

"I must apologize, Lord Curdoz. I don't believe I understand what you and the Mother Idamé are saying. Have you seen my son and daughter before this evening? There was the time when Kodi went with his father to the port of Ross on the ambernut trade, and Lyndz appeared at the duke's court in Cumpero only last year," she offered. "Were you there as well? She didn't mention it."

She felt the need to suppress the strangeness, searching as she was for explanations that might fit, resisting her heart telling her something more complicated was going on.

Curdoz turned to his hostess. He had anticipated such a moment. Speaking with kindness, he said, "No, Lady Elisa. No, that is not how I know them. I haven't traveled this direction in over four years. We have never really met one another face to face. But we have, in a manner of speaking, met in another way." He looked at Lyndz again, but she appeared almost as uncertain as her mother. Which told him something. But when he looked at Kodi, it was obvious. "I see it in your eyes, young man. You have not spoken of it to your mother, have you? Tell her then how you know me. Do not hold back. She deserves to know."

Kodi's usual self-confidence appeared diminished, but then his twin stepped over and stood beside him. His sister's firm hand on his shoulder was enough to give Kodi the wherewithal he needed. He looked at his sister, breathed very deeply, and then looked from Curdoz to his mother. "A Vision, Mother. A Vision from the Guardian Meical."

The Sage nodded.

"What?" responded Elisa. The information was just too exotic. "What did you say?"

Kodi looked down. He was at a loss how to explain himself further, knowing the ramifications this revelation would bring, and it gave him no pleasure to upset his mother. He wished now he had followed Lyndz' advice days ago and said something to her already.

"Young lady," Curdoz said, turning his focus upon Lyndz. "You yourself have had a Vision like your brother?" Though he thought from her face he knew the answer.

Lyndz was startled by the question. "No, m'Lord, I have not. Why would I have a Vision?"

"Well, of course the question is, why did your brother have the Vision? It seems just as likely you would have had one, too. You are twins, am I correct?"

"Yes, m'Lord." she replied.

Then the Sage looked again at Elisa. She was obviously not happy. Elisa at one level wished to resist what she was hearing, but at the same time she was a perceptive person. In her heart of hearts she knew there was something here that was unique, and it required her to respond with some semblance of objectivity.

"I still do not understand, Lord Curdoz. Kodi is saying he had a Meicalian Vision and that you were in it? And I guess you had one with Kodi in it, since you recognize him as he does you?"

"Yes." He turned back to the twins. "*Kodi*. Kodi is your name, is it? It is a good name. It means 'warrior'. Interesting. And what is yours again, young lady?" he asked.

"Lyndz, at your service, m'Lord," she replied, though quietly.

"Ah, that is a name rooted in *wisdom*." He winked at Idamé who nodded knowingly, and then he turned back to Elisa. "Yes, Countess, I have seen both Kodi and Lyndz in a Vision from the Guardian. However," he looked around at everyone, "this will certainly take time to explain adequately. Maybe we should all sit down?"

At that moment Ansy came back in from the kitchen and stood next to Yugan. "Madam! We have guests, I see! Will they be staying for dinner? I can add two more to the table, I believe we..." She dropped off as she now looked more clearly at the two guests.

"Yes, Ansy." Elisa realized the best thing to do for now was to first have dinner, and then afterwards hear the explanations she needed. "His Lordship the Sage and the Mother Matrimonial were the ones I went to meet. I invited Lord Curdoz and Mother Idamé for dinner, knowing we would have plenty for Pap's birthday."

"Lord Curdoz, the Sage?" Ansy was dumbfounded as she looked more closely at him. She curtsied. Then she looked at Idamé standing beside him and the shawl around her shoulders. She curtsied to her as well. "Mother."

On top of the strangeness, when Idamé saw Ansy standing with Yugan, she developed a rather large grin, and coming from such an immensely pleasant and homey face, Ansy could not help but to grin right back. "Mother? I beg your pardon, but why are you looking at me that way?"

"Oh! Did I have a *look?* Oh my!"

Everyone was puzzled by this. The twins were uncomfortable with the whole interchange of the past several minutes and this just added to it.

"What is it, Mother *Idamé,* did I get your name right?" Ansy inquired again.

"Oh!" said the Matrimonial, still grinning. "I'm so sorry! I know I must appear very silly! Yes, you have my name right. What was yours again?"

"Ansy, Mother."

"Well, dear lady, Ansy! I will be glad to tell you why, but I...I do believe it needs to wait, too! But sometime this evening we could get together and chat for a wee?"

Not knowing what else to say, the cook answered, "Certainly, Mother Idamé, if you wish!" She was confused still, but she did not lose her smile, Idamé's own being as infectious as it was. Really, this last seemed for whatever reason to lighten the current mood slightly. It certainly brought Elisa back around to herself again, and she thought it best to forego explanations and long conversations for a while at least.

"Yes, we shall have dinner first. Ansy, go add two more settings. Lyndz, bring your Grandpa a bowl of water and soap for his hands."

Kodi then realized he still needed to wash up from his day's labor and gratefully took the opportunity to disappear to the room behind the kitchen that held several buckets of water used for various purposes. He splashed his face repeatedly to try to get a grip on himself. *I can't believe it,* he kept telling himself over again. *What am I going to say? What am I going to do?*

No immediate answers were forthcoming. He finally managed to wash his face and upper body sufficiently with some soap, dried himself, and donned one of his clean shirts that Ansy had laundered and had hung on a row of hooks in the wash room.

When he emerged, the others were sitting down to a beautifully laid table in Yugan's dining room. Candles were lit all around. After several trips Ansy returned with the last of many scrumptious dishes. Often Ansy ate in the kitchen by herself, but it was understood that for special occasions she was to enjoy eating with the family. Yugan's birthday was certainly special. Yet with the arrival of a Matrimonial Mother, and no less the Sage of Solanto, this would likely be the most important dinner ever served in Yugan's home.

Elisa was determined not to allow her own unsettled curiosity interfere with her duties as hostess. She knew that, for the moment anyway, she must set questions aside while they all enjoyed a feast to celebrate her father's special day, and to act warm and welcoming of the two important guests. Nevertheless, she couldn't help but every minute or so to look at Kodi with frustration, wondering why he had never mentioned to her the unusual dream.

Curdoz and Idamé refused to usurp Yugan's and Elisa's positions at either end of the table despite their protestations. Rather, the two guests sat next to one another on one side of the table, while the twins and Ansy sat on the other. Ansy happened to be sitting at the corner next to Yugan, and oddly throughout the dinner Idamé continued to look at those two with that grin on her face.

Idamé's friendly chatter and the old man anecdotes offered throughout by Yugan were enough to open everybody's hearts a bit and make the little feast cheerful. Lyndz spoke up from time to time, despite her underlying angst.

Kodi, however, remained silent.

Chapter 7—Explanations

Finally, dinner ended, and they moved to the parlor. Kodi added more wood to the fire and set his grandfather's chair closer to it. Musca was curled up in a vast lump close by. Ansy brought out a tray of silver goblets and served Escarantine wine, opened at Yugan's orders. She also passed around a tin of sweet butter biscuits, a local favorite.

Idamé was complimentary of the treats, and had her hand in the tin more than once over the next hour. And if she was delighted with the butter biscuits, Curdoz acted overwhelmed by the wine.

"Oh my! Dear Yugan! This is fine!"

"Thank you, Lord Curdoz. The honor is mine to have you and the Mother Idamé to share it with, and on my birthday, no less."

Curdoz was not exaggerating. If anything, the Sage was a connoisseur. He had a large cellar stocked to the ceiling at Villa Saundry, and indeed most of the selection was from Duranti or Escarant with a number of bottles imported from faraway Nant. However, as far as he was concerned, that which was made in Escarant, the land of his friend Grand Duke Mannago, was by far the best. He was used to the vintage, but apparently the bottles Yugan had Ansy open for their dessert were of a particularly good year.

Kodi and Lyndz sipped theirs. Kodi, although he far preferred ale, made some effort to appreciate it. It was quite strong, and after a glass or two and light conversation, he and his sister both felt a bit more relaxed.

Elisa, though, was the first to bring the talk back to the necessary business. "Lord Curdoz, I believe we should talk now about exactly what brings you here. I realize now that your coming was not simply to accompany the Matrimonial Troupe."

Curdoz took another sip and set down his goblet. "No, Lady Elisa, it is not coincidence that we met at the inn tonight, though I'll be honest we didn't know that we had finally come to, I guess you could say *the right place,* until I saw Kodi and Lyndz here in your house. I was called to come to Tulesk, certainly, and I intended if necessary to travel to Cumpero to Duke Amerro to see if he could help me, but now that is not necessary. Meical the Guardian has set in motion something that we must follow through on. As it was, the side road here to Felto intrigued me, for it came to mind the new manor being constructed and your husband's reputation, so the Troupe and I chose to come this way. The Troupe was assigned to Tulesk; I happened upon them in Thorune, although even that was more than happenstance, and so I came with them. And though I'll explain more later, you must first know, yes, that in my Vision I was shown both Kodi's and Lyndz' faces, was given in my mind the idea that they are twins, and was told that I must seek and find them in Tulesk." He then looked at Idamé and nodded for her to explain her own position.

"M'lady," she said after swallowing the bit of biscuit in her mouth. "I have also had a Vision. It seems an extraordinary thing that the Guardian should divine upon Lord Curdoz, your son Kodi, and myself, interconnected Visions, and that Meical should bring us together. There is a purpose behind it all. Like Lord Curdoz said, the Guardian has set something in motion."

The Sage continued, "I must warn you that we don't know the full reason why we specifically are needed for this task, and I feel that no matter what I say, it will not, Countess, put you at ease, but your son, and your daughter too, are both required to respond to these Visions, and though you will not like to hear it, you must come to realize that they will have to leave home and come with us."

Elisa frowned. Yugan shuffled in his chair, rhythmically pressing together and relaxing his fingers. Ansy stood behind, rubbing his shoulders.

"Me?" chimed in Lyndz. "But…but I didn't have a Vision!"

"Yes," continued Curdoz, "but it is clear from *my* Vision that you are important to this." He then looked at Kodi. "Isn't that what you believe, too, Kodi?"

Kodi looked first at his sister, then down at the floor. "Er, Lyndz was in my Vision, too, yes, m'Lord."

Lyndz dropped her jaw and looked at her brother, and before she could stop herself said, "You didn't tell me I was in it!"

Elisa couldn't help herself, either. "Lyndz, you mean to tell me that you knew about Kodi's dream, too, and yet you nor he chose to tell me anything!"

Lyndz looked down at the same floor her brother was already regarding with deep interest. "But…" she trailed off.

However, Lyndz' anxiety at her mother's chastisement was exactly what was needed for Kodi. He was a man, and it was time to act the part. He looked up and took upon himself a mature tone. "Mother, it was this very afternoon that I decided I would finally speak up about my Vision. Besides, it was my place to tell you anyway, not Lyndz', so you should not be hard on her. In fact, it was she who convinced me finally to speak about it. It was my plan to wait till after Grandpa's dinner."

Kodi saw no need to indicate that he intended only to tell his grandfather, and Lyndz had no intention either of elaborating. He continued. "I'm sorry. I didn't expect it to all come out like this, with all these people here, you know. I didn't know they were coming. I guess the timing of it all just didn't seem important, about me telling you about the dream right away. I had to work a lot of it out in my own mind."

"Lady Elisa, surely you can understand why something of this nature would present a dilemma for your son with regard to discussing it with you. Don't you agree? It is likely that it is only now, now that the Mother Idamé and I are here and Kodi is seeing me face to face, that he begins to understand more the reality of the Vision."

Curdoz was playing a delicate game. He had learned much since his arrival, from words spoken at dinner but also from observation. There was some tension it seemed involving Kodi and the twins' father. Hess had apparently required Kodi to remain home despite his age and his wishes for himself. Kodi was a man who needed to expand outward and find his own way, yet Hess was using his own absences as an excuse to make Kodi stay. Then also the idea that Lyndz as a young woman was being drawn into something that would surely appear dangerous made the whole situation with Elisa very tricky indeed. The mother was the key.

Elisa recognized what Curdoz was doing in his diplomatic attempt to soothe, and she wanted to respond, but found herself only nodding.

Curdoz looked at Kodi. "Young man, the time is now, now that Mother Idamé and I are here. And perhaps," he looked at Elisa to emphasize the point to her, "just perhaps, Kodi, it was also meant for you to wait until tonight just as your own instinct has suggested. But I think you should tell your tale first, and I'm sure it will help Mother Idamé and me to better interpret what was going on in our own Visions. And she and I will also tell you ours." He then looked at Yugan's mantle clock. "Though, it is somewhat late already, and we may not finish it all up tonight, but we can certainly gather here in the morning again if it is all the same to you. But go ahead now, Kodi. We will at least commence."

Kodi breathed, took a rather large swallow from his goblet and began. Though his eyes were mostly on the Sage, he deliberately looked at his mother from time to time in a rather conscious attempt to 'come clean' with her, and as his story unfolded even Yugan's face turned from puzzlement to amazement. In great detail he described everything—every place and each person: the sorcerer and sorceress, their castles and the gray cities, the sea and the yellow-sailed ships. He spoke of the young man by the fountain next to the grand palace in the bright city by the sea. After that he described the strange human-like figure on the plateau in the forest, how the white bird seemed to speak with her and how sad she seemed, and even the emotions he could tell she was feeling and her probe of his mind. At this, Curdoz and Idamé looked at each other with curious expressions, but as neither interrupted, Kodi plunged ahead. He told them how he himself felt during each 'scene' and how he knew instinctively that he was somehow called to meet the young man and this last female figure at some point in his future. Finally, he spoke of his airborne flight over the great mountains and his coming to the beautiful Valley, but when he got to the end of the Vision and the Valley Lake and spoke of hearing the Guardian's Voice, he grew quiet all of a sudden.

Curdoz seemed to understand, and he looked at Elisa. "When one hears the Voice of Meical in a Vision, it is an intensely personal affair. It is difficult to describe. But young man, we need to know what His words were."

Kodi gazed into the fire burning unconcerned in the fireplace. He sighed and said. "Every word is really clear in my mind." He repeated the amazing conversation he had with the Guardian Meical and concluded, "…so though I did not see your face, Lord Curdoz, when you stood by the lantern light, I…just knew."

"He called you His *brother?*" asked Curdoz for clarification. "That is, eh, curious."

Kodi nodded.

There was a minute or two of silence before anyone spoke. Finally, Lyndz said, "You said I was in it, but you didn't say where."

Kodi had deliberately avoided it, but Curdoz looked at him and nodded as if to coax him into revealing it. Kodi responded, though he couldn't look at his sister. He had shared with her about the Vision, but in his desire to protect her, he had purposely left out the one part that involved her, and he now felt ashamed of himself for having done so.

It was wrong to underestimate her, and he knew it. "When I was looking at the sorceress on the tower balcony there was a moment when I saw you, too. You were not necessarily there *with* her, but I saw you there. It was like you were in a circle of light, like in a portrait or mirror frame…"

Yugan interrupted. He had not spoken since Elisa first steered the conversation. He leaned forward intently. "A circle of light? What color was the light?"

Kodi looked at his grandfather and wondered. "Green. Why, Grandpa?"

Elisa's brow wrinkled as she duplicated. "Yes, Pap, why? Why is the color important?"

Yugan was agitated and would not respond right away. He was gripping the arm of the chair and his hands were shaking. Ansy was sitting now beside him and reached over and rubbed his shoulders again. But when it was clear that Yugan would not answer, Curdoz chimed in.

"It is important, Lady Elisa, because," and he looked at Lyndz—she was wide-eyed and wondering—"green is the color that represents the Gift and the use of magic. Meicalian-derived magic, by the way. A good thing."

Elisa nor Lyndz could say anything. Idamé spoke. "Green light is a sign of the Gifted, Lyndz. The stole the Sage wears is green, and so is the banner that represents the Orders."

Lyndz was dumbfounded. "You mean to say that I am Gifted?"

"It is *possible*, Lyndz. It is not clear yet. But your brother is Gifted, as he has shown by being given a Vision in the first place. Monastics have Visions and no other Gift, but I think it safe to say that the servant life of a Monastic is not Kodi's Calling. Nor yours. If you are Gifted, it sounds to me that it hasn't manifested yet. In neither you nor Kodi. It can take time to discern it, and so you wouldn't know it right away, unless the Vision happened to explain it." Then he looked over at Yugan. "Yugan, you act as if you suspected this. How so?"

The old man was still gripping the chair. "I…I wondered, because my mother…my mother was a Seeress." He looked up anxiously at his daughter.

Elisa took in a startled breath. She was clearly shocked by this revelation, as were the twins. This was a family history fact of which she had been kept in the dark. "I…I didn't know this." She stared at her father.

"I'm sorry. It has never seemed important till now."

Curdoz raised his eyebrow. It appeared this was an evening filled with revelations. Something clicked in his mind as he heard this, and it was one more realization that something greater was going on that was somehow tied to past events as well. *That would explain some things.* Still, he had to be sure. He turned to Yugan. "It isn't common for the Gifted to Bond, but when they do, Giftedness can certainly run in the family. What was your mother's name, may I ask?"

Yugan, though, grew silent and clearly did not wish to say. The Sage looked at him kindly as he realized the old man's difficulty, but in a low voice he persisted. "Yugan, may I offer a name?"

The old man immediately looked up at the Sage. "No, m'lord, wait!"

"It was Trevisté," said Elisa.

"Yes and no," said Yugan with a troubled face. "Sweet daughter, I need to tell you something I haven't told you before. I always used my mother's…your grandmother's middle name, Trevisté, when I would talk to you about her. But no one knew that name aside from me, as she never used it. I am so sorry to have kept it from you all these many years, but I …but so many people think that a Gift like that is *always* inherited. If anyone had found out it would have been the end of our family's privacy. We would have been bothered by everybody with any problem, coming to us and getting us to try to tell them their future. It is an awful thing. No one would leave my mother alone until she moved us to a village in the deep forest in Hesk. I did not want that same life for us."

"So that's why you left Hesk and moved here to Tulesk, isn't it?" asked Lyndz, perceptively.

"In part. Even after my mother died, people would come to me. I could tell them nothing. I am not Gifted, but they would not leave me alone. I joined the Hescian army, as you all know, and fought in the war for a time. But then I quit it, went home, packed my things, and did not tell anyone where I was going. I moved here and helped settle Felto, since by then the Ice Tribes had been chased out. I soon Bonded, and we raised Elisa, and we were content here."

"And no one here knew who you were. Or rather who your mother was," said Curdoz. "You changed your surname, too."

Yugan looked at the Sage. "Yes. I had her surname, and I believe it was her family name, for I never knew my father. I started going by the name *Lunder,* a very common name in northern Solanto, of course." He paused for a moment but then said rather imploringly, looking straight into Curdoz' eyes. "My mother was a good woman…"

"She was, in her way, resistant to her Gift, and did not go study in the Valley." Curdoz looked at the old man. "But I understand. A Seer or Seeress does not enjoy glimpsing the future. I think I know who your mother was, Yugan. The time frame in which your mother must have lived...well, there was only one Seeress who lived in this part of the world then."

Yugan finally spoke. "Kalemna Deroge, m'lord. Her name was Kalemna Deroge."

Idamé raised her eyebrows and spoke next. "But Yugan, Kalemna Deroge disappeared around forty years ago. They never found her, yet you're certain she died?"

"It is what I believe. The war and all. That bit of Hesk was overrun by the Tribesmen for a short time. I believe she was captured and killed."

"Others believe so, too," said Curdoz. "Deroge was resistant to her Gift, and like I said, never went to the Valley of the Gifted. Yugan, I don't understand your tone and the point you are trying to make. Giftedness certainly can run in families, though not always— it isn't in my recent ancestry—but you seem to think it is a bad thing. To be Gifted..."

"To be Gifted means that you are at everybody else's mercy," said the old man with conviction. "You have no control over your own life. Everybody will try to use you for their own purposes." He looked at his grandchildren pleadingly. It was almost pathetic to see such a pained expression on his old face. "I am so sorry."

The twins were silent; they were very unnerved by all of this.

"Yugan, obviously I know much about this subject. And being a Sage has many disadvantages. Yes, there are powerful people in the kingdom that try to manipulate me, just as you say. And in my case it is mostly about power—the desire to have political control. Noblemen try to use me to side with them. But there is something else you need to know about being Gifted." He looked at Idamé.

She took the cue. "To be Gifted means to be in a very particular relationship with the Guardian. We enjoy our family and our friendships, but with the Gifted, Meical Himself *becomes* a friend. Deeply personal and difficult to describe, just like Kodi being at a loss to describe the emotions he felt when he heard the Guardian in his Vision. It gives us a kind of strength." She looked over at him. Their eyes met. "I understand, Kodi, what you felt in your Vision."

Kodi nodded out of politeness, but didn't respond.

"I understand though, Yugan; don't get me wrong," continued Curdoz. "In the case of a Seer or Seeress like your mother, I can see your point. But Kalemna for some reason chose not to go to the Valley. She remained in Hesk. A number of her writings are in the great library in Aster. I've read some of them. She was quite scholarly, and her education implies she came of a noble family. But most Seers or Seeresses remain in the Valley after their course of study. In any event, her choice to stay probably made it hard for her, just as you say. The Healer pairs get a good dose of bother. The Matrimonial Troupe Sisters are rather used to couples approaching them." He winked at Idamé. "It's just part of who we are, Yugan, so don't think so much of it. I don't know what Meical has in store for Kodi and Lyndz, but the Guardian knows what He's doing. You have to give them their chance."

In the silence that followed, eyes drifted toward the fire. After a minute or two Kodi got up and added another log. With an iron poker he rearranged the logs. Curdoz watched him closely.

When he had finished, Kodi stood up straight and looked at his mother.

Elisa was struck by how much he looked like her husband; tall, handsome and strong. His face was ablaze with the reflection of the stoked fire. He had changed in the last few minutes. She could see it in his face—determination. His earlier embarrassment was cast away. She seemed to know what he was about to say.

"Mother, I will be leaving with Lord Curdoz. I can't stay in Felto any longer. I hope you understand. Father made me promise to wait till he returns, but I can't now. It's all different now with Lord Curdoz here. You can give me the Familial Blessing since Father isn't here, and let me go. You must do it."

All she could do was nod in recognition of what she realized now was a foregone fact.

"Me, too, I suppose," said Lyndz. It had been awhile since she had said anything.

Every part of Elisa's heart resisted this idea, but she had deciphered enough of the information to realize that there were events she could not control. It was obvious Kodi had to follow the demands of his Vision, and though Lyndz had had no such clear-cut evidence to support the idea that she, too, was required to go with Curdoz, there was still plenty to suggest she was important to it all. She was in Kodi's Vision. She was recognized by Curdoz. She was Kodi's twin, and so they were connected at a certain level. Elisa, therefore, did not argue, but the realization hit her hard that not only was her son leaving—and she knew in her heart this was long past due—but so too was the daughter that had been at her side since she birthed her.

Idamé's face took on the most compassionate expression, as she immediately stood up, went over to Elisa, knelt down and took the woman's hands into her own. "You know, dear, of course I have no children, but I am going with Lord Curdoz, and, with your permission I will watch after your daughter as though she were my very own." She beckoned Lyndz to come over, which she did, and she knelt too, and Mother Idamé wrapped one arm around her, as she still held on to Elisa with the other.

Though she felt as certain as her brother did on the necessity of the task at hand, Lyndz too shed tears at the thought of leaving her mother. Ansy came over as well and stood behind Elisa and held onto her mistress's shoulders. The four spoke to one another in soft whispers that the men in the room could not easily hear. In fact, the three men looked at one another. Yugan nodded, and with his grandson's help, he hobbled up and the three of them headed for the kitchen.

On their way to the rear of the house, Yugan described for Kodi something he wanted him to retrieve from his bedroom, and to bring it to the kitchen for Curdoz. Kodi thought it curious, but did as he was asked, and walked down the hall to his grandfather's room. This had once been Ansy's, but when Yugan hurt himself they switched in order for him not to have to manage the stairs. The room was warm, but not as warm as he knew his grandfather liked it, and so Kodi added more wood to the small fireplace and stoked it into strong flame. He then went to the dresser. In the bottom drawer near the back lay the requested item. It was a small wooden box, hand-carved in beautiful ambernut, obviously his grandfather's work.

Back in the kitchen, Kodi laid the box on the table. In the stronger light of the kitchen lanterns, he paid closer attention to the intricacy of his grandfather's carving. Ambernut was the most highly prized of all wood due to its golden beauty, the luminous depths that could be achieved through polishing, and its ease of cutting and wonderful carving properties. It was only plentiful in Tulesk. It was known there were stands near the drop of the Escarpment in the neighboring Principality of Hesk. But because of difficult terrain very little was harvested there, so before Tulesk was settled, ambernut was limited to the creation of small objects, such as jewelry or keepsake boxes, and turned and carved bowls and goblets. Only after the discovery of large stands in the eastern Tulescian forest region following the war did its availability and demand increase. With it, larger objects such as furniture could be produced, even paneling. Only the wealthy could afford these large pieces, and it could be found in the palaces of the barons and dukes of Solanto. They would trust only the finest carpenters and carvers in the kingdom to create objects from the precious commodity. Here in County Fothemry, especially among those involved in the timber trade, it was reasonably common, though still highly appreciated even by those who could get as much as they wanted, like Yugan.

Yugan was highly skilled. He had once made very fine furniture: tables with matching chairs, and desks, not only cut and pieced with much skill but also decorated with his remarkable carving, or inlaid with dark walnut, and these were sold at great profit. It was a slow business, though, as he was a perfectionist in his work. But since his fall he had limited himself to crafting that which was small and easy enough to handle as he sat in the parlor or at the kitchen table. He would direct Kodi as to the size—width, depth, and length—of the pieces he needed for carving. Kodi would cut the wood with Yugan's tools. Then Yugan would take it from there, and with carving implements regularly sharpened by a blacksmith friend he could still craft superior pieces and sell them.

This box was lovely, displaying intricate geometrical patterns on all sides, with a curved top and inlaid with burl walnut which created a fine contrast with the golden ambernut. It was quite small, perhaps seven inches across and two inches deep.

"This is beautiful, Yugan. You're a master, I see. In fact, I've never seen a finer piece."

Yugan then opened the box on its tiny hinges. Perfectly fitting inside it was a rather plain, leather-bound book. It was very small, in fine condition, handled very little over the years.

He handed it to the Sage. "I had the pages trimmed and bound by a bookmaker long ago. He was expert at what he did. They are in the order my mother had them in—they are all in her very handwriting. I will be frank, I do not know if all of it is Prophecy. It is in code."

"You...you mean you've never read it?" asked Kodi.

"I cannot decipher the code. There had to be a cipher, but I feel confident it was not in the old house when I packed and left Hesk." Yugan looked then at Curdoz. "I want you to have this. Somehow you will have to decode it. You are the Sage of Solanto, and I know you are a more worthy keeper than I."

"More worthy? No, I doubt that. But thank you, Yugan Lunder. You honor me with such a gift! This is unexpected. Yet auspicious. This could be very valuable to us." he said. He began turning through the pages. "I brought a cipher book with me, but who's to say that any of them are the correct one? I don't recognize some of these symbols. Some of the writing on certain pages is styled like poetry. Those are almost certainly Prophecy, but other pages appear to be common prose. There are probably seven or eight Prophecies, though difficult to tell. Yugan, there could be secrets in here. Secrets about her. Are you absolutely sure you..."

"Yes, Lord Curdoz. I want you to have it. Find the cipher, decode it, and if it holds helpful information then all is well."

Kodi held out his hand for the book, and the Sage handed it to him. "Can you explain to me more about codes? And what is a cipher?"

"Well, these writings are all in code," Curdoz said as he pointed to the page that Kodi had opened. "You see, these letters and symbols don't make real words, but rather the letters and numbers and symbols would match up with the correct letters and numbers and symbols on a table or chart, which is called a cipher, so you can determine what they really stand for. The problem is trying to determine what cipher is appropriate. And it is possible that more than one cipher was used. There are a dozen ciphers in the book I have, and they are useful in decoding secret letters, and I have people who send me coded letters even today. Hopefully one of them is correct. It'll take some time to figure that out. There's the possibility I won't have the right one."

Kodi thumbed through the pages, and then handed it back to the Sage. "Why would she have used a code? It's meant to keep it secret, isn't it? I mean, did she write anything else in code?"

"Good thinking, Kodi. Not that I know of. But we're not likely to know the answer to why until we decipher it."

"Can the Gift be used to figure it out?"

"Umm. No, Kodi, there's not a Gift for that. I'm afraid it's just a matter of time and research."

"M'lord, if you say that most of my mother's writings are in Aster, maybe the cipher is in the library there."

"Nothing else she ever wrote was in code, like Kodi alluded to. If it weren't for the fact her own son gave this book to me, and that the writing does seem familiar, I would be skeptical they came from Deroge. What you say is plausible."

He made to put the book in his pocket, but Yugan shoved the small box over to him. "They go together. I want you to have it, m'Lord."

Curdoz nodded and placed the book back into the ambernut box. "It is a treasure for sure! Thank you again, Yugan. I feel confident that at some point I'll decipher the writing. I think all that has happened has been for a purpose. Not just the Visions that Kodi and Idamé and I had, but also the fact Idamé and I met up on this journey the way we did, the relative quickness in which we found the twins, because I thought we might have to search all over Tulesk, and because of the fact that Yugan, and you, Kodi, descend from a Gifted Seer, and because of this tiny book Yugan kept of his mother's writings. It has all worked out rather neatly. So I think there is Something at work here. The Guardian has moved events."

"You think the writings in the book are that important?" asked Kodi.

"Possibly. Likely—I should say."

Kodi seemed to understand what Curdoz meant, but he still remembered the chill in his heart over the two evil beings in his Vision. "Lord Curdoz, those people I saw in the Vision, though. I want to believe what you say, but I don't think everything is going the way the Guardian wants it to."

"No," Curdoz agreed. "You are absolutely right, but I'm speaking mostly of ourselves—of us here. It is the choices we have made that have brought us to the events of today. No doubt there are Dark Powers at work again in the world, but that is why Meical has worked our own situation the way He has. It is why, of course, we call Him the Guardian. Dumhoni is His world to watch after."

He reached over and put his hand on Kodi's shoulder and continued. "Let's not talk anymore tonight. Tomorrow we will talk more and determine a plan. We need to get your mother's formal Blessing, and despite her nods tonight, I suspect she will need to know more information before she bestows it. I know a great deal about what you saw in your Vision, and it has confirmed what I saw in mine, and in Mother Idamé's. Mother Idamé and I need to return to the inn and rest." He then stood. "Oh! I forgot that Idamé means to speak with your housekeeper. Yugan, I believe she intends to speak with you as well."

Kodi wondered at this. "I usually help Grandpa get ready for bed."

Yugan was a bit confused as well, but he deemed it wise to hear what Mother Idamé had to say. "Hmm, don't worry about it tonight, Kodi. You go on; I'll manage."

Kodi got up from his chair and left the two older men and made his way to his bedroom. In the upstairs hallway he ran into his sister. They looked at one another rather intently. It appeared to Kodi she was waiting for something. Finally, he spoke.

"I'm really sorry, Lyndz. I'm sorry I didn't tell you I saw you in the dream. It just didn't seem important. You weren't involved in any action in it, if you know what I mean. It was just your face."

"I think you just didn't want me involved in something you thought might lead to danger."

Kodi thought for a moment. Honesty. He looked into his sister's eyes. "You're right. It was the wrong thing to do, and it really caught you off guard tonight. I'm sorry."

His sincerity was obvious, and she couldn't fault him anymore. "Well, I'll admit I'm not at all happy about leaving Felto. It's going to be really hard on everyone with both of us gone."

Kodi too knew he would miss his home and his family. Nevertheless, he was finally coming to grips with the idea that he would be leaving Felto shortly to pursue the mystery of the Vision. Recalling the end of his Vision and the lake water and the Voice, his confidence had begun to build again. "It'll be fine, Lyndz."

Lyndz shook her head. "I don't have that same confidence, Ko. Don't you see? Think about it. There will be danger, just like you expect, and hardship. Maybe you're ready for it, and I believe you are. But I don't know that I am."

She walked past him to her own bedroom and softly shut the door.

Kodi swallowed. For the first time since he had his Vision, he realized this was definitely not just about him. He went to bed, and by the time he fell asleep hours later, he was a wiser man.

The twins understandably slept little, and the same was true for their mother. Elisa had at first resigned herself to her son and daughter leaving, and by all traditions both were of age and could make their own decisions. During the night as her thoughts made circles in her mind she had misgivings. There was rumor of war in the distant east, and based on Kodi's Vision there would be great dangers to be faced. The obvious fact that there was really no knowing when she would see them again was perhaps the most difficult idea to deal with.

On top of those worries were her father's revelations regarding her grandmother, a woman she never knew, who apparently was a noted Seer. Elisa's realization that her own son and daughter may have inherited from the woman Meicalian Giftedness was a great challenge to her dreams and hopes for their future. She knew Kodi expected to train with Duke Amerro for knighthood, and though she understood there were inherent dangers associated with such a choice, the fact Solanto had been at peace for over a quarter century had always somewhat relieved her of considering the worst of those dangers. Lyndz she was grooming to be a talented lady of class, capable of managing an estate for a nobleman Bondmate. Elisa really had hoped to have Lyndz with her when the family moved into the manor, and looked forward to her assistance for at least another year or two.

She was very resistant especially of letting Lyndz leave her side. Sure, she knew of plenty of young men and women the same age as the twins who had left home already and established homes and families. Elisa and Hess themselves were somewhat younger than the twins when they fell in love and began their life together. When the Matrimonial Troupe performed the rites, the Sisters declared that there was an Aura. But this was different. Very different. Giftedness would to some degree dictate the direction of her children's lives. There was an old saying that Aura Bondings resulted in children especially blessed by the Guardian. Was that the case here? Was there really something in the old proverb?

She greatly desired the presence of her husband, but he was far away, somewhere in the Tolosian Peninsula. So, when the morning light peaked through her window and she finally arose from bed, she had little choice but to put on her best show throughout breakfast and through the activity presented by early morning chores. Her wrinkled brow, though, was a telling sign to Lyndz and Kodi, and neither said very much to her.

Ansy for whatever reason was bustling about cheerfully, humming a tune in the kitchen as she prepared everyone's breakfast. Elisa did not seem to pay it any mind, but the twins thought it odd. Even odder was that Yugan too seemed different. The old man was rarely *un*happy, but this morning—despite the revelations of the night before—he was rather chipper. The twins could not help but to notice that he and Ansy often looked at one another, pausing in their speech momentarily, then looking away. The housemaid's face seemed rosier than usual.

When Lord Curdoz and Mother Idamé reappeared at the door having spent the night at the village inn, the twins and their mother ended their morning chores and they sat together again in the parlor. It was brighter, of course, with the daylight streaming through the windows. Ansy and Yugan, believing they could add little to the discussion and, uninvolved in any decisions to be made, remained in the kitchen.

Curdoz nodded to Idamé to begin explaining her Vision.

"I did not see Kodi and Lyndz in my Vision," she said. "But I did see some of what Kodi saw. The drear stone city of the sorceress were as he described, but I saw it in great detail, and I also I saw more of the lands about. It was far south, rainy and wet, and there were vast fields of crops and livestock. Many of the crop fields were flooded with shallow water, and I do not know what they were growing. There were many farming villages and the livestock were nearly all cattle and pigs, and I don't recall any sheep or goats. The people were bowed and sad as they toiled the fields. There was great traffic of black and yellow-caped riders on horses on numerous roads, soldiers and messengers. Their capes bore a wolf insignia which Curdoz tells me is used by the Khestadone realms. I remember thinking it odd that they wore such capes, because it seemed a very warm clime, for all the peasants working the flooded fields appeared to wear only towels around their waists. There were also expanses of forest, though I knew from my studies in the Valley that these were not the great

Jungles described by the Etoppsi in the Southern Continent. Lord Curdoz explained to me that the Jungles lie even further south."

Kodi broke in. "The Etoppsi! But I thought the Etoppsi were just in storybooks!"

Lyndz nodded her agreement.

"Oh no," said Curdoz. "They are many and maintain a very great kingdom called Berug, and they have been there for an age and an age. In Solanto we are often unaware of what goes on in other parts of the world. It is true no Humans have traveled to the lands in which they live for many years. But from what I hear, some few of them every year fly to the island Kingdom of Nant for the annual Meicalian Feast."

Kodi was not particularly interested in the feast. "So the Etoppsi really do fly? They have wings and are huge beasts just like in the storybook drawings?"

"Well, of course they fly," said the Sage. "How do you think they built Guardian's Gate so high, and the Emperor's Palace and the Great Library in Tirilorin, if they couldn't fly? You must get it into your head, Kodi, the Etoppsi are not beasts. They are of the Mold. They are very large persons, certainly, and their unfolded wings are vast, and helping one another with ropes and cradles, they can lift great blocks of stone and support beams to great heights."

Kodi was intrigued. He had never believed the Etoppsi existed, though he knew about Guardian's Gate. A massive three-armed structure, it traversed the narrow waters between the Guardian Lake and the Western Sea and connected three lands: the Duchy of Duranti on the Solantine mainland, the island Duchy of Donesk, and on its southern side, a mostly uninhabited land that led southwards to Lorinth, the old Imperial Domain, now the Republic of Tirilorin. He had seen drawings of it, too, in books. The legend claimed it was built by the Etoppsi hundreds of years ago not long after the Anterianhi kingdoms were established. But as far as he knew, nobody really believed it, but rather that it was built by Human hands alone.

For the moment, though, he asked no more about the Etoppsi, but wondered what other revelations about the world were to be revealed as he stepped outside the familiar.

Idamé continued her tale. "This land on the Southern Continent was very great. I was lifted up miles above the land, and it was the same as far as the eye could see—fields interspersed with forests—and greater hints of green on the edge of sight. By the sea there were other cities besides the first gray city, the one I know Kodi saw. I saw the yellow-sailed ships upon the water, too. Altogether, it was a great region.

"Then I traveled northward to the beautiful green forest land that Kodi described, but my Vision showed a number of the inhabitants boarding ship with us."

Mother Idamé stopped momentarily and looked straight at Kodi. "Guess who they looked like."

Kodi thought for a moment, and then it hit him. "Tanned skin and black hair? And there were flocks of birds?"

"Yes! The people had medium-brown skin like the female you described, and some were obviously communicating with the birds. Their faces were serene and very beautiful. Can you guess who they are?"

"No. I wish I could."

The Sage chimed in. "Maybe you should think again about those old story books your grandfather read to you when you were a boy."

Kodi wondered, but he still did not answer.

Lyndz knew. "Qeteral! They are the Qeteral! They live in deep forests and talk to the birds, according to the books!" She looked at her brother. "Now why didn't I think of them when you told me about the woman in your Vision?"

Kodi looked from her to Curdoz, who nodded.

"That people live northeast of the abandoned kingdom of Lintiri and had contact with them before the last southern war when Lintiri was overrun by the Khestadone. The Qeteral withdrew to their own land and isolated themselves when the last emperor abdicated. No one has seen them in a hundred years."

"Why?" Lyndz seemed as interested in the Qeteral as her brother was in the Etoppsi.

"They have always been a secretive people. They only had connections with the Anterianhi Empire because of their loyalty to the House of Terianh. They assisted in the Ralsheen downfall, although it's unclear how. They may have defended their own, but they did not send any armies to Terianh. By all accounts the Qeteral avoid war. But with the emperors gone, it is possible they feel no obligation to maintain contact with Humans. They were never very tolerant of Humans until Meical came, probably because of the excesses of the Ralsheen whom they feared and hid from." Curdoz concluded.

"The question, really, is why they are important and appear in the Visions," said Elisa all of a sudden. She looked at Curdoz and Idamé. "Do you know?"

Idamé shook her head. "Lord Curdoz and I have talked, but we just do not know for certain. There is little more of detailed interest in my Vision. However, Curdoz has more."

All now looked at the Sage as he took up the tale with pieces—those he was willing to share, anyway—of his own Vision.

"First of all, it's important for you to know that it is only with Idamé's and Kodi's Visions that I have understood more of my own. So, as I go along, I am also going to offer what interpretation I've been able to discern from all these tales just to save some time." They all looked at him and nodded.

"Meical spoke to me at the beginning of the Vision rather than at the end like with Kodi. We Sages have been better trained than most in the emotion of the contact with Him. It is intense, though. In fact there is nothing like it. Had the Guardian spoken to Kodi at the beginning of the dream, he would have been too overcome with the emotion. With us Sages, however, we are more used to the intensity of that Presence, and it doesn't interfere, well not too badly anyway, with our ability to handle the rest of a Vision. Mark you we don't get them often. Visions are rare everywhere and at all times even among the Sages of the kingdoms. For most of the Monastics and the Gifted their first Vision is also their last. Through it they feel a Calling to join the Orders, travel to the Valley of the Gifted to study and then they are assigned to the various lands to begin their work. I'm not going to go into a lot of detail about Visions right now, but I want you to know that most Visions are personal and of very limited scope. A Vision of *events*, or, it would be better to say the possibility or likelihood of events, is unusual even for a Sage. So the fact that the three of us here had such Visions is remarkable.

"When this one came to me I was shocked. *'Find the Twins,'* He said to me. *'You will find them in the north of your country, in the land you call Tulesk. Find them, lead them, befriend them. They are for Me. There are those who move against Me and these two are needed.'* That is what He said, and it is all He said. He showed me your faces as plain as day."

The twins looked at each other, and a cock of her head made Lyndz look slightly more ready to cast aside lingering doubts.

"Now what I saw afterward were 'events' rather than mere scenery. The first event I saw was that of a Council of the Kingdom of the nobles of Solanto, with the king at his palace in Ferostro presiding. The one thing that struck me was the presence of Prince Filiddor of Hesk. Now I remember believing that odd, because it has been four years since he has attended the Kings Council—he and all the princes before him have been rather distant and concerned only with events in their own Principality.

"Then the scene changed and I was in the imperial city of Tirilorin. Now, I think you know that the last Anterianhi Emperor Zarelio abdicated long ago, but his descendants still live, and I years ago met Genehbro, who was the emperor's last descendant. He was a young man then, recently Bonded to a beautiful lady. She died a few years after I met them, unfortunately. I think they may have had a child or children; I'm trying to recall information from letters to me from Enric the Sage there.

"I wander. Anyway, they no longer recognize any noble titles in Tirilorin, however Genehbro is one of several councilors of the city, they call them Masters, but he does not head their Council. Now, he is a scholar, a very wealthy man, and in my Dream I was with him again, though he was twenty years older than I remember him. We were in his study and discussing information, but I do not yet know what that is. So, it is pretty clear that we must go to Tirilorin, probably as our first destination once we finally leave Solanto. I think Kodi's Vision confirms it, for we are to find the young man he saw.

"I remember seeing a harbor briefly, which I believe to be Sevarr on the Kingdom of Nant. Then I was on a ship among others as in a convoy, and they were almost certainly Nantian. The Nantians maintain the greatest naval fleets in all the world, and there were seven or eight ships in the convoy, maybe more. There were Qeteral on the ships with us, and many birds flying to and fro. We traveled far south. Now then a map came into my mind, for the other places shown me were rather incidental. But this is where it became, ah, new for me. The map enlarged itself in my mind upon the Khestadon Sea and the Sea of Siriné, which divide the Southern Continent into eastern and western halves. On their western shores are the land of the Alkhaness and on the east that of her cohort the Alkhan. It is a dangerous Sea, the Sea of Siriné, according to tales, for sea serpents enter from the Jungle rivers there, and the Spinning Pool of Siriné which no ships can escape. It is believed that the ancient goddess is herself entrapped within that great pool. Few have ever ventured there and returned to tell what they saw. Even further south on the eastern shore of the Sea, however, was a green forest of strange trees that are probably only common in those tropical climes. I am not familiar with that sort of forest, although the Etoppsi could probably describe it to us. Anyway, I set off into that forest. I saw Kodi's face quite clearly again. He set off into the forest with me, although there were others besides.

"Now, what I've described for you is rather a journey, and the route to get from here to there was at least in part clear to me. We will travel to Tirilorin first. I must see Genehbro, and the young man in Kodi's Vision apparently is to become a part of our quest for some reason. Then, we will travel to the Island Kingdom of Nant I think to acquire ships of transport. I have a small ship with which we will probably travel to Tirilorin—that is my plan at the moment. I think

Idamé saw my small ship in her Vision. Maybe even to Nant, but it is not meant for long travel on the open oceans. With the larger Nantian ships we will hunt for the land of Ulakel, the land of the Qeteral. There, if not before, I suspect we will learn the essential nature of the quest Meical has placed before us. Then we travel again by ship to the deep south to the land where it must be that the other Qeteral can be found."

He ended. He had left out much, scenes of battles and other dangers, the land of the Alkhan and the deserts and mountains. Some of it he had not even told Idamé. But it was all he was willing to share with Elisa present. He worried already that his description of the Sea of Siriné would cause fear and hesitation.

The others too were quiet for some time. Kodi had been looking at and listening intently to what Curdoz had to say. Lyndz looked down, for she was thoughtful.

Curdoz now felt he should say a little more. "Idamé is both courageous and highly Gifted. She was one of our best Discerners of the Gifted, of women, back in the Valley when we were both there. I believe part of Idamé's task is to mentor Lyndz, and I am meant to work with Kodi, and the four of us will travel to Tirilorin and beyond. But it is also important to note that if the Guardian is moving us, it is also very likely that He is moving others and other events in important ways as well. Meical is calling us now to aid Him. It is a high Calling."

Idamé seemed to sense the emotion in the room. "Lyndz and Kodi, I see much in you. Kodi is anxious to go, but even in you, Lyndz, there is courage you may not realize you have, and a serious sense of purpose that is well beyond what others so young typically have. Like Lord Curdoz has said, Meical has chosen both of you for a high purpose, and unfortunately we cannot see exactly where you fit in. We don't even know our own roles beyond that of helping. But wherever our journeys may lie, whatever the quest is, it will not get far without you, or at the very least, this is some sort of training ground for us all by which we will master skills needed for an even more distant future, a future that Meical may see something of, but which He has not shared yet with us."

"Why won't He share it, so we know more about the dangers?" asked Elisa.

Idamé looked at Curdoz, who cleared his throat. "Meical is the greatest being to have ever come to Dumhoni. Most in the Valley believe that he is ancient beyond all reckoning, a Servant sent to our world to aid the Three Peoples of the Mold against the evils of the world. He holds a special relationship to the Creator, and it is for this that we revere Him. Nevertheless He has limitations. Meical can see into the future only so far. But as events unfold in our World and create more and more complexity, the future becomes more clouded, making it more difficult for even Him to see. He has shown us what He thinks is important for us to know and only to the extent He is somewhat certain. If He were to show us that which is uncertain, even if He could do so, it would only confuse us."

"But it doesn't protect them from danger. It puts them in greater danger as far as I'm concerned, not to know," said Elisa.

"You're right, Lady Elisa," said Curdoz sighing, and he knew the time had come to tread carefully without being deceitful. "There are dangers to be faced, for sure. I don't know quite how to reassure you, for I'm afraid there are no guarantees for the safety of any of us. If we do nothing and we all remain in Solanto, I suggest that eventually those dangers will come to us. It may be this errand will forestall such dangers. It is difficult to know, and I'm expressing a hope in that regard. You're entrusting Lyndz and Kodi to us. You're giving them the Parental Blessing which we all know is a sacred thing without which one leaves home with doubts and a clouded sense of purpose. I don't want that for Kodi and Lyndz. I'll share something personal; my own father refused his Blessing when I left home. It was an awful time, and doubts persisted for years. It was many years later that he finally came around, but before that it was very hurtful. In some ways it still is hurtful. But it doesn't have to be for the twins. Idamé and I have entrusted you with information because you deserve it and so you know somewhat what Kodi and Lyndz are up against."

Elisa was silent for a while, and yet all were waiting essentially for something from her, now she had heard all the information she was going to get.

The fire was dwindling since no one had bothered to add wood; even Kodi was too intent on what the two visitors had to say. Finally, after long minutes, Elisa got up and stood by the fireplace, looking into the embers. "If my husband Hess were here, he would listen to all of this you have said, and I know in my heart he would sense the spirit of adventure and the call of the Visions, too, and send Kodi with Lord Curdoz with his Blessing. Kodi is ready for many trials. I love him, and I've watched him. He's ready to move on, I know. I know that my husband intended to let him go to Duke Amerro upon his return to pursue training for knighthood. He requested Kodi stay until then, but of course that was only to watch after the rest of us and to be here for our needs. Kodi was, in all honesty, quite generous and obedient to his father by agreeing to do so. It was also hurtful, for he is almost three years past the time when most young men are given permission to lead their own lives, and when many of

them choose to leave home. The time has come and it is past due."
She looked warmly at her son and Kodi smiled in return. He seemed
even taller to her and more proud than ever, very much as she
remembered his father when she first met him. "I believe, based on
all that I have heard, that it may have been the Guardian at work in
my husband's hesitation when he made Kodi promise to stay here,
even to this very day in order for you to find him, Lord Curdoz.
Otherwise, you would have had to travel to Tolos and search the
wilderness for long months in order to find him, for his father
considered taking him with him. It was very hard on Kodi to promise
to stay here considering his eagerness and maturity, and I honor my
son for having been so good as to choose obedience.

"As my husband's Bondmate, I release Kodi from his
promise. He is a man, now, and he must go, and I give him our love
and our Blessings." Kodi leaned over and she then kissed her son on
the top of his head.

Kodi stood back and could not speak; he was so grateful for
his Mother's words. He had wanted this for himself for the longest
time.

She then turned to Curdoz and continued. "I'm not at all
happy that Lyndz should go. But I'm not unwise to the importance of
Visions, even though I don't understand them. Yet, I realize now as
we have talked that this may be the one good thing by which her
father was *not* here, for if he were, I am certain he would withhold his
Blessing in order to discourage her from leaving. The danger to his
daughter would be at the forefront of his mind, and he would want to
protect her, for that is of course the especial nature of fathers when it
comes to their children, particularly their daughters. As it is, though,
he is not here to stop her.

"I will not stop her either. I have always believed my daughter
is meant to achieve great purpose, just as much as I have my son. You
will not find a young woman more capable or with more resoluteness.
If she is Gifted like you insist she must be, then I will say that she is
ready to find that Gift and use it. Idamé promises me she will try to
take my place, and I will admit that if Idamé were not a part of this
undertaking, I know I too would do my best to stop her from going
with only men, off into unknown dangers in foreign lands. But as it
is, with Idamé's help, I suspect Lyndz will achieve great things. I
don't want to prevent any of that. She is a grown woman, and I give
her our Blessing as well." At this she went to her daughter and kissed
her on her forehead.

Lyndz may not have felt quite the self-assuredness that her
brother did, but she nevertheless felt just as grateful for her mother's

words. Those words would be a powerful driver for Lyndz' future decisions.

Curdoz nodded. This from Elisa confirmed a suspicion he had. He was now convinced Idamé's very presence made a big difference. It was a certainty her mother would have tried to prevent Lyndz going otherwise. And if he were in her position or that of the Count Hess, her father? In his own heart, despite all his training and wisdom and Giftedness and his mystical connection to the Guardian, he might also have refused his Blessing. At least at first. Perhaps now he understood just a little of what his own father went through forty years ago, having to give up his only son, the only person, despite their differences, that he cared about.

Curdoz wanted to say something of wisdom at this moment, but he couldn't find the words. Did that mean he himself doubted the wisdom of the Guardian—to call a very young woman to face unknown and yet certain dangers in a world that appeared to be gearing up for some inevitable great conflict? Lyndz was not like Idamé or the other Sisters when they were novitiates going off in perfect safety to the Valley of the Gifted to study for seven years. Lyndz, like her brother, was being called to dangerous purpose. But for the moment all he could do was to brush aside this thought. It was critical Lyndz should come, and he was grateful it didn't have to come down to coercion by way of his authority as Sage of Solanto. Thankfully, with Elisa's formal Familial Blessing, at least they would not experience the depression and doubts he himself did for long years. Such self-doubts about their place and purpose could cause failure at a critical point. They needed to go forth in the world as equals to the ones who bore and raised them. Conflict was the partial result of unblessed, insecure people attempting to alter their world to make themselves *feel* more secure. And such alterations usually resulted in suffering. As he looked into the faces of Lyndz and Kodi, it was of a certainty that these two would not be altering the world for their own self-serving benefit.

Their purpose would be to make the world a better place.

At this point all Curdoz could do was assume practicality. He stood up, looked around at everyone and said. "Then it behooves us to prepare and pack. In two mornings we will leave."

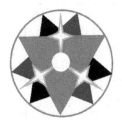

Chapter 8—Surprises

There was much to be done to prepare the twins for their journey, particularly Lyndz. Kodi had his great pack and much gear that was sufficient for traveling, having gone on many outings with his father when he was home, or on camping journeys with his friends to the river and beyond, and even on lone hunting expeditions with Musca. But Lyndz had next to nothing for a long journey, having traveled only to Cumpero the previous summer, and so some time was spent in procuring for her in the village the items needed.

None of the pack animals used by the Matrimonial Troupe could be spared, so they set about finding a useful beast to help carry all their things. Though the Fothemrys stabled two perfectly good riding mares, it seemed unfair for Elisa to have to part with them. It was simply not necessary, according to Curdoz, because for now he preferred walking, and even if he changed his mind, they could borrow horses or hire a carriage once they returned to Ascanti. But by the end of the day, they did acquire a good strong pony from the stablemaster in the village.

Food was not an issue, for they would be able to fill their packs in every town. Kodi was such a big eater, however, that he did include dried meats and fruits, and a large quantity of nuts, in his own pack. He was never one to let himself go without, even for short periods of time.

Elisa offered Lyndz her own recently-acquired traveling cloak. It was of very fine make, and she wanted her daughter to have things that would always remind her of her mother, and Lyndz was grateful.

There was more. That afternoon Elisa invited Lyndz and Mother Idamé into her bedroom, whereupon she presented her daughter with a small package that had been hidden away, a gift Lyndz' father had procured for her some time ago, which he had been saving for an appropriate occasion. Elisa felt Lyndz should have it before she left, not knowing when they would see her again, and she knew Hess would have been disappointed if the opportunity to give it to her slipped away. Lyndz carefully opened it and her eyes grew big as she took in a huge breath. In the package she beheld a medium-weight necklace made of gold and a pendant containing a faceted oval jewel the size of a sparrow egg.

"That is stunning, Lady Elisa," Idamé exclaimed. "Lyndz! It is a gift for a queen! That is the prettiest and most crystal clear emerald I have ever seen!"

Lyndz was shocked at such an unexpected and extravagant gift from her father, and shed several tears. "Oh, Mother! Please tell him how grateful I am! I will always treasure it! I have your traveling cloak and the quilt you made me last year, and now this beautiful thing from Father! I am so proud to be your daughter!"

Elisa had given up on tears and she refused to shed more, although it cost her. So she simply smiled and said, "Of course I will tell him, my dear. He will be so glad I went ahead and gave it to you! Your father found the stone already faceted in a ruin near the mouth of the Tolos River where he believes the Ralsheen had their main shipping port. The gold for the chain came from there, too, from a small pile of gold coins he collected. He had the chain made and the pendant set by a jeweler in Cumpero whom your cousin the duke recommended. Put it on!"

And so she did. With a hand mirror from her mother's dresser, Lyndz looked at herself. "Oh, I've never seen anything so beautiful! But…but why did he not give it to you, Mother?"

"Ah, now don't you worry, dear. Your father has given me many fine things, and quite likely," Elisa said with a laugh, "he has other gifts he has set back to give me at celebratory times! He admitted to me that for whatever reason when he saw the emerald he thought of you. I think it is wonderful he did so. That he keeps each of us close in his heart when he travels says much as to what a good man he is. Now you keep it tucked under your shirts and display it only when you are in safe places and among those who will admire it and won't try to steal it. No point in drawing danger to yourself."

"In Solanto she will be safe," offered Idamé. "No one would dare touch her as long as she is with me or with the Sage, of course. But yes, I will remind her to keep it well-hidden in foreign lands."

Later, Lyndz showed it to her brother and grandfather.

"Amazing, Lyndz!" said Kodi. "I know you will love it always." He indeed thought his sister looked very striking wearing it.

"You two have a good and thoughtful father," added Yugan. "I know Hess can be stern. And he is often gone, but he is a great man and Amerro depends on him. But he has shown his devotion to you in many ways. Come with me. As a matter of fact, I have something, too, for both of you." The old man took them to his own little over-warm bedroom.

"Grandpa, you are walking well today," Lyndz remarked.

"I feel very well, Lyndz. I seem to have a bit more energy," he said.

Taking his granddaughter's hand, he continued. "Dear, sweet Lyndz! Now I have several things written down in a list that I have acquired over the years that I have every intention of giving you, but they are large items, furniture for the most part that I made, or books I have purchased. You were to receive it all when you Bonded. And I expect it will still be yours in coming years! But you cannot travel with it, so I want you to have something that I made that you can take with you and remember me by.

"Now let me find it. Where is that thing? Ah, here it is." He was feeling around behind a set of books on a shelf for something he apparently liked to keep hidden.

It appeared to be a wooden box, smaller though similar to the one he gave to Curdoz containing Deroge's book. It contained a few trinkets, but he dumped those on the shelf, and took a cloth and wiped the box clean of any dust and handed it to his granddaughter. "If I had known about the chain and pendant, I would have made you a new one. But this one is special to me. It was one I made for your grandmother many years ago, and she kept a few tiny things in it. Your mother has those now, but I kept the box. You may have it, my dear one, to carry that necklace at times you'd rather not wear it."

If possible, the detail on this box was even finer than the one he had given to the Sage. On all sides, except for the mirror smooth bottom, the ambernut was carved in minutely intricate patterns. But it was unlike the other which emphasized only geometric patterns, for it contained no inlay, and in the center on the top was carved a tiny hummingbird sipping nectar from a morning glory flower. Lyndz took the box with more tears dripping from her eyes, as Kodi looked over her shoulder at it. Finally, Lyndz said, "Thank you, Grandpa. It really is wonderful! I will keep it and remember you always!" Whereupon she gave him a grateful embrace and kiss. "Why look! It's lined with purple satin! This is perfect, Grandpa. Thank you so much!"

"Now let me speak to Kodi alone for a short while."

Lyndz kissed him again and left the two men alone.

Yugan took a long look at his grandson. "Kodi, I am not a Seer like my mother, Kalemna. I cannot see into the future with Visions. But I can tell you one thing I see in you, and I know for a fact your father sees it, too, and that is this. You will be a great warrior someday. I know it! You heard the Sage. The name Kodi is shortened from ancient Ralsheen 'ka awodan' which translates 'man of battles'. Don't turn up your nose that it's a Ralsheen derivative, for the language developed centuries before the Dark Times! I helped your parents with the name, and I have always been very proud that they chose to use it! Now, I do not have any idea what battles you will be forced to fight, or what other trials you may have to face, but as soon as you have the opportunity, get the training you need to be a fighter! If I were still young I would have trained you myself, or at least I would have begun it anyway. I was once quite good with a sword!"

Kodi was silent, for he was so surprised to hear his grandfather talk to him this way. No one had ever before openly encouraged him in this direction, although it was his strong desire. Even though his father was willing to send him eventually to Amerro to train, he never tried to make Kodi feel as if it were his calling.

It was as if Yugan could discern this thought from Kodi's silence. "Your father, like I said, believes it too, and I know much of what he thought about you. But your father is an explorer, not a warrior, although he'd be about the last person I'd ever want to face in a fight! But he knew about you, Kodi, both of us knew, from the time you were a small boy, that you would be a *fighter*. You excel in all competitions, and you're full of courage and self-discipline beyond the ordinary.

"I know your father would send you off with many fine things. He is not here to do so, but I have something of great value that I have been saving for you.

"Now, I am sorry I didn't keep my sword from the Ice Tribe war, for you should have one, but I sold mine soon after the war, for I needed some money to buy woodworking tools." Then he stood up from the chair and put his hand on Kodi's shoulder. "But I have something else for you. I made it for you when you were but a boy, and I wanted to give it to you at some point in the future, although I was never sure in my mind exactly when. When you turned sixteen I almost gave it to you, for that is manhood according to our traditions, but something held me back. I then thought maybe I would save it as a reward after your future training with the duke, or even as a Bonding gift.

"But you're leaving now, and Son…" Yugan abruptly broke down and collapsed into the chair. The tears began to flow, and Kodi knelt down close to him and reached up and held the old man. He couldn't recall ever seeing his grandfather cry, but the intense emotion so transferred to Kodi that he could hardly hold back himself. Yugan finally completed his statement. "I…I do not know if

I will still be here when you return to us, that is all, you know. You have been a solid rock for me these last few years, Son, and I will miss you more than you can ever know!"

Kodi continued to hold him close, and said words of comfort to help calm his shaking grandfather. But it hit Kodi hard when he realized that there was the possibility it could be years before he returned to Felto, and though there was every expectation he would find his mother and father, who were still quite young and perhaps residing by then in their new manor, Yugan was in his sixties, and though that was not ancient by most standards, he had not been in the best of health the last years since his fall, and struggled much more so than most others of his age.

After several minutes, Yugan regained his composure, wiped his tears on his handkerchief and looked up again at his grandson. "I'm sorry, Kodi. You must know, that though I was blessed with your sweet mother, the best daughter anyone could wish for, it has been the most joyful thing of my life these last years to have you all living here. We have grown close, you and I, and because of you, Kodi, I haven't felt deprived of the son I wished for but never had."

Kodi knew Yugan thought of him in this way, and for his own part, though he honored his father they had their differences, and he felt a stronger emotional attachment perhaps to his grandfather who was always there for him and loved him unconditionally.

Finally, Yugan stopped shaking and stood up, wiped his face again, breathed deeply and resumed his usual cheerfulness. "Ah, the gift. Like I said I made it for you years ago just before you all moved into the house." He walked over to his large wardrobe. He opened the door, and shoved aside several hanging garments, reached to the back and withdrew something tall and bound tightly in cloth. "*Now*, of course, is the time for you to have it." Yugan took it and laid it upon the bed in front of Kodi.

With high curiosity, Kodi unwrapped it carefully.

It was the most stunning bow he had ever seen. It was solid heartwood ambernut, obvious from its deep, golden-orange luster. Kodi owned two other yew bows with which he hunted regularly, and had even set one out to take with him on the journey. But they were nothing as fine as the shining implement before him. "By the Guardian, Grandpa! It's...it's amazing!" He held it and studied every inch of its shaped and beautifully carved surface.

"I fancy there is not another like it anywhere. Your father helped me find the perfect piece of ambernut heartwood. He's the only other who has seen the finished product. He tested it for me when I finished it, for of course no one knew whether or not ambernut was of the right strength and flexibility to be used as a bow, but Hess said it was perfect. He said it shot long and straight. He declared to me, and I know he is right, that there is probably not a hunter or soldier, prince or king in all the world who has an ambernut bow!"

Kodi had been around the ambernut business enough to understand that the rarity and beauty of it created a market among the wealthiest for items of show: namely furniture, paneling, floors, and small, hand-carved artistic items such as those that Yugan still made. He had never heard of anyone purchasing ambernut lumber for the purposes of making an item for a hunter or a soldier, nor even a knight. With the exception of a few people in Felto who could get some of it every now and then, such as his grandfather whose son-in-law owned the business, ambernut was for nobility and royalty, and the wealthiest tradesmen. To use a sizeable piece of the highest quality heartwood to carve out and shape a bow was an extravagance that only his grandfather could have perceived and executed.

"It's amazing!" Kodi repeated, for he was too overcome to think of any words more amazing than 'amazing'.

"It needs stringing, of course. You will have to manage that on your own. It was years ago when Hess tested it, and the string he used would not have lasted anyway. But the strings from your other bows should work, for the size is standard."

Kodi practically reverted to boyhood in his excitement. He couldn't wait to test it. He muttered something inaudible to his grandfather and raced upstairs to his own room to retrieve the string from one of his yew bows and also his quiver of arrows. He returned, strung his new bow quickly and drew it back with his strong fingers and let it go with a twang that was more like a song. He then coaxed his grandfather into donning his heavy coat to follow him into the back yard.

On their way through the house, he called out to the others to whom he excitedly showed his grandfather's gift. They all exclaimed at the magnificent implement and followed Kodi out the kitchen door into the backyard which extended to the woods, although there were a number of shade trees between the house and the woods. He picked out one of these, an elm, perhaps thirty yards distant. Kodi was an expert marksman, the best in the county, having won every archery contest in Felto for the last three years. It was perhaps his greatest skill, for he practiced ritually. From his quiver he chose an arrow, fitted it in place, drew the string back with perfect confidence and let it go. His aim was right on. The arrow struck the tree's center beautifully.

"Way to go, Ko!" exclaimed Lyndz.

"Beautiful work, Son!" agreed Yugan, nearly as excited as his grandson.

Elisa, Ansy, and Idamé applauded.

Curdoz was highly impressed, but not surprised, "Ah, just as I expected."

"I love it!" proclaimed Kodi, studying the bow again. "It's wonderful, Grandpa! Thanks again! I will treasure it and carry it with me."

By noon the day before they were to set out, the twins declared themselves ready to depart. It gave them the afternoon and evening to spend with their mother, grandfather, and Ansy, too, whom they had learned to love over the years she had served the family.

Lord Curdoz came by with Mother Idamé again and insisted they all walk to the manor building site together, saying he wanted to see it. They were all willing, for the weather was pleasant enough for earliest spring. Since Yugan was going they all rode together in a two-horse-drawn wagon that they borrowed from the stablemaster. When they arrived at the site, about a mile west of Felto, Curdoz proclaimed a formal Blessing over it. It was a brief rite and all the workers stopped what they were doing to attend. Most of these were quite awestruck at the presence of the Sage of Solanto, and he spent several minutes placing his hands on each of their brows and pronouncing the Meicalian Affirmation. Mother Idamé walked the grounds with Lyndz and Elisa, and the two older women listened as Lyndz declared her intentions for grand formal gardens and trees. Elisa promised she would do her best to carry out her daughter's wishes, continually expressing her hope that Lyndz would indeed return to her in the not too distant future.

The afternoon grew warmer as they wandered the site. Kodi showed the Sage some of the stone work he had himself helped place and even the curved design of the exterior staircase that led to the main entryway. The Sage was quite complementary.

"This is good design work, young Kodi. Excellent job. You're gaining a knack for engineering, I see."

"Thank you, m'Lord."

The Sage chuckled. "Kodi, that will get old. There may be times in the presence of other nobles while we are in Solanto that it would be quite polite and appropriate for you to address me so, because they themselves will, but at all other times from now on, just call me 'Curdoz'. Or 'sir,' if you feel you must."

"Sure, Curdoz, sir," Kodi replied and grinned. Curdoz laughed and slapped him on the back.

After a half hour of wandering the area, Kodi watched as Curdoz approached Elisa a short ways away. Those two spoke for a minute and Elisa pointed in the direction of a hillock upon which stood a grouping of massive Northern Pines. Curdoz nodded and then, mysteriously, nodded at Mother Idamé and pointed at the same hillock. Mother Idamé then gave a shrill whistle.

From within a set of trees, an outcropping of the forest close to the building site, a laughing group of women emerged—the Sisters who made up Mother Idamé's traveling Troupe. In contrast to Idamé's multi-colored, gold-tasseled affair, the Sisters wore plain white shawls with no decoration. They walked promptly towards the hillock. Their two Kingsmen guards were with them, but then they stood back and remained to themselves.

"What are they here for?" asked Kodi of Lyndz who had just stepped up to him. The women bore branches of greenery, tiny bouquets of the earliest daffodils, along with decorative ribbons. Too, they carried with them a pair of elaborately embroidered robes, one white and decidedly feminine, the other a deep blue and of a masculine cut. "It almost looks like they're going to perform a Bonding rite. But who?"

Then they saw that Curdoz was helping Yugan out of the wagon, and was walking with him towards the pine tree hillock. Elisa was escorting Ansy in the same direction, whereas Idamé went directly to her Sisters and began to chatter away with them. Curiosity overcame the twins and they too walked towards the gathering group.

"Oh!" cried Lyndz. "Don't you see, Ko!"

"What? What is it? I don't get it."

"I knew it! I just knew it!" she replied ecstatically.

"But..." started Kodi, but then his jaw dropped as it finally dawned on him.

They had now all gathered at the hill. Upon the pine trees, the Sisters had now strung ribbons, and in a circle between them they placed the greenery and most of the yellow flowers and branches of sweet-scented winter honeysuckle. Kodi looked at his grandfather, who was standing as tall as he had ever seen him, and his face seemed at least ten years younger. Two of the Sisters were placing on him the deep blue robe. Close by, two more were doing the same with the white one for Ansy.

When they placed the lovely white robe on Ansy, her face beamed. She appeared more beautiful than the twins had ever seen her.

"I don't believe it!" whispered Kodi to his twin. "Did you know about this?"

"No! I didn't know! But you saw how they've been acting ever since Mother Idamé came. It makes perfect sense. I've always wished they'd get together, haven't you, Ko?"

Kodi replied in the affirmative, not to appear an idiot, but in actuality the whole thing had gone completely over his head. Till now.

The Sage of Solanto, and Elisa too, now walked back to stand with the twins. Kodi expected one of them to say something, but they were all smiles and remained silent. The workmen and the cooks from the building site had also come up behind and made themselves into a very attentive witness section. In front of the family group, in the circle of greenery under the trees now stood Yugan and Ansy, and those two had eyes for no one else but each other. One of the Sisters now handed Ansy a large bouquet of the yellow daffodils and winter honeysuckle, a hallmark of early spring and new beginnings. Mother Idamé was now also outfitted in a lovely mantle of green, embroidered with multicolored silk flowers, and with her colorful shawl draped over all. She stood in front of the couple as they now faced her, and then there was silence for a long minute. Finally, the Matrimonial Mother launched into a brief monologue while all listened.

First, she talked about the Creator and Meical the Guardian and how the Creator had designed the magnetic interplay of the male and the female. The Guardian had planted the Gift among the Matrimonials in ages past to determine the Bonding of all couples. The wording was all very formal. It was the same as all Bonding rites that the twins had attended in the past. Then, Idamé made some personal comments.

"It was a grand moment for me two evenings ago when Lord Curdoz and I arrived at Yugan's home, for as soon as I saw Yugan and Ansy together in his sitting room, the Aura of Bonding appeared above them, and I had the privilege of being the Witness of this. The Aura as you know does not appear for all, but with some couples that the Guardian has brought together for especial Blessing. After talking to them later that night, it became apparent that indeed these two before us have had a great love for one another for some years, and yet neither had spoken thus to the other. This is a great blessing, for the surprise of the Aura can be a great joy to an unsuspecting couple, as it was for Ansy and Yugan. It is therefore my privilege to bring the two together today to experience the Affirmation of the Creator upon their Bonding. It is likely my last Bonding over which I will preside for some time, as the Lord Sage has called me to other work. My Sisters present know this, and I will miss them, for soon we all will part and go our separate ways. And though the next days will be a time of many partings, this afternoon is a time for celebration."

At that point the Troupe of Sisters encircled the three in the front and started to dance. It was lovely to watch, and after a minute, they stood still, and one and then the other, and finally Mother Idamé, too, began to sing a very ancient song to a very ancient tune.

In rapturous morning, under golden sun,
The One stood in a Valley of Gold.
There was joy in the heart of the One,
And from that joy sprang the Mold.

With clay at hand, the Mold was imbued
With the shape of two, yet the essence of One.
Female and Male mirrored the Mood,
She was called Daughter and He was named Son.

Daughter was draped in garments of white.
A mantle of blue was born by the Son.
Together they stood in the morning light.
One had made two. The two now became one.

Side by side they wander the Earth.
The Son is the hunter and fights the foe.
Daughter is gatherer and to their children give birth.
Together they love. Together they grow.

The song was old and derived from a reading in the Ancient Book. Kodi had heard it before, but since it was his own grandfather who was partaking in the rites, he actually listened this time. Not since his Vision had he been so moved, for even though the song was sung by women, the words themselves spoke to his own deep longing as a young man. It now hit him that the following morning he would be leaving his home and heading off into a challenging future.

Lyndz, too, was listening, and all along was humming and swaying to the tune. She felt joyful despite the other concerns that had consumed her the past few days. It would bring her happiness in the days to come to remember this last family gathering and celebration. To think of a new beginning for her aging grandfather and for Ansy the house servant whom she had loved would in a small way lighten the burden on her heart on the road ahead.

Upon returning to Yugan's house, Kodi, Lyndz and their mother worked hard in the remaining light of the day to re-order Yugan's bedroom. They emptied it out almost completely, cleaned it thoroughly, and then furnished it again. Kodi man-handled from upstairs the various parts of Ansy's larger bed and put it back together. Elisa applied fresh linens and retrieved from a chest some fine lace curtains to decorate the window. Being springtime now they would soon be replacing the heavy winter-time draperies in the house anyway. Elisa and Lyndz had together only recently completed a beautiful new quilt. It was intended to be saved for Elisa and Hess's own bed in the new manor, but mother and daughter happened to think on it at the same moment while they were cleaning Yugan's room, and it was agreed it should be presented to the couple as a wedding gift. It was used then to top the clean linens and other blankets on the bed. Though his wardrobe and a chest remained, some of Yugan's other furniture, such as the trunk and a large bookshelf had to be moved out to make room for Ansy's dresser, chair and vanity table, and there was room in the wardrobe for some of her clothes to hang beside her husband's. The daffodils and winter honeysuckle from the ceremony were gathered into two vases. One was placed on Ansy's vanity, the other on top of Yugan's wardrobe. Elisa replaced the space rug with a newer, much brighter one from her own bedroom.

It was certainly a transformation. They had let the fire burn out while they were cleaning and redecorating, so Kodi was in the middle of rebuilding it when Elisa and Lyndz led the new couple to their now joint bedroom. Both were very pleased by the effect and thanked them all many times.

It was their last evening together as a family, for Idamé and Curdoz had declined to reappear until the next morning and had returned after the ceremony with the Sisters to the village inn. Emotions were mixed. It was difficult for all of them knowing that the twins would be leaving home the next morning, and much advice was given and reminiscences were exchanged. But the new joy being shared by Yugan and Ansy was contagious, even for Elisa, and she was as cheerful as she could reasonably be. They all shared a late dinner by many candles in the dining room which the three women had prepared together. Ansy adamantly refused to take a break from cooking, and in any event she wanted to prepare a ham pie for her new husband, his favorite dish, which he indeed exclaimed over when it arrived at the table. But even as they sat down, there was a knock at the door. A special confection had been prepared that day by the village baker at the order of Idamé and the Sisters, and was now being delivered. A rare, sweet treat, it was enjoyed by all.

Shortly after dinner, for it was really quite late by that time, Yugan and Ansy retired together to their new bedroom. Ansy told Kodi she could handle the fireplace, which of course she could. And yet it struck his heart realizing now that he would no longer be present, or even needed, to help his grandfather anymore.

Elisa looked at the twins and spoke. "I want you to promise me something."

"Of course," said Lyndz.

"Sure, Mother," replied Kodi at the same time.

There was a long pause before she spoke. Elisa had a number of promises in the back of her mind she wanted the twins to make, about not deliberately seeking out dangers, about making good choices, about returning home when the quest ended, and there were others, too, and she was almost about to launch into each of them. But then her mind made its rounds. It felt wrong to place limitations or demands of any kind on her children. They were grown, now, and apparently had a destiny beyond what she had once thought possible for them. She had taught them all she could, and she decided she had to trust them to adhere to the lessons she and Hess and Yugan had taught them over the years. Besides, the specific things she wished for might not even be possible. Asking Kodi never to seek out danger when he was as strong and energetic as he was, or thinking that by making either recite a promise they would always make the best decisions. No. And even insisting they return to her when their quest was ended—this didn't seem to work either. What if this was a journey the Guardian had set them on that was life-long? Returning to provincial Felto, despite their likely inheritance of the Fothemry estate and name, might not be within the realm of their choices.

Finally, she sighed. "Watch out for one another, Son and Daughter. Promise to help each other."

The twins looked at one another and like children replied in unison, "We promise!"

Chapter 9—Leaving Home

Weather being unpredictable in early March, it was foggy and somewhat colder than the day before as the twins, the Lord Curdoz, Mother Idamé, and her Troupe prepared to leave Felto. The Sisters had performed some seventeen Bonding rituals in the village and surrounding countryside besides Yugan and Ansy's, though only theirs was accompanied by an Aura of Bonding and conducted by Mother Idamé herself. A number of villagers and friends had come to bid farewell to the Troupe and to Kodi and Lyndz. None but the family knew the details, only that the Fothemry twins were leaving home with Sage Curdoz. Some speculated they were to be further educated in Ferostro, or that their presence might be desired by the king to be honored, or of other elements of the life of the nobility that most knew nothing about. A handful might have thought it had something to do with the Orders of the Guardian, though no one really believed the twins were being Called to join the Orders. Most presumed they would eventually return. Though there was sadness at the separation, all offered only cheer and well wishes upon the twins. Elisa played the countess, thanking the Lord Sage and the Matrimonial Mother in gracious words for honoring their town and their home with their presence. She kissed Kodi and Lyndz one last time and presented each of them with a sizeable bag of gold and silver coins. Curdoz had said he intended to provide all their needs, but Elisa knew having their own money would allow her son and daughter a bit of independence during their travels.

Lyndz made unnecessary promises to return to her mother as soon as might be, for it was indeed her intent. In Kodi's mind he assumed he probably would return someday. The presumption always was that he would inherit his father's titles and positions. But that would likely be many, many years from now, and there were a thousand possibilities between now and then. So, with no intention of committing himself, he made no such promises as did Lyndz. Thankfully his mother did not request them.

Ansy and Yugan too stood by and participated in the final goodbyes, although Kodi could tell that Yugan struggled mightily when Kodi gave his grandfather one last embrace. Kodi whispered, "Everything you've ever done for me, Grandpa, I will never forget it, and thanks for my ambernut bow! It's my treasure, you know, like that emerald Mother gave Lyndz."

Yugan beamed, but could not speak at the moment. Though his step had improved a bit upon his recent happy nuptials, in the immediate moment he looked old again.

The pony chosen to carry baggage for the twins, the Mother, and Curdoz, was loaded, but Kodi was carrying his hunting knife, and across his back was cast the magnificent bow. In addition to these items he also carried his own pack and some camping gear, for these were from his father, and though his relationship to his father had its strains, he nevertheless honored him and wanted to keep him close in spirit.

It was not, of course, the only gift from his father.

There had been no question that the Elentine Noble, Musca, was to travel with them. It wasn't even necessary for Kodi to insist upon it, since Curdoz himself proposed it to Kodi. In private he said to him on the afternoon after they had come to Felto, "There could be times we are in the wild, and a great animal like Musca will be a useful protector and warn us of danger. Nobles have a superior reputation. He is independent and can find his own food in the wilderness and help us discover food, too, if it should become necessary." And though he did not say it, Curdoz had also been intrigued by the dog from the moment he set eyes upon him, with its size and strength, rare silver coat, knowing face, and unfathomable green eyes.

The animal was at present nosing around from person to person, licking the hands of the family members he seemed to understand he was leaving behind.

Lyndz donned her mother's heavy traveling cloak, and upon her bosom, hidden under all, was the necklace. Otherwise she carried nothing, for in her practical way, since she was not used to long hikes, she saw no reason to burden herself like her brother, and so the rest of her belongings were on the pony.

There was one final exchange, however. Ansy came forward and presented to Mother Idamé a round tin of her famous sweet butter biscuits, a gift for having performed the Bonding rite.

Idamé laughed. "Sweet Ansy! How did you know I liked these so much?"

Curdoz kissed Elisa's hand and then bowed to Yugan. "You are a sire of a great family, Yugan. These two leave you now, but have heart that you have done very well indeed by them!"

Yugan squelched the tears that desperately tried to show themselves, and looking at both the twins for the last time, he gathered himself together.

"Yes. I know I have."

They set off at a good pace and before the end of the first day they reached the Northern Road. The right-hand way led north to the ducal capital of Cumpero and the more populated northern counties. Upon the left was the return route to Ascanti. The tiny village of Meleto stood here. It was a part of County Fothemry, and though it stood on the main route it was nevertheless that much farther away from the ambernut stands eastwards near the Escarpment where the lucrative lumber mills had caused Felto to grow so rapidly. All in all the southern half of Tulesk was sparsely populated. Heavily forested, and even during the time the Ice Tribes held sway in this region, it contained few people. It was only in the northern portion of the duchy where the North Inlet reached its long finger inland that the land opened out and where it was more suitable to intensive farming and the building of towns and cities.

All that Meleto consisted of was a blacksmith shop, a tanning shop, two or three houses and a sizeable inn with connecting stables. There were a few homesteads with tiny farms carved into the forest round and about, but otherwise it was merely a stopping point for travelers.

Room was made for them all at the inn, and after they had seen to the ponies and set their things in their rooms, they all met in the common room for supper. It was to be the last night together for Idamé and her Sisters, for the Troupe was assigned to travel to Cumpero and those populated northern regions of the duchy, whereas Idamé and the others of course were returning south. Though the women were nearly always cheerful, tonight they were somewhat subdued as they shared stories. Lucchenda was looking through the record book with Idamé, by which all Bondings the Troupe performed were recorded.

Musca had realized as soon as they arrived that they were staying here, and in his independent way disappeared into the woods bordering the village to hunt his own dinner. It was only as they were all preparing for bed the great dog returned, and the fat innkeeper allowed him inside, which, based on her sour expression, was something she would likely not have done for anyone in the kingdom but the Sage of Solanto. The dog's rare pedigree and disciplined behavior were irrelevant to her.

It was a different sort of arrangement than was typical of the older more established parts of Solanto, for there were three large rooms full of bunks for men on one side of the inn and a similar arrangement for women on the other. The innkeeper was willing again—for they had indeed stayed here, sans the twins, the night before taking the Felto road—to give her own private space to Lord Curdoz, but he refused for the second time. However, he, Kodi and the two Kingsmen Troupe guards were able to share one of the men's bunk rooms alone among themselves.

As they were preparing for bed, and while the Kingsmen were inspecting Kodi's magnificent ambernut bow, he asked them some questions. He learned that the two each had a family in Cumpero, and they were looking forward to seeing them again after they had finished their assignment. They explained to Kodi they preferred this arrangement to that of common barracks soldiers. For though they were away from home part of the year, at other times they were able to spend long stretches uninterrupted with their families. Importantly, they were paid better than common soldiers. Not only did they receive the ordinary soldier's stipend, they also received twelve gold marks extra from the Matrimonial Order for their services. It went a long way to make life better for themselves and their families. Kodi asked them if they knew his father, Hess, the Count Fothemry, to which they both replied in the affirmative, for he was always well-received when he would attend to his cousin the duke in Cumpero, but they admitted they had never served with him otherwise. He was famous as the man who had determined that the Dragons in Tolos had died out and for opening the peninsula to exploration and settlement, so they had seen him at Amerro's castle.

"And ye be the spittin' image of 'im, I'd say," said one of them by the name of Yaguro as he sat on one of the lower bunks and took off his muddy boots to set by the fire. "When I saw ye at that new manor house they're a'buildin' for yer dad and ma, I figured you was his."

"Ya," said the other one, Teegriss by name. "Wha' Yaguro says be true, that be for sure. Good proud faces and fine bearing! Stern but noble, like yer cousin his lordship the duke. How close be ye to he, young man?"

"Father and he are first cousins, though Father's probably ten years or so younger than Lord Amerro."

"Well, ye be a mighty fine, handsome lot. Me own son be your age, but ye be twice as big and strong, I'd say. Wish he'd ha' been more like ye. He won't never be no soldier. He left home last year, and he be apprenticin' w' a bootmaker. 'Bout all he's good fer, that one. Oh well. I try to remember me grandpap always sayin', *All work is good work.*" Teegriss trailed off.

"Ya, 'tis quality in this one's bones, for sure, mate!" said Yaguro reaching up and squeezing Kodi's sizeable bicep with his massive hand. Kodi laughed.

"Bet ye have ter fight off the women don't ye, young'un?"

"Shhh, mate!" said Yaguro quietly to Teegriss, pointing over to the Sage who was sitting in a ladder-back chair quietly by the fire smoking his pipe. "Don't ye be a'talkin' 'bout such as tha' 'round his Lordship, mate!"

"Ar! Sorry 'bout tha'!" Teegriss whispered back but threw a knowing wink at Kodi.

Kodi chuckled. So instead of women, the talk returned to his bow which the two soldiers remarked upon endlessly in their commoner accents. The two reminded him of the men with whom he worked on the manor in Felto and the lumbermen employed by his father. It occurred to him he was going to miss the informal tease and banter with the stone workers and his village friends as the days went by. Until he got to know him better, he presumed Curdoz was above this sort of thing, not to mention Mother Idamé.

The following morning many goodbyes were said and tears were shed among the women, and for some hours after they parted and were on the road southward, Idamé was silent. From time to time Curdoz, who was leading the pony, would reach out with his free hand to grip Idamé's own when a tear would fall from her eye, but the twins were keen to allow her the privacy she needed. For Lyndz in particular, it reminded her of her own separation from family the day before. So, for the most part, she and her brother walked somewhat ahead of the other two, while Musca tramped tirelessly and endlessly back and forth across the roadway, into the forest and out, across the few farm fields they passed, scouting ahead and returning to ensure the presence and safety of the twins. This pattern of the beast's constant movement continued forever after on their travels and reflected his innate eagerness for continued adventure.

This eagerness was shared by Kodi, though not by Lyndz. If anything, Kodi felt almost guilty for the emotions he was currently experiencing, glad as he was to have finally left home. He knew he would miss many things, his horses, the river, friends, and his grandfather, but he was practically ecstatic to know that his Vision had a serious purpose, confirmed by the Sage of Solanto, and now he was on a path to uncover its many mysteries. It was much easier for him anyway than for his sister, for he had been wanting to leave home long before, a wish always delayed. Kodi regretted he was leaving without his father's knowledge and express paternal Blessing, something sons usually preferred as that masculine connection had conscious and subconscious implications, but he rested on the assurances of his mother and grandfather that he was doing exactly as his father would have wanted him to do considering the immense importance of a Meicalian Vision and the request of the High Sage of Solanto. In any event, he felt as though he was becoming the man he was meant to be, and in his own case he had always felt in his heart that being his own man and making a mark in the world would take place far away from Felto.

Their connection as twins was in a way not unlike the emotional communication shared occasionally through Gifted magic between Curdoz and Idamé. Kodi was aware of his sister's opposing emotions, and he remembered her words before they went to bed on the night of their grandfather's birthday. Rather like Curdoz comforting Idamé, Kodi would sometimes walk right next to Lyndz and put his arm on her shoulder, or like now she had reached out to grip his hand and he had obliged. Lyndz for her part had shed the last of her tears long before and refused to display anymore signs of sadness, but she was certainly not as eager for adventure as her brother, though grateful for his presence.

"You know, Ko, you've got wonderful hands," she said abruptly.

He laughed as he squeezed her gloved hand with his bare right hand and looked interestedly at his left one having never paid much attention to them before. "What are you talking about, Lyndz?"

"Well, they're big. And they're kind of leathery and soft at the same time. They're always warm. Your hands are never cold. I can feel the heat of them even through my glove. And they're just a handsome brown color. They're just like Father's, you know. And you have a real, brotherly, healing touch."

Kodi laughed at this revelation, exploring his free hand even more closely. "If you say so, I guess. That's funny, but thanks. The Kingsmen last night were telling me how much I look like Father."

"Well, it's true. Mom says you look just like him when she first met him. Though they were younger. Both were fifteen when they met and fell in love."

"Yeah, I know. I expect to find a great woman, too, like Father did, you know, but for now I reckon you're the most important lady in my life!"

"Thanks," she laughed. "I'm glad we're together, Ko. At least right now we are, anyway."

"You think we'll get separated?" Though Kodi was intelligent, he was still sometimes subject to a confined thinking common to young men. He had dreams and goals, and had visions in his head of what sort of feats he might achieve in years to come, but he gave few thoughts to the steps that would need to be taken between here and there, the consequences of most of his choices or even the serious predicaments he might be in only this afternoon. He simply took it all as it came and adapted accordingly, a story unfolding page by page. As far as he was concerned they had just left home; they were all traveling together, heading south towards a new life full of adventure.

Many say that the minds of young women mature more rapidly than their male counterparts, and in some ways they do grow up faster. This advanced maturity was evident in Lyndz, no doubt. She was always pondering the future, and she considered the possibilities of the next hours and days as clearly as she dreamed of a detailed far-off time. Those dreams of the future had been radically altered in the past few days and seemed far more uncertain now, and she struggled with that. She didn't like uncertainty. Consequently, she remained more thoughtful than Kodi and more logical. "Yeah, I really do. Eventually. I think Curdoz is expecting big things from you down the road. Well, I guess me, too. I still have a hard time with that idea. But anyway, yes, I'm sure we will separate at some point, although I hope it's not too soon. It's just not likely that we will stay together every minute of every day, despite what Mother is hoping."

Kodi knew in his heart she was probably right, although unlike her he had not pondered such detail. His own goal was to train and become a warrior, and he still hoped, despite whatever Curdoz and the Vision had in store for him, that he would soon have the opportunity to learn the skills of a knight and maybe even fight in the eastern wars.

It was a dream that stemmed from his closeness to Yugan in the too often absences of his own father, and the stories his grandfather would tell of his time as a soldier in the last Tribal War decades ago when the Ice Tribes were finally eliminated from Tulesk and the northern mountains for good. Although Kodi very much admired his father the explorer, the life of his soldier grandfather appealed more to him and seemed more real.

It wasn't just the stories told by the fireplace, either. Five, six, seven years ago, when his grandfather was more agile, he would take his impressionable young grandson tromping through the forests around Felto. They would explore open glades, remnants of clearings made during the war, and hunt for battle artifacts, as all of Tulesk had been the scene of war even in these remote forested areas. Even in the caves near the river, they would sometimes find rusted knives and rotted bows, and even pots used for cooking. Some of the implements were Solantine, but others were clearly Tribal, and Kodi relished his grandfather's interpretations of the evidence. He would describe what must have happened on those very sites and of the brisk battles that had been fought here and there for control of the land between the vicious, pale Ice Tribesmen, descendants of the evil Ralsheen, and the noble, civilized Solantines. His grandfather could always weave a harrowing tale, and Kodi would wrap his mind around it and take it all in.

Kodi couldn't really think of anything particularly philosophical or create words that sounded especially wise in order to reassure his sister. Instead, he resorted to the emotion of the moment. "Well, I plan to stick with you as much as possible, Lyndz, and protect you, too. If we ever separate I'll do everything I can to find you again." It was certainly a safe thing to say, for it was unlikely that Curdoz as the leader of the group would leave the women without some serious protection if he chose to take Kodi off in a separate direction.

The sentiment was sufficient to satisfy Lyndz for the time being, and for the next couple days, she, and Idamé too for that matter, began to perk up and enjoy their travel through southern Tulesk. Lyndz enjoyed the ferry ride over the broad and rocky North River as she had never been out of Tulesk before. A bridge was being built here on the King's orders to encourage easier travel and trade between the Kingdom and the relatively remote Tulesk. Close to completion now, it had not even been begun when Kodi had last been this way with his father two years earlier on their journey to sell ambernut in the port city of Ross. Though Kodi appreciated the engineering and the stone work, he felt a little sorry for the ferry master, whose job would soon be coming to an end.

Amazingly, the idea of separation came more abruptly than the twins expected, for as they rested in Somme that night, Curdoz surprised them with a proposal that he had not mentioned before.

"It's about this little book from your grandfather. From the moment he gave it to me I suspected that it might be of importance to us and our journey. Yugan's suggestion that a proper cipher could have been deposited in the Aster Library by Kalemna makes some sense to me."

"So the ciphers in your book don't work, then?" asked Kodi.

"They do not. The librarian in Aster is a very old man by the name of Theneri. He is a Monastic, and he has been there since long before I was installed as Sage of Solanto. I am hoping he can help us. It is worth the side trip. But it might add a couple weeks more to our journey."

"I've always heard Aster is a beautiful city," said Lyndz.

"It's full of old Ralsheen buildings, though, isn't it?" asked Kodi skeptically.

Curdoz thought it interesting the twins had opposing views on such an obscure subject. "It is, Kodi, that's true, but don't hold that against them. Ancient Ralsheen architecture appeals to some. Just because the Ralsheen nobility were wicked in their last century doesn't mean they were not capable of great feats of engineering and artwork. And there were happy centuries of peace and prosperity before their dark days came upon them—before the goddess Siriné corrupted them. Aster is, like your sister said, a very beautiful and ancient city. Of course it's the tail end of winter, there is probably still some snow on the Highland, so it's not the best time to visit, but that's beside the point. The library especially is grand. I've been there several times. However, I don't think we need all go together."

The twins looked at each other.

"What are you suggesting, then, Curdoz?" asked Idamé.

"I don't trust Prince Filiddor, and I don't want to take Kalemna's book with us. The Princes of Hesk have been allies, of course, in war, and have always been reliable in our conflicts with the Ice Tribes. But they can be devious and self-serving. Anyway, I think it best we separate for a short while. Kodi and Musca and I will travel to Aster, and Lyndz and Mother Idamé can travel to the Convent in Ferostro and await us. The ladies can take Deroge's book with them, and I won't have to worry about it. Most likely it would remain safe in my pack, but, especially since Filiddor appeared in my Vision as an antagonist at a Council of the Kingdom, I simply don't want to risk it. I'll copy down two or three lines from the book on a piece of parchment and take that instead. It will be sufficient for Theneri to determine if there is a cipher for it. When we get to Thorune, I'll hire a carriage to convey the women to Ferostro, and Kodi and I will borrow horses at the Kingsmen barracks."

"Are you sure it is worth sparing the time, Curdoz?" asked Idamé.

"There is another reason I feel compelled, I must admit. We are friends, are we not? We must trust one another."

The Sage went on to explain himself as the other three listened carefully. Even Idamé had not heard of Curdoz' encounter with Xeno and Danly and their tale, for he had deemed it unconnected in any way to the Visions and didn't bother to share it with her before. They were all shocked by the idea of Ice Tribesmen in Aster, despite Curdoz telling them that their presence could very well be no more than some connection to the fur trade. Even that, however, seemed sinister to Kodi, for he had inherited his grandfather's deep hatred for Tribesmen.

"I'm all for it, then," said Kodi eagerly. "Let's see what we can find out!"

Curdoz laughed. "You know, I think we will need to go under other pretense. If anyone asks about Kodi I'll say he is traveling with me as a Novice who has recently had a Meicalian Vision and that we are pilgrimaging to the Monastery in Aster to commune with the Brothers and Sisters there. I will claim Musca as my own, simple enough. We will stay at the Monastery, so little of what I say would be untrue. It's not out of the ordinary for a Novice to do so and to see more of what life is like for Members of the Order before traveling to the Valley of the Gifted for study." He looked at Kodi. "But I am also going to hide your parentage from Filiddor if I may."

"Why!" exclaimed Kodi, surprised. "I am proud of my heritage and my family!"

"Of course you are, but there is something you don't know, although your father almost certainly does whether he's told you of it or not. Prince Filiddor resents that Duke Amerro was given control over the Tolosian Peninsula due to your father's exploration and discoveries. The Prince made it clear in Council that he should have been rewarded with Tolos as a consolation for his father not receiving the land of Tulesk after the last war. The Prince will know of your father's name and reputation and is likely to hold strong antipathy towards him...and his family."

"You think he would hold me hostage or something like that?"

"No, not while you're with me certainly, and probably not otherwise, but he would almost certainly question you, question your business with me, perhaps even send informants to Felto to attempt to learn more about you, because of who you are and find out exactly why you're connected to me. Now you're up to this, aren't you? You're a part of my alibi to go over there."

"Yes, sir. I'll do it, sure." Kodi, of course, was game for any sort of venture. This appeared to him as if it was to be their first one.

"Good man. Now, while there we will see Theneri and find out if he can help us. For me to go to the library is not at all unusual, for I have been there several times. Maybe a task will present itself for you, Kodi, while we are there. But most likely I will learn all I need to know from Theneri, whether the presence of Ice Tribesman was of legitimate purpose or not. Hopefully it was legitimate, or related to the fur trade and thus unimportant otherwise, and I won't have to worry about any of that and focus on finding the cipher. Theneri has special skills. He is an informant and sends me reports on Filiddor. Only a handful of people know he is what is called a Moment Master, a very special Gift."

"Really?" Idamé was shocked. "I've not heard that there are any in the world today! Of course in the Valley, we didn't discuss that Gift very much since it is so rare."

"Rare, yes, and yet the last I heard, Theneri was having difficulty with making use of it."

"What is Moment Mastering?" asked Lyndz, intrigued.

"He can capture a moment in time, like a painting, and explore it thoroughly and all the details of it. It's a very powerful gift. He can spend hours in the moment on his own time, but in our time, in real time that is, it only takes a few moments."

"So he spies for you?" asked Kodi.

"I suppose you can call it that," said the Sage with a chuckle.

The twins were amazed at this information. It never would have occurred to them that the Sage of Solanto would be someone who would rely upon a sort of intelligence network. Kodi thought spies were only something kings and generals used during a time of war to get information about the enemy, of plans and the movement of troops.

"But I am worried," continued Curdoz, "That he may soon not be able to function in this role much longer. I need to check on him, quite frankly, and that really gives us a third reason to go to Aster. It is an old proverb that if you have three good reasons to do something…"

"You'd better do it!" said Kodi, laughing and looking at Lyndz who was laughing along with him. "My father has said that to us a hundred times over the years!"

"Then you should certainly go to Aster," agreed Idamé. "Just think, Lyndz, maybe you and I will have a week or two at the Convent to try to discern your Gift!"

Lyndz raised her eyebrow. "All right, then." Though she had doubts, the idea did seem intriguing.

When they arrived finally in Thorune next day, Curdoz made a second request for a carriage from the accommodating Captain Santher. In his sense of duty he did not question the Sage's reasoning or need for two guards instead of one. He then said, "By the way, m'Lord, I have the information ye requested."

"Thank you, Captain! What did you find out?"

"As a matter o' fact, Lord Curdoz, the very day that you left from here, Onri, he shut down the Fox and made off again."

"Indeed!" exclaimed Curdoz. He had talked himself into believing he had all along been overreacting to the innkeeper's oddness. He was rather surprised to realize he wasn't. "And which direction did he go?"

"He took the eastward road, m'Lord, towards Hesk. I must admit, this has all made me right curious, Your Grace, as to his motives for his leaving so often. If ye recall, Grand Duke Mannago has a deep distrust for Prince Filiddor, and maybe I'm biased against the man because of it. I hope ye don't find me thoughts out of order, m'Lord."

Curdoz looked at Idamé, who raised her left eyebrow. He then said to the Captain, "No, Captain Santher. His Lordship the grand duke is a great friend, and he and I share much with one another. Your thoughts are perfectly in order, though you should probably keep them to yourself. When did Onri return?"

"He had not yet returned as of a few hours ago. Shall I send someone to see if he has returned since then?"

"Yes, while we wait here to send off the two ladies; that would be good. Thank you."

Santher managed all these requests adeptly. It only took a quarter hour to receive information that Onri had indeed not returned. "Lord Curdoz, if ye wish to have him questioned, it is certainly within your authority. As soon as he returns I can have him brought to me…"

"No," the Sage interrupted. He had something else in mind. "It really isn't necessary. You've provided all the information I need, thank you, Captain. However, I need to borrow a private space for a half hour and parchment, pen and ink."

Curdoz then retreated for a short while, but when he came back outside to the others as they stood by a waiting carriage he spoke privately to Idamé. "I need you to do me a favor." He then told her to take the time necessary to find the whereabouts of the Brothers Xeno and Danly, and gave her specific instructions to have them square away their business in the counties they had been assigned to and to meet Curdoz in Thorune in ten days' time for reassignment.

"I think I need more eyes and ears in Hesk, and they are willing, and I trust them. I told them to check in with the innkeeper in Davos, so you might stop there first. He might at least know where exactly they are. It might cause you to have to backtrack some, but…"

"Oh, I'll find them, Curdoz. You know I'm really quite shocked that you have a web of informants."

"What is so shocking about it?"

"What is so shocking to me is that as long and as well as we have known one another, that you have never made use of me!"

Curdoz snickered. "Ah, but who's to say I haven't? Not all of them *know* they are informants."

Idamé was confused. "What do you mean by that?"

"I glean a tremendous amount of knowledge on the workings of the Matrimonial Order and particularly the Mother Superior from your letters to me."

Idamé stood there silently for a moment digesting this truth. Finally, though, she could not help but to burst out with pleasure. "Oh, Curdoz! What a joy to have you in my life again!" She then kissed him on the cheek.

"I've never left you, Ida, in my heart."

She giggled a bit like a girl and went on separating out Lyndz' and her belongings from among the pony's baggage.

Kodi didn't like it, but Curdoz had him deliver up his ambernut bow to the care of his sister, for a Novice of the Order was not allowed to carry anything that could be perceived as a weapon.

At this, Lyndz asked a question. "Sir, Kodi has had a Vision from the Guardian, and you've confirmed that, so perhaps he truly is considered to be a Novice in the Order?"

"You're not wrong, Lyndz, but in his case it is quite different, you see. His Vision implies danger and conflict to be confronted. It is very different than the typical spiritual-type Visions that most Order members have. Everything about this situation is different. For example, he nor you are going to be traveling to the Valley of the Gifted for the ordinary study and training. Instead, we are going on a quest appointed. No, when we leave the country, perhaps when we get to Tirilorin, I want Kodi to train as a fighter. We must prepare ourselves for the dangers in the far south and in the wilderness. But it's not necessary here in Solanto, and it would raise questions that I don't wish to answer." To Kodi he added, "You can keep your hunting knife if you want, but I'm sorry that the bow is just too obvious and questionable. I know we could say it's purely for hunting, but the fact that it is made of ambernut unfortunately speaks of wealth and rank, and I would just presume Prince Filiddor think of you as a merchant's son or commoner. Probably an educated merchant's son considering your more proper language."

"I ken change me tone, m'lordship, if ye like!" Kodi expounded with a put-on accent in perfect accord with that of Yaguro and Teegriss or Captain Santher.

They all cackled, but it was Idamé who replied. "The problem with that, Kodi, is that you're just far too handsome, and you walk tall as if you own the world! Nobody would mistake you for a typical commoner!"

"Ah, ye jes' havin' a misunderstandin' 'bout us common folk! We's all right good-lookin' when we shave! I'll jes' let me scruff grow on me face, Mudder Idermay, 'n ye'll see! It'll make me look right common and rascally!"

"It really will, Mother Idamé!" agreed Lyndz. "Of course, even when he achieves the 'scruffy rascal' look he's much too handsome for his own good!"

Additional laughing ensued, but Curdoz reiterated that such efforts would not be necessary.

Kodi kept it to himself for now, but he was thrilled at the prospect of training in Tirilorin, and was willing to do whatever Curdoz asked of him. So he requested some cloths from inside the barracks and carefully wrapped and bound his bow and quiver of arrows to protect them from the weather and from anybody who might see the bow and try to steal it, and Lyndz stowed it under the seat of the carriage.

"Take care, Lyndz!" Kodi called out. "Everything will be fine. We're still in Solanto, you know!"

"I'm not anxious," she replied truthfully as she reached out the window to squeeze her brother's hand. And though it was her first time not to be near family, she felt no fears. "Don't worry about me. It's you who'd better stay out of trouble!"

Kodi laughed. He and Curdoz watched as the carriage carrying the two women made its way through the open gateway of the old fort.

Chapter 10—Wisdom Exchanged

Now, after having traveled for weeks on foot, Curdoz finally requested a horse for himself and one also for Kodi, and these were provided by Captain Santher. "I'm rather tired of walking; what about you, Kodi?"

"Sure enough, sir."

Kodi was pleased enough with the horse that was loaned to him, a well-trained gelding. Kodi had learned superior skills from his father over the years, and the training and keeping of horses came natural for him, not to mention riding. He could have managed a spirited stallion, but he knew he wasn't about to charge like some hero into battle.

They left the baggage pony they had brought with them from Felto with Captain Santher, who could always make good use of such animals. Then the Sage and Kodi took to the road.

Curdoz proved as adept at riding as the far younger Kodi. Musca, for his part, seemed to be pleased with the opportunity to move at a faster pace as well.

For some time on their way eastward, the two men shared stories. Though there was some traffic—the pace of trade had begun to pick up now that the port of Ross had re-opened for the year—and there were occasions in which the Sage was recognized by his green stole and felt obligated to stop, dismount, and pronounce Affirmations from time to time, there were long stretches when they would neither pass by nor see anyone. Curdoz was glad of the relatively private opportunity away from the women to focus on Kodi and learn more about him. Since he had not had the privilege of meeting Kodi's father, he asked Kodi to describe him. Though Kodi talked with proper respect for Hess it wasn't difficult for the astute Curdoz to perceive the resentment the younger man harbored towards his father.

The older man nodded often as he listened, and it reminded him keenly of the time when his own father had refused to acknowledge his sense of Calling through his first Vision. At the time, he was two years younger than Kodi, and in Curdoz' case it was worse, for his father could be very severe. For all practical purposes Curdoz had to walk away, without the traditional Familial Blessing, in the care of his uncle. Hess, in contrast, allowed Kodi many freedoms at home, and he clearly took deep interest in his son having taught him many manly skills and having trusted him with various responsibilities.

The Sage attempted to offer some wisdom to Kodi, who had grown silent. "I'm not a father, of course, but I certainly remember my own quite well, and I've observed this in others, too. Particularly when a man has an eldest son or an only son, he tends to have in his mind some perfect idea of who and what that son ought to be and do. It sounds to me, though he was eager at first to prove himself to Duke Amerro, your father eventually grew to have misgivings about leaving home so often. A man can sometime feel enslaved to his sense of duty, and perhaps even more so in Hess's case as the duke's cousin. I suspect he sees the same sort of drive and eagerness in you, and in some way he was attempting to rein you in, perhaps? I suspect he was trying to make you feel content with your lot at home. From what you're telling me, and from what your mother has said, Hess knows what a capable man you are, and he didn't want you to leave home and get caught up in others' grand schemes, as he has done with Duke Amerro."

Kodi remembered his father speaking words to him of this sort, such as 'be content with what you have' and 'don't seek too hard after adventure, for trouble may come unbidden.' But they were words that always seemed a bit shallow and hypocritical to Kodi, for it appeared his father did not necessarily follow his own advice.

"I'm not going to find what I want in life by staying in County Fothemry, sir."

"I know it. Trust me, I do. Some sons over time look back and appreciate the firm guidance given them by stern fathers, and following in their footsteps turns out to be good. But a great many do not. I wasn't content with being a farmer. Don't deny what you're being Called to. Fathers, even in their love and wisdom, can make errors where their sons are concerned. And let's also not forget—remember what your mother said. If your father had taken you with him to Tolos this time, or even if he had allowed you to leave home years ago to train with Amerro, it would have made it that much more difficult for me to find you. You were meant for something very different."

"Thanks, sir. I appreciate you coming to find me, by the way, I really do. And Lyndz. She didn't need to stay there anymore than me. She could rule a kingdom, you know. The Guardian knows how smart she is! She doesn't need to be stuck in County Fothemry, and she doesn't need to be Bonded off to some rich merchant or even to some baron or baron's son."

"Hmm, yes. I think I see what you mean. I've known her a short time, but I know she has a high Calling."

"Sir, she's never had a Vision, though. Is it a problem? I mean how will she know what she is meant to do?"

"Even with our three connected Visions we are unclear about many things, but I can almost guarantee you at some point on this journey of ours Meical will communicate with her somehow. I believe, now I have met her and gotten to know her, the reason she hasn't had a Vision *yet* is because she hasn't needed one. So far, she has been willing, as we say, to 'play along' with the rest of us. But even the Guardian Himself doesn't know the whole. It is rather like a puzzle as I have said before."

The conversation then began to lead in the direction of Prince Filiddor. Kodi wanted to know exactly what Curdoz knew of the prince, what he was like, what the politics of Solanto were concerning the events of the last war and Tulesk and Tolos. It was important to him to know why the prince thought that Tulesk and then Tolos should have been added to the principality.

He learned much. He had never really understood before that the principality was in any way different than one of the duchies, like Tulesk or Ascanti. He was surprised to learn how independent the principality was in its relationship to the King of Solanto. He'd had some rather vague dislike for the Principality of Hesk, due to his grandfather's reminiscences, for Yugan had often made it clear he didn't like living there, nor having had to participate in the Hescian army in the war, for their generals were severe taskmasters, publicly whipping soldiers for even minor indiscretions. Kodi also had heard enough history to know that Aster was once an ancient Ralsheen city, and he'd always thought that a bit sinister. But in general, he'd not really thought of Hesk being different than any other part of Solanto.

"But why do they act so much different than other Solantines, like you say? The princes that is."

Kodi was shocked to learn that Prince Filiddor's ancestor, before he had been granted Hesk as his principality to rule by Emperor Terianh, was a minor Ralsheen nobleman. Curdoz suggested that a bit of ancient Ralsheen pride and ambition may have made its way down through the centuries. To this Kodi asked, "If the first prince was Ralsheen, then why did he fight on Terianh's side?"

"It's often hard to understand a man's motives. They're often hidden. I don't know that I know the answer, Kodi. I don't think it has been discussed much, frankly, for it was so long ago. Society was ready to discard its Ralsheen past. We must presume Terianh trusted the man at the time, and all accounts do say he was critical in helping conquer this part of the country and liberating it from the Ralsheen. After they took this region, Tolos was all that was left to the Ralsheen Empire, along with some islands, and of course their navy. There were still many years to go before the Conquest came to an end."

"And aren't the Ice Tribes descended from the Ralsheen? Wouldn't that make them related to each other? Does Prince Filiddor have bright white skin and pale eyes?"

Curdoz laughed, "No. Not all the Ralsheen looked like that, although that's what we tend to hear about in the old tales. Keep in mind, Kodi, that almost everybody has Ralsheen ancestry, though not so much from its nobility class. And it's only the leadership class of the Ice Tribes that are like that with the bright white skin. I'll admit the traits are understood by some as a sign of evil. The histories say it was a sign of the corruption of the Ralsheen upper classes, tainted as it were by the wicked goddess Siriné. In part I think that the deliberate reproduction of those traits is wicked, for it clearly does not take into account true love between men and women. Arranged couplings are rarely good things. However, the albino traits appear in the natural population, too. There is nothing inherently evil in natural albinism. I have a friend or two among the Monastic Orders that I knew and were friends of mine back in the Valley of the Gifted. We have to have a care not to judge people by their looks alone. The former Anterianhi realms contain many ethnic groups. Most Solantines and Elenites and Barantines are light-skinned like your mother Elisa. You twins and your father and Amerro display the darker complexion common to your Escarantine ancestors, and they themselves came from Nant centuries ago. When we travel to those places, you will find you will fit in very well in looks. The Hralindis and the Essemarians in the Far East—I knew many from my time in the Valley—are very dark-skinned, nearly black. On occasion we will receive delegations or traders from those faraway places in Ferostro. Although not so much since they are now at war. In any event, variety is a good thing in this world, don't you think?"

"I do, sir. And I look forward to meeting different peoples, and the Qeteral and maybe the Etoppsi someday. But the way my grandfather talks about the Ice Tribesmen, you should hear him."

"Well, he's probably not wrong. Though we should feel sorry for their peasants who probably look at the world little differently than poor folk here, the Tribal leaders are definitely cunning and vicious and not to be trusted. They would often take Solantine children and women hostage during the wars in their raids, and kill them when we could not ransom them. Anyway, Kodi, you'll find that in looks, Prince Filiddor looks no different than any Solantine. All I'm saying is that Filiddor and his ancestors have always been strong-willed and ambitious, and though that was a trait too common among the Ralsheen, it is not unheard of in Anterianhi history either. But maybe, Kodi, there is some dash of Ralsheen heritage that comes through in the princes. The idea of a superior race of Humans, perhaps, for the princes are strongly prejudiced. And they treat women very badly. But the princes are ferocious enemies to the Ice Tribesmen."

"Yes, sir, I guess that's why I don't understand, like you've heard, there were Ice Tribesmen visiting Prince Filiddor in Aster."

Though Curdoz attempted to explain again to Kodi the possibility that it had to do with the fur trade, Kodi was definitely not convinced. And Curdoz had to admit that over the last couple weeks since he had heard that report from Danly and Xeno, he wasn't entirely happy with his initial presumption. He concluded, "…but, hopefully we will find out one way or the other."

With the aid now of horses, the men arrived in the morning, two days after leaving Thorune, at the edge of the Grand Escarpment which marked the boundary between the Duchy of Ascanti and the Principality of Hesk. To their left in the distance could be seen the North Falls. A wide expanse, it was the largest waterfall in Solanto. A hundred feet it fell into its stony basin, and the North River continued its rocky course westward towards the Bay. Yet the Escarpment itself rose again another three hundred feet above the head of the falls to the top of the plateau-like Hescian Highland. Particularly in this region the Escarpment was sheer, and the only way onto the height was by way of a magnificent cutting and Ramp, in part made by the convulsions of the world long ago, or perhaps the gouging fingernail of one of the world gods, but then enhanced by thousands of slaves during the Ralsheen era. Where the road met the wall of the Escarpment ancient gates stood open, beyond which the Ramp rose slowly upward. Hescian guardsmen operated a toll business just outside the gates. There were no levies on incoming trade goods, however there was a flat toll to make use of the road itself.

The guards stood and saluted the Sage with proper respect, for with his stole they recognized him.

"Lord Curdoz, you have not visited us in some years. Are you making your way to the Monastery in Aster?" Kodi noticed that though the Hescian guardsman was respectful and used an educated form of speech, he did not appear to have the same friendly tone typical of Solantine Kingsmen such as Captain Santher.

"I am indeed, thank you. This here is Kodi from Tulesk. He is a Novice in the Order. He is accompanying me to the Monastery."

"Very good, m'Lord. There is of course no toll for Order Members. You may proceed at will, Your Grace. I will send ahead a message to His Highness of your arrival. I'm sure he will most graciously receive Your Lordship at the Palace."

"It was not my intention to call upon His Highness. We will be staying at the Monastery and I need myself to research certain information in the Library in Aster. Probably stay two or three days at most, and then we will return. You do not have to bother with announcing us to His Highness."

"Your pardon, m'Lord, but His Highness has issued a recent order to send word of the arrival in Hesk of any Solantine of the rank of baron or higher."

Curdoz thought for only a moment before responding. "Am I required to call upon him? That would indeed be a change in the freedom of travel within his domain."

"No, m'Lord. There is no change at all on that. However, since he will know you are staying at the monastery he might possibly send for you."

"Of course, then. If that is his desire. A quick question however. Does this new rule include those of the Orders? I don't mean myself, of course."

"Not of Healers and Matrimonials or Monastics, Lord Curdoz, only high officials in the Order such as Your Grace. I believe 'tis only His Highness's desire to extend cordial greetings to those of, er…"

"Influence, yes. I should not be surprised by the new rule." Then he turned to Kodi. "Let us then be on our way, Novice Kodi."

Though the Hescian guardsman's face was stoic at this response, Kodi grinned at the Sage's sarcasm. They then began to make their way up the Great Ramp. It was an interesting climb through what was essentially a straight canyon, the walls of which grew gradually shorter as they continued ever higher. It was noisy. The walls echoed and magnified the sounds, and there was a rivulet of water rushing downward on one side. There were a number of people, some walking, some riding, mules and horses pulling carts down the Ramp, and others struggling with their loads upwards. Kodi and the Sage had to go around these. Curdoz was pleased by Kodi's knowledge, for the young man pointed out where the softer limestone at the base of the cliff, a hundred feet from the top, switched over to the harder sandstone capstone. It was very obvious here as it was so abrupt, and the gray of the former gave way to the more colorful sandstone. "You know quite a bit about the geology, Kodi. How is that? Your grandfather's books?"

"Partly." Kodi then explained that the Escarpment backed up to the edge of County Fothemry, a fact that Curdoz knew of course, because it could be seen in Felto. But Kodi went on about the Wolf River where he often swam with his friends, and the various deer trails that lead beyond it up into the Escarpment, for it was less sheer there, more rocky, with many cutouts and tiny ravines. His grandfather perhaps five years before, when he was more able, had taken Kodi back there in order to explore rock shelters and caves, and even a trail that climbed to the top of the Highland. All that region was densely forested, and there were no people.

Curdoz was intrigued by this information. "So there is a trail onto the Highland from behind your home? That is fascinating, Kodi. I never knew there was any other way to the top besides the Great Ramp that we are traveling on now! From King's Valley there is a set of hills that separate it from Hesk, and those could be traversed, but there is the great Durn Swamp on the other side, so no one goes that way."

Kodi was pleased he possessed information that Curdoz thought interesting. "Grandpa showed it to me, like I said. He said he first found it years before right after the war when he lived in the forest in Hesk. He went down it mostly just for fun and to explore, but when he discovered the stands of ambernut, he decided after the war to move to Tulesk. He had a feeling the lumber trade would become really big, and he was a master woodcarver already and wanted to try his hand at cabinet making. He was one of the first to settle in Felto, and he knew it had to be close to that trail. He was pleased when he found it again with me that time. But anyway, yes sir, that's when he showed me about the difference in the kinds of rock, because you can see it there, too."

"Probably some ancient way of the Ice Tribesmen, or even the Ralsheen."

"Grandpa said the same thing, sir. If you ask me, though, it's really quite a natural pathway, because there's a creek that runs down through it to the Wolf. So maybe they used it, sir, but I don't think they made it."

"Is it still a secret, do you think, Kodi?"

"Some of my friends I've taken up there and we've camped in the caves and on top of the Highland. We'd uh…" but Kodi grinned and checked himself as he was about to accidently confess to a high Sage of the Guardian that he and his friends usually had with them some kind of ale or liquor they'd acquired and how drunk they'd get on these excursions. "Funny, because the times we were up there we never really thought of it as being in Hesk, but I suppose it is."

If Curdoz noticed the cover, he said nothing. "Well, that's very interesting, Kodi. I bet it's quite secret otherwise." There was no more to be said about it, but Curdoz stored this intriguing tidbit in the back of his mind.

Five more minutes had not passed, however, when a most interesting person on horseback was just about to pass them heading down the Ramp in the opposite direction. Curdoz would quite often avert his eyes from strangers in the hopes they would not recognize him and request an Affirmation; he didn't always appreciate the distraction and how it slowed him down. But since Thorune, though he had not said so to Kodi, Curdoz was on the lookout for someone, someone in particular that he was expecting.

Curdoz put on a face so knowing—almost sinister—that Kodi was taken aback. However, he quickly learned what the Sage was about, for he was present when Captain Santher supplied the information back in Thorune. Kodi considered at the time it was not really his business, but he certainly paid attention now.

"Onri! The innkeeper at the Fox! How fascinating it is to see you so far from home! How interesting you have, er, dealings with the Principality of Hesk!"

The man who Kodi realized was probably no more than five or six years older than himself was clearly caught off his guard, and did not return the Sage's smile. He stopped his horse abruptly and stared with startled face at the Sage of Solanto. Before he could respond, however, Curdoz continued.

"And such a fine horse! It is such a delight to see that your business is flourishing so much that you have been able with your own coin to acquire such a one as this! Particularly, as I have heard that your inn is often closed! A Hescian Trotter, my word! I didn't even know His Highness allowed the breed to be sold to those outside the Principality. 'Tis fascinating, yes?"

Even if Onri could have come up with an excuse on the spot, he would have had a hard time getting a word in edgewise, for Curdoz plunged on unabated. Kodi watched with astonishment as the Sage played the man for all it was worth. "Yes," the Sage agreed with himself. "It is remarkable that an innkeeper would close his doors the moment his important guests leave and make his way to the Principality of Hesk. One would almost think the man had certain, shall we say, 'news' that he wished to convey to other 'important' persons. You know what I mean, say, one of the noble cousins of the prince, eh? Or perhaps His Highness himself? Yes, 'tis interesting. Now, of course, I can't imagine what information such an innkeeper could have learned from me that would cause him to feel the need to convey it to the prince, could you, Onri? Of course there was the unusual fact that I was on the northern roads at the tail end of winter, and that I met with a Troupe of Matrimonial Sisters, and had a long, private, conversation with the Mother of the Troupe, who I had declared was a friend of mine, and then there was the rather deliberate attempt on my part to avoid prying questions, and then also the fact that I took the Northern Road out of Thorune with the Troupe towards the Duchy of Tulesk which I haven't visited in many years."

The man continued to stare silently, and Kodi thought he'd never seen a face as nervous and beet red as Onri's. Kodi thought the man might faint and was really beginning to feel sorry for him. Musca stood by obediently waiting, panting. A couple of drivers on carts went past at this point, but they pointedly ignored the angry-sounding Curdoz.

And he wasn't quite finished. "Yes, fascinating information for someone who perhaps pays gold to such people to gather information. 'Tis a good thing I know my conversation with the Mother was private, as I put up a deliberate Block so that certain nosy innkeepers could not hear what we two old friends were talking about. Of course, there was not much information of importance. Maybe the innkeeper had been ordered by his employer to simply report what information he could on the movements and motives of people 'of influence.' Whether such information is truly important is to be determined by the employer himself? All the innkeeper is required to do is report. And I thought I was resting in a peaceful inn in the kingdom where I serve the king and its peoples—including its innkeepers by the way—by the Guardian Meical! Hmm, I bet you are about to leave this fine animal they *loaned* you with the guardsmen at the bottom of the Ramp? That would explain the timing quite well.

"You walked to the Escarpment. You borrowed a horse and rode to Aster and delivered your pathetic information, then you returned by horse just in time to pass by me. I am Gifted, as you know, and can sometimes understand the thoughts of others. Pleasant journeys back to Thorune, Master Onri. And by the way, I suspect your current, eh, *position,* has been, shall we say, *compromised.* I think Captain Santher has now become more wary of your odd habits. I told him not to bother with you anymore, but Onri, you especially should know how curious some people are. Being a paid informant does not gain one very many friends now, does it?"

But before the innkeeper informant could arrange the first phrase on the end of his tongue, Curdoz reached into his breast pocket and retrieved a curious parchment sealed rather like a letter. "Here, Onri."

The man seemed to feel he had no choice but to reach out and accept the thing. And as he did so, Curdoz' tone changed abruptly from cynical accusation to that of an army captain spitting orders. "Listen to me, Onri, by the Guardian! I don't know the motives behind the fact that you have become a paid informant or how long ago you began such nonsense. Maybe you were struggling, and the prince's agents made an offer that at the time sounded good to you. Perhaps it seemed to you to be perfectly innocent. The truth is you are interfering with the freedoms of innocent people. And what is there to inform of in a time of peace? Whatever your struggles might have been, you no longer have to deal with them. When you get home I want you to open that letter and read it. Your response to it will determine your future. No one in Thorune will trust you now that Captain Santher suspects you. Your reputation will suffer and you will lose business. If you take the offer in that letter, you will have the opportunity to begin anew."

Curdoz ended the diatribe, signaled to Kodi, and the two of them trotted past the man. Musca followed, unconcerned. Though Curdoz did not look back, Kodi turned to see that Onri still sat there on his fine horse with the letter in his hand and his cheeks were still fiery. Kodi could hardly believe what he had just witnessed and had questions, but Curdoz had grown silent and didn't seem to want to talk anymore just now.

It took the better part of a day, altogether, from the gates at the bottom of the Ramp to reach the flat. Kodi looked back through the narrow gap made by the Great Ramp. He could see for many miles out onto the plain, but it was impossible to make out any detail, and the late afternoon sun was in his eyes. He then looked all around him. Though all snow had melted down on the plain, up here there were still many patches. At this higher elevation, winter lingered longer than even it did in his own southern Tulesk.

This part of the Highland was fertile enough, but there were no yeoman farmers, no thriving homesteads and bustling towns. Curdoz had warned Kodi that all the land remained in the hands of the wealthy barons, for Filiddor and Lanwi before him had refused to institute the Reforms. There was a large and stately palace off to the left about a mile away, probably quite close to the river canyon, and a village near to the road that contained a few dozen dingy hovels. Though there was traffic on the road, it seemed to be bypassing the village and there was not much movement there. The peasants were apparently sheltering inside against the last of the winter winds. Indeed Kodi found the winds up here on the flat to be quite brisk and chill. He decided there was still potential for late snowfalls here.

To his right the land was open and wide and Kodi imagined that it could be quite beautiful in other seasons. There were mixed forests interspersed with fallow fields patched with snow. Several miles off to the left, beyond what he knew must be the ends of the canyon of the North River, were dense forests. However, being the end of winter, and with the lack of cheer in the nearby village, he really didn't feel he liked the place.

"It seems a really sad place, Curdoz," he said, pointing at the village. Dense smoke poured from gray brick chimneys. Peat was a common fuel in Hesk, for it was cut in massive quantities in the southern parts of the Principality. There were few windows, and Kodi imagined these homes were just as dreary on the inside as they were on the outside. The peasants who lived in these hovels probably couldn't afford the luxury of glass windows. Here and there were some cattle and goats, but they looked rather forlorn, standing idly by stark trees and rickety fences.

"Aster and the other cities appear quite prosperous, but there is a tremendous amount of poverty in the countryside. The peasants in these villages work for the barons, like Baron Gant who lives in that manor that you see. They have precious little to do until the snows are gone when they can start plowing the fields. *His* fields. It looks much better in spring and summer. In fact, this land is quite beautiful and productive, but most of what they harvest is sold by Gant to the cities. The peasants keep barely enough for themselves to last through the winter, though you would find Gant's own tables well-stocked. They're allowed a small amount of land on which to raise produce to sell in the marketplace, but they remain quite poor. And that is what you will find over the whole of Hesk. It is not a very nice place to live."

"I'm surprised they don't move away, sir, and find something better."

"Easier said than done."

"I suppose."

Curdoz looked over at Kodi, the epitome of health and confidence. "Kodi, I'm glad you grew up in a place like Felto! Your grandfather knew exactly what he was doing when he quit the Principality and moved. You had a good family, you had your land and your horses and your river and your friends. All very right and proper for a boy growing up in the good kingdom of Solanto. Just what the Guardian wishes for everyone, and it's what I've worked hard to bring about in the Reforms. But the Principality of Hesk remains a gloomy sort of place, and unfortunately there is almost nothing this Sage can do about it. The princes haven't wanted the peasants and city commoners to gain freedoms, because they know they will lose a certain amount of control over them, and his barons—nearly all of them are cousins of his—don't want to give up even a square inch of their land."

Kodi pondered this. He was grateful, assuredly, for what he had grown up with. He nodded his comprehension. Finally, though, he brought up the subject of Onri the innkeeper. "Curdoz, what you did back there...I just don't understand. What was in the letter? What were you offering Onri, sir?"

The Sage pursed his lips and sighed. "I don't think stirring up trouble is really Onri's goal. He just wanted the extra gold, which is why he works for Filiddor. He has poor social skills and doesn't communicate well with people. He's odd and he probably realizes it. He's a loner according to Captain Santher. Onri isn't especially brilliant, either, for as you see he had not even come up with any sort of alibi in advance for what he was doing away from his inn. He's a simple fool with little going for him."

"But you demolished him, sir! I thought he was going to fall off his horse!"

"I know I did, Kodi. I did not enjoy it, despite the sarcastic tones. I was calculating. I spoke to him that way so he would clearly, very clearly understand that I was on to him, that I suspected what he was up to the morning after I met him, and that he had no more future as an informant, and very little future as an innkeeper. Given the timing and the facts, it seemed likely to me we would see him on this road, and I wrote that letter in Santher's office before we left Thorune. With it I've offered him a way out, Kodi. It's the Way of the Guardian. Onri is not at all a bad man, just a foolish one working for the man he is. Filiddor is a thorn in the side of the king and this kingdom. If Onri accepts the offer, he will have to sell his inn and move to Island Saundry and work at my estate. We can perhaps find if he has any other talents and apprentice him to someone, for he is still young. He will have a peaceful and contented life there if he wants it, and he'll be far away from people like Filiddor who would try to use and abuse him for his naivety."

Kodi thought all this remarkable. He paused before responding. "Sir, do you expect him to take it?—your offer that is?"

"We'll find out when we travel back through Thorune on our way south."

Kodi trusted Curdoz, but his conflicting behavior towards the innkeeper was an eye opener. He was silent for a while, but finally Curdoz, sensing Kodi's discomfort, spoke again.

"Kodi, we have to have opportunities to redeem ourselves when we've fallen, or we can travel down a road to despair. I know how I treated Onri was harsh, but fools can't see the broader picture unless you scream it at them sometimes, and I judged him to be such a one. What I'm truly hoping, Kodi, is that he doesn't go one inch lower than he has now gone. I brought him low in an instant, and from now on it should be better. If he comes to Saundry, he will have plenty of good work to do...even friends. There are nobles and princes, even kings out there in the world who have to travel long dark paths of their own making and fall in pits they have to climb out of if they can. That road to despair is traveled by the strong and powerful as much as it is by the poor and weak. Typically the great fall harder and deeper than the rest. But with the great we can only offer help to them when they ask for it, otherwise they only resent us for trying. Onri is better off, for his low road will be brief, or hopefully so if he makes the right choice."

Kodi thought about this. "Yes, sir. But if you don't mind me being so bold, sir, I thought what you did was not what I would have expected from...from a Sage, that is. You're Meical's Representative to us, right? You are as a Father. That's the way I learned it."

"Yes, Kodi."

"And what I'm thinking is that the way He made me feel at the end of my Vision was really just the opposite of what you did to Onri. Meical raised me high. I felt trapped in Felto. Anger too—I guess you figured that part out. But I, er, uh...made some mistakes a few years ago that really messed with me, and I've been trying hard since then to avoid the, er, same sort of thing..."

As Kodi paused, Curdoz reflected. As a man himself he thought he knew what Kodi meant by 'mistakes'. In a small setting like Felto there really weren't all that many 'sorts' of mistakes young men like him could make. It was obvious to anyone that both Kodi and Lyndz were an especially handsome set of siblings. A young woman of Lyndz' social status, particularly in the traditional atmosphere of a Solantine small town, had a certain amount of protection; no man would dare violate the count's daughter without themselves getting a public flogging and prison sentence. For Kodi as a young man it was different. For eighteen he was as large as most men in their twenties, virile and fit, with a somewhat deep, confident voice and a compelling personality. Young women were attracted to these traits, and some would deliberately want to place themselves in Kodi's path. Or it may have been that he had been the one pursuing— more likely a combination, considering his words.

The males in Kodi's family, like his father Hess and their cousin Duke Amerro, found mates and Bonded young. Curdoz had always been of the opinion that there were at least a couple real and legitimate differences among men that created sort of a spectrum in this arena, and both seemed to represent different elements of the

Great Design. It was all true of women, he felt certain, but Curdoz believed he understood his own sex better. Most of the men who joined the Order tended to be rather internal and cerebral, like himself, and with the exception of a very few, they were willing to take the Vow of Chastity. The High Priest in the Valley would grant Dispensations, but it was not common, usually only when there was an Aura. Curdoz had considered upon a time requesting it for himself and Idamé, but eventually decided it was not that important—not Bonding made no difference in his close friendship with Idamé. For men such as himself, it was a high Calling to spend their lives with a focus on serving the Guardian and the kingdom to which they were assigned, reading and studying and using their Gifts to bring teaching, healing, or Affirmation to the people.

But for men on the opposite end of the spectrum, charismatic leaders, warriors, adventurers, Curdoz knew that the physical aspect of bonding was critical to their overall sense of well-being and achievement, aiding them in their goals and giving them further confidence. That physical and emotional link to the feminine was a source of healing and fulfillment for such men. It completed them. Hess was apparently even younger than Kodi when he Bonded Elisa, and the handsome Kodi's drives and desires were surely not a whit different than his father's.

He knew he was insinuating a great deal from a handful of Kodi's words, but then it occurred to Curdoz that getting away from a village full of young women, almost none of which were of the quality and manner of Kodi's mother or his sister, was probably one of his very reasons for wanting so strongly to leave home. Kodi would be on the lookout for a suitable mate. It was one of those things he sought for—one of several themes maybe that characterized and drove him. Despite Kodi's Call through the Vision, Curdoz doubted that Meical would expect Kodi Fothemry to take the Vow. It was certain Kodi would refuse, for he was too independent to see the need to make such a concession, and it would go against his nature. By leaving Felto, Kodi was attempting to nobly steer his desires rather than be entrapped by some young village or farm girl who could not help him grow into the man he aspired to be. Curdoz had tremendous appreciation for the attempt, because in his experience far too many women were treated far too poorly by far too many men, because in addition to those two legitimate ends of the spectrum, there were several illegitimate realms of Human male expression not even on the spectrum that were way too common. Their sexual natures were more Fallen than that of their Etoppsi or Qeteral counterparts. Both the other races were determinedly and devotedly monogamous according to what he knew of their cultures and reproductive differences in comparison to Humans. In any event, Curdoz' conclusions seemed to fit well the one riding beside him. Kodi perhaps had had a taste from one of those other realms, but he found it lacking.

"...I was just kind of at my wits' end when I had that Vision, sir. I wasn't going to describe it in front of the women, you understand, but I stripped off and was naked when I plunged into that Lake. That's typical for all the men and boys at home when we go to the river, but this was different. It seemed really important to make the choice to jump in completely free like that, even though it was a dream, to cast away what I was before, stripping away the past, and then I felt like my whole body grew into a giant or something, a great man, you might say, but of the best sort. Made me feel like my father as the famous adventurer or Grandpa as the soldier—the awesome stories they tell about themselves, anyway. Like Terianh the Great or even better, really, if it's possible. You know the song the Sisters sang at Grandpa and Ansy's Bonding? It was as if I was that very First Man. The great hunter and warrior. Does that make sense, sir? I know I didn't deserve it, you know, what Meical did for me when I jumped in that Lake. Every time I think about it I feel really strong, like I've turned a corner in my life." Kodi was silent for a brief moment, then concluded, "But, anyway, I know Onri may have been foolish, but I guess I wish for him, for everybody really, what I felt."

As they rode along, Curdoz thought about Kodi's words very carefully before responding. The young man was remarkably self-aware, and he clearly had many other strengths which the Guardian knew of and was latching onto. The detail of the emotion Kodi was describing was intense. Curdoz realized that whatever woman out there in the wide world should actually win Kodi's favor, she would be blessed to have such a mate who harbored such passion and was actually willing to demonstrate it.

Too, Kodi wasn't just feeling sorry for the innkeeper, but was rather putting himself in the man's shoes. He was comparing Onri's bad choices with those of his own and wishing for him the same sort of freedom and enlightenment that Kodi had himself received through his Vision. Curdoz found himself amazed that one so young, particularly a man, harbored this level of empathy towards others. It was uncommon, and suggested a maturity well beyond his not quite nineteen years.

There was nothing wrong whatsoever with the way Kodi was thinking about Onri. In fact, he was right on target with the way the Guardian Meical preferred to operate. Kodi's only fault was lack of experience. "Like I said, if Onri follows what's in that letter, he will be lifted up. Maybe now that I consider what you say, I might have

acted a tad bit differently, eh? Taken a warmer approach? Hmm. I
have strong doubts, though, that it would have worked. I think I've
acted with wisdom, with the Gift Meical has given me to be a Sage.
The words rather flowed from me when I spoke them, you
understand. I believe they will have made the appropriate impact.
However, if I am wrong and Onri is still there at his inn when we
travel back through, perhaps we'll stop and chat with him again, you
and I. I hear what you're saying, Kodi. For now, though, let's not talk
about Onri anymore."

"Yes sir."

The evening was darkening, and Curdoz began to watch for
the Hescian barracks where he intended for them to stay the night.
Kodi only paused for a minute before continuing their conversation,
though without reference to the innkeeper. "Curdoz, have you ever
dived into that Lake in the Valley? Is it really like in my Vision?"

Curdoz didn't mind at all talking of and thinking more about
Kodi's Vision, for there was symbolism Kodi was alluding to the
Sage had not considered when the tale had been told back in Felto.
Some of these new details were telling. He was intrigued by Kodi's
honesty. Few men had it in them to share their inner thoughts like he
was doing. "It is called the Valley Lake or sometimes the Lake of
Life. All the various little streams from the surrounding mountains
flow into it just like you described before. It is a fantastic place to
swim in the middle of the summer, and it really does have healing
properties. It is used for ritual purposes, too, for those who study in
the Valley. The Ancient Book holds that the Creator used the water
from the Lake and mixed it with the soil in the Valley to create the
Mold. The first Male and Female were named Modelo and Modela,
and their children were shaped into the Three Peoples. It is a holy
place, and your Vision confirms that if you think about it.

"But what you described is a surprise to me. Your Vision
altogether had some elements in it that were unusual. For example,
the Qeteral woman that you saw seemed to actually acknowledge
your presence. You say that element switched from daylight to
nighttime, just as it obviously was as you were sleeping. That is a very
telling detail. It was as if she were having a Vision at the same time
as you. I frankly think that's a pretty good guess as to what happened,
and Meical almost certainly directed it. I rather don't think her
sensing you was important for you, because I don't think it makes any
difference in how we manage to go about finding her, but it does
make me think that it may have been specifically critical to her. The
Qeteral have a different manner of understanding Meical and have a
sense of fate, more so than we Humans who feel we are more in
control of our destiny. You said she suddenly had hope, and I think

Meical saw a need and was offering that hope to her by letting her feel you.

"Then, yes, what you experienced at the end of the Vision seems to me…well I don't really know, Kodi. It was obviously a very powerful spiritual experience. It is common for Meical to speak to the Gifted in their Visions, but it was as if He were connecting Himself to you in a different sort of way. He Called you to dive into the Lake water?"

"Not exactly. I wanted to jump in. Whatever it was about that Lake I wanted it, and without actually saying anything He implied I could go right ahead, so of course I did. I stripped and dived. Now that I know the legend you're telling me, maybe I was being— drinking that water—I don't know, re-made? Into a better or new man, I hope. Kind of like that First Man from the Song."

Curdoz fully agreed with Idamé back in Felto when she told the twins they had a serious sense of purpose. "I think you're right. In fact, you should always look back on that and consider it in exactly that way. I really believe you've discovered the metaphor of that element in your Vision. Symbols are critical to our lives. You're a pretty smart fellow, Kodi."

"No. Lyndz is the smart one."

"Well then you're doing a good job of fooling me. That doesn't happen often! But listen. You need to know you're a good man already, Kodi. I'm not saying that just to build you up. I don't think you need that very much, frankly, you're fully confident and competent. What I am doing is expressing a truth that deserves to be expressed from what I see in you, from your demeanor, your character, and your words. If you've made errors in your past, Kodi, I would suggest that so far they are few, and little harm has come of them. You hear me? Maybe you were lucky, or maybe you were blessed. However, every person in Felto that I spoke with talked admirably and with great enthusiasm of you and your sister. The reputation the two of you have for character is the best. One would be hard-pressed to find it at your young age anywhere.

"Meical has connected with you in a unique way, but I would say the Guardian knew exactly what He was doing. The fact that you listened for and searched for His Voice and followed it over the mountains to the Valley, and that you wanted with all your soul to jump into that water says something about you: willingness, boldness, risk, desire for that which is good, a penchant perhaps for, at least most of the time, making right choices. Meical needs you, Kodi, you hear me? You say he called you His *brother.* That is rare. You're young and you've perhaps indulged in an indiscretion or two, sure. You're not perfect and nobody is. Some who have great regret request formal Absolution, yet you don't need it, and the Guardian seems to have renewed your spirit in His own way anyhow. There is a wisdom and graciousness about you that is unusual, even for those with more experience of the world. And I know we don't know what your Gifts are yet, but whatever your particular tasks are Meical is telling you you're the man who has what it takes to complete them."

Kodi looked over at Curdoz and nodded his heartfelt appreciation for his words. Kodi did not often need the confirmation of others, for his self-confidence, like the Sage admitted, was perfectly healthy, but he was not deaf to such high praise from the Sage of Solanto. It meant something to Kodi, and if he did harbor any lingering doubts about his current path, or regrets pertaining to his relationship with his father, they were now dispelled.

Chapter 11—The Principality of Hesk

On the Hescian road, far fewer people recognized the Sage or his green stole, and those few who did were tradesmen from other parts of the kingdom, and they greeted him with as much delight as they would have elsewhere. Curdoz inevitably acted cheerily, dismounted and pronounced the common Affirmation upon them.

They passed several estates similar to Gant's and villages little different than the first one Kodi saw when they topped the Highlands. Curdoz told Kodi the names of each of the barons who dwelt in these and a brief bit about them. The younger man was surprised by how much Curdoz knew, as Curdoz admitted that almost never would any of these barons travel to Ferostro to sit on the King's Council. The Sage finally related to him that there was a period of years long ago in which he visited Hesk more regularly in an attempt to persuade them to the cause of the Reforms, and so he had stayed with many of them, or their fathers in some cases, on their estates. He had some hopes they would listen and then in turn persuade the prince, but it was all a great failure. Since then, Curdoz refused to allow them to provide him hospitality since the source of their wealth and prosperity derived mostly from poor, peasant labor. He then ordered all those in the Order never to yield to the invitations of the Hescian barons but to stay either at inns, though these were very few, or at the soldier strongholds, on their pilgrimages to and from the monastery in Aster.

None of this information, of course, gave Kodi any greater love for the place or its leadership. His pity for the peasantry, however, continued to grow. He considered what Curdoz said about his grandfather. Yugan had been very open with him about his life as a soldier, but some of these insinuations of Curdoz' had not occurred to Kodi before.

The traffic increased markedly as roads from cities further south in the Principality merged with the road to Aster. Each evening the Sage stopped for the night at strongholds containing barracks of Hescian soldiers, not unlike the one in Thorune. Though the captains at each of these acted with proper respect towards Curdoz when he introduced himself, and offered the travelers sufficient food and warm lodging, they were not as open or friendly as Captain Santher or other Kingsmen by a long shot. Occasionally, a young soldier would attempt to make conversation with either Curdoz or Kodi, but inevitably an officer would come by and order the soldier to some duty.

The one thing, however, that did elicit some friendliness on the part of the Hescian soldiers was the presence of Musca. Without fail, the soldiers would remark upon the beautiful animal, for though nearly all had heard of the reputation of Elentine Nobles, few had ever seen one unless they were older soldiers who had trained with the Elenite army in the few short years following the last war when there was more friendly contact between the two peoples. They allowed the dog a break from his typical late evening hunting exploits by providing him with as much meat from their kitchens as he could possibly want. There was no doubt that Musca proved more popular than his human masters.

It rained cold and heavily on the second night, and by morning there was no more snow visible anywhere on their route through the Highland. On the third day from the Ramp, in the morning, the travelers began their approach to the city of Aster. The traffic was much greater with constant coming and going of all sorts of people from very rich to beggarly, along with soldiers, and tradesmen with their goods loaded on great wagons. Kodi hadn't seen as much activity since he had traveled to the port of Ross with his father two years prior. By the fourth hour they could see the domes of the bright city resplendent in the sun. Kodi had never seen a city so large. He was surprised when Curdoz told him that Aster was actually more populous than Ferostro, the Solantine capital where King Carlomen had his palace. Despite Kodi's dislike now for all things Hescian, he had to admit that upon first sight, Aster was indeed impressive.

Curdoz pointed out the golden dome of the Prince's Palace.

"So it is Ralsheen, then, is it?" asked Kodi.

"Around six hundred years old, built at the height of the Ralsheen era. It is a splendid place I must admit, on the edge of the river which spreads out wide like a shallow, though picturesque canyon. You will find the palace smaller than King Carlomen's castle, but certainly more sumptuously decorated. There is enough gold on that dome to feed all the peasants in this principality for a hundred years. I'm not opposed to art and magnificent architecture, by any means, but there is a difference, say, between the splendor of the old emperor's palace in Tirilorin that was built freely by the Etoppsi and decorated with gold given in free tribute by the nations of the world, and a place such as this that was built at the beginning of the Dark Times and the slave era of the Ralsheen long ago and continues to be enhanced with wealth drawn partly upon the backs of peasants.

"I'm not implying it should be torn down, either. I just wish...I just wish, Kodi, that they would spread the wealth some. If they had implemented the Reforms, they would have gained greater wealth in time through increased trade, although at the loss of some of their rigid control over the people. Oh well. Maybe someday, Kodi. Maybe someday."

"Sounds to me there would have to be an overthrow of the princes, sir, considering everything you've told me about them."

"Perhaps so, Kodi. Don't speak such thoughts too loudly here, though. All these people traveling, particularly some of the wealthy tradesmen or soldiers that have passed us would likely take those words directly to the prince, not with deliberate attempt to cause us harm, but rather to try to gain some advantage with the prince. You can presume that many you see that have wealth here are unscrupulous bastards," he ended with a whisper and a scowl.

Kodi laughed.

Curdoz then pointed to another vaulted structure with three smaller domes, and being turquoise in color Kodi knew they must be fashioned from copper. "Yes, sir? What is it?"

"The Aster Library. You won't find a finer collection except in Tirilorin. Not even the Valley of the Gifted can boast such a collection."

"Are we going there first then, to see your friend?"

"No, we will go to the monastery and clean up. You nor I have had a good bath since Felto. I want to find Novice robes for you there and speak to the Head. We will have our midday meal and then spend the afternoon at the library."

"Very good, sir. Can I see the monastery from here?"

"No. It is situated on the edge of the river canyon, but it is slightly east of the city. We have to go through the city to the other side."

They came to the city's western gates. They were of bronze and were similar to the ones at the base of the Ramp. However, these bore impressive moldings of a battle scene. Kodi was instantly reminded of his Vision and the gates of the keep of the Witch-queen.

But thankfully there were no monsters or mutilated bodies depicted. He studied them for a moment.

There were many Hescian soldiers just inside the city gates. Some were inspecting merchandise on wagons, while others were spread out at a number of large tables, for just within the gates was a large open area. Unlike cities in the kingdom proper, traffic in Aster was required to stop and the people to declare their business, but since there was so much of this the work had to be delegated. Perhaps twenty-five tables were manned. If someone had a cart or wagonload of merchandise he was subject to inspection, and even those like Curdoz and Kodi who were without much baggage had to dismount and give their names to be put in a ledger.

They approached one table where a Hescian captain sat. His work kept him so busy that he did not even look up until Curdoz declared himself. Whereupon the captain and those others within hearing distance stood to salute the Sage of Solanto.

"Your Grace! We had word from the staff at the Ramp that you would be coming to our city. Welcome! You and yours have the freedom of the city as always, My Lord."

"Thank you kindly, Captain." This man was at least friendly, Kodi thought, and his words suggested more education than that of a common soldier, rather like the man at the toll booth at the Ramp. Of course, he knew how to read and write since he was assigned to ledger duty. Nevertheless, Curdoz did not offer him much information. The Sage pronounced the Meicalian Affirmation, to which the Captain nodded and expressed appropriate thanks. But then, as the Sage was about to walk away, the Captain spoke up again.

"Oh, My Lord. I apologize, but before you go, I am required to take down the names of all who come to the city. What is the name of your servant?"

"Kodi Lunder of Tulesk, Captain."

Kodi instantly realized that the game was on, and he had to play the part. He was only slightly taken aback at Curdoz' use of his grandfather's adopted surname. Curdoz would not use the Fothemry surname, which would have caused great scrutiny by the servants of Prince Filiddor. Kodi nodded at the captain who looked at him and who wrote down the name in the ledger. "He is a Novice in the Order. We are on our way to the monastery where I will have him fitted in robes. And this is my dog. Am I required to give you his name?"

The captain actually laughed. "No, Your Grace. Beautiful animal, though. Very good, My Lord Curdoz. I have written down Master Lunder's name along with your own. Please wait a moment, however. We were asked to inform the major when you arrive. Major Gendurn is the keeper of West Gate." The captain then bustled off to a small stone structure just to the left of the gate. Within a minute he had returned with Major Gendurn.

The Sage took all of these delays in stride and of course Kodi had no need to intervene and kept quiet. The major's greeting was just as cordial as that of the captain, although his tongue was a bit more honeyed.

"Thank you so very much for the blessing, Your Grace!" he said after Curdoz again made his customary pronouncement upon the man. "His Highness asked me to deliver a message to you upon your arrival."

"Oh really? And what would it be, Major?"

"His Highness is of the understanding that you intend to make your way to the monastery, but he asks that you come to dine with him upon the second evening of your arrival. Will you still be present tomorrow evening?"

Curdoz sighed. He was not pleased with the idea of attending to Prince Filiddor. Nevertheless, he was not entirely surprised by the invitation.

"Express my gratitude to Prince Filiddor for the invitation. You may tell His Highness that I will gladly attend, but I am not inclined to a grand feast with many people present. Tell him my preference would be a private affair. I am not in the mood for grand gestures and displays. I am here on business of the Order, and do not wish to engage in show. Tell him just that, Major."

"Er...yes, Your Grace." The major's face flushed. He appeared petrified he had offended the Sage. Curdoz saw this but chose not to say anything that might ease his mind.

"May we go on about our business, now, Major? I wish to arrive at the monastery before the noonday meditations."

Gendurn allowed them to do so, and Kodi and Curdoz remounted their horses, and with Musca running behind they made their way down the main thoroughfare of the city. They did not speak, for Kodi could tell that Curdoz was a bit annoyed.

The young man contented himself by looking around everywhere. The city was indeed stately with wide boulevards, although the buildings were tightly compressed and Kodi thought it cramped. Nevertheless the architecture was interesting. Being an ancient city of the Ralsheen, most of the larger structures carried domes and their doors and windows were contained within curved arches. Some of the domes were copper, turquoise in color like those of the library, and others were bronzed and burnished. Only the Prince's Palace had a gold dome. In contrast to the country villages, all the buildings contained many glass windows, and there were hundreds of fireplaces spitting out heavy smoke. This was probably the major drawback of the city, particularly this time of year, for on occasion the travelers found themselves in clouds of smoke drifting on low breezes across the avenue. It never occurred to Kodi that cities could be so smoky. He coughed.

There were hundreds of people milling about, and Kodi noted the variety in class. Most were poor city dwellers wrapped in heavy rags against the chill, and a few of these were begging at corners. Others were of the merchant class, store owners sweeping the sidewalks and trying to keep the beggars away from their storefronts. Too, there were shoppers going into and coming out of shops, and including a few obviously wealthy people in carriages. Few were on horseback like Kodi and Curdoz, with the exception of some soldiers going here and there. All were busy about their day and few looked in the direction of the visitors, and Curdoz' green stole went unnoticed even by those who had to step aside in order to allow the horses to go by.

They finally came upon the central square where many hundreds of noisy people bustled about on their business, and to the left along another wide avenue could be seen again the massive golden dome and the accompanying minarets of the Palace of the Princes. To the right another lane led to the smaller but stately, three-domed library. The fountain in the central square was empty of most of its water. Kodi presumed that in far northern climes fountains had to be emptied in winter in order that their mechanisms and pipes not be frozen. Nevertheless, the statue of rearing horses in the center of the basin Kodi thought impressive. He wondered how old it was.

Curdoz allowed Kodi a moment to look all around, for this was an important perspective, and after a minute finally spoke.

"What do you think, Kodi?"

"It's all beyond me, Curdoz. I'm not used to such grand-ness, I guess."

"I am used to it, but I am not a city man, either. I grew up on a farm. Aster is a great city, but it is not a particularly happy one."

"No. I can see that. People aren't very friendly."

"Say rather that they are indifferent. They don't welcome strangers. Except for trade merchants and Gifted on pilgrimage to the monastery, few from Solanto come to Aster."

"Why is the monastery here, then?" asked Kodi.

"Oh, very good, Kodi! You do see the oddity, don't you? But really, it is for one reason, the library. But the Gifted needed their own space so as not to feel obligated to the princes, and after much negotiation about ninety years ago, the prince at the time finally allowed the Orders to establish the boundaries of a monastery within which the Gifted and the Monastics can order their own lives outside the rule of the principality."

"Interesting, sir. So you mean that those who stay in the monastery are not subject to the laws of the principality?"

"Exactly so. By treaty."

"By treaty! They insisted upon an actual treaty with the Orders?"

Curdoz laughed, pleased with Kodi's awareness. "One would think that open and friendly relations with the Meicalian Orders would be a given, and a treaty should not be necessary. Actually it was the Orders that insisted on the treaty. The time that led up to the treaty was a bit contentious, and the Orders almost pulled out of the principality altogether. Of course that would have denied the services of the Gifted. No Bonding ceremonies, no Healings, no more educated Monastics providing scribe services and teaching the children of the nobles. The prince at the time finally came to his senses, but we insisted upon a treaty. Remind me in the future around a campfire, Kodi, and I will tell you more. Let us go. It is another quarter hour ride to the monastery."

Finally, after much finagling through the city they came to the East Gate. Less traffic implied to Kodi that there was less trade coming in off the eastward road. There were fewer attendant soldiers, and there was no requirement to have your name listed in a ledger upon leaving the city, only upon coming in. A captain acknowledged them and nodded, but Curdoz ignored him, and he and Kodi trotted through, Musca following. There was some exclamation among the soldiers at the gate at the presence of the Elentine Noble, and though one or two nodded at the Sage, most avoided even looking at him.

Outside the gates, which were as equally impressive as the western gates, Kodi spoke again. "The people seem more excited about Musca than they do you, Curdoz. I don't understand. Do they not know who you are?"

"They sometimes show appropriate respect towards my Office, but unlike in the rest of Solanto, being Sage doesn't mean much to them. I have no authority here at all. I cannot issue judgments, and I cannot give orders. Except within the monastery, of course, I have few privileges in the principality. Oh, yes, and the library. The Sages may make recommendations for scholarly applicants for the head librarian's position, for virtually all the most scholarly are members of the Orders. However, Theneri has been librarian for so long I myself have never been required to make a recommendation."

Not a quarter mile from this gate, on the edge of North River Canyon stood the monastery of the Orders. A dry-laid sandstone wall enclosed a huge space with the exception of the furthest side where the edge of the canyon dropped some hundred-fifty feet to the river below. It was an attractive location with its view of the wide forested canyon and open sky. Cold breezes, however, met the travelers as they approached and entered the open gateway. There were no soldiers to stop anyone here, but there were a number of Gifted and Monastics moving to and fro between various buildings. These were not of Ralsheen architecture, constructed as they were within the last century using Classical Anterianhi. It was the style, though on a much smaller scale and interpreted in brick and timber, reminiscent of the stone buildings and palaces of Tirilorin, Ferostro, and other cities in the more recent empire, featuring pointed arches, tall windows and high-pitched roofs. There was no gold to be seen here, as that would have been extravagant for the Orders, but details in carved columns and colored brick created attractive art. Many of these structures were situated quite near the edge of the Canyon, and Kodi could see that several terraces were built out behind them. It was too cold for Order Members to linger outdoors, but Kodi could see a number of stone tables and seats with the implication that in summer the Gifted on pilgrimage could sit and look out upon the view as they meditated or contemplated Meicalian Principles of nature, service, and relationship.

When Curdoz entered what was clearly the largest and grandest of these buildings, Kodi's eyes were drawn upwards, for there was a tremendous amount of light coming in through the lofty windows, these being of a mix of multicolored and clear glass. Massive wooden beams crisscrossed the central hall, and large chandeliers full of candles hung from these, apparently only lit at nighttime. As was typical for Kodi he was intrigued by the engineering and he was automatically peering around trying to determine supports and structure.

It was of course odd for a dog to enter into the grounds let alone inside one of the monastery's buildings, so eyes began to turn towards the creature and his attendant travelers, and within moments they all saw Curdoz' stole and recognized him for who he was.

The cry, "Lord Curdoz!" made its way around the great hall, whereupon dozens of Order Members stopped whatever they were about and rushed to extend their respects and greetings. Kodi had the last week been on such friendly terms with Curdoz that all the bowing and reverence towards the man took him aback momentarily. But here was demonstrated the reverence the Sage actually commanded among most Solantines, enlarged further by the fact these were Order Members. As High Head of the Orders in the Kingdom of Solanto, Curdoz was to them a prince.

These were his people.

They were given a guestroom containing two beds with a partition between. The fireplace was quickly lit and before long the room began to warm. Male Monastics bustled in and out of the bathroom and filled two tubs with kettles of warm water for the travelers to bathe. Kodi had never experienced such a luxury, although the new manor in Felto was being designed with such amenities. He was used to bathing near the kitchen fire with a washrag and bucket, though in summer he would take soap whenever he went to the river. He adapted quickly and had a hard time making himself get out of the warm water.

The soothing comfort of the bath, however, did not last very long. In short order, Kodi was fitted out with a double layer of Novice robes sewn from itchy brown woolen sackcloth. Curdoz laughed.

"Etoppsi in clothes! I doubt any such specimen as yourself has worn such robes since the days of the First Sages."

Kodi looked at Curdoz. He did not understand the reference, unfamiliar as he was with Etoppsi society.

Curdoz explained. "Etoppsi do not wear garments, for their bodies are covered with short, dense fur. Clothes are unworthy of their race. I am complimenting you, for you have a toughness and masculine quality that just doesn't fit the typical Novice. Ha! Brown sackcloth is not what the ladies especially would expect to see on one such as you. Meical tends to choose those of us for the Orders who are quiet and contemplative by nature. Of course many of us worked hard when we were young, and are fit enough, but you have sculpted yourself and have inherited mannerisms that conform to a manly image, like Idamé was trying to tell you back in Thorune."

Kodi grinned. He was not unaware of his own looks, and certainly he had built a strong figure with his father's and grandfather's encouragement through years of deliberate exercise. At the fairs held in the summer in Felto every year, Kodi usually won every test of speed and strength among those his age. Few wanted to compete against him. "Thanks, sir. But are you saying I'm not meant to be in the Orders, even though I've had a Meicalian Vision?"

"Like I told Lyndz, you are meant for something distinctive. You were named *Kodi* for a reason, I think. Meical called you by that name in your Vision."

Kodi was confused but said, "He did, yes."

"You have repeated to us already the conversation, of course. I haven't told you before, but for many of us He gives us new names and never uses our old ones when he speaks to us in Visions."

Kodi was amazed. "Is Curdoz not your real name?"

"Well, from my perspective Curdoz is my *true* name, since Meical gave it to me. But I was given another as a babe. As the farmer boy I was Luvin. It was also my father's name. He expected me to be like him and named me accordingly. It means 'of the land' in old Anterianhi."

"Then what does Curdoz mean?"

"I didn't know until I went to the Valley and studied languages and root words. It is not unlike your sister's name, for the 'd' and 'z' close together come from the High Anterianhi word 'andz' which means 'wise' or 'perceptive'. I suspect when Meical does finally speak to your twin, He will use 'Lyndz' just as He used 'Kodi' when He spoke to you. Who named you anyway? Your father?"

"Grandfather Yugan, sir. He told me so just before we left Felto."

Curdoz raised an eyebrow. "Interesting. And in that case he likely chose Lyndz' name, too. I'm beginning to think that the Giftedness of your great-grandmother Kalemna did not skip so many generations. In some way, even if very limited, your Grandfather had foresight. The birth of you and your sister touched something in the back of his mind. He deduced your true names when you were born."

In order to keep up the appearance that Kodi was indeed a Novice, Curdoz had Kodi attend the noonday meditations. "Remember, you are supposed to be coming to the monastery to learn a bit of what life is like for Order Members, and if anyone asks, from here you will be traveling on to the Valley of the Gifted soon for the appropriate course of study. Tell no one anything about your Vision, and while we are here, pay attention. Learning to empty your mind in meditation can be of value for someone such as yourself who needs to find his Gift. You are meant for more than having Visions. You have a deep magic that must be discovered. So, do your best to follow what the others around you do."

Though the Head of the monastery typically led these, Curdoz as Sage and Head of the Order took precedence. Kodi, expecting more ritual, found the noon rite was not especially complicated. Men and women comingled in several rows of ordered semicircles on the floor of the main building, with Curdoz sitting on a simple wooden seat in the center of view. Perhaps a hundred and fifty persons were present, which included mostly pilgrims on vacation from their duties—Monastics from other parts of the country, and Healers, and now Matrimonials, too, though these last were not so common in the past—in order to rest and to renew their focus, but also to spend time studying in the library. All of these wore clothing common to their particular Order, practical enough. There were, however, at least four dozen Monastics in robes like those given to Kodi. These men and women actually lived at the monastery and cared for its grounds, planted its gardens, cooked for and kept clean the sundry chambers and apartments of the other Order members who visited on pilgrimage. Many also worked in the city in order to care for the poor, manage the orphanage, and to visit prisoners. Curdoz had told Kodi that none of the Monastics had any sort of magical Gift beyond Meicalian Visions. They were called to serve others, both lay folk and other Order Members, and to meditate regularly, offering thanksgivings. A number were scribes and many were great scholars. Only Monastics used thrice-daily meditation, but other Order Members were expected to participate when visiting the monastery.

Curdoz spoke a few words of greeting. Then, he raised his forefingers in what was his typical symbolic gesture of Affirmation, but when he did this, all those present closed their eyes and lifted their hands just above their knees, palms upward. Kodi followed suit, however he would quite often open an eye to ensure he was still doing what everyone else was. He found that following Curdoz' advice was not working for him. He began to wonder how long this would last, wondered where Musca was, figuring he was wandering around outside, looked up at the great windows for a second or two, pondered structural supports again, before he realized he was supposed to have his eyes closed and he snapped them shut. The silence lasted five minutes, although to Kodi it seemed like at least a half an hour. He gained little from the experience but a slight cramp. He was never one to sit for long unless he was doing some task with his hands like shelling peas or breaking beans, or applying finishing oil to some of his grandfather's carvings.

It ended when Curdoz pronounced the longer, more formal Meicalian Affirmation. There was some shuffling, and Kodi made to stand up, but he checked himself as no one else was doing so. Rather, all remained in place, their arms down and relaxed, though still attentive and quiet. Kodi saw that one of the Monastics then brought to the Sage a medium-sized book. Kodi was sitting somewhat to the rear, so it was a bit too far for him to make out what might have been printed on the cover, though it appeared to be decorated with gold tracery. Kodi noticed Curdoz look his way momentarily, and then the Sage began thumbing through the book as if he were deliberately looking for a particular passage. Kodi discovered later that it was from the Book of Histories and Prophecies, a book he had heard about, but of which most lay folk didn't read.

"The great crowd from the city and its surrounds came at Meical's bidding to take up arms against the Ralsheen. They gathered in the great court before the palace of M'gnani, a relative of the Emperor's. She and her Court had fled north at the approach of the Guardian. It was now dark and many thousands of torches had been lit. The High Guardian stood before them, and the Eight Chosen were with Him at His side. A green light shown around Him. A chant was then lifted up by the crowd. Conquer! Conquer! Conquer! And they repeated it for some time. Finally, Meical lifted his arm and admonished the crowd to silence, and His voice carried far. "No! I tell you all! I am not calling you only to conquest! You do not yet understand. These years have created among you such a thirst for vengeance and power over those who have wronged you. Though it is the Ralsheen nobility who have made you slaves to their will, you have nevertheless taken part in their savagery against one another. Because of that you do not understand the purpose of war." Some cried out, "Master, if You are not calling us to rise up against our oppressors, then what would You have us do?" With great dignity in His voice the Guardian replied to them. "You shall indeed rise up, and I have called you to do so, and we shall fight the oppressors, and the Ralsheen will fall. But the purpose of war is not conquest!" One of the Chosen, Lphai, the one who later became first High Priest replied, "Tell us, then, Master, what is its purpose?" Meical replied again to the people, "The purpose of war is not conquest but to return freedom to a people from whom it was wrongly taken, to bring order out of chaos, and to make your world a better place for your children. You cannot do this as slaves to evil masters. If you will it, you shall freely serve a new ruler, one who will provide proper leadership and bring peace." The crowd cheered. There must have been at least twenty thousands, but all replied in one voice, "We wish to serve You, Meical, our Good Master!" For they at first believed He was talking of Himself. But he replied, "I will be here only a little while," and He pointed to the Chosen standing behind him. "These Eight you will acknowledge, whom I have called and who have served me faithfully and will serve you. They shall anoint Kings of several Kingdoms. And you shall have a new Emperor, and he will keep the Kingdoms united. Your slave markets and temples of evil sacrifice shall be utterly destroyed. You will have peace for many long years. But do not be complacent, but be diligent, for though we fight now, we will not destroy all evil." They questioned Him further, but He refused to answer. Lphai whispered to Him, "But Master, they wish to know more of those times." The Guardian smiled at Lphai, and said quietly to him only, "I cannot foresee that far. I cannot answer all questions. I do not know all answers." "But you are our Guardian," said Lphai. "I am of many

worlds and my cares are great. I serve the Maker, who is greater than I. You know this." "Yes, Lord, You have told us so, and You said so, too, in the Ancient Book." "Then you also know that evil is inherent in your world since the Rebellion of the Earthbuilders, and though a thousand of your years have passed since I imprisoned the Rebellious Ones behind the Guarded Teeth, still they are a part of this world. The Maker put them here." Again, Lphai responded, "If you stay You can protect us, Lord." Meical replied, "Perhaps I could, but it is not my Purpose. I cannot stay! The evil in your world must be conquered by those who live in it. I can only help, and only for a short while." "But Lord! No one in our world has Your power!" "You are not wrong insofar as what you think of as 'power'. Not yet, anyway. I will plant seeds. You will have Gifted ones with power, but the greater power is that of the hearts of all the peoples of your world." Lphai was perplexed. "Lord Guardian! How do you mean?" "Exactly as I have said." Lphai looked down. One question from the front of the crowd then caught the Guardian's attention, and he turned to the crowd again. A woman's voice it was, and she had asked, "Who will be our new Emperor, Lord Guardian?" The Guardian then demonstrated his Authority, found the woman with His piercing eyes calling her by name. "Moronia Terianh, you know him best of all!" And He smiled at her as He said this. She was astonished beyond all measure, and she looked around at those near her, but it seemed as if no one but she had heard the Guardian's voice. But Lphai too heard and wrote down these words."

Leaving Musca at the Monastery, in mid-afternoon the two men walked together back to the city. It would have been difficult for Kodi to ride anyway with his new Novice robes. It took longer, but they had time to converse quietly as they walked. Kodi asked Curdoz. "Sir, why did you choose that reading?"

Curdoz placed his hand on Kodi's shoulder. "It seemed fitting. It was for you, actually."

"I saw you look at me. I liked it. Grandpa doesn't have a copy of the Book of Histories and Prophecies. I've never heard that story before. I've heard stories about Terianh, but I haven't really heard about how Meical chose Terianh. Moronia was his mother?"

"You remind me when we speak to Theneri, and he'll have the Scribes make a copy of the Book and I'll have him send it to your Grandfather. It isn't typical that lay people should ever read it."

"He loves all books. Over the years he's spent a good deal of his profits from his woodworking on books. I'm sure he will appreciate it."

"I owe him perhaps a 'replacement' for Deroge's little book," said Curdoz. "But yes, I thought you would like that passage. It spoke of seeds planted and leadership. It also spoke of the purpose of war. I wanted you to hear it. But rather than me analyze it for you, I'd prefer that you ponder it on your own. I have asked the Head to have the passage hand-copied for you by one of his scribes. You shall have it before we leave. I want you to read it from time to time."

As they walked, Kodi did ponder. Was Curdoz saying that he, Kodi, was a 'seed' planted by Meical? That was the thought that continued to run around inside his mind.

Coming again to the great horse fountain in the central square they made a left turn toward the great library. The street was lined with attractive hedges and yew topiary that even in winter created an orderly and attractive garden-like avenue. This street was quieter, for there were no other businesses off this avenue and anyway, few Asterians would make use of the library except the well-to-do and of course Order Members. The noise of the busy square was left behind. Soon they found themselves climbing a short set of broad marble stairs and entered an attractive set of bronze doors opened by a solitary Hescian guard. Kodi wondered at his presence, but Curdoz whispered. "He ensures no books or manuscripts are taken from the library. You can hand-copy materials and take away your copies, of course, but the Princes have always maintained a policy that nothing original can leave the building. Not even I can borrow a book. It is not a bad policy, for such a collection needs to be protected, yet it is sometimes inconvenient. The Order Members on pilgrimage must walk here from the monastery to read and study for at least five hours each day. Knowledge is crucial to Members of the Order, for through it we gain wisdom. Or, at least it helps, anyway. The wisest also gain their wisdom from experience and even revelation. There is no one book that holds all answers. The wise allow for change and for the discovery of truth through the working of the mind."

"The Ancient Book and The Book of Histories and Prophecies are not considered to be enough?"

Curdoz chuckled. "Long ago, a number of the early Sages believed it was. However, it was soon determined that there was far too much emphasis placed on a book, when really a book is meant to point to something Greater than itself. And there were Visions, too— the Guardian made them understand their error. Now, we read and study, consider, speculate, and meditate. There are many hundreds of books and scrolls that have great value. If we presume all relevant knowledge comes from the Book of Histories and Prophecies or The Ancient Book, then, quite frankly, we simply do not wish to walk with open eyes. We would simply prefer it if others always dictate to us what is good for us and what isn't. Always, always have an open heart and mind, Kodi. Never allow yourself to be stuck in dogmatic thinking. Relationship. Love. These are the everlasting truths evident in the Creation."

They entered a massive central hall, square in design, but overhead was the large central dome. Windows encircled the base of the dome giving it light. To Kodi's surprise it was painted. Having only seen paintings in frames in a handful of grand buildings, he had never imagined that anyone could create a vast panorama on such a large scale. He did not at first understand what was depicted, but Curdoz called it 'The Condemnation of the Earth Gods,' and said it was a famous work by Zagrem, the greatest artist of the early days of the Anterianhi Empire, painted shortly after the Conquest after the library was built. Having only heard His Voice in his Vision, Kodi did not recognize at first that it was meant to be Meical. Yet here He was with stern expression pointing over the heads of a group of beautifully painted, fierce-faced muscular nudes both male and female, cowering under the gaze of the Great Guardian. Meical seemed to be pointing at a distant mountain range of unfathomable height.

"He…Meical has wings!" Kodi exclaimed.

"The Etoppsi insist they see him with wings, and Human artists often depict Him that way as a way to enhance His image. However, there is no Human account that mentions wings. It is believed by some that Meical appears to each of the Three Peoples in their own likeness."

"His face was not in my Vision."

"Sometimes He shows himself and sometimes He doesn't. With many, like in your case, it is only the Voice. Also, the gods as depicted express the imagination of Zagrem. They, too, could take on various shapes and skin color. Who's to say how they actually appeared, though as Zagrem was of northern stock it makes sense he would depict them with Human bodies and whiter complexion."

The room itself was huge though warm enough, with two enormous stone fireplaces. On either side of these stood attendants who not only kept them roaring but also were responsible for ensuring the fires stayed in bounds. Buckets of water sat in alcoves next to the hearths to be used in an emergency. Kodi had never before heard of such unusual precautions being used anywhere, but it certainly made sense here. On every wall were many hundreds of books, and in orderly bins were cylinders of wood or hard leather, clearly holding scrolls. Some wall spaces were open, and in these hung large maps in frames. All around them were large walnut tables with matching armchairs, and near the fireplace were leather-upholstered lounge chairs. Several Order Members sat in these and at the tables looking over volumes of various sizes, or even some of the old scrolls. There were also a handful of what appeared to be youthful, richly-dressed students also perusing through stacks of books, some at tables diligently copying passages under a Monastic tutor's guidance. These were boys and girls from some of the local noble families and of a handful of wealthy merchants, the only class of the prince's subjects allowed to use the library.

They approached a large, ornate desk of solid ambernut in the center of the room. Behind it sat the oldest man Kodi believed he had ever seen, and yet to his eyes the man seemed almost familiar. Though his hair was long and gray, as was his beard, there was nevertheless a twinkle in his deep blue eyes which was so lively and engaging it made Kodi laugh nearly.

"My Gracious! Lord Curdoz!" The man put up his arms in a show of surprise and nimbly stepped out from behind the desk and bowed to the Sage of Solanto. "Why, I haven't seen you in over three years, my friend! I had heard you had come to Aster. Come, come!"

He then gripped Curdoz' arm and practically dragged him across the central room to another domed room to the side. He had much strength for someone so old. Kodi thought him funny.

This section was smaller, though still lined with hundreds of books, and against another wall was a doorway. He took them through this and promptly shut the door behind them. A stone fireplace kept this room warm as well. One could see other doors off this room, and Kodi then realized it must be Theneri's living quarters. Evidently he did not live at the monastery with the other Monastics.

The man then bowed again, this time kissing the Sage on both cheeks in a greeting Kodi understood was common among high Solantine noblemen. He could not help but to like the old man. Something about how he walked and talked reminded him keenly of his grandfather Yugan. "Brother Theneri!" said Curdoz, finally. "How glad I am to see you again! Why, you haven't aged a day!" He winked.

"Interesting, as it would be hard for me to age any more than I already have and still walk around!"

"You seem as healthy as ever, I must say."

"Ah, but you only see the outside!" he quipped, then looked at Kodi. "And who is this young man? In Novice robes, eh? I don't believe it for a minute. Who are you trying to fool, Lord Curdoz?"

The Sage laughed. "The disguise doesn't work on you? Prince Filiddor is the one I'm hoping to fool."

"Of course. As he is the only one around who needs to be fooled! Ah, Your Grace, you and your tricks! Well, it shouldn't be too difficult. His Highness never looks below the surface. The robes should suffice. But, I say, you haven't introduced me, yet. Who is the sporting lad? You stripped a young knight of his gear and put him in sackcloth, did you?" He then walked over to Kodi, put his hands on his shoulders and shook him as if to see what secrets might fall out upon inspection.

Kodi understood Theneri to be a confidante of Curdoz', and as he thought the man so warm and friendly, he introduced himself. "I'm Kodi, good sir. Of the House of Fothemry in Tulesk."

"Oh, yes! I have heard of the young count! Hess Fothemry would be your father? The one given credit for opening Tolos to settlement? Oh, my, Lord Curdoz! I can see why you'd want to hide this one from His Highness. The Fothemry name is well-known, and I must say, not so well-appreciated around here. The question is why did you risk bringing him, of course? Kodi. Good, strong, name. Ancient Ralsheen, you know. 'Warrior'. Yes, sir! Rock solid. Novice, my bony ass!"

Kodi chuckled as the ancient man kept pinching his shoulders and squeezing his arm muscles through his Novice robes and slapping him on the back.

"Ever the perceptive one, Theneri! But he is here to learn a bit of the world. We are traveling together. Despite his looks, this one has had a Vision."

"A Vision! You don't say! Why would the Lord Meical present a Vision to a warrior?"

"I am not a warrior, sir. At least not yet. I hope to train as one, though."

"Would be a waste of material otherwise, I should say," offered Theneri, looking at Kodi keenly. "Oh well, Lord Curdoz knows what he is about. Am I to be in the know on this, Your Grace?"

"I think so, but only over a goblet or two."

"Of course, Your Grace! Make yourselves at home here in my apartments. The wine is in the decanter there. And I daresay you'd like a smoke. Help yourself. Let me go out and tell Thersa that I am to be occupied for an hour or two. She can handle the library. Indeed she handles most of the administration already. I have pretty much assigned myself to research and translation. I have plenty of work to do with that. Master Kodi, would you mind adding a few pieces to the fire? Just watch the hem of your robes!"

He bustled out, and Kodi was left breathless. "He sure has a lot of energy, sir! How old is he?"

Curdoz laughed. "He does indeed. Hmm, I don't believe he has ever told me his age, although I suppose I could look it up in the Records at Villa Saundry. At least eighty-five, I should say."

Kodi carefully added to the fire as instructed. The act reminded him of home, and he thought again of his grandfather. It seemed sad to him how age had come upon Yugan so much sooner than it apparently had old Theneri who was assuredly twenty or even twenty-five years older than Yugan, and yet who was clearly quicker and more hale. "I like him, sir. He's funny."

"He is full of joy, Kodi. He is a bright star in the principality; that is a certainty."

Kodi looked all around. Books by the dozen lay scattered on all the furniture, along with loose pages on two large tables. Kodi looked at these. It appeared Theneri was in the middle of translating into modern Anterianhi some very old documents.

"Wine, Kodi? We will be here awhile."

Kodi took the proffered clay cup with appropriate though non-committal thanks. He preferred ale like most lads, or something stronger when he could get it and when he could camp at the river with his friends, but he decided if he was going to travel in Curdoz' circles it was time he learned to appreciate some of Curdoz' activities. Curdoz found a comfortable chair in which to sit in Theneri's parlor and reached into his pocket to take out his pipe. Kodi realized something. "You haven't smoked the whole time we've been in Hesk. Is it against their laws?"

"No. I suppose because it is such an indulgence in front of Hescians who, aside from the nobles, never get to indulge much in anything. Theneri has that celebratory attitude, however, that tends to open one's heart, you see. But I'd better keep the fire away from his precious manuscripts!"

Kodi laughed as he sipped his wine, puckering at the bitterness. He sat at another chair at one of Theneri's work tables.

The old man returned momentarily with bread and cheese, talking cheerily and continually. After a few minutes he finally sat, and listened resolutely for the next hour as Curdoz explained all about his business and the Visions. Theneri was enraptured by the whole tale, nodding profusely.

"Unbelievable, Your Grace," he said when Curdoz appeared to be done. "Tell me, then, why you have come to Aster. Sounds to me you have gone out of your way. Must be important, though."

"Two reasons, really. First of all I need to question you about something. Perhaps you can clarify and ease my mind. That is at least what I am hoping." Curdoz then went on to explain the tale told him by Danly and Xeno.

Theneri remembered them clearly, remarking upon their scholarship. "Oh, yes! I liked those two very much. Brilliant minds, both of them. Few have entered these doors so willing to learn, who already knew so much, and with whom I actually enjoyed conversation! Brother Danly even knows Ralsheen!"

"Then do you have something to offer on the presence of three Ice Tribesmen in Hesk? Is it, as I suspect, something to do with the fur trade?"

The librarian looked at Kodi and grinned. "Does this here overeager, aspiring knight hiding behind Monastic sackcloth know of my especial *nature?*"

Kodi chuckled, full-willing to engage the old man's humorous side. "That you're not really an old man with a long gray beard and hair, but rather a young princess in masquerade?" Kodi reached out and yanked familiarly on Theneri's whiskers. "How did you glue those on then, sir? I need to learn your tricks!"

The man guffawed with unrestrained glee. "Thank the Guardian, His Grace is taking up with a clown or two. He can use a laugh!"

Curdoz chortled. "All right, you two! Speak your mind, Theneri. The clown knows your secrets."

"At least the ones I've told His Grace, eh?" Theneri calmed down and continued with his take on the Ice Tribesmen. "The Brothers' information is curious. I have sent to you a coded report, but obviously you have not received it, yet. I knew the three foreigners were here, Lord Curdoz, but I have not been able to achieve the state of mind needed for Moment-mastering. I wanted to gain access to the Palace while they were meeting with the Prince, but my skills eluded me. It is difficult now, for me, and I admit my worth to you as an informant is very limited these days. I can get into the Mode, but once there I cannot move out of the Dome of Light. I cannot go anywhere. I used to use it all the time, you know. I could sit at my chair translating, and if I needed to reference something, I could enter the Mode and go hunt for whatever it was anywhere in the library, come back to the real world and keep working. Such a time-saver! Of course, it could make me quite lazy! Ha!"

Kodi thought all this fascinating. He had heard of Moment-mastering, but had no knowledge of how it worked. Here was the only known living Moment-master in front of him, but apparently he had lost his Gift due to his extreme age. He wondered what "Mode" and "Dome of Light" meant.

"I knew it was becoming more difficult for you," said Curdoz. "Can you tell me what you put in the report I haven't yet received?"

"It is limited, I must say. The three did stay as the guests of the Prince inside his palace. Close guard was placed on them at all times. They would on occasion move about the city in the quiet of the night, which is apparently when the Brothers saw them. Finally, they left the city on the eastward road under escort at night. What minimal information I have gained is from servants in the palace, and only the Head of the monastery, Jarom, knows I am your informant. He was the one who told me of the Tribesmen leaving the city, but I'm thinking now it is likely he gained that knowledge from the Brothers, for the story is the same."

"Did you see them? How would you describe them?"

Unfortunately, Theneri had no new information to offer Curdoz other than what was already told by the Brothers. He did, however, offer an opinion.

"I will say this, though. A palace servant told me they were here on negotiations for the fur trade, for that is what he was told by the guards, but despite that, I have doubts. Which is why I sent you a report."

"What do you think, then?"

"I think they were here for the purpose of negotiating something else. Something secretive. Danly and Xeno were right to be suspicious. There was a summons issued to the nobles who live near and are close to the Prince. Ultrech, Funeas...the usual cabal! They met in private council while the Tribesmen were in the Palace. I have not one clue what it could have been about. But the fur trade cannot be the issue here. For that, His Highness would have delegated one of his cousins to meet and negotiate at a border post far away from Aster."

"Even if it were for the purposes of making it officially legal?"

"Yes. It is risky to bring Ice Tribesmen on a purpose to Aster, although very few of His Highness's subjects are likely to question anything he chooses to do. There are others outside the principality who come here on trade who would take enormous offense at the presence of Tribesmen. The only reason they were out and about at night is because of the city curfew, which the Brothers were not subject to, as Members of the Order. Otherwise, hardly anyone was likely to see them as they explored the city in the dark. In all likelihood the only people to see them were people inside the palace, and any Order Members, like Danly and Xeno, who happened to be leaving the library to walk to the monastery late at night. I'm sorry, Lord Curdoz. I have nothing more to offer you. But you can be assured if I should find out anything more I will report it to you.

"There was another suggestion that I made in my report, and it was the presence of the Ice Tribesmen and my inability to gain any useful information that caused me to suggest it." At this, Theneri paused and sighed deeply. "You need to replace me, My Lord. And I don't mean as Head Librarian, but as an informant I am of no more value with Moment-mastering. I have contacts but they are few. I've outlived them all! These old whiskers are not glued on for show, unfortunately!" He winked at Kodi. "You need someone young, Your Grace. You send them here, and I can help them somewhat, and I can continue to send you reports, but I cannot spy anymore."

Curdoz thought for a moment before responding. "There are no more Moment-masters, which is the one way by which we have been able to gain information. What if you had a Healer Brother to lend you the Gift of Mind Support while you engage in Moment-mastering?"

Theneri considered. "I actually do have my secrets that even you are not privy to, Your Grace, and I would not be happy if they gained access to them, which happens in Mind Support. I don't know. But you already have somebody in mind, don't you? None of this is especially new to you, is it?"

Curdoz puffed happily on his pipe. "You might not achieve Moment-mastering, but there is quite obviously nothing wrong with your mind, Brother Theneri. You are sharper than Kodi's razor. I was thinking actually of Danly and Xeno. In fact, I've already sent word to them to prepare for reassignment. I will be sending them here. I was also thinking Danly could serve as an apprentice to you."

Theneri paused before responding. "I've been here for over half a century. No one can translate as well as I, and I enjoy the work tremendously. But, I am only here until the inevitable. I cannot deny that age is catching up with me, and my inability to use my Gift demonstrates that. I know I don't look old on the outside," he winked again at Kodi who chuckled, "but I am beginning to feel it on the inside! I am willing to train someone new to work with me. The prince would have to approve, however, even an apprentice for the library. Now that will require some maneuvering on your part. He will listen to your suggestions, because the only scholars who could understand this place have to be Order Members. Danly would prove a superior choice, no doubt about it. It's a bit atypical to choose a Healer over a Monastic Scribe."

"But not too much out of the ordinary. I am meeting with the prince for a private dinner tomorrow evening. Perhaps that is the opportunity I need."

"If he wants something from you, then perhaps you could work a bargain?" suggested Theneri. "Otherwise he is not likely to give you a quick answer. But on the use of Mind Support, Lord Curdoz, I would like to think on it. I ask that you not order me to do it."

"Such is a personal decision. But I would indeed order such a person to keep your memories private, not even to share with me.

Xeno is of course the one I have in mind for that purpose. Father Marco believes that Xeno's magic for Healing is maybe the keenest since the time of the Great Sages, with Mind Magic to match. He is of such character that he is unlikely to ever speak of your private matters."

Theneri pondered. "I did like Xeno. He was quiet and kind, subtle, and like I said, brilliant. It makes much sense to keep the pair of them together. I promise to give you an answer before you leave town. Now, what is the second reason you have come here?"

"Ah, now on that I need the library and your guidance!"

Curdoz removed from his pocket the scribble he made of the short passage from Deroge's book and handed it to the old man.

Theneri took it and looked at it. "In code, is it? Oh, of course! You need a cipher. I made that book of ciphers for you many years ago, Lord Curdoz. Do you not still have it?"

"I do. The correct one is not in the compilation. I was so disappointed in discovering your lack of infallibility, my friend." Curdoz winked at him.

"Really!" said Theneri, laughing. "Well, there are others here, but I need to know more about it to begin a search. What is it about, precisely? You copied it I suppose from what?"

"I copied it from a small book given to me by Kodi's grandfather. I left it with Kodi's sister Lyndz when we parted company in Thorune. It is a short passage, for I deemed the book to be of such unique value I didn't want to run the risk of it falling into Prince Filiddor's hands."

"I will buy into your reasoning. Very good. Do you know who wrote the original?"

"As a matter of fact, I am curious if you actually knew her once upon a time. Surely you at least met one another long ago. Kalemna Deroge."

Kodi happened to be looking at Theneri. When the name was said, it looked as if the old man's wrinkled face paled a bit. But there was only a very short pause before Theneri responded. "Yes, Lord Curdoz. Famous Seeress. I met her…long ago. She would indeed come to the library from time to time during her life. She was not a Member of the Order, but I would allow her to study here. She was Gifted…and scholarly. It was sufficient reason."

"She was my great-grandmother, sir. Can you tell me anything about her?"

"Your great-grandmother!" Theneri's eyes seemed to shift as if he had grown suddenly uncomfortable. He then stared at Kodi as if he were a new person who had just walked in the room, dwelling on his face for several seconds. He stood up, drained his still half-full goblet as he did so and walked to a window looking out upon a cold, late winter garden. "I…I had not heard that she had any children. Eh, tell me, Kodi."

Kodi thought Theneri's behavior and question a bit odd, but as Curdoz did not seem to notice, sitting back in his armchair as he was, smoking and enjoying his wine and looking at a small painting on the wall above his head. So Kodi replied, "My grandfather, Yugan, sir. He was her only child. He has not told us very much about her I'm afraid. Other than that she was a Seeress. He joined the Hescian army after she disappeared, fought in the last war, but then left Hesk to help found the town of Felto, our town in Tulesk."

Another pause. "And how old exactly is… Yugan, did you say?"

"Sixty-one, sir. Born in year 430."

Theneri swallowed hard, and he gripped the window sill.

Curdoz did notice, then. "Is there a problem, Brother Theneri?"

But before Curdoz could set his pipe down safely and get up from of his chair, Theneri turned around, all smiles. "Problem, Your Grace? No. No problem. Kalemna Deroge, yes. She was an interesting character by all accounts. But no, sorry, Kodi. I am afraid I don't have anything to tell you about her. Eh, when she would come to the library to study, we spoke very little. She was, ah, very secretive, you see."

For some reason Kodi felt that Theneri wasn't being entirely truthful. Yet the man was all exuberant business as before.

"So, Lord Curdoz, you are hoping there might be a cipher here? I am not aware of a cipher invented by Deroge and placed here, if that is what you are expecting. I will look diligently, however. There are many ciphers here, some very ancient that I didn't think useful when I made that reference for you. If you leave that scrap with me, I will see what I can do."

"Certainly. May we return tomorrow around the same time?"

"Yes, but…but please don't leave," he said, looking quickly at Kodi again, happy as before. "Stay a bit. Have more wine. Sorry I have no ale, my young lord, and a tall mug!"

Kodi chuckled. The old man seemed quite himself again. "Er, and how did you know that's what I was wishing for, sir?"

"Because at your age that is what I was wishing for!" He laughed. "Wine is for old men like Curdoz and me!"

Curdoz was amenable to this, saying there were few in Aster with whom he enjoyed the company. He filled his pipe again and relaxed as Theneri refilled everyone's goblets.

Theneri seemed oddly and inexplicably fascinated by Kodi, questioning him about his family and background. Kodi didn't mind telling him about himself, for he knew that Curdoz trusted the old man. He was only slightly disconcerted that Theneri would peer into his face as if to see if he could decipher some secret code behind Kodi's eyes. Yet he was warm and encouraging, and went out of his way to make Kodi feel at ease otherwise. Kodi still felt drawn to the old man despite the oddity of the earlier moment. Theneri seemed very interested in hearing about Elisa and Lyndz, as well, though not so much about the Baron Hess, interestingly, although Kodi reckoned it was because his father was already well-known. He asked Kodi to describe the ladies' looks and personalities, and was quite intrigued to find that Lyndz was a voracious reader and was thought to be highly intelligent and perceptive, an observation that Curdoz was able to confirm. But he would quite often bring the conversation back to Yugan and wanted to know where he lived while in Hesk and the circumstances that caused him to remove himself from the Principality and settle in Tulesk. Kodi didn't know very much about Yugan's early life other than that of being a soldier, but he described what he obviously knew of the kind of man his grandfather was.

"A Master woodcarver is he! And ambernut furniture maker?" asked Theneri, obviously intrigued.

"He only hand carves small items now, but he used to make large pieces long ago. Rather like the desk in the front of your library."

Theneri paused. "Did he ever speak to you…of his father?"

Kodi thought the question a dash odd, wondering why Theneri was so curious. "He said he died before he was born. He does not remember who his father was."

Theneri breathed deeply, then said, "Hmm, yes, like I said, Kalemna was quite secretive. And it sounds to me he is the one who likes books?"

"Yes, he has about a hundred books at home."

"No doubt educated. Is he Gifted like…like Kalemna?"

Curdoz interrupted. "Yugan is a gem, Theneri. I know you and he would get along well! But he is self-taught, through and through. Remarkable man, rather like you in many ways! He might have a touch of Kalemna's Gift, for he is quite perceptive, but nothing extreme. He looks a dash like you, frankly. That northern look with the light skin and blue eyes."

Theneri seemed to pale again at this comment, but smiled anyway. "Perhaps so! I…I wish I could meet him and all your family, Kodi! Thank you for telling me about them! I can see why Curdoz here believes you and Lyndz to be special, Visions aside! What, eh, are your Gifts? Yours and your twin's?"

Kodi had to admit that these were as yet undiscovered, but Theneri said, "Ah, they will be known in time. I wholeheartedly agree with Curdoz that even though your sister has not experienced a Vision, it seems entirely likely to me that as your twin, she will at some point. The two of you must be a counterpoint to the Dark Powers in the deep south, isn't that what you think from the Visions, Lord Curdoz?"

For several minutes the Sage and the librarian discussed this point. Kodi had not until now quite grasped this possibility, although as he played with it he realized that maybe the thought had crossed his mind once or twice, particularly when he would recall the point in the Vision when Lyndz' face appeared next to the witch on her balcony and the surge of hate Kodi felt in the presence of the Alkhan. He felt a bit uneasy at the casualness with which the two men spoke about it. With a bit of gumption Kodi poured himself a third goblet from the decanter and began to drink more resolutely. He ate some bread and cheese to try to keep the effects from going to his head, although another part of him didn't really care. He was getting a bit bored now, and wondered how much longer Curdoz intended for them to stay. Finally, he interrupted them, "Sirs, am I allowed to explore in the library?"

Curdoz nodded. "Certainly, Kodi."

Theneri looked at him knowingly. "Warrior Kodi! The books about Terianh the Great and the Great War are straight ahead as you walk out the door! I think I can tell what subjects interest you!"

Kodi nodded and went out. He spent a minute or two looking around at the fantastic support columns that held this smaller domed ceiling, but decided that Ralsheen architecture was not so much to his liking. It was heavy and cumbersome, he thought. There were two other persons in this back room, but there were no tables. Here, one would find the volumes of interest and then take them out to the other room in order to read by the fires or at the tables. The two he saw were Order Members, and they nodded at him in a friendly way but went on perusing volumes. Kodi then decided to act upon Theneri's suggestion and walked forward to the selection ahead of him on the wall. It did not take even a moment to find the books on the Conquest and Terianh. Most were written in High Anterianhi, the old formal language which Kodi had never bothered to learn. Finally, however, he discovered what appeared to be an almost new book, opened it, and was relieved to see it was written in the modern dialect. One of the first pages contained a pasted-in woodcut depicting the statue of Terianh the Great on his horse in front of the imperial palace, the very one from Kodi's dream. Believing this rather portentous, he took it from the shelf, went out to the great room, sat in a large leather chair close to one of the fireplaces and began to read.

It was at least two more hours and approaching dinner time before Curdoz and Theneri emerged. By that time, Kodi had become engrossed in his volume. Terianh was his greatest hero, and he devoured the pages as readily as Lyndz did books on gardening. It contained great biographical detail, and even appeared as though later on might go into details of battles and strategies. Yugan had no books with this much information on Terianh.

He was mildly startled to realize Theneri was peering over his shoulder.

The old man whispered, "Kodi, I have my own copy of that book, for I made two of them. Would you like to borrow it while you are here?"

Kodi answered in the affirmative and before he and Curdoz left the library, Theneri returned and had come to the front door, explaining to the guard that it was his own book that Kodi was taking from the library. The guard nodded unquestioningly. He seemed a bit nervous with Curdoz present, and he hardly looked at the book. Curdoz reminded Theneri they would return the next day, and he and Kodi made their way back to the monastery.

As they walked, Curdoz spoke. "Interesting character, isn't he, Kodi? One of the most intelligent people I know. He was very intrigued by you. He agrees with me that your Vision destines you for great things."

"I like him very much, sir. He reminds me a lot of Grandpa."

Back inside the library, the old man's face had turned from his typical cheeriness to one of stunned apprehension.

"Is there a problem, Brother Theneri?" asked Thersa, the Monastic clerk. She was sitting at the large ambernut desk, in the spot where Theneri himself usually sat.

"No," he lied. "But I could use your help for a moment, Sister Thersa. Help me find the maker's name on this desk."

"The maker's name! Whatever for?" she asked with a laugh.

"Just curiosity. Now. It would be under the bottom, or perhaps inside a drawer."

Thersa continued to make snide remarks to the old man with whom she had grown to have such friendly rapport, but she did as she was asked. They worked at this task for several minutes, removing some of the contents from the drawers, with Thersa crawling under and around the huge piece of furniture with a lantern, but finally, upon opening one of the cabinet doors on the right side, she pointed at something. Theneri stepped closer. In the jam of the cabinet door was carved in small, bold Anterianhi script, a name.

YUGAN LUNDER A.Y. 479.

"Does that name mean something to you, Brother Theneri? If he is the maker, he does very fine work, doesn't he? A master cabinet maker, I should say. And the carved moldings are superb. I've always thought this piece was a bit princely for a Monastic! I suppose it well-fits our library, though. When did you acquire it?"

Theneri stood, unresponsive for a moment. As Thersa had vacated the chair, Theneri sat down in it and reached over again to feel with his own fingers the letters carved in the jam.

Finally, he spoke, though it was barely a whisper. "I ordered it several years ago from Tulesk. I...I never realized..." He trailed off.

Thersa looked at her mentor with a sudden bit of concern. "You act like you've seen a ghost, Brother Theneri. Who is Yugan Lunder?"

But Theneri could only play with the answer in his now troubled mind.

Oh, Kalemna! Why? Why did you never tell me!

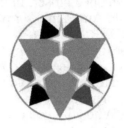

Chapter 12—Kodi's Adventures

If the Head of the monastery was skeptical of Kodi being a Novice, it wasn't evident. He apparently took Curdoz at his word. Father Jarom was not one of Curdoz' confidantes, though he liked the man quite well. Kodi asked him why he had not placed another informant in Jarom's position, to which the Sage replied that until now Theneri had been sufficient.

"Jarom's character and discipline are impeccable. He deserves his position, and the Monastics here love him. His regular reports to me include enormous detail which adds to what I receive from Theneri. But he's an innocent, Kodi, not the kind of person I need to put at risk and use in that sort of way. Do you know what I mean?"

Kodi thought he did. He had certain friends for whom he had high regard, but would never invite on his camping trips where some heavy drinking and bawdy talk were typical. "But this tour is deception, in a way."

"Only in part, and there is no risk to him. I really want you to learn what you can about Monasticism and its place in the Meicalian Orders."

Therefore, when Curdoz left Kodi with Father Jarom to tour the facility and grounds, the Head communicated with Kodi as if he were indeed a typical Novice, describing the daily routine of the Monastic life from the moment the Brothers and Sisters would awaken at cock's crow to when candles were extinguished two hours after sunset.

"...so, as you see, once you begin your study in the Valley and they work with you, it may be that they find you are a Healer and you will not live either here nor in the monasteries at Karuna or Guardian's Gate. That is, of course, if you are even assigned to return to Solanto. You may go to one of the other kingdoms, or Tirilorin. Yet even Healers maintain a serious routine, Brother Kodi. Your position in the Order depends upon your Gifts. But, if Lord Curdoz brought you here, he must be of the opinion that you have the Monastic bent…"

And so on. Kodi would nod at these sorts of comments, playing his part by asking questions he deemed appropriate, and he did learn a little.

At one point, however, Jarom asked Kodi a question that threw him off his guard. "…and therefore un-Bonded men and women serve together closely in the Orders. On occasion a woman demonstrates the Gift of Healing, and there are a number of them among the Healers, although never would one find a man serving as a Matrimonial, of course. But probably half our numbers in the Monastic Order and of the Scribes are women. So you have come to the conclusion you are willing to take the Vow of Chastity, Master Kodi?"

Kodi choked. In all their conversations, Curdoz had never once mentioned the Vow to him, although Kodi was well aware of it. The Vow of the Orders was one of those delightfully loaded topics the lumbermen and palace builders, not to mention his camping friends back home, would joke about on a regular basis, jokes to which Kodi himself participated in extravagantly. But not once had Curdoz mentioned it since they met. He wondered. If the Sage kept repeating that Kodi's Call was 'unusual,' maybe he didn't think the Vow was relevant in Kodi's case?

He certainly hoped it wasn't. He had promised himself since his tryst with the stablemaster's daughter three years before, that though he would do his level best from that point forward to avoid such a situation again he knew that once he did find his true Bond-mate, he intended to keep her, as his male companions would joke, 'well-satisfied.' Besides, he envisioned his future with a family. He was young, yes, but he maintained an undercurrent desire, one he had never spoken much about—he wanted to be a father, in addition to being a good husband.

Chastity was for real Monastics. Not pretend ones.

He coughed to cover himself. "Sure, Father Jarom! I've thought about it and don't have any problem taking the Vow." Though he was growing used to his false role-play, this was certainly one of the most wholeheartedly deliberate lies he'd ever told.

"Very good, Master Kodi!" replied Jarom with satisfaction, patting Kodi warmly on the back. "That is what I like to hear from a Novice!"

Kodi chuckled to himself. He hoped this tour would end soon.

When it finally did, he was left barely twenty minutes before designated bed time. When he arrived in Curdoz' rooms he found the Sage snoring softly. Musca was curled at the foot of the man's bed, though he flapped his silver tail once in greeting when he saw Kodi.

He took a moment to add wood to the fire, stoking it until it began to roar again. He then removed his double layer of Novice robes, which he found to be the most absurd and obnoxiously hot and scratchy things he'd ever put on his body. He went to the guest alcove around the partition next to Curdoz' own space, stretched and exercised for a few minutes, glad to bare his chest to the cool air, and finally tumbled into bed. After reading for perhaps a quarter hour Theneri's translation on Terianh, he dimmed the lantern and promptly fell asleep.

A low growl awakened him in the dead of night.

"What is it, Musca?" It was rare for the great dog to demonstrate displeasure of any sort. Kodi sat up. Musca looked at the door to the hallway and growled again, then he came over to Kodi's bed, looked at his master in the face and yipped once. "Shhh! Don't wake Curdoz! You need to show me something outside?"

Again Musca went to the door and clawed it quietly.

"All right, buddy! I'll come. Let me put on some clothes." He presumed there might be non-Monastic Order Members who might come in late from studying at the Library in the city, so he reluctantly put on the Novice robes again. "You'd think they would at least wear a linen shift under these stupid things." At least they were warm, particularly if Musca needed to go outside. After donning his boots he grabbed his hunting knife for good measure and tucked it into his belt with some attempt to camouflage it with a fold of the outer robe.

Near the front door of the dormitory a sole lamp cast shadows on the ceiling above. The dog trotted straight for the door, clawing at it as well. He clearly expected Kodi to follow him outdoors. It was curious. Obviously, the dog thought something was important.

"You'd better not be hunting!" Nevertheless, when they went outside, Musca led him straight to the gate. This Kodi found shut, but not locked. No one was around; the Order hadn't seen the need to engage Hescian guards to man the gates and walls since the last war with the Ice Tribes.

Man and beast made promptly for the main road. Kodi looked to the right towards the city only a quarter mile distant and was intrigued by the many lights upon its great walls. Here Musca turned as if to ensure Kodi was still following, and, satisfied, he led his master across to a patch of woods that bordered the road on that side for some distance, and then away from the Monastery and the city.

Without Orohmoon's yellow glow lending its dim hues to the forest floor, it would otherwise have been pitch under the trees. Kodi found himself becoming concerned as the dog followed beside the road under the cover of the trees for a mile or more eastward, stealthy maneuvers that seemed to Kodi unnecessary.

"Musca! What is it, buddy?" Kodi whispered. "I don't have my bow! We don't need to go hunting even if you've found some awesome twelve-pointer! 'Course it's kind of late for a buck to sport antlers. And how would you know anyway, since you've been inside all this time!"

He laughed at his own speculation, but when the dog looked back at him, he almost cried out in shock. Musca's eyes flashed bright green!

"By the Guardian!" Kodi exclaimed, although he did so in a whisper, as he felt an urge to maintain caution. However, the moment passed so quickly that after a minute or so Kodi found himself wondering if he had imagined it, musing it had been a reflection of Orohmoon or something.

They finally arrived in a thicket overlooking the road again, and Musca sat on his haunches facing it. The city's gates had long ago closed, so there was no traffic way out here on the approach road at night. Kodi stood next to Musca and looked all around, seeing nothing that could have caused the dog's urgent attitude, but then Musca nosed Kodi's hand and whimpered. "You want me to get down? All right, all right."

It was all very odd. Much of the dog's manner was familiar to Kodi, as the two would hunt together. Plus, they would hunt at night on occasion, so being out in the dark was not unusual, either. However, Musca had never before awakened his master and urged him out of bed in order to follow him.

They sat on the ground for long minutes, Kodi stroking Musca's silver coat. He had a good view of the road. A nearly full Solvermoon had just arisen above the tree line on its swift orbit, and there was now plenty of light for Kodi's sharp eyes. They were well-hidden, though the dog was panting slightly and his warm breath was visible as a mist on the cold air.

Shortly, Musca growled low again. Then, to Kodi's surprise he heard boot steps—quite a number of them—mingled with the clip clop of hooves. Before long, a troop of twenty Hescian soldiers appeared, marching along the road, their helmets and other gear glinting in the moonlight.

The captain of the troop spoke. "We approach the city, honored guests, and will shortly pass by the Hescian Monastery of the Meicalian Orders."

A guttural voice answered in a strange accent. "I remember it from before, Captain. Of course, Chieftain K'natel has not seen."

Kodi stifled a cry and crouched lower. He was astonished to see in the midst of the troop not three but four stark faces, much whiter in tone than that of their Hescian escort, almost ghostly in Solvermoon's light. It was the first time in his life he had ever seen Tribesman, though they had been described to him thoroughly by his grandfather. As his face was now right next to Musca's head, he heard the deepest, yet most discontented growl he had ever heard come from the beast. However, the snarl was so quiet that the sound would not have traveled much further than Kodi's own ears.

"By the Guardian, Musca!" Kodi whispered. "Ice Tribesmen! But how did you know?"

"Interesting," said another voice of the same accent as the first foreigner, though of a higher pitch. "There dwell those who actually worship the false god Meical."

The captain responded. "You misunderstand the Orders of the Guardian, Chieftain. The Principles and the Disciplines point to the Creator. Meical is the Guardian sent to our world by the Creator."

"Of course," snickered the man. "I…beg your pardon. We of the Tribes do not believe in…"

He was interrupted by the first Tribesman. "What the Chieftain means to say is that we have never experienced in our country beyond the Mountains the presence and workings of the Great Meical. The Orders do not function there. But it is understood by us that Solantines…and Hescians, do hold Him in the highest regard."

"Yes," agreed the snide Chieftain, pretending to accept the correction. "Ambassador K'trek speaks well our thoughts on the matter of…the Great Meical."

Kodi snorted. The conniving cynicism even through its foreign accent was obvious to him. How the Hescians could be fooled by it was a wonder.

Just as they were passing adjacent to Kodi's hiding spot, the Captain spoke again. "His Highness Prince Filiddor will gladly tell you more of Meicalian History, Chieftain."

"I look forward to that," replied the white-skinned man, although Kodi knew he said it only in order to please the Captain. In Solvermoon's brighter light Kodi saw the man and his companions were adorned from head to toe in rich furs. Their capes were fastened with elaborate gold brooches. With them were four stout mountain ponies loaded down with many fat bundles. Kodi wondered what they could be carrying. Or delivering.

Kodi waited with Musca as the troop and the four foreigners filed past. After about ten minutes, when he could no longer detect in the distance any boot steps or the clopping hooves of ponies, he stood. "Good going, Musca! Thanks for showing me! But how'd you know about it? You've been in our bedroom all this time haven't you?"

For a split second he imagined he saw the dog's eyes glow bright green again, but just as quickly the illusion was gone. The dog licked Kodi's hand and led him back through the woods, more slowly this time. There was no reason to catch up with the troop on the road. Eventually they came again to the point where they had crossed it. The wall of the Monastery was visible just beyond. Kodi looked, but enough time had passed that the troop had by now entered the city gates.

Making for the small gate of the Monastery, they had barely traveled ten yards when Musca growled viciously and barked once. Kodi reached for his hunting knife.

"Who goes there!" asked a commanding voice. Two Hescian soldiers emerged behind a group of trees, swords at the ready. Musca's stance was one of attack, but Kodi held him in check with a snap of his fingers. The dog came and stood in front of Kodi, but the fur stood on his back.

"Just myself. No need for concern, sirs," said Kodi, withdrawing his hand from his knife hilt and making great effort to appear at his ease. He knew the story he was about to use, some truth and some untruth, and it would do no good to appear nervous.

"Who are ye?" said the soldier. "No one is to be out of doors after curfew! Especially if ye came from the city. The guards at the gate allowed ye through it?"

"I am Kodi, and I am staying at the Monastery. I am making my way back from the Library. We were there earlier this evening, you see."

The second soldier spoke to the first. "We are outside the city, Garru, and the Order is not subject to curfew anyway. He is within his rights. The gate guards always allow them through."

But the first soldier looked at Kodi skeptically. "Monastic robes, of a certain. Though ye look rather young for a Member of the Order. Is this here your pet? Elentine Nobles are worth a right fortune in this country!"

"I am a Novice in the Order. The dog belongs to Lord Curdoz, the Sage. I came with him to the city last morning. Lord Curdoz knew I had become fond of his dog and allowed me to take it about with me."

"Lord Curdoz! I had heard His Lordship had come to Aster. Of course, he could afford to acquire…" The man sheathed his sword; the other had already done so as soon as he saw Kodi's robes. "But why are ye out so late, Novice Kodi? Did ye see a group of soldiers pass by 'bout twenty minutes ago?"

"No, sir." Kodi said coolly. He then explained that after he and the dog left the city earlier, they tramped the fields southwards scouting for a spot to contemplate the stars for a few hours and to watch Solvermoon's moonrise.

"We have no authority to question an Order Member," reminded the second soldier. "Let him pass on."

The one named Garru looked at Kodi. After a moment he nodded and appeared satisfied. "I have great respect for the Order. The Noble is a beautiful animal. I can see why ye would attach ye'self to it. Ye do have a honest face, Novice Kodi. Ye be from the south, perhaps? Ye look like an Escarantine."

Kodi knew his father's forbears originated from Escarant, nevertheless, he didn't wish to give such specific information that might in future connect him to Duke Amerro or his father. "I am not. Perhaps my ancestors lived in Escarant, I do not know for sure. Are you a captain, good sir?"

His own question, designed to steer the subject away from his origins, was calculated too as flattery. He knew the man was not a captain.

"I am not, Novice Kodi," the soldier said with a laugh. "We are assigned to watch the approach road tonight. Well, then. We are sorry to interrupt your nighttime wanderings. It is cold. I am sure ye wish to go to your bed. There are only a few hours remaining for sleep. Father Jarom will have ye up at the crack of dawn!"

Curdoz sat in his night clothes and listened intently to Kodi's revelations. Musca was asleep at their feet by the fire. Since Kodi was uncertain about the dog's flashing green eyes, he made no mention of it. But the Sage's eyes were wide as he looked down at the animal and offered a theory as to the dog's awareness.

"His kind were bred by the Elenites specifically for their wars with the Ice Tribes. He may have senses acute to their presence. It was smart to bring him with us, wasn't it? And by the Guardian, Kodi! You are the cool one. The story you gave to the guards! And I heard you from time to time earlier in the evening with Father Jarom. Excellent acting, I must say, though I hope you never try to deceive me! The question now is where we go from here. This is all very much out of the ordinary. The use of the title 'ambassador' and the presence of one of their Chieftains. Yet I bet most of those bundles on the ponies were furs as part of a cover."

"It's really bad that Theneri can't use his Moment-mastering, sir. But you will be going to dinner with Prince Filiddor."

"True, but it will not be the sort of situation in which I can wander the palace and search for clues, nor even ask direct questions. Theneri, though, you're right."

"Is there no Healer here on pilgrimage you would trust to lend him the Mind Support you talked about?"

Curdoz considered a moment. "Not without getting to know them better. The problem is that during Mind Support the Healer can read the other's memories. You heard Theneri. He is not prepared for that. But there is another way. I think he is afraid to use me, otherwise I think he might have offered up the idea himself. He could use you, though."

"Me? But I don't know anything about…"

"You misunderstand, Kodi," interrupted Curdoz. "What I'm thinking of is a different method altogether. You see, Theneri has no problem in accessing the Mode. His problem is that once he accesses it, he has no control. He can't exit the Dome of Light. That's the area of magical light into which the Moment-master enters a portrait of the moment. It's a confined area just big enough for two people, maybe three. That's where you come in. He can take you with him into the Mode through a simple magic called Melding. You would be able to move out of the Dome of Light into what is called the Sphere of Movement. It's the total area that surrounds the Dome about a half mile in all directions. You could then access the palace as his surrogate." Curdoz explained to Kodi what he could of the theory of Moment-mastering. "Theneri can tell you more, though. He will have to get much closer to the Palace. He surely has a secure spot near it that he has been using all these years to spy on Filiddor, and there is also a good possibility that through some of his servant contacts, he can find out in advance which rooms the Tribesmen are using. It is critical we look for clues. There may be papers spread about on tables that they will be perusing. You could even get into their packs and describe for us everything they have brought with them."

Kodi nodded. "That's amazing! I'm all for it, sir! But what if I can't read any of it? All I know is modern Anterianhi. I don't even know the High language, sir. I certainly don't know the Ice Tribe language!"

"Which is derived from Ralsheen, by the way. Another reason why the first method of Mind Support is better, since Theneri knows them all. You will just have to do your best. Nothing you take with you can be left there. Or it will simply disappear upon return. But you can take some parchment for copying and then bring it back with you. Of course, it could be that there will be no papers of any sort, but I think now the first meeting a month ago was to negotiate something in secret, just as Theneri believes. This meeting, particularly with a Chieftain present, is probably meant to seal a deal." He paused. "But you need a bit more sleep, Kodi. You need to be well-rested tomorrow afternoon when we try this."

"I'm too keyed up. I'll never get back to sleep, sir."

"Come." Curdoz stood. "Get into your bed. I can fix that."

For the second time that night, Kodi removed the scratchy Novice robes and fell into bed. As he lay there, Curdoz spoke.

"You've never seen me use the Gift before. Don't be startled. You won't feel anything."

Curiously, he watched as Curdoz then placed his right hand on Kodi's forehead. The Sage closed his eyes, and suddenly a green light emanated from his fingertips and sank into Kodi's skin down through his skull. He felt nothing. He wanted to ponder the green light and his first experience with the use of Meicalian magic, but within a few seconds after Curdoz removed his hand, the uncontrollable urge to sleep came upon him.

"Thanks, sir," he yawned.

"You're welcome, Kodi."

When he awakened, it was long past cock's crow. He looked out the window and knew by the light it had to be mid-morning, and decided Curdoz must have given Father Jarom some sort of excuse as to why he needed to sleep in. He certainly felt rested, ready for another day's adventure. Today was the Spring Equinox which marked the new Anterianhi year. He would miss the house-to-house Walking Feast back home in Felto when all the well-to-do families in the town would cook special foods and open their doors to all the villagers who would wander through and socialize and partake in eating all afternoon. It was one of Yugan's favorite things to sit in his chair in the parlor and greet the townsfolk, giving out tiny carvings of wooden animals to all the children, while Ansy filled the dining room table with delicious treats, her butter biscuits being the famed provision at their house.

Yet A.Y.492 seemed to have an interesting beginning, despite missing out on the old home celebration, and Kodi wondered how the year would progress. He used cold water from the wash basin to wash his face, then found that a fresh set of Novice robes had been laid out for him at some point. He picked them up. He looked longingly at the open trunk at the foot of his bed, where they had also returned his own clothes: a tightly woven linen shirt, his tunic of fine Scantian wool, famed for its smooth nap, and his matching wool breeches, all of which the Monastics had apparently laundered carefully and dried the afternoon before. Looking at the robes in his hands, he rather loudly and with disgust complained, "A Vow of Chastity would be less sacrifice than being forced to wear these stupid things the rest of your life. Bunch of knuckleheads forcing themselves to wear this stuff! And chastity! For life? Are you kidding me? I don't get the suffering and sacrifice all the time! What's the point?" He wanted to fling the things in the fire.

"The point is that you do that which you feel personally Called to do by the Guardian!" said Curdoz with a bit of snap in his voice. He had just stepped into the door quietly just in case Kodi was still asleep. "You think their own Meicalian Visions and Calls are less important to them than yours are to you?"

Kodi looked at him regretfully. "Sorry, sir. Er...New Year Greetings to you?"

Yet Curdoz had no intentions of letting him off that easily. "Don't try to change the subject! We live in a world of overindulgence, Kodi. Don't you see? Rich men spend gold to embellish their palaces and do it not because they appreciate the artists and artisans, wishing to give them an outlet for their expression, but in order to show off their wealth to their neighbors, and they do it while peasants go hungry in winter. And here in Hesk they make their gold off the peasants' labor. Too many high lords all around the kingdom treat their wives with the utmost disrespect and refuse self-discipline by taking lovers whom they lavish with jewelry and servants and fine clothing! Or much worse by using them as sex slaves. And there are those who are not rich who nevertheless imitate them by wooing young maidens whom they have no intention of Bonding, or paying prostitutes in the cities! Monastics are Called to live in contrast to the evils that wealth and envy often bring. They set an example of simple living and servant-hood. To you it seems a bit extreme, but you do get used to it in time and it becomes a part of who you are."

"Yes, Curdoz. Sorry. I understand the idea of servant-hood, just the robes and the...the Vow, seem unnecessary to me."

"It's not about what's necessary or not. It's about the Disciplines! You don't see what you're doing, Kodi. You're building up excuses in your mind not to have to follow the Call of the Monastic life, and criticizing others who do. You must be careful about this. So often when we criticize, we are separating the other from us, putting them into a category less worthy or less important than the category we believe we ourselves are in. You must still have a dash of fear that Monasticism is where you're headed, or being a Healer or something similar. I know it's not what you want, so let me ease your mind." The Sage's annoyed tone made Kodi feel ashamed, though. This was similar to how he spoke to Onri back on the Ramp. "You remember what I said about how Meical typically Calls those of us to the Orders who are more contemplative by nature? Heavy woolen sackcloth clothing, thrice daily meditations, even the Vow, I'm telling you right now that these things are not for you. Not all the Disciplines are the same for everybody! That's very important for you to understand. Yet there are certainly Disciplines for you! We don't know where you're headed, but very likely there will be sacrifices of other sorts, you hear me? War, pain, maybe torturous pain, and even death, since we seem to be on a quest to dangerous places with deadly enemies! There will come a time when sackcloth and the Monastic life will seem blissful by comparison."

Kodi swallowed. "Yes, sir. I expect to take all that as it comes."

"Yes, I know you will, for if Meical Himself has confidence in you, then I do, too. But complaining about minor discomforts along the way is weak. Keep above it. And I don't ever want to hear you ridicule the Vow of Chastity again, not even in a joke! It's obvious it isn't meant for you, anyway. I have a strong feeling that your life-mate awaits you somewhere in this world, maybe even on our journey, and I expect you to reserve your passions until then and make yourself worthy of her!"

"I intend to do that, sir!" said Kodi with an amount of heated sincerity. "I am not a cad, sir. Please don't think so of me!"

"I believe you." Then Curdoz spoke more softly. "But you need to understand that for those of us who have accepted the Vow, it opens our minds to Meical's Voice and makes us more in tune to our Call. Romance and family can be a distraction, and they commit our time and talent when they are required elsewhere, do you see?"

Kodi nodded. He'd reverted to selfish boyhood, forgetting momentarily who he was and the man he was striving to be, the man Meical was building him into. His successful role-playing of the night before, his discovery of the return of the Ice Tribesmen, and Curdoz' praise afterward; these had caused him to feel a bit big-headed. His juvenile outburst was atypical of him, and he regretted that Curdoz had heard it.

He donned the robes again. He tightened and tied the laces this time, deliberately making the garments hotter and scratchier than ever before. *'It's not about what's necessary or not. It's about the Disciplines!'* Kodi would remember these words forever, and he would apply them.

When he was ready he nodded at Curdoz who finally smiled and then did offer Kodi the traditional New Year greeting. The two left first for the kitchens for Kodi and Musca to eat, and leaving Musca behind, they left for the library.

"You could use your Authority and question His Highness. On the King's Council your position in judgment is higher than Filiddor's."

"He, nor his predecessors, have ever accepted the supremacy of the Council in the principality. You know that."

"I didn't mean *here*, Lord Curdoz!" Theneri laughed. He and Curdoz were debating the news of Kodi's discovery, and Theneri was trying to offer alternatives to the Meld and the use of a surrogate, an idea he seemed to think dangerous and wasn't keen on. "In Ferostro! Call a High Council and debate it. You said such a meeting appeared in your Vision. Quite likely this is what it is about!"

"The thought has certainly crossed my mind, but…"

"I see. It is a delay. You and the twins and Mother Idamé need to depart the country. But remember, you're on the Guardian's time, not your own. Based on all you've told me, your movements have been quite precise as far as that goes. Did you think the Council meeting in your Vision would take place after you leave?"

"It's a serious matter to call a Council, particularly one of Judgment. My uncertainty is that though the Vision showed Filiddor in a Council meeting, I did not see *me* there."

"But it doesn't mean you weren't there," put in Kodi.

"No. No it doesn't," admitted the Sage.

Theneri offered sound advice. "It is perfectly clear that a Council is to be called. The question is who is to call it. For all you know, when you get back to Ascanti or to Ferostro you might receive messages that the King has called it, or one of the other High Lords has. However, if not, then you must call it, otherwise you cannot guarantee the action presented in the Vision."

Kodi interrupted. "I'm not understanding something, sirs. Are you saying that events in a Vision don't necessarily happen?"

Curdoz clarified. "Ah. Kodi, the pictures Meical showed *you* are real. You can presume the enemies stood on their tower balconies, or will at some point, that the young man in Tirilorin did or will throw an apple. All independent of you. The action for you personally is implied in the emotions you experienced. You felt the urge to fight the Sorcerer-king, you told me. You felt with certainty that you would meet the young man and the Qeteral woman. But, no, the action is not a given. You must choose to go."

"You mean I could have chosen not to go?"

"Always free will, Kodi. Correct. You could have remained in Felto. But it would have been a denial of your Calling, and the Guardian's Work would be made more difficult to achieve. Perhaps even disastrous for the cause of good."

Kodi nodded. "I wanted to go, of course. But your own Vision, sir, showed…what am I trying to say? *Action* that is more obvious? Like getting on a ship and traveling, a mind map showing you where you are to go, walking with me, and things like that."

"You're thinking is good, Kodi," assured Theneri. "Curdoz' Vision was different in that way, just as you say. It demonstrated some future elements that are as yet uncertain until he follows through with them. Which brings us back to the Council. The Council must be called, and I think the Guardian expects Curdoz to ensure that there will be such a meeting. Whether he is the one who does the calling or not is really only a matter of reading clues. The only disagreement we have is that I believe the evidence for him to call it is obvious and sufficient…"

"…and I believe I need more." Curdoz said.

Kodi was confused by this. "What difference does it make who calls it?"

"Council meetings must be called for specific purpose, you see, and if I call it, its purpose would be a Judgment Council to present evidence to prove Filiddor is engaged in unlawful action."

"Oh. You don't just call Council meetings to bring the lords together to discuss, er, how things are going around the Kingdom?"

"King Carlomen can do that, and he does nearly every fall, and at those Councils we discuss the status of the kingdom and make new laws, but no, we other High Lords cannot call general meetings like that. Prince Filiddor virtually never comes to those Councils in any regard. But for a High Lord to call one we must have particular reason. And so I have hesitation to call it and bring an accusation against another High Lord. Such would be a supremely serious matter."

"Would it hurt you in some way?"

"It would not hurt me, perhaps Kodi, but it could permanently damage current relations with the principality. For all we know still, this whole situation could be related to the simple matter of making the fur trade legal. I don't believe that anymore. There is enough evidence for us in the know to believe otherwise. But there is not enough evidence yet to prove it to the lords in Council when Filiddor protests the accusation, and claims even in a lie, that it is in regard to the fur trade."

"I get it. Thanks, sir. All right, then. So, we, er, need to get more evidence?"

"Precisely. We need to get more evidence." Curdoz looked at Theneri. "So, are you going to help me and use Kodi in a Meld?"

Theneri frowned. He was clearly unhappy with the prospect.

"You understand there is real danger involved? Kodi's very life could be at risk. If I lose the Mode, Kodi would be lost forever."

"Have you ever in your life lost the Mode, Theneri?" Curdoz asked skeptically.

"No, of course I haven't!"

"That's because you can't lose the Mode unless you die just then or someone with great forcefulness interrupts you. All within those very few seconds! So, tell me honestly there is real danger to Kodi!" Curdoz admonished the Moment-master.

Theneri sighed. "No. There really is no danger to Kodi unless he himself does something stupid."

"I'm not stupid, sir."

"You know, I'm convinced every man under thirty years is stupid," Theneri replied, laughing. "When you're young you inevitably take unnecessary risks."

Kodi grinned at this, but replied, "What's the fun in life without a bit of risk?"

Theneri snorted. "See? He admits it. All right, Kodi. My biggest concern I suppose is that you may sense my emotions. And I, yours."

"Ah, so that is your real fear," inserted Curdoz. "But he cannot read memories in a Meld. Meical trusts Kodi, Theneri; you must see that in his case you may set aside your hesitations."

"Yes." Theneri stroked his long whiskers as he looked again into Kodi's face. "I'll do it, of course. Well, then, Kodi! Let's experiment."

Kodi had to endure a half-hour lecture on the theory, however, before Theneri was prepared to take him into a Meld. He told Kodi everything that Curdoz told him the night before, but added much, much more.

"…a Moment-master captures a moment of time so that he can examine it in detail at his leisure. But it is not the actual moment, Kodi. It is an Image of that moment. Rather like a very realistic painting of a scene, but it is a scene with every detail possible that could actually be found in the real moment. You can open and walk through doors, you can read through books, you can search through baggage. You can remove someone's hood to get a better look at their face. You can empty their pockets to see what they're carrying…"

Kodi sat there listening to all this. To him it sounded like the most incredible sort of magic he'd ever heard about. "And the person would feel nothing?"

"Remember, this is an *Image* of the moment. If I painted a portrait of Curdoz sitting still with his hood on, it would be as though you were removing the hood from the portrait of Curdoz, rather than the real Curdoz. It is all an Image, basically, in your mind, Kodi. Actually, it will be in *my* mind. It's not the real thing."

"And yet I could lose things in it?"

"Yes! There is great danger in Moment-mastering, for whatever you take with you, if you leave it there, whether you do so by mistake or with deliberation, will be lost forever once you return through the Dome, and I let go of the Mode. You would never want to take anything with you that is important to you and risk losing it. And of course, nothing can be brought out of the Image, not even into the Dome."

"But I can take my own quill, ink and paper, and copy, and bring it back."

"Exactly. If I've done that once in Filiddor's palace I have done it hundreds of times. The man and his father have hardly been able to do anything that I haven't known about, as long as it was something written down in a scroll or on parchment or in a ledger. Until recently, of course. The biggest limitation of the magic is that I cannot hear conversations. For example, until Curdoz told me of this innkeeper informant in Thorune, I was unaware that Filiddor used informants. He has certainly never kept a list of them. Again, unless it is a recent development."

"And you won't be on the 'excursion' with me?"

"No. You will be on your own once you step out of the Dome. Since everything outside the Dome has become invisible to me I won't be able to see you, although I suspect I will be able to hear. I should be able to talk with you as long as you are within hearing distance, for distance does affect the magic, but I cannot exit the Dome anymore. When you return to the Dome, then we can return to reality. And when you do, of course—this is the oddest thing to the uninitiated—you will realize that for everyone and everything else barely two seconds of real time will have passed. In your mind you will believe you have been gone for quite a while, but to any person present, it will appear you never left. And in reality, you never did leave, though even that piece of it must be qualified, as that is fact based on not losing the Mode magic, for if I did, you would disappear based on theory, if you are outside the Dome of Light. Where your body and spirit would go is unknown. But technically Curdoz is correct, for the Mode grounds you safely to the real world. Anyway, you were simply perusing an Image of a moment inside your mind. I mean *my* mind. However, my sense of the time taken will be the same as yours."

Kodi couldn't help but to grin in wonderment at all this. "That's…that's amazing!"

"Now listen. Our minds are connected in a Meld, and though you will not see my thoughts nor read my memories, we will sense one another's emotions. For example, if you come upon something that causes you to be startled or angry, I will sense it. If you sense my emotions, no matter what they are, I expect you to ignore them and focus on your task."

This last statement seemed to present itself to Kodi with a certain amount of vehemence on Theneri's part. Clearly, the older man felt a strong need to retain his internal privacy, despite how social and gregarious he might appear on the surface. Kodi felt, however, that maturity on his part was required in his response. He must reassure the older man. Remembering one of the most important truths his father taught him, he said, "Emotions come and go. They do not define a man."

He looked at Curdoz when he said it, remembering his own outburst that morning and winked at him.

Curdoz nodded.

When Kodi turned back to Theneri, the old man replied. "You are only partly correct, Kodi, but there are perhaps a couple levels to emotion. There is that which surfaces constantly based on what events are taking place around you at the moment. Someone insults you and it makes you angry, for example. You stub your toe and it hurts and annoys. A lovely young woman flirts with you and causes you to lose a bit of control, yes? So you are right by saying such emotions do not define us, for they disappear almost as readily as they appear, and one would be a fool, and less of a man, if he acted upon such emotions without thought. Insult does not warrant a murder. A flirtation does not warrant a mating or a Bonding. Our *response* to emotion can define us, and the axiom you quoted is really about being careful not to respond to emotion without care. Perhaps more importantly though, there is the other level of emotion that runs deep and actually does shape our character. It can include deep longings and loves, for example let's say for your twin sister, Lyndz. I suspect you feel a deep attachment to her and there is an unbreakable bond there between you. That love is an undercurrent always present and likely influences you in ways you are unaware. 'Twould be the same for a Bond-mate or for a mother or a father. And pains, too, deaths one has experienced, and resentments or regrets that go deep and are hard to let go. They affect us, you see."

Kodi listened. "So, you're saying we will be able to detect those deeper things, too, during the Meld?"

"Yes."

"I'm prepared, sir."

Curdoz laughed. "'Twould be nice to be young again, eh, Theneri?"

"Aye, 'twould indeed." But the old man shook his head and looked at Kodi. "Just remember to ignore all of it, right? Sticking to your first wisdom on the matter is sufficient, in retrospect, for the purposes of the Meld."

For some reason Kodi had doubts that Theneri meant what he said on that last, but rather that it reflected still his hesitation.

It was determined that the chair in which Kodi sat would be the Origin of Departure. Theneri brought a stool and sat at Kodi's immediate side.

The initial magic was similar to what Curdoz employed the night before when he put Kodi to sleep. With Theneri's hands on the top of Kodi's head, the green light surrounded his head and seemed to enter down through his skull. However, from here it spread outward, encompassing all of Kodi's body, and Theneri's, too.

He blinked, and Kodi knew something extraordinary must have taken place. He was inside the Dome, apparently, for everything was green. Curdoz had told him that green magical light indicated Meicalian magic. He wondered what other colors of light might represent magic from other sources. Everything except Theneri seemed perfectly still, frozen in place. Curdoz looked as still and unblinking as a statue.

Something else was strange, too—a lightheaded feeling that reminded him very much of the times when he would drink that second mug of ale that would cause his head to start stirring. Though it wasn't quite as pleasant as that. After a moment he became aware that something, or someone, was inside his mind. Was that Theneri? Kodi closed his eyes and dwelt on the sensation. There was anger, there. It reminded him of the time many weeks ago when he had asked his father Hess if he could go with him to Tulesk, but he refused. It did remind him of that situation, yes, but there was more to it than just anger. Rather, it was the resentment afterward. *Hmm.* He couldn't put it into words exactly, but he began to feel as if it reflected that whole situation, both the anger and the resentment in combination. Yet, it was very deep, as if the emotions were enhanced multifold.

So, this is what Theneri fears. Something happened to him in his past, like he warned me about, that affected him. He doesn't want it to get out.

"Is there a problem, Kodi?"

Kodi opened his eyes again and looked at Theneri. Kodi couldn't help being curious, wondering what a man who had lived as a Monastic and librarian for over fifty years could have experienced that would create such a strong combination of emotion. However, he knew he was making a judgment that was not warranted. He had not a clue what sort of life Theneri had led. Curdoz' chastisement that morning was about more than just enduring hardship without complaint. He remembered too Curdoz asking him if he thought the Calling of the Monastics was less important *to them* than his own Calling was *to him*. Such Callings came with profound sacrifices and choice-making he now realized. Certainly Theneri had lived a very long time and experienced a great many things, and as a spy he had involved himself in a certain amount of danger and deception. So, if these deep emotions and conflicts that partly defined Theneri were something the man was trying desperately to keep to himself, fearing to make use of a Healer for Mind Support—because it would allow the other to read his memories of these events—then Kodi understood why.

Theneri was suffering some deep pain and regret, far deeper than Kodi's own with his father. He knew his own was nothing to what Theneri was enduring.

And Kodi knew now that he needed to give Theneri his space. Kodi realized that if he himself suffered at such depth, he would very likely want to keep it to himself as well, or be especially careful whom he shared it with.

"No, sir. No problem at all. Just trying to get used to…the stillness of everything, that's all."

He set the shared emotion aside. He needed to concentrate through the lightheadedness that he was feeling, rather like he had to do when he was tipsy coming home after an evening of drinking ale with the palace workers and having to communicate with his mother or with Ansy in that state. It wasn't too difficult. In fact, after a moment or two he found it easier to do than the other.

Theneri laughed. "I sense both confusion and resolve in you, Kodi. Now, I presume you can see the Image outside the Dome?"

"Yes, sir."

"Then everything is working with the magic. That is good. Get up and step out of the Dome."

Kodi did as he was told. As he stepped away from the Dome, all was clear again. Looking back, the Dome itself was quite obvious with its giant, half-egg perimeter of green. Now only Theneri appeared green as he sat there under its light, though he knew the older man could not see him.

"Why can't you come out of the Dome, Brother Theneri?" asked Kodi.

"I think my age has caused my mind to be confused by a separation from reality. As if it were dangerous to me for some reason. I think my old mind is trying to protect me, which is quite nice of my mind to do that, don't you think?" He chuckled. "Inside the Dome, I am still connected to reality, and my mind understands I am perfectly safe here."

"But out here, I am…?"

"Out there you are inside an Image of a moment."

"An Image. But it's real, isn't it."

"It is more than an Image perhaps, for it contains most dimensions, but it is less than a moment of time, which is a necessary dimension for reality. It is as though you are separated from all time whatsoever. Time has no meaning there, but there is danger. You could indeed hurt yourself, or even climb and jump off the library's roof and be killed. You are subject to gravity, though the objects in the Image, less so."

"Then what would happen to me in normal time if I died here?"

"Well, in that case, you really would disappear as I said before. One moment we would see you, the next moment you would be gone. Forever."

"Have you ever almost died in an Image?"

"Umm, once or twice. When I was young I took more risks." He laughed. "But Kodi, when you think about it, you have all the time in the world to peruse the Image. There is no need to get in a hurry, to believe that you must accomplish a deed there quickly, or something of the sort, and thus put yourself at risk. You can take all the time you want to be careful. Nothing there is capable of reaching out and hurting you deliberately. Except me. If I were out there with you, I suppose I could punch you in the face!"

"And I could pull that old beard!" Kodi laughed. "Do you think I will be a Moment-master?"

"It is a very powerful magic, no doubt. Curdoz suspects you are meant to be a fighter for Meical in a future conflict with the Khestadone Realms. It is what you believe, too, is it not?"

"Yes. I think so, sir."

"Meical likely has something different in store for you." Theneri smiled very kindly in Kodi's direction. But it was warm and beautiful, even from such a wrinkled face, and his eyes twinkled, and accompanying it Kodi noticed another emotion.

He has a lot of pride…and even love for me.

Kodi admitted that he felt drawn to Theneri for some reason, liked and trusted him, but it seemed a bit strange that considering how brief a time they had spent together that the old man would feel such a strong attachment already like the one Kodi believed he was sensing. He would expect it from someone he was closely related to.

He had come to believe, though, that people could become especially sentimental in their old age.

"I told you to try to block emotion, Kodi. It is not useful for Moment-mastering."

Kodi grinned. "I...I'm sorry, Master Theneri. I...I feel your kindness. It is towards me, isn't it?"

"I think the older I get, the more I appreciate the young. I feel your emotion, too, and there is much...I think the best word to describe it would be 'genuineness' and perhaps a playful innocence and eagerness. It is all quite refreshing. You are so far unburdened by very much pain. There are hints of regret, bits of anger, but none of it has...damaged you. You seem a better man than I was at your age. There *is* more, Kodi, but...but I regret I cannot tell you of it. But you are like a hope that comes out of my pain. I know you sense the pain. You almost have to. Unlike you, I have a great many regrets. I trust you to tell no one that, not even Curdoz. Besides that, I can tell you have experienced joy before, and it seems to be what defines you best. And it rather transfers itself to me, and causes me to feel the joy myself. Which is very, very nice, almost making me feel young and strong. It was from your Vision, wasn't it? It must have been powerful."

"Yes, sir. The end of it was."

"Have you and Curdoz explored it together?"

"Yes, sir. He said certain elements of my Vision were unique."

"Try to keep that joy in front of you Kodi. Now, enough with the shared emotion. We had assured one another we would ignore it. And yet perhaps a bit of this speculation helps build trust...and a happy connection between us. Now, let us get to business. Do the task you were assigned and come back to the Dome."

Kodi then walked across towards the door. As he passed the fireplace in the center of the room, he felt no surge of warmth.

"What would happen if I put wood chunks in the fire now?"

"Nothing."

"But the wood chunks are real."

"Only *within* the Image. You could, however, knock yourself on the head with a chunk of wood, and the pain would still be there when you re-enter normal time."

"So I can only make changes to myself, and that which I bring with me."

"Correct."

"What if I brought with me tinder and flint? Could I set fire to my surroundings?"

"It is a good question, Kodi. Fire cannot burn without air, and the air in the Image is not quite like real air. It apparently lacks what is needed for burning. Even if you could make a fire it wouldn't burn the items there, I don't think. Fire would alter its nature, turning it into ash and smoke. You cannot do it. I've experimented with many things, and there are many interesting aspects to the magic of Moment-mastering. But there is no reason for you to learn it all." Theneri laughed. "Any more questions?"

Kodi shook his head, although Theneri couldn't see him. He grabbed the door latch and pulled. The door leading out to the library opened readily enough.

"Just one more, Theneri." Kodi couldn't help himself. It was all so unusual. "You can't throw objects, can you?"

"You figured that out, did you? The door only swings to the point you let it go, didn't it? You're right. You can pick up and move and use objects, but they will not fall to the ground if you let go of them. Even if you throw an Image object as hard as you can, it will freeze in the space right where you let it go. It's rather like molding thick clay. However, the items you bring with you do conform to normal nature, and you could throw that ink bottle in your pocket and crash it against a wall."

Kodi walked through the door and away from Theneri and the Dome of green light. There were several people out here, and all were frozen in various positions. One Monastic was halfway up a ladder with one foot on a rung and the other not. Since he appeared to be looking down, Kodi believed he was climbing down rather than up, otherwise he really wouldn't have been able to know for sure. A female Monastic was standing with a book open, her hands frozen in place while she turned a page. Another person, an Asterian boy, had apparently been holding a large book and it had fallen out of his hands and was half-way to the floor. The book was frozen in mid-air. Kodi chuckled. He decided he didn't need to tell Theneri that a clumsy boy had just dropped one of his precious books.

He walked into the front room under the great painted dome. He made his way around a couple of frozen people statues towards the large ambernut desk where Thersa was sitting. She was perfectly still with a quill against a ledger. She was entering names of books from a large stack on the desk into the ledger. She was blocking the drawer he was supposed to open, but he was able to shove the woman out of his way. He didn't much like it. Her body was like a dead lump, though more flexible than a statue. *This is just an Image. It is not the real person.* Kodi had always been one who refused to be squeamish about anything. He had no fear of picking up harmless snakes or doing filthy tasks, no qualms about gutting his kills after the hunt. But having to manhandle Thersa's Image was very strange. He did his best to smile his way through it and then opened the now unblocked drawer.

Inside was a stack of letters. As he picked it up and began thumbing through it, the letters wanted to separate and float motionless, based on how he moved them around. Only if he lay them on the desk would they appear to conform to gravity. He tried lifting the books on the desk, but he could not drop them. Just like the boy in the other room whose book was floating above the floor, these were, too. Everything he tried to move adhered to the spot where he let it go just like Theneri had said. He took one of the letters at random and opened it, allowing it to sit motionless in the space in front of him. From a pocket in his robes, Kodi withdrew a large tablet of paper, a bottle of ink, and a quill. Theneri had told him that he must use his own paper and ink that he took into the Mode in order to bring it out.

Just as Theneri had said, his own supplies did conform to gravity. He set the tablet and the quill on the desk as he might in reality. The more Kodi thought about the magic, the more strange and eerie he realized it actually was.

Diligently, he copied every word in the letter. It was a short letter from a local nobleman requesting Theneri's help with information which the man hoped could be found in the library. In about five minutes, Kodi had completed this task. He replaced the stopper on the ink bottle and returned it to his pocket along with the tablet. He had begun to refold the original letter, gather up the stack, and put it back in the drawer when he realized it didn't matter, really. He had no need to hide anything he was doing, for no one would ever know.

The large fireplaces were frozen. Orange and yellow flames stood resolutely like swirled glass. Sparks stood like frozen fireflies in the air. On a whim, he strode over to the side where they kept buckets of water for emergencies. He looked into one and saw the water there. He reached his hand into it. The feeling of the water was strange. It felt wet, but it didn't have the coolness to it one might expect. When he pulled it from the water his hand was as dry as before he put it in. He then reached into the fire. His hand waved through the heat-less flames, and they seemed to move aside and dissipate.

He had never experienced anything so surreal. When he returned to Theneri, he said, "I don't really like this. Nothing feels right. Nothing moves right. The air is stifling, even though I don't feel the need to breathe."

"I can understand, Kodi. However, it could be that what you have observed here is not especially interesting to you. Um, what place do you enjoy the most near your home?"

Kodi considered. "There is a rock in the middle of the Wolf River. I enjoy sitting there alone sometime, and everywhere I look is a great view. Or I will sit in the water in the rapids as it pours over me. I love it all best when the sun is hot."

"You might find that if you were there and you entered a Moment-mastering experience, you could enter the Image and explore every Dragonfly flying through the air, every fish swimming in the water, every bird in mid-flight, every tree and rock. It can be used for meditating on a moment. I used to find it very peaceful when I could easily exit the Dome."

Kodi could see the potential, but to him that which was real in normal time seemed more powerful to him. "But you would not be able to feel the heat from the sun, or smell the woods."

"True. I suppose for me, that which I can see with my eyes, or even my mind's eye, has extraordinary meaning. The other senses are less important to me when it comes to meditating. But it is definitely not the same for everyone. Come back into the Dome."

Kodi did, and after he sat back in his chair, Theneri released the magic. The green light faded quickly.

Kodi breathed deeply. It was startling to realize he had not breathed proper air the whole time he was gone.

"We're back, Curdoz," said Theneri.

"What? Extraordinary, of course. I've always envied your ability. I didn't notice you were gone!"

"Did you notice the green light?" asked Kodi.

"Maybe the briefest flash, but often as not only those involved with the magic tend to even notice it."

"Well, Kodi, you managed that? Let's see the tablet and ink bottle and quill."

He handed over the tablet and the ink bottle. "Oh, no! I forgot the quill!"

Theneri looked at him with an annoyed smirk. "Those things cost me eight coppers!"

"I'm really sorry about that, Theneri, I can pay you for it!" said Kodi.

"It is not necessary." Theneri opened the tablet. "Just remember, Kodi. Never take anything with you that you consider so important that you might forget it, or it could be lost forever. All in order here. Good copying. Fine handwriting, Kodi. It…it looks rather like my own."

"Yugan taught me how to read and write. I will be more careful next time about the quill, sir!"

"I know you will," Theneri winked at him. "Next time, we will be more deliberate, and when you get back to the Dome we will run through our mind everything we brought, for if you forgot something, that is the time to go back and get it, before I drop the magic."

Curdoz asked, "And the Meld, Theneri? The sharing of emotion?"

Theneri leaned back and breathed deeply. "Kodi is a true-hearted young man. Good as gold."

"Likewise to you, sir," said Kodi.

Theneri looked at him, "I...no...never mind. Thank you, Kodi. I trust you as a surrogate."

And so they made their plans for the evening. It was agreed that Theneri would take Kodi with him to what was once a side entrance gateway to the formal garden attached to the Prince's Palace. He said it was always kept locked and that no guards were stationed there. "If you're a good climber, which I suspect you are, it will be easier for you to get over the gate and let me in. There is a tiny guard room just inside with a bench, used to hold garden tools now, and we will use it as our Origin of Departure. It is close to the kitchen; the cooks leave the doors open so as to let the heat out from the fires, and you will be able to gain entrance easily enough." And he assured the two that by the time they returned that evening in order for Curdoz to make his way to the Palace for his pre-arranged dinner with Prince Filiddor, he would have determined which rooms the Ice Tribesmen would be assigned to. "Or at least which hallway. 'Tis likely the western wing where they stayed before, for they can keep it guarded. And it is far from the dining room in which His Highness will host Lord Curdoz for dinner."

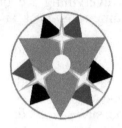

Chapter 13—Secrets Revealed

Later that evening, Kodi and Curdoz again walked from the Monastery to the city. They parted as planned at the horse fountain, Curdoz in the direction of the Prince's Palace, and Kodi to meet Theneri at the Library.

It was barely a half-hour later, just as the sun set, when Kodi, now with Theneri, made his way along another city street that paralleled a tall yew hedge and outer stone wall that lined a large pleasure garden attached to the Prince's Palace. No one was nearby to notice the young man hoist his Novice robes rather revealingly and climb the wall with muscular ease and slip into the small guard house. He quickly unlatched the creaky gate to let the librarian through.

"The prince doesn't keep a strong guard except for within the palace. He has nothing to fear from his subjects, for no one dares to cross him. I have a friend in the kitchens who lets me in regularly, for he is under the impression that all I want to do is wander the gardens. I wander the gardens, yes, but I would also sit here and go into a Moment-mastering excursion and scour the palace for useful information to send to Curdoz. Of course, no one would really suspect anything, for in real time it only took a few seconds. No one remotely suspects that I am an informant. Anyway, like I've told you, the maximum distance one can travel in an excursion is about a half-mile in all directions. The library is too far away, of course, or I could simply sit in my study. From this point, though, I can cover the entire palace with space to spare."

"Have you never run into the prince while wandering in the gardens?"

"Never. He spends a small fortune maintaining them, but he cares nothing for the value of gardens to the human spirit. Probably the gardeners and I are the only ones who really appreciate it. I like coming here in the warm months; it's one of the most beautiful places in the city. If it weren't so dark, we could walk around. I'm sure the prince knows I visit the garden, but I'm sure he just believes I am meditating. And sometimes that really is what I'm doing. Most gardens remind me of the Valley of the Gifted, of course."

"My sister Lyndz loves gardens. She practically has an obsession with garden layouts and flowers."

"And what about you, Kodi?"

"I like them, but I guess I sort of prefer buildings and bridges and construction."

"What do you think of Aster?"

"It's interesting, sir. I don't know the right word. Maybe, 'heavy' or 'bulky'. Too much weight in all the support."

"Yes. It is grand, but it does not lift the spirit, does it? You will like Ferostro. And you will love Tirilorin. Your sister will like Tirilorin, if she likes gardens. Now, let us sit here on this bench."

The tiny guard house now served as a tool house for the gardeners. Spades and clippers and barrows stood neatly on one side, all kept oiled and clean and in good order. On one wall was a large bench. It was getting quite dark now, but it didn't matter. Kodi's main thought was the knowledge that in less than a real minute, they would be finished with their task and they would let themselves out the narrow side gate and make their way back to the library to await Curdoz.

As before, Kodi found himself in the Dome of green light.

"Take your time, Kodi," offered Theneri one last time before the young man stepped out of the Dome. "If you need advice, you can come back of course, and begin again."

Kodi confirmed his understanding and took off in the direction of the kitchens. Theneri had made it clear to Kodi that without keys, locked doors and compartments, trunks and cabinets would still be impossible to open, but the kitchen doors were always open, for there was constant movement in and out due to the size of the palace cooking operations. Hundreds of people had to be fed, soldiers, servants, in addition to the prince and his relations that lived there, and all the palace fireplaces and kitchen fires even at night had to be maintained. Kodi followed his instructions and found the garden pathway that led to a rear entrance, quite close to the drop-off of the North River Canyon. He didn't bother, however, to look in that direction, intent as he was on his task, and besides, beyond the half mile defining the limits of the magic, nothing could be seen in any regard.

All was still and quiet as he entered through a mud room and into the kitchens. Dozens of servants in black and white uniforms were frozen in place at their various tasks. Motionless boys were frozen in the act of turning spits of meat in front of frozen flames. A still woman was dumping cut potatoes into a large pot and the pieces were captured in the air between the cutting board and the inside of the pot. At least a half dozen bizarrely statuesque cooks were gathered around tall tables, putting various foods together. Another was placing trays onto a mechanism built into the wall that had ropes visible. Kodi was intrigued. He had heard of these contraptions intended to lift food from basement kitchens to higher levels in a palace or manor house and was quite fascinated by it. Just like the fancy bathrooms, these were also planned for his parents' manor in Felto. He wanted to study it all, but decided he had better things to do. Though no real time was passing, he knew that Theneri shared the same amount of excursion time as did he, and there was no reason to dawdle.

He found the servant stairs that led to the upper stories and had to worm his way around more black or white-garbed servants, some going up and others coming down. At the top was a room surrounded by counters, above and below which were shelves lined with fine porcelain and silver utensils and platters. Some items appeared to be made from gold, like candlesticks and vases. They were at least gilded. Kodi discovered where the food-lift mechanism ended, and realized he must be just above the kitchen. He made his way through a short hallway to a door that was closed. He opened it.

Kodi was quite surprised to see Curdoz himself sitting rigid at one end of a large white-clothed table laden with fine china, silver goblets, and a centerpiece of miniature gold statuary with candles surrounded by small branches of greenery. The Sage's hand was frozen in midair, holding a wine goblet on its way to his lips.

And at the other end of the table was surely the Prince of Hesk, Filiddor, in garments of rich, red velvet. He too was frozen with a fork full of food half way to his face.

He was younger than Kodi expected, of similar age to his parents Hess and Elisa, maybe a bit younger. No one else sat at the table, although there were eight servants who stood by against the walls, ready to pour more wine or to remove plates as necessary for the prince and his distinguished guest. Kodi was glad, because he knew that Curdoz had feared that the prince would want to host a showy dinner party, and even though the Sage had made it clear in his message that he wanted no such affair, Kodi had still presumed that there might still be two or three others of the household that would have attended the prince at dinner anyway. Kodi presumed he must not even be Bonded yet, or surely his wife at the very least would have been present. He couldn't recall if Curdoz had ever made mention of whether or not the prince had a wife. He rather didn't think so, though.

The man was of stern expression, Kodi thought, and he seemed to be looking intently at the Sage even as he ate. His eyes were dark, but his thick hair was cut short and was light brown. His skin tone was typical for Northern Solantines, and he looked no different otherwise than most other Hescians that Kodi had seen. If there were Ralsheen traits, he certainly could not discover them. The man looked nothing like the Ice Tribesmen. But Kodi realized that after five hundred years, there was no reason for him to believe that this descendant of a Ralsheen nobleman should look at all like what he supposed his ancestors might have looked like. But then he remembered Curdoz telling him that not all the Ralsheen nobility had the bright white skin and yellow eyes, a trait deliberately duplicated each generation since by the Ice Tribe ruling classes through arranged pairings.

Nevertheless, there was definitely something in the man's eyes and bearing that in Kodi's mind had a sinister feel. It was not the face of a man who valued compassion, but rather one of calculation.

Kodi's emotion upon seeing the man, though not anywhere near as strong, was reminiscent of how he felt when he saw the Alkhan of Eastrealm in his Vision. He wondered if Theneri would pick up on his feelings. When he closed his eyes, he did indeed sense that Theneri's so far muted emotion seemed now to express a bit of curiosity. Quite likely the old man wondered what it was that Kodi encountered that made him feel so tense all of a sudden.

Pondering Theneri, however, reminded Kodi that he had work to do. With one last look upon the prince and the Sage, he left the dining room and began again his search for the Ice Tribesmen and their apartments.

It was quite a distance from the dining room to the west wing of the Palace, but Kodi knew he had finally found his way there by the far larger number of armed guards. At every corner and hallway entrance, indeed in front of several doors, Kodi found Hescian soldiers in place. Now it was a matter of trying various doors until he found the right ones. He surmised that the doors immediately in front of which stood guards were probably not the ones that housed the Tribesmen. These were likely in place to keep people, quite possibly even the Tribesmen, out rather than in. There were, however, a set of double doors half way down a long hall that looked promising, as a guard stood on either side and also across the hallway facing it.

He found the set of doors locked. Looking at the guards however, he noticed one held a set of three keys. Untying it from the man's belt, Kodi was again struck by how weird it was that objects only moved to the position where he let them go. The keys did not really jingle unless he specifically knocked them together. He tried one key, but it did not work, but the second one turned the mechanism. He opened the door. He was about to put the keys back, but he remembered again that this was an Image of a moment, and not the actual moment. He left them in the lock.

He did, however, open the door with some slow deliberation. He frankly didn't know if upon opening he might push the door into the Image of someone standing in front of it. He did not. However, he immediately realized something.

He had come to the right apartment.

He was in a large room with a fireplace. It was filled with fine furniture and was richly decorated. Several other doors, most of which were open, led off of this central parlor. Through these could be seen large, fancily-made, four poster canopy beds. However, all four Ice Tribesmen were in the center room, interestingly all standing near to the fire, frozen in the act of engaged conversation. They had all removed their heavy fur cloaks and were wearing wool clothing of good quality. Their strange eyes stood out distinct. Kodi felt a strong upsurge of hate. He didn't really know why, other than some instinct that caused him to feel such a strong sense of separation from them. He felt as though they had come from some other race of being, barely Human, if at all. The bright white skin and odd eyes of the Tribesmen were so foreign to Kodi's senses that he felt they symbolized evil in some way. Not so much the fact that it was perhaps a form of albinism, a natural though uncommon trait Kodi had at least heard about, but rather that they continued to maintain the trait deliberately through inter-bonding. With the realization that mutual love could hardly be the reason behind the vast majority of such pairings, it seemed to Kodi horribly unnatural. To be a woman in Tribal society was very likely an unhappy prospect.

He forced himself back to the task at hand and removed from his pockets the quill, tablet and ink bottle that he had brought with him. There was a desk with an elaborate chair and he set all these things down, sat in the chair and began to write. He described the color of the Tribesmen's clothing, and the necklaces and other decoration they wore. He noted that nothing really stood out, with the exception that the Chieftain, whom Kodi recognized from the previous night, had upon his hand a large signet ring. He knew what it was, for his father had one by which he formalized documents and letters. Kodi didn't like touching the man, but as he had done when he had to move Thersa's body out of the way from the library's desk, he squelched the eeriness and set about to remove the ring from the man's hand—it was tight but he managed it—and set it on the desk.

The shank was plain gold, but the top of the ring appeared to be made of some black stone with characters that stood up, strange letters. He had an idea. He very carefully covered the raised tracery on the ring with a shallow coating of ink, and then pressed it into the paper. It imprinted a strange script which he believed must indicate Tribal lettering. It seemed possible to Kodi it might in some way help to identify the man.

Having done his best to describe the four men, he went into each of the bedrooms looking for items he thought the tribesmen may have brought. In one room were several large stacks of furs of various types. Kodi felt these. Like many things of texture that he had experienced in his two excursions, the furs did not feel quite as he expected them to. The nap would not rise again after he pressed them, and they were not especially soft. Kodi was beginning to realize that almost everything in an excursion that was not actually 'hard' had a very strange, unreal, tacky feeling. He listed on his tablet that there were several stacks of furs, but to describe the various types and colors he believed was not relevant. In one of the bedrooms he found a pack made of leather, but within he found nothing that seemed remotely important other than clothing garments, and even food wrappings of what Kodi believed were traveling biscuits and jerky of some meat, perhaps seal or walrus. Kodi sniffed them but there was no aroma, and he put the biscuit and then the meat to his tongue but tasted nothing, bland as paper. Only an Image, he reminded himself.

In each of the rooms he found the rest of their packs, but he found nothing in any of them that seemed remotely important. No documents, no scrolls, no books, no strange packages. He opened bureaus and cabinets, and though he found their fur traveling cloaks, he found nothing else that he believed belonged to the Tribesman. He went back out to the parlor and looked again at the statuesque men. If they carried something important, where would they keep it, he asked himself. Close to them, perhaps? On their person?

It seemed his last hope. He tried the Chieftain first, rummaging through his clothing, looking for hidden pockets. He did find a small purse of coins in a pocket of the man's woolen tunic, and though he listed on his paper that they were coins minted in Solanto, and the amount, he knew it was not important.

He searched the man that had been referred to as the ambassador, and finally Kodi came upon something. In a breast pocket of the ambassador's tunic was a small tube of white leather. Kodi knew it probably contained a scroll, and indeed it did. But when he unraveled it and began to look at it, he raised his eyebrows. It appeared to him exactly the sort of coded writing that his great-grandmother Kalemna used. In fact, though he couldn't remember specifically, he thought it looked a very good deal like her handwriting.

Could it be? It was truly unfortunate that Theneri was blind to the Image, otherwise Kodi could take it back to Theneri to look at it. He suspected he would recognize it if it were Kalemna's writing. It was all up to Kodi, he realized. He took it to the desk, and with great care he copied every symbol and letter with all the spacing and lines just as it appeared on the scroll. Yet it was impossible, really, to copy the writing style. He made a deliberate study, though, of the different letters and symbols in order to try to memorize what they appeared like.

The lines of the piece appeared to be organized rather like a poem. He remembered Curdoz saying that he could tell that some of the writings in the book that Yugan gave him appeared to be poetry. After perhaps a half-hour, and after looking it over several times to make sure he had copied it right, he was satisfied.

He then decided that maybe he was onto something, and decided to check for hidden pockets more carefully. However, there was definitely nothing else hidden among the Ambassador's clothes, and after more thoroughly examining those of the Chieftain, he found nothing more there. This left the two other Tribesmen, whom Kodi believed must be high-level attendants of the other two, since they were also Of the White.

Again, he achieved a bit of luck. In an inside pocket close to one of the men's back left hip was a leather pouch. Inside was a piece of folded parchment, and on it Kodi was certain he was looking at a cipher, just like Curdoz had described one should look. In a column on one side were approximately four dozen letters and symbols with lines that connected them to other letters, combinations of letters, numbers, and punctuations of common Anterianhi script, all in a second column. It also appeared to be in the same handwriting as the poem he had just copied which the ambassador carried.

Was it a match? In his excitement, Kodi couldn't wait. He decided he would attempt to match up the symbols of the first line of the "poem" and see if they were actual Anterianhi words.

He took his time and forced himself to be patient, and as the minutes went by as he constantly compared the two, he was convinced the handwriting was the same. He believed he had a good vision in his mind so he could check Kalemna's book when next he got a chance. He matched symbol to letter, and letter by letter, as real words began to appear, he became more and more excited. Finally, the first line was obvious.

The Door is shut, the Dragons sleep

"It works!" he said aloud, though of course no one could hear him. In the back of his mind he could tell that his excitement had registered with Theneri, for he could sense Theneri's curiosity again. With tremendous diligence he began to copy the cipher. "If this happens to work on Deroge's book, wouldn't that be something!"

Though he was also aware of how unbelievably curious such an outcome would be. For the Tribesman to have the exact cipher needed to translate Deroge's book was far-fetched at best and would create more mystery. Nevertheless, he was precise and careful, and every time he thought his scribble wasn't precise enough, he scratched through it and did those particular symbols over again. He knew it was critical to get it right, otherwise any translation might have indecipherable errors, and that just wouldn't do. He then realized that Monastic Scribes were required to be equally precise. "But I bet they at least know the languages they are copying." Nor did they necessarily rewrite coded letters or messages. Nevertheless, he realized how important it was to get things right each time something was copied, otherwise errors could produce more errors in time, and eventually the original meaning of something might be lost. Kodi was determined to get it right.

Finally, he was finished. He again examined their clothing, but found nothing more. What he found so far he thought important, yes, but there were certainly no documents that cast any light on what the Tribesmen were up to, unless it was contained within the coded poem, but he'd have to decipher the rest of it later. He took one final look around the parlor. Nothing looked out of the ordinary to him. There were vases and candelabra, objects of silver, a chess set carved perhaps of walrus ivory, and alcoves containing decorative objects. Two held marble statues of human figures, one held a vase made of fine porcelain, gilded and painted, and another held a pedestal upon which lay a rather large, black cube, carved perhaps of shiny onyx. He concluded that a stone cutter with precision skill must have fashioned it and presented it as a gift to the prince or one of his forebears.

Nothing seemed unusual, and he believed he was done. He carefully placed his own things in his pockets, took one more glance at the Ice Tribemen and went in search of Theneri. He did not choose to look anywhere else. Curdoz had said that if they had brought any important documents that they would have brought duplicate copies, and even if Filiddor had one somewhere else in the Palace, the Tribesmen would have the duplicate in their possession until it was time to sign them, and then each party would have an official copy.

To search anywhere else would almost certainly have been unnecessary. Kodi hoped so.

There was not very much room inside the Dome of green light. Nevertheless, Theneri thought it important to look through Kodi's tablet before he dropped the magic of the Mode. Sitting in the cramped space, they spoke of the young man's findings.

"Yes, yes," said Theneri. "Much of this is probably not important, just as you say, but at least you were thorough. The scroll and cipher you copied are undoubtedly important. I suspect your copying is very good. I have other materials that demonstrate Kalemna's handwriting. You can look at those and tell us what you think. All appears to be in order. You did a fine job. Let's end the excursion and go back to the library. By the time Curdoz meets us we might have this one piece deciphered."

The Dome of light fell. It seemed much darker than it had under the green light. So, hardly had five minutes of real time passed since Kodi had climbed the garden wall when the two let themselves out of the gate, which locked behind them, and began to walk back to the library to await Curdoz.

"Fantastic, Kodi!" exclaimed the old librarian. "You've apparently done a perfect job copying the poem and the cipher!"

Theneri had taken Kodi's findings and sitting at one of the wooden tables in his study recreated the poem that Kodi had found on the ambassador. In his excitement, Kodi had been peering over Theneri's shoulder as the older man wrote out the poem, letter by letter.

"Read it out loud to me, Kodi! Sometimes the reading of a poem can help in understanding its meaning."

And so Kodi read it aloud to the old man, unaware of course that the ambassador had recited the same to Prince Filiddor over a month before.

The Door is shut, the Dragons sleep
Their last sleep. Their prey is dead. They famish.
Meical's Scourge ends.
One claims Tolos. The Usurper, his child will defeat.

The Door is shut, though look deep.
Look very deep. The child, a scion of Ch'ndra. No blemish.
Time bends.
Old Empire renewed? When New and Old meet.

From the North they will come to set it aright.

With alliance of Princes they will fight.
South will bend to the will of the North.
New kingdom will now spring forth.

When he was done, he handed it back to Theneri. "Is it a Prophecy, Brother Theneri?"

"It is definitely a Prophecy."

"And do you understand it?"

He laughed. "Oh, Kodi! Maybe pieces of it, but the unfortunate thing about Prophecy is that you quite often don't know what it is referring to until the events spoken of have long passed. Especially when they are written in this way—cryptically."

This made some sense to Kodi, but it was not especially helpful. "Then what..."

"I think it best to discuss it when Curdoz arrives. Now, follow me."

With curiosity, Kodi followed Theneri from his study to a different room, the third of the large domed rooms which Kodi had not been in as yet. It was apparently dedicated to scrolls and maps, rather than books, and it was full of bins, some large and some small, which contained hundreds of materials. Most were rolled up very neatly into vellum tubes, but there were also deep, layered shelves of large parchments, mostly maps lying flat. Though it was late, there were two persons, a man and a woman, both in Monastic robes, peering at a map together. They nodded at Theneri, who waved a hand at them across the room.

He walked to a small bin, one of many, on the north wall. After looking at the labels on several tubes, he pulled one out, opened the flap on the end and extracted a rolled scroll. He handed it to Kodi.

Kodi unrolled it. He peered at the writing. "Is this Kalemna Deroge's handwriting?"

"It is. What do you think?"

"I think it's the same! I really do! I made an effort to study some of the letters, and how the person drew them. I'd almost swear it was the same. What do you reckon, Brother Theneri? Do you think she wrote that Prophecy poem?"

The old man sighed and looked away from Kodi. "There was a rumor that Kalemna was captured by the Ice Tribesmen. It was during the earliest stages of the last war, forty years ago. There is one more thing to try."

He led Kodi back to his study and pulled out of a drawer in a side table the tiny slip of parchment upon which Curdoz had scribbled the line from Deroge's book. He pointed to several ciphers on the table. "I've tried all of these, and none of them work. I didn't really expect them to. Let's try the one you discovered on the Tribesmen, shall we?"

"Some of those symbols are the same, don't you think?" offered Kodi, expectantly.

"They do appear so, yes." Theneri took it over to the larger table where the tablet and the transcribed poem still sat. "Why don't you try it, Kodi?"

Kodi sat in the chair and picked up a quill and began on a separate piece of parchment to see if the symbols and letters matched up with Anterianhi characters from the cipher he had discovered. Theneri watched him with his hand on his shoulder.

... From the North they will come to set it aright. With alliance of Princes they will fight....

Kodi beamed. "I don't believe it, Theneri! It's the same! It's the same! Curdoz will be ecstatic!"

As if his name had been called, the Sage himself walked into the room and closed the door behind him. "And what am I to be ecstatic about, Kodi, my man?"

The discussion went long into the night. Nor was it mostly between the two older men, for they made Kodi an integral part of the discussion. His own thoughts, in addition to his discoveries among the Ice Tribes, were listened to and debated, nor did he feel the least bored like he did the day before when they were discussing his Vision and he had chosen to go read a book instead. Here were presented new clues, relevant to the tasks ahead, and yet there were many new mysteries as well.

Curdoz, and Theneri too, believed Kodi was absolutely correct in his view that both the poem and the cipher originated from Deroge. And the short phrase Curdoz had copied from the little book proved it. It appeared as though the cipher was invented by Deroge solely for the purposes of decrypting some of *her* writings. Some of the symbols she used appeared to Theneri to be unique, having never seen them used in any other coded writings that he had come across in his years as librarian.

"It may not prove she was captured by the Ice Tribesmen, but it certainly points to that as a likely scenario," Curdoz added. "It solves that mystery, partly. They certainly acquired the poem and the cipher from her. We can presume she did not give them to them freely. She might or might not have had other writings on her when they searched her, but it seems clear that this one particular Prophecy they believe they have interpreted or are attempting to interpret and believe it to be of immense importance to whatever it is they are up to."

Curdoz admitted that some of the Prophecy was obvious to him. Particularly that regarding the Dragons. It was clearly a reference to recent events. Kodi's father's discovery that the Dragons appeared to have been starved out in their competition for food and lack of prey was presumed to be correct by most of the Solantine leadership based on his findings. "The Dragons having been brought to Tolos were often referred to as Meical's Scourge, and it references the fact that the Guardian set them loose in Tolos in order to destroy that last holdout of the Ralsheen. The Anterianhi did not have the engineering at first to build a fleet, and there is no land route over the mountains into the peninsula. The Ralsheen cities there seemed perfectly safe. What has never been known is how Meical introduced such a large number of Dragons to Tolos in the first place. They are only known to live naturally in the Infested Jungle on the Southern Continent, south of West Khestadon and the Kingdom of Berug."

"You think this 'Door' may have been how He did it?"

"I can't imagine the magic required! When Meical returned to our world that time he deliberately avoided showy demonstrations. Even against Siriné herself. He always preferred to channel power through others...others that He trusted like Terianh and the Sages. But the fact the Dragons appeared has always been attributed to some miracle on Meical's part. Some sort of Doorway might have been His method. It might not be important, now, particularly the reference that it is 'shut'. It is quite possible it is figurative—that a return to the past is not practical. I believe the reference to a 'Usurper' and a 'scion of Ch'ndra' are perhaps the most important."

"The reference to the Dragons being gone simply sets the stage for later events," added Theneri, agreeing.

"Then who exactly is this Ch'ndra person?" asked Kodi. He looked at the Sage who in turn looked at the librarian.

"You're the one who literally lives in a monstrous library!" Curdoz joked.

"See, he does jest sometimes, Brother Theneri!" quipped Kodi.

Theneri chuckled, but came to the point. "I do not know. The name is unequivocally Ralsheen. Feminine. *Snow child* or *Child of the Snows* is how it would be translated; I know the language quite well, but I have not seen reference to such a person. A woman likely of some note, for the prefix *Ch* was used within the elite classes. Possibly a noblewoman or even a princess. There are a great many very old works here that are written in Ralsheen, but I have only translated a few dozen of them. I...well I have avoided the works from the Dark Times of their last century, unwilling I suppose to bring their hateful philosophies to light! I'm sure you can understand my reasoning. What I already have translated from Ralsheen is from a time much earlier, before the wicked world goddess Siriné came among them. Looks like I have more work to do. I doubt, Your Grace, I will be able to offer you any insight on her before you leave town. It could take weeks or months before I run across some reference."

"It would be helpful, for sure, but quite frankly, the Usurper and the child are quite likely the ones to be concerned about. Nevertheless, knowing who Ch'ndra was might help us to identify."

"Do you think they reference people on Meical's side or not?" asked Kodi.

"It is hard to say," said Curdoz. "My instinct tells me that the Usurper is not, but that the child is. My feeling is that the reference 'no blemish' implies someone good and pure. Clinging to older tradition—not uncommon with those who wrote Prophecy—it might have referred to someone who has not engaged in the mating act, virginal, but if we think it might be Deroge's and only a few decades old it could reference rather an individual with uncorrupted motivations. It is even possible it refers to someone who has flawless *physical* features, someone very beautiful with no scars or blemishes on face and body. Male or female."

"It is vague," Theneri added, "but it is not a description a Seer or Seeress would use for an enemy. Time Bends' could be simple. It could be a reference that additional time will go by before the events of the next line. But there was a time when Moment Mastering was referred to as Time-bending, but that would be a very obscure rendering. Few would know it. Although, Kalemna…never mind. She…never went to the Valley, of course, so she wouldn't know that reference."

Kodi couldn't help wondering if Theneri's statement was to cover something he was about to say.

Curdoz seemed not to notice. "The next line is very uncertain," he said.

"Why would it not mean a renewal of the Anterianhi Empire?" asked Kodi. It seemed one of the most obvious references, and yet it was a puzzle to the Sage.

"It might be, Kodi, but it is fearsome, nonetheless. The Ralsheen ruled an Empire, too. Some of the wording in the poem reflects the perspective of the Seer or Seeress. Since Deroge wrote it, and we presume she wrote it forty years ago, then to consider what she meant by 'no blemish' and 'old empire' could be the key. The same with 'usurper,' which presumes someone without legal claim from Deroge's point of view. The last four lines, though. Look at them again. Theneri, keep quiet. Let us test Kodi's thinking." He looked at Kodi. "Kodi, compare them to the previous. What do you see?"

Kodi re-read the lines, then he looked again at the first two verses. "Er...they don't really read the same, do they? The rhyming is different. It's a bit more sing-song. Is that what you're getting at?"

Theneri nodded. Curdoz replied, "Precisely, Kodi. And yet, considering that it was all written on the same piece of parchment, I bet you anything...anything...that the Tribesmen believe it is all connected. I would be willing to say I know more about Prophecy than anyone in the lands of the Ice Tribes, and..."

Kodi interrupted, "They're two completely separate Prophecies!"

"Yes! They may have a connection to one another, but they refer to different events."

"The second one definitely speaks of war, doesn't it?" asked Kodi. He became quite serious all of a sudden, looking down at the words again.

Curdoz replied. "Yes, and yet I think they are hopeful words. Keep in mind, though, that Prophecies rendered by a Seer or Seeress do not always come true. Since Kalemna wrote this, we can presume that through her Gift for insight, she could see something of future events, based on her experience and her study of past events. All in all, I think Kalemna's Prophecies, both of them, should give us hope. We cannot focus on them, though. We have to plunge ahead with what we're doing."

They were quiet for a moment, but then Theneri spoke. "Some would argue, Lord Curdoz, that Kalemna was not Meicalian Gifted."

"Do you believe that?"

"No. No, I don't. I never could understand why she did not pilgrimage to the Valley. But she...she was a very good woman. The Guardian moved her then as much as He does the three of us here and now. I truly believe that. What I am thinking, however, is if the Ice Tribesmen are giving this Prophecy significant weight, then it is almost certain that they themselves believe she was not. They hate and ignore everything connected with Meical, for they don't follow Him. They must be under the impression that she was either a Seeress of ancient Dark Prophecy, connected with ancient World God religions, or something else. It would be curious to find out *why* they consider *this* Prophecy important, and of course, how *they* have interpreted it." Theneri sighed. "All right, Curdoz. I'll allow it."

Kodi looked up at Theneri, confused by this statement. Apparently Curdoz was, too.

"What, Theneri?" the Sage asked.

"Xeno, of course. I see there is a real need for us to continue to gather information. If you send Xeno to me, I'll allow him to use Mind Support on me so that I can continue working as an informant. There are things we need to know. I do, however, expect him to keep my memories private."

The Sage offered his gratitude. "Thank you, Theneri. You have a unique Gift! I don't think Meical wishes you to stop using it just because you're old."

Theneri actually grinned. He seemed happy and resolved about something that may have been troubling him before.

Then Kodi remembered. "Curdoz, you haven't told us about dinner with Prince Filiddor. What did he say when you asked him about making Danly an apprentice?"

He shook his head, which at first Kodi believed to be bad news. "I don't understand, frankly. As it turned out, Filiddor was quite amenable to the idea and gave permission for it."

Surprised, Kodi asked, "Then what's the problem? You seem, er, dissatisfied?"

"The problem is that it was too easy."

Theneri puckered his eyebrows. "Consider, Curdoz. Was his attitude upon your recommendation one in which he was listening carefully to your reasoning, or was it one that appeared to be humoring you? I think it's important."

"I agree, old friend. Actually, it was neither. I admit I brought up your age and of coursed played upon Danly's scholarship, yes. But it was rather as if Filiddor were *uninterested*, like he didn't really care what my reasoning was on the matter. He waved his hand to interrupt and said simply, 'If you believe he is well-qualified, Lord Curdoz, then I have no objection.'"

"What is wrong, then?"

"Well, Kodi, I would think he would take a change in the status quo more seriously. Theneri here is in a position of authority within the city. If Danly takes his place someday, then I would think Filiddor would care very much about the sort of man he would be. I would have expected him to ask questions."

"I've never given him a reason to distrust me," offered Theneri. "Of course, I've been here fifty years. But you're right. It is odd."

"Did he ask you for anything, Curdoz?"

Curdoz smiled oddly and looked up at them. He breathed deeply before he spoke. "Well, no!"

Puzzled expressions met him at this. He continued. "Filiddor did not ask me for any specific favors. In general, he was quite gracious, though of course he has never been a warm sort, and I had to suppress my discomfort in his presence. But I found out I have no reason whatsoever to call a Council of the Kingdom."

Kodi was more confused than ever. "But you don't believe all that about the fur trade, do you?"

"Of course, I don't. I still believe that is a story he is telling his guards and his servants to justify the presence of the Tribesmen in his palace. The man himself has called for a Council of the Kingdom."

"No kidding!" exclaimed Theneri leaning forward and with both eyebrows hitting the ceiling.

"To be held next month. I am probably the last of the lords to hear of it, for since I have been traveling, I have received few messages of import."

"Curdoz! That is remarkable! A Prince of Hesk hasn't called for a Council since the last war!" The old man actually stood up and began to pace around the room. "Well, that explains it, Curdoz! The reason he doesn't care whether you install Danly here is because it really *is* unimportant to him! It was more of a distraction. He has some other trick going on that is *extremely* important to him."

"Yes," said Curdoz. "I believe the same as you, and it involves the Ice Tribes."

"What did he tell you about it, Curdoz?" asked Kodi.

"All he would say was that he had something of critical significance to present to the King and the Council, and wanted to know if I would be attending."

"Did you say you would attend?" asked Theneri. "You want to be out of the country before then, do you not?"

"I was able to avoid making a specific commitment, and he offered no information in order to gauge my opinion…on anything. And I didn't ask, for I felt quite confident he wasn't going to give me prior information. It seemed inconsiderate on my part to probe, for it would have appeared accusing."

According to Curdoz, all the Prince seemed to want to do was to pretend to be lordly and friendly, and that the majority of their conversation focused on trivial matters. He asked Curdoz for no favors, he did not question him very deeply about his business or the purpose behind his travels, and he made no mention of Kodi having traveled with the Sage to the Monastery.

"More mystery," said Theneri.

"Yes," said Curdoz. After a short pause, he continued. "Expect Danly and Xeno to arrive within the next couple of weeks. I expect to find them in Thorune when Kodi and I return that way; I will explain to them everything, and then send them on. And as soon as they arrive, I expect you to put them to work."

"I will. But when you leave the country, with whom should I correspond?"

"Father Marco and Grand Duke Mannago. Considering everything, I fear something dangerous is coming. Something is in the works, I can feel it. Filiddor is operating under some kind of plan, a plan he will not divulge, obviously, but one that is not likely to benefit the Kingdom of Solanto. There may come a time, as a matter of fact, when the Prince may begin to scrutinize more closely Order Members living in, or pilgrimaging into, his domain. At the least he is gathering information on the movement of High Lords outside of Hesk. He likely thinks the rest of you are not especially important. In time that may change. Keep your eyes and ears open, Theneri. The instant anyone starts to ask you leading questions—servants, soldiers, Asterians who come into the library—you should be suspicious, and that should indicate a tightening in Filiddor's strategy. It means he is developing a system of gathering information here in his own city. Trust no one but Danly and Xeno, put up voice Blocks, and keep your discussions private."

"I'll manage it, Curdoz."

The Sage and Kodi took their leave for the night. They intended to come by the library one last time before they left the city the next morning. After the East Gate guards allowed them through, but before they arrived at the Monastery, Kodi spoke to Curdoz.

"Sir, there is something about Theneri that I just can't put my finger on. I shared his emotions, and I have trust for him. It's not that. The man seems to have a great deal of affection towards me, and I don't quite understand why. He hasn't known me but two days."

Curdoz listened to this and was silent for a moment before he responded. "And how do you feel towards him?"

"I feel connected to him, sir, but maybe it was simply the sharing of emotions during the Mind-mastering excursion. I feel, though, like he's keeping something from me. Something important."

There was a pause. "Well, I'm not going to deny your instinct, Kodi, because it has proven itself to me already as being quite reliable. Though it's obvious to me that Theneri has taken to you, I admit I don't see anything especially unusual. There were quite a number of elderly people back in Felto, as I've mentioned already, who spoke very fondly of you. You have a knack of reaching out to them I think with a sense of warmth and respect. They also see how good you are to Yugan, and naturally they respond to that with affection towards you. I suspect Theneri's taking to you is no more than that, Kodi. And keep in mind this, too. Those who have experienced Visions have a link with Meical, and that mystical connection tends to open our hearts to care more deeply, perhaps more naturally than some who don't."

"Yes, sir. Maybe so," replied Kodi.

But later as he sat up in his bed and as he read more of Theneri's translation of Terianh's history, his thoughts retuned again and again to the old man. He couldn't help thinking that maybe he could see something that even the wise Sage could not. He was convinced Theneri was hiding something, and the thought kept crossing his mind that it had something to do with his great-grandmother Kalemna. There was something about her he believed Theneri didn't want him to know.

The following morning they were awakened by Monastics, and after they had dressed they packed their bags and made their way to morning meditations and then to breakfast. To Kodi's annoyance, though he was determined to hide his emotion, Curdoz insisted that Kodi continue to wear the Novice robes as they traveled in the Principality. "It will be presumed that I have officially installed you as a Novice in the Order. If Filiddor is keeping track, it will create much curiosity if you start wearing your ordinary clothing again."

"Yes, sir. It's not going to be easy to ride; er, my legs will sort of stick out, but I can do it."

Father Jarom and others stood at the Monastery gate to bid them farewell as they rode out. The man handed to Kodi an envelope.

"This contains the passage that Lord Curdoz asked me to have copied for you. So long, Novice Kodi! Enjoy your years in the Valley of the Gifted!"

"Thank you, Father Jarom!" Kodi said, placing the envelope in the pocket of his robes. His lower legs did indeed stick out from his robes as he sat on his horse. It was cold, but not enough to bother him. He knew he must look quite silly with bare legs and boots, but he presumed the other Monastics understood. Yet he was even more self-conscious at East Gate as the soldiers stood by, and on his way through the city. Finally, though, he resolved that he had very decent and very muscular legs. What was he self-conscious for? When he realized it had more to do with his obvious connection to the Monastic Orders due to the robes he was wearing, he tried to squelch his emotion altogether. *I am a statue of a virile general on a warhorse.* He chuckled to himself and decided that was the best thought to grasp hold of in order to proceed without embarrassment. He just wished he were holding aloft a sword.

With an eager Musca running behind them, the two rode first to the library. They found Theneri at the ambernut desk working on some project. Other than servants tending to the fires, no one else had arrived yet this early to study in the library.

Theneri stood. "Ah, my friends! It has been such a pleasure!"

Curdoz replied. "Indeed it has! And I appreciate everything. I need you to complete a task for me. Have some scribes make a complete copy and have it bound of the Book of Histories and Prophecies. I want you to have it delivered to Kodi's grandfather Yugan in Felto in Tulesk. Use money from Jarom's funds; I've already spoken to him, though he knows nothing really of Kodi's family."

"Certainly. It may take several weeks, but I will have it done."

Kodi then handed the librarian the book he had borrowed. Instead, Theneri said to him, "I have decided I want you to have it, Kodi. Terianh is a man worth emulating, particularly someone such as yourself. I expect great things from you!"

He winked at Kodi and then took the book and wrote a message on the front, inside page and handed it back. Kodi looked at it, smiling as he read.

For Kodi, Meical's Warrior. Read and learn. With gratitude, Theneri, of the Order of Meical the Guardian. Remember me.

"It's beautiful, sir. I know this represents a lot of work on your part, the translation and the scribes writing it out. I suppose this is the first book I've ever owned myself! Thank you, sir. I will certainly remember you, Brother Theneri. But I don't know what about me you are grateful for."

Theneri reached up and put his hand on his shoulder. He squeezed it and looked steadily into Kodi's brown eyes with his piercing blue ones. "For that sense of hope I mentioned to you yesterday noon."

Kodi nodded. If anything, Theneri's statement only added to his belief that the old man was holding onto some secret.

With Musca trotting behind, the travelers left the library and made their way to the west gates of the city.

Chapter 14—Independent Moves

The return journey to Thorune was uneventful. Though only eight days had gone by since they had passed this way before, as they descended to the plain from the Great Ramp, springtime was more strongly evident. Trees were budding and other wildflowers besides daffodils were in bloom: hellebores, hyacinths, pansies and bloodroot. No snow remained anywhere, and farmers were making early progress preparing fields. Traffic on the road had picked up enormously the last week, and Curdoz had dispensed with dismounting every time someone recognized him and requested his Blessing.

He said to Kodi, "It is more polite and respectful to get down and engage them, but every year it is the same. As travel increases and the weather becomes more pleasant, so do the requests. Just remember to consider each opportunity that you relate to someone. You have to make choices, but whenever possible be as polite as the circumstance will allow you to be. We often feel the need to hurry and rush when it isn't necessary. But if I dismount each time, we'll never get to Thorune, let alone Ferostro."

Musca seemed pleased with the change in weather, and whenever they crossed a small stream, the dog would splash through it delightedly. It rained again, and so instead of camping they stayed in the home of a large farm family the first night, for there were no inns, but on the second evening from their descent on the Ramp they arrived in Thorune. They chose a rather large inn on the east-west road; Curdoz was certainly not going to stay at Onri's place on the south-bound road. The first thing Kodi did was wash and shave.

The second thing he did was to put on his own clothes and pack away the Novice robes—for good.

A tired Musca chose to nap in their room by the fireplace while the two men went to the common room for dinner. It was a busy place, and Curdoz was obliged to greet and bless several travelers and locals. Kodi was feeling so good and so much more himself he didn't even bother to inform Curdoz. He had his own money with him. Leaving the Sage momentarily at their table, he stepped up to the bar.

Curdoz raised his eyebrows.

When he returned he presented the Sage with a decanter of wine and a goblet, and for himself a pint of dark ale.

"Been keeping you from enjoying some of your favorite pursuits, Kodi?" Curdoz asked, eying him as the young man looked lovingly at his pint.

Kodi winked and drank a quarter of it in one magnificent gulp. "Just celebrating, sir, that's all. I am Kodi Fothemry again. Wish I'd left my bow with Captain Santher instead of sending it on with Lyndz. I feel like it's a part of me and I miss it."

"We'll be in Ferostro in less than a week," said the Sage. He nodded his gratitude for the wine and poured his goblet full. Sitting back, he drank with slower deliberation than Kodi. In another minute a barmaid presented them with several plates of food. She looked at Kodi with a twinkle in her eye; he nodded his thanks but then picked up his knife and began cutting into a large ham steak. The barmaid walked away disappointed.

"And I just bought our drinks, Curdoz. I'll let you cover the food." Kodi said with another wink, holding a big chunk of meat on the end of his fork which he then plunged into his mouth.

As they ate, Curdoz couldn't help but to ponder more the young man sitting across from him. He wondered much, especially what sort of Gifts Meical intended to bestow on this one. It wouldn't do to reveal too much too soon in case he was wrong, but he had certain suspicions, and was glad Kodi could not see the mental debate going on in his mind.

'He's young. Terianh was over thirty when Meical Called him.'

'It doesn't matter. The Guardian isn't going to make it happen until he's ready.'

'And it's a very dangerous proposition.'

'But if anybody is willing to handle danger, it's Kodi. He is fearless.'

'He has had little to fear so far. But no doubt you're right.'

'Meical knows what He's about choosing Kodi. Look at him. Listen to him. He has supreme self-confidence.'

'I was never that way. Certainly not when I was young.'

'No. You were full of fears, and you were repressed.'

'He's not quite nineteen, and there he is talking with me, a high lord and the Sage of Solanto, as if I am a close friend. He orders himself an ale like an off-duty soldier.'

'He's a man three years by all traditions. The young women notice him, don't they? Not only that, he bought you a drink, too.'

'Thoughtful. But I would have been too self-conscious to order and drink an ale in front of my elders.'

'Does it bother you that much?'

'No.'

'You say that but you're having a difficult time with his youth.'

'Maybe. Frankly, the more I think about it, the more it doesn't bother me one whit. And I am a friend, certainly. It's just that...I don't know.'

'A bit of envy? You wish you had been more like him back then. You never felt equal to anyone until you went to the Valley. Your father never made you feel as though you were a man on a level with him and capable of making decisions for yourself.'

'We've had this discussion a thousand times before. And I was somewhat younger than Kodi. Anyway, Kodi is...what am I trying to say?'

'A specimen of confidence. And a damned good-looking young buck.'

'It is more than that. There is almost no hint of boastfulness, a trait that too often parallels such confidence and great looks. It says something about his character. I certainly do NOT want to repress him. I'll let him enjoy his ale. He probably drinks like a sailor in the right company. I myself don't care, of course. Better not around Idamé, though. She'll give him that look she has; she thinks wine is the only civilized option. I'll warn him later. I wish I had been as he is. Maybe I would not have been so bothered by what my father thought of me.'

'You say that, but Kodi himself, as self-assured as he is, still has some tough thoughts regarding his own father.'

'It doesn't show anymore, though, does it?'

'He has come to terms with it better than you did. You should give yourself some credit for that. And more than anything, he just needed to leave home to discover himself and be his own man. He's come a long way the last two weeks. He listens to your words. He believes you are wise. Uncle Normene tried to help you in the same way.'

'I was full of anger.'

'Your time in the Valley softened you, thankfully. Kodi, on the other hand, is not naturally an angry man.'

'No. Another mark of his character. But it does come out.'

'Impatience, rather. It is different. You're thinking of the Novice robes. You know, he's somewhat right about that. You sure you didn't snap at him because you feel the need to defend the tradition out of pride?'

'I said good words.'

'You did. And he learned a good lesson. Like I said, he thinks you're wise. But he was still right about Novice robes. The discomfort is not necessary. The symbolism of wearing them is lost on most. You remember how much you hated them, too. And he is probably more right than not on the Vow, as well. Dispensations should be easier to come by than they are. Being a Member of the Order can be lonely. Such alone-ness does not suit everyone.'

'If I am ever made High Priest, I will grant more of them. Not just the Aura ones.'

'Probably. But you won't be High Priest. You're too much a political man.'

'I have been, that's true. But I'm leaving Solanto. Politics will mean less to me.'

'Maybe. Maybe not. You're leaving at a strange time, too.'

'I know. I don't like it—not one bit.'

'You'll have to rely on Marco and on Mannago to aid the king. They are good men. Marco is highly regarded. He'll make a good substitute while you're gone.'

'He's not politically subtle, though.'

'No. That, he is not. He is, however, highly intelligent and perceptive. Are you going to tell him everything?'

'I think I'll have to tell him and Mannago both, everything about this situation with Prince Filiddor. I can't tell the king all this. He would not approve of my methods—he's too good of a man. The king's goodness could trap him. He has become rather soft in his old age. At least the others need to be on their guard at this Council.'

'So, you've made the decision not to stay for the Council, have you?'

'I think it is more apparent now we need to move on. I may tell them somewhat more about the Visions. Marco has probably figured some of it out, though. He'll likely discern much from what little I've already told him.'

'You were thinking about Kodi.'

'My mind is wandering, isn't it?'

'At least your mind still works! You suspect his Calling will be similar to Terianh's.'

'It disturbs me to think that times might be that desperate. The Alkhan and Alkhaness must be far more powerful than we had *thought. Walking the roads of Solanto one would never believe such threats existed, would they? Except whatever it is that Filiddor is up to.'*

'The bigger danger is in the south. And the east. Solanto has been isolated from the threat.'

'I hope so. Anyway, I'm not happy that Kodi might have to deal with all of it. He is eager, sure. And if that is his Calling, I don't know what good I am to him.'

'Stability and friendship. They will mean much as time goes by. You stick close to him.'

'Of course I will. Like glue. I am concerned he needs more than me, though. He needs training. Who's going to provide him that? Terianh was already a military captain, and the Guardian Himself taught him how to use his magical Gifts. I know nothing of warfare except what I have read in books, and the magic of the Sages is muted since the early days. So even if I help him discern his Gifts, I won't know how to help him use them, particularly if it's the Calling I suspect, anyway.'

'But there is a very good chance Kodi is a natural warrior. He's already a superior archer. They told you in Felto how he wins nearly all the contests that the men compete in at the fairs. When he acquires his first sword, I bet you anything he'll be superior in a matter of weeks. How many times have you said it to yourself? Meical knows what He's doing. Kodi's reading that book Theneri gave him, and at some point he's going to really start wondering about himself. He'll see things.'

'I...I just...fear. I fear for him and I fear for Lyndz.'

'You fear, because you care.'

"Curdoz, you're mighty quiet."

"Hmm? Ah, Kodi!" the Sage said. "I have much on my mind."

After they had eaten their meal, Kodi ordered a second pint and sat back while Curdoz loaded his pipe. Kodi asked, "I've never smoked, sir."

"Tobacco grows in southern Duranti and on Donesk. I've been smoking since I was quite a bit younger than you. All the farm boys I grew up with, and all their fathers, too, and some of their mothers, for that matter, smoked pipes. It isn't allowed in the Valley, for it doesn't reflect very well the Disciplines adopted by the Orders. Picked it right back up when I came back from the Valley. It relaxes me, particularly when I'm anxious, and it helps me think. I like it, but I don't recommend it to you. Bad habits are hard to break the older you get."

"It's carved out of ambernut. May I see it?" Curdoz handed the pipe over to Kodi. "How old is this? You know I wouldn't be surprised if Grandfather Yugan made it. It looks a lot like his older works, like the box he gave you with Kalemna's book. He was one of the few that worked with ambernut thirty years ago. Now all the best wood carvers do."

Then he gave Curdoz a rather wicked grin and took a draw on the pipe. He coughed rather violently.

"Give that back, you rascal!" Curdoz exclaimed, laughing. "That's what you get for your daring! Takes some getting used to."

Kodi chuckled, handed it back to him, and took another mouthful of ale.

The two engaged in conversation for quite a while. Kodi tended to talk more after a couple pints, yet Curdoz was perfectly willing to listen as the young man rambled on about his home and family, his interests and goals for himself. The Sage felt he had come to know Kodi quite well after their several days together, and obviously Kodi was becoming more comfortable around him. Curdoz was glad for it. Friendship and loyalty meant much. They made life meaningful.

He knew he had to trust him with more. At the least he was to grow Kodi into the leader that Meical wanted. "I have some tasks for you tomorrow, while I stay here in the morning. I have a number of letters to write." He then told Kodi what he needed him to do. "…and then we'll try to get out of here in the early afternoon."

"I'll handle it, sir." Kodi claimed confidently as he finished off his pint and went off to bed.

Curdoz remained awhile, thinking and smoking, and studying more closely the pipe that Yugan might have made.

The next morning, before Curdoz had awakened, Kodi was up and about. Musca remained asleep next to Curdoz' bed. After breakfasting in the common room Kodi saddled his horse and rode around the town to various inns requesting information. It took the better part of an hour before he discovered what he was looking for. Two men, one decidedly taller than the other, both in heavy brown woolen traveling robes, were exiting an inn on the western edge of the town. He hailed them.

"Would you be the Brothers Danly and Xeno?"

"We are indeed!" said the shorter man. He had a cheerful expression, rather like a male version of Idamé, though there was nothing effeminate about him. "I am Brother Danly, and this is Brother Xeno." He indicated his companion. "And I bet I know just who you are! The resemblance between you and your sister is striking! Twins, she said you are."

"I am Kodi, yes! Lord Curdoz asked me to look for you. Mother Idamé and Lyndz found you, did they?"

In a quiet corner inside, Kodi and the two Brothers talked at length. Curdoz had entrusted Kodi to describe for them all that had taken place on their journey to Aster. Xeno often nodded, but for the most part it was Danly who engaged. He would interrupt often and asked many questions.

"Well, that explains much! It made no sense that those Tribesmen were mere fur traders. So, they are plotting something with the prince, are they?"

Kodi then did his best to tell them what their tasks were to be—that Danly was to apprentice under Theneri to, in time, become the head librarian, and that Xeno was to operate within the Monastery as a Monastic and to provide Mind Support for Theneri so that the old man could continue his secretive Moment-mastering excursions. Kodi told Xeno of Theneri's hesitations and strong desire for privacy. The tall man then spoke up for the first time. He had a quiet, but very deep voice, which fit well his large size.

"Master Theneri has nothing to fear from me. Old men carry old secrets…and old regrets. They should not be tampered with. I will keep his memories to myself."

Kodi liked both Brothers quite well. Danly was full of exuberance, and Xeno a shy seriousness. Kodi could easily imagine as a Healing Pair that their very presence would do much in bringing health to the suffering, whether they employed their Gifts or not. He noticed too they had strong hands, and underneath their layered garments Kodi deemed them to be tough as soldiers. They were not the most typical of Order Members like those he had met at the Monastery. "Lord Curdoz asks that you call upon him at the mid-day hour. He's busy, but he wants to give you a few more instructions."

"We will go to him," said Danly. "And we wish you and your sister well in whatever the Lord Curdoz and Mother Idamé are planning for you!"

In a special gesture of goodwill, Danly and Xeno together placed their hands on Kodi's head. He felt as though warm water flooded over his body, and though he was not sick or suffering in any way, every minor muscle ache abruptly disappeared, causing him to feel as refreshed as if he'd had a late evening swim in the Wolf River in summer after a hard day's work. It was the first time he'd ever experienced the Gift of Healing, though he'd heard many stories of the miracles Healing Pairs could perform. He thanked them kindly and took his leave.

From there he made his way to the southern road and followed this about a quarter mile. He stopped just outside another inn on the east side of the road, an inn that Curdoz had described for him.

There was no activity of any sort: no patrons or horses or wagons. The Fox was quiet. He tried the front door without success, although he noticed smoke rising from one of the chimneys to the rear. He ensured the horse was secure and walked around to the rear of the main building. He found the stables, but there was only one large and sturdy carthorse there. Presently, a man stepped out of what Kodi presumed was the rear kitchen door. When the man saw Kodi, he started.

Kodi put on a cheerful face and spoke quickly. "Onri! My name is Kodi. We were not introduced the other day. Lord Curdoz sent me to look in on you."

Onri stood still as stone, looking Kodi over, uncertain at first how to respond. Kodi however walked over to the man and held out his hand. Reluctant at first, Onri reached out and took it.

Finally, the man spoke. Kodi had not yet heard the man's voice, for the other day Curdoz had not really given him a chance to speak. It was quiet and nervous. "I…ye may tell his lordship that I accept his offer. I am, as a matter of fact, choosing which possessions I wish to take with me on the journey south."

"Is there anything I can help you with, Onri? Did you sell your inn?"

"It is sold, yes. I purchased me a good new cart and horse…as ye can see." Onri pointed to the horse in the stable. On a wagon close by were loaded a couple of large crates that appeared to be full of Onri's belongings.

Kodi, determined to be friendly, walked over to the stable to take a look. He gave the large beast a few strokes on his large face. "Fine animal, Onri! I know you will miss your inn, though. It belonged to your folks before you?"

Though he was still nervous, the man was being drawn into Kodi's warm manner. He answered. "Yes. But…but methinks I may not miss it so much. Me father…he was not a very kind man. He could be cruel to me mother. Me memories of this place are not very good ones."

Kodi reached out and grabbed Onri's shoulders in a friendly manner. "I'm sorry, Onri. Your future should be a brighter one!"

For the first time, Onri smiled and the anxious crinkle between his eyes seemed to smooth. "Would ye care to come into me kitchen and have some chicory coffee, Master Kodi?"

"Sure!" said Kodi. "That'd be great!"

For the next quarter hour, Kodi listened as Onri the innkeeper opened his heart to him. He spoke of his history. He apparently had no real friends, and yet Kodi could tell that it was because the man's nervous way did not lend itself to making friends easily. Kodi, however, looked beyond it and discovered underneath a man of some pain. The man appeared close to tears as he spoke of the death of his mother only the year before, the only person in the world whom he loved and who loved him in return. He expressed shame for having acted as an informant for the Prince of Hesk. "Didn't believe I was really harming anyone. Methinks I just wanted...I don't really know what I wanted."

"Sounds to me like you were having a rough time after your mother died. You just wanted to feel important," offered Kodi.

"Yes. But I was a fool."

"What sort of information did he want you to report?"

"If anyone of unusual authority, such as a High Order Member, an official of the king, a baron or duke was to come to Thorune, I was to do me best to find out why, what his travel plans were, and who and what sort of people he spoke to and what his business was."

"Are there other informants that you know, Onri?"

"I wish I knew, though methinks there are none other here in Thorune." Then he said, "Wait here a moment, Master Kodi."

With that Kodi watched as the man disappeared from the kitchen, but he returned quite soon and handed him a tiny bag.

It jingled.

"That is the money Lord Ultrech gave me when I brought him word of Lord Curdoz' travels and business. Pray give it to Lord Curdoz. I be too ashamed to keep it now. I wish now I could be helpful to Lord Curdoz instead."

Kodi doubted that Curdoz would choose to use Onri as an informant of his own. Onri needed emotional healing and to distance himself from his previous life. "I've heard that Island Saundry is a really fine place. I bet you will like it there."

Onri sighed. "What I really would have liked years ago, Master Kodi, would have been for me dad to apprentice me to a master cabinet maker. I believe me work is good, but without a master's reputation I can't sell me wares. At least not at fair prices."

"Really?" Kodi asked, surprised. "Show me some of your work, Onri."

The man stood and had Kodi follow him across the backyard to an outbuilding, where inside, quite surprisingly, were a great many quality woodworking tools.

But there was more.

"You made this chest, Onri? And these chairs?" Kodi, who of course had already learned many skills from his grandfather was the perfect judge for Onri's work. "But they're excellent, Onri! Fantastic dovetailing and molding. You carved these medallions?"

On a work bench were several detailed pieces intended to be fitted as decorations on larger items.

"The work takes me mind off meself."

"Are you sure you haven't tried selling these?"

"I…er, have a hard time promoting meself, and like I said before, without the reputation that comes from apprenticing with a master I would not receive fair value."

Kodi picked up a horse figurine. It was a fine recreation of a rearing animal with a flowing mane, carved from blond walnut. Kodi was flabbergasted that someone with such talent could not find a market for his obviously quality wares. Perhaps his carving skills were not quite the caliber as those of his grandfather, but the furniture he made was of exceptional skill and could hardly be equaled even by a master. The only thing that kept them from being highly valuable was that they were made of common Northern Pine rather than a quality hardwood. Yet even on the walnut carvings, with the exception of his own grandfather's, Kodi had rarely seen better.

"You purchased all these tools over the years? Your father didn't have these as an innkeeper!"

"Like I said, it has become rather a passion. Yes, sir, Master Kodi, I purchased each tool as I could afford to."

Kodi looked at Onri keenly. There was clearly more to the man's soul than the acquiescent shyness and odd social skills. The man had some ambition, he had goals and dreams, yet he had kept the inn apparently out of obligation. His heart wasn't in that.

His heart was in creating beautiful things out of wood.

A sudden thought came to Kodi, and then too he felt a powerful Voice in his mind urging him, a voice saying, *Yes, Kodi! Trust your impulse on this, Brother.* Kodi wasn't sure he really heard such a Voice, yet for some reason the moment he dived into the Valley Lake came into his mind again, and that powerful sense of 'bigness' came over him. He knew just what to do.

He looked squarely into Onri's face and spoke firmly.

"You have paper and quill, Onri?"

"Certainly, sir," the man said, curious. "Though me own writing isn't very good, sir."

"Doesn't matter. Now listen to me, Onri. I'm going to write a letter to my grandfather and mother. I have something better for you than going to Island Saundry!"

Perhaps an hour later he took Onri's hand and patted him firmly on his shoulders.

"It'll be like having a family, but a good one this time, Onri. And my grandfather will be pleased to have someone as talented as yourself to help him, I'll say! You show them this letter from me, and they'll watch after you. You pack up all your tools and all these carvings and furniture and take them with you. My grandpa will find a market for them!"

Onri had such a grin, and though his cheeks were flush they were in marked contrast to the pained embarrassment back on the Ramp. He waved as Kodi rounded the back corner of the inn to return to his horse.

One task remaining, Kodi rode straightaway to the center of the town to the Kingsmen barracks to find Captain Santher.

"Ah! Lord Curdoz' friend! Kodi is your name, if I remember rightly?" Santher was in his office as usual, writing reports and issuing orders to Kingsmen soldiers.

"Yes, sir! Lord Curdoz wants to know if you need the horses back, or if we may ride them south. He will have them returned to you in two more weeks."

"'Tis perfectly well, Master Kodi! Send His Lordship my regards!"

"Thank you, Captain!"

He found the Sage concluding a conversation in their room with Xeno and Danly. Musca was gnawing a meaty bone beside the fireplace. Kodi handed over the moneybag, explaining where it came from and telling him something of his visit with the now former innkeeper.

The Sage tossed the moneybag directly to Xeno. "You may find a use for that. So, it is Filiddor's cousin Lord Ultrech who is gathering information for the prince? Xeno, have Theneri begin an operation to look in on Ultrech. He has an estate far to the south in the Principality, but he has a manor in Aster where he stays much of the time. He has always been Filiddor's closest confidante. If these informants like Onri are reporting to Ultrech, then he may have a list of them, and you can discover how widespread this arrangement is. Father Marco can make use of the information."

"We will do, Lord Curdoz."

"And Kodi. You just never know how information like that might be useful someday. I want you to tell the Brothers as much as you can about that trail onto the Highlands from behind Felto."

Kodi did, though he had to draw on parchment a map based on the knowledge in his head. "You can find it easy from the bottom, using this map and my descriptions. But from the top I've never traveled to any forest village or anything in order to get a good bearing. Grandpa would know better. It's all forest up there for miles and miles. My best guess is that from the Falls it's probably at least twenty miles north if you follow the edge of the Escarpment. The falling stream, if you can find it, will lead you right to the trail. The shelf that juts outward where we used to camp is stark and pretty obvious. It's shaped kind of like a hunched up triangle or the keel of a boat, that's the best I can tell you. Maybe you can find that, and the creek and the trail are just north of it."

Xeno pocketed the map and the Brothers took their leave of the Sage and Kodi one last time. The latter two finished packing their belongings. After a late lunch, Curdoz paid his bill to the innkeeper, the two mounted Santher's horses again and, with Musca well-rested and well-fed, they made their way to the southbound road.

Passing by Onri's inn, Kodi described for Curdoz the details regarding his encounter with the man that morning.

Curdoz was somewhat ambivalent to Kodi's proposition to Onri.

"The offer speaks well of you, no doubt, Kodi. But I really wanted Onri to be much further away from Lord Ultrech and Prince Filiddor. Felto is hardly any distance at all."

Kodi, however, expected this response. "Just like you said you felt compelled to offer him a way out, so did I. It was absolutely the right thing, you'll see. It was as if the Guardian told me to do it. No, it was more like I thought of it on my own, and then Meical confirmed it. It was as if He was expecting me to think about it and then pressed me to act on it. I discovered what is really important to Onri, and Grandpa can help him. And he can help Grandpa."

Curdoz looked at him unsure whether he should be pleased or exasperated.

"I sent you without me because I believed Onri would have been too ashamed to speak if I had come. I believed I was doing the right thing on that, and was basically giving you permission to handle the communication. I don't think I would have done the same as you, but nevertheless, I grant it was your place to do it. It would be wrong for me to go back there now and undo it. I'll just have to have trust on this. I certainly can't deny your sincerity. And as it is, you were able to find out that bit about Ultrech. And you told him to keep his destination to himself?"

"Yes. He sold the inn already, but he has told no one his plans, and assured me he won't."

"Better for him when Ultrech realizes he is gone."

"I think he thinks so, too. He's a lot smarter I think than you give him credit for, sir. Just a bit slower. I think he's one of those sorts of people that if you give him enough time, he can see through a stone wall."

By dinnertime they had arrived in the village of Davos, and Kodi was surprised to find out that this was actually Curdoz' hometown. To Arturo's delight, the Sage chose to stay the night at his place. The two travelers were treated to some of Arturo's best cooking, and a trio of local fiddlers provided entertainment to a full house of locals eager to see the Sage again, even if it had only been a few weeks since he had come through before. Kodi pleasurably enjoyed the brew here, too, deciding it was some of the finest he'd ever tasted.

It rained cold the next day and their going was slowed. When evening came, Curdoz requested lodging at the home of a widowed farmer's wife with two strapping sons who gawked at the Sage. They had never met anyone so important. The woman was a jovial character and very pleased to entertain the Sage of Solanto. Kodi got on well with the boys, and Musca went off hunting half the night, returning wet and tired, though apparently with a full belly.

The rain was heavy the next morning, but by mid-afternoon the sun popped out and it proved to be the warmest day so far that spring. When they arrived in Trimm, Kodi was introduced to Curdoz' friends, Anni and Leskin at the Laughing Dog. The inn was now busy with the increase in travel, but with one room left, indeed the same tiny room that Curdoz had used before, they were made to feel as much at home as could be even though it was a bit cramped and Kodi had to sleep on a makeshift pallet on the floor. The sweet old couple showered Musca with meaty leftovers and bones, and they doted on Kodi like grandparents and gathered all sorts of food to stuff into his pack, making funny statements about growing boys needing to eat. Kodi laughed and was reminded keenly of home. Old folks in Felto were always pressing food on him with similar commentary whenever he would pass by their doors.

The road from Trimm to Ferostro was broad and carried even more traffic than the east-west road in northern Ascanti. Curdoz was determined as usual to bless everyone who requested it, and indeed more people seemed to know him, green stole or not. Yet, like before, he refused to get down off his horse. Rain the second day out from Trimm caused some decrease in traffic and those few who still endured the wet were less inclined to want to stop the Sage. There were more towns and fewer forests, for here in the heart of the kingdom more of the land was cleared into many hundreds of farms. On the fourth morning after parting from Anni and Leskin, the skies cleared, and beyond a large blue lake the massive gray walls of a great city with its many tall watchtowers stood, and a large and stately castle on top of a hill reared high in its very center.

Everything about the capital city of Ferostro was splendid, although Kodi was surprised to find that the streets were a bit narrower than those in Aster, and therefore it felt more crowded. However, the people were far friendlier, reflecting the beautiful spring weather which was now in full swing and a happier and healthier populace. The buildings were tall and charming with pointed arches reaching skyward, townhouses with towers and pennants flying, and trees planted in park-like intersections surrounded by flowerbeds being filled now by laborers with cuttings of flowering summer plants. Kingsmen marched splendidly through the streets on their way to their duties. There were more horses and carts, but the cobbled streets were kept reasonably clean by even more laborers. However, it was all very orderly, the laborers were not ragged and beggarly like those in Aster. There were street vendors by the dozens, and everyone was bustling and busy. Curdoz was hailed often by people who knew him.

Though Curdoz said it was his first duty to call upon King Carlomen whenever he appeared in the city after an absence, he felt it important for the twins to be reunited as soon as possible. Besides, the Sage wanted Lyndz to attend when they went before the king.

"My biggest concern is being dragged into a long conversation with the Mother Superior," Curdoz said with a sigh after explaining these plans to Kodi. "I will just have to arrange a meeting with her later in the afternoon. Oh, Kodi! I almost forgot. As Sage, I am one of the few men allowed to enter the Convent, and even so, only to the offices of the Mother Superior and the Chapel of Song. You will have to wait elsewhere. Eh, just stay away from the taverns, will you?"

Kodi joked. "It's a bit early. Maybe later!"

Musca followed them, drinking at every fountain they passed and many eyes turned his way, for he was a large and handsome animal with his thick silver coat. Other city dogs would bound up to him and bark, but the Elentine Noble ignored them all like a snooty nobleman. Finally they arrived outside the iron gates of a large complex of impressive stone buildings. Two Kingsmen stood guard and hailed the Sage.

"Hail, Lord Sage!" said one of these. "We have been expecting you! The Mother Superior is eager to see you!"

Curdoz nodded, though Kodi noticed him rolling his eyes as he dismounted and walked alone through the gates. Kodi tied the reins of Curdoz' mount to the pommel of his own saddle and led both horses and Musca down the lane to a busy bazaar where several vendors displayed their wares and clowns performed in the middle of the street for laughing children. He strongly doubted there were clowns in Aster even in high summer.

A young boy ran up to him. Perhaps confused by the horses, he asked, "Are ye a knight, m'lord?"

Kodi squatted down to be at his level and scruffed the boy's curly brown hair. "No. As you see, I have no sword! I'm not even a soldier. Not yet, anyway! I plan to start training real soon, though, how about that!"

"You look like a knight! I was sure you were! You better get you a sword, then!" The boy ran off, leaving Kodi both cheered and wondering.

A flower vendor called out to him, "Lovely tulips for your lady, young squire?"

"For my sister, yes!" exclaimed Kodi. He handed over a few coppers to the woman who eyed him up and down.

"Your sister! A man such as ye should have a lady in your life to kiss that pretty face! If I wasn't Bonded I'd do it meself!"

Kodi laughed jovially, "Thank you, my dear!" He bowed caddishly as the woman laughed and he then walked away.

There were minstrels playing and singing, and he stood with the small crowd that had gathered. He listened for a few minutes, dropped silver piece into their collection bucket, then turned away. His steps took him to a man who cooked sausages on an iron grill fixed neatly to the top of a wheeled horse cart. Though his pack was still half full of Anni's food gifts, the cooking meat smelled so good he couldn't help himself. The man put the hot sausage in a roll and handed it to Kodi. "Rather not be paid in tulips, mind ye!" he said jokingly, looking at Kodi holding the bouquet. "Have one I dropped in the dirt earlier, not fit now for a person! Yonder pup looks hungry! Handsome fellow it is. Sell it to ye for two coppers!"

All in all, the contrast with the gloom of Aster was refreshing, and Kodi decided it was more than just the fine spring weather.

He led his menagerie of animals to a stone bench by a fountain and sat down to eat his sausage roll. He threw the cold one to Musca who gobbled it down in one bite. He had just finished drinking from his water bottle when he heard a favorite voice.

"Ko!"

Lyndz had come from the direction of the Convent gates, running to find him.

"Oy there, Lyndz!" Kodi stood and picked his sister off the ground in a huge bear hug. "Got something here for you!" He added, handing her the tulips he had set upon the bench while he ate.

"Oh, Ko! They're so sweet! Musca! Oh, I missed you, you big ole bear!" She bent down and gave the Noble a great squeeze, who barked twice and then set about licking her furiously in the face. "You smell like sausages!"

The two sat together on the bench and talked. Though Kodi was able to tell her some about his time with Curdoz, the Sage didn't want them discussing important information out in public where other ears might overhear. "And what about you!"

"Oh, we haven't discovered my Gifts, yet. Although, I feel like I'm becoming quite adept at meditation and concentration! All the Sisters have been really friendly, yet they all seem to think that Mother Idamé brought me here as a Novice!"

"Have they made you wear stupid brown sackcloth robes?"

"Novices who come to the Convent wear white linen robes! Though they only stay until the weather is good enough to travel to the Valley. But no, Mother Idamé hasn't made me wear them. Ko, the Convent is so nice! It has pretty gardens, and I've been helping the Sisters plant the flower beds. They've taught me probably thirty plants I didn't know before! And they've got a huge glass house for growing things in the winter. I love it, of course!"

"Have you met the Mother Superior?"

At that, Lyndz frowned. "Oh, Ko! She is a ferocious one! Don't get me wrong. She has been quite polite to me and can be quite gracious, but she has been giving Mother Idamé a terrible go. She is really angry that Idamé is leaving the country with Curdoz."

Kodi whispered, "What about her Vision?"

"Oh, she believed Idamé that she had one, but of course Curdoz ordered her not to tell the Mother Superior anything more about it, and that just infuriates her. She doesn't want to believe that Meical would present a Vision to a Matrimonial that would cause her to have to take leave of her duties. She's convinced that Idamé has interpreted her Vision incorrectly, and she hardly listens when Idamé tells her over and over that Curdoz interpreted it for her. I dread the thought when she and Curdoz meet later. Thankfully, we don't have to be there for that!"

"Curdoz is going to present us to the king, did he tell you?"

"Yes! I am so beside myself! This is exciting, Ko! And we have such a famous father, you know!"

"Well, let's go, then!" said Curdoz, standing suddenly in front of them.

"Curdoz! We didn't see you!" said Lyndz, standing up. "Is Mother Idamé not coming with us?"

"She is packing. Your things, too. And she will not forget Kodi's bow." He added this before Kodi could even ask. "She cannot wait to leave the Convent now I am here. I have rooms in the king's palace. She met the king long ago, so she doesn't need to go with us to meet him. She will see us there later in the afternoon. You have some flowers to put in water?"

Kodi lifted his sister onto his horse, and he then sat behind her. They rode further down other roads until they came to a main boulevard that zigzagged up the central hill containing the palace complex.

Enormous black iron gates stood wide and some dozen Kingsmen guards in bright blue uniforms greeted Curdoz with due reverence. They promptly took charge of the horses and the baggage and even Lyndz' tulips. Musca too was led off with the horses, though they promised to look after him. A servant ran off to announce the arrival of the Sage of Solanto.

Before them stood the seat of King Carlomen. Built over three hundred years before in high Anterianhi style, half fortified castle, half palace, it was a series of towers and buildings containing numerous arched windows, countless trefoils and quatrefoils, and surrounding a high, pointed-arched dome in the center. It had a lighter feel to it than the Ralsheen-built Princes' Palace, but it was far larger. Everywhere floating in the breeze were bright blue pennants, and high above on the tallest tower flew an enormous blue flag bearing a white stag. In the courtyard was a large flowing fountain featuring also a magnificent antlered stag cast in bronze.

Kodi was moved by the immensity and the grandness. He thought of his father and of what Lyndz had said, and for the first time since he left home rather wished his father were with him now.

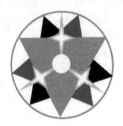

Chapter 15—Royal Greetings, Royal Gifts

The three of them ascended the stairs and two enormous doors swung back revealing a well-lit and grand hall beyond. More guards stood here and saluted the Sage very formally. When they entered the hall, the proud chamberlain stood forward to greet them.

"Honored Sage! His Majesty will be delighted you have returned so soon! He always looks forward to your presence and good counsel!"

"Thank you, Liddeus! I am glad to attend him as always. But I have two here I wish to introduce to His Majesty. Is he available for a brief audience? And then, yes, I need to speak with him on certain matters."

"He has been made aware you have arrived and wishes you to appear before him at once. He has just finished the noonday meal and awaits you in the Chamber of Fire. Her Highness the Princess Isatura is with him."

"What a pleasure! Shall we follow?"

"This way, Lord Sage."

The three followed Liddeus down the entrance hall through another set of doors and into another hall. Everywhere were hung gorgeous tapestries of various scenes, and many paintings of Solantine royalty. Statues of sundry kings and queens stood regally in alcoves set off in the walls and lit by quatrefoil windows of sunlight. High above were more windows, some of colored glass and some clear. The columns that held up the ceiling were spaced widely, and the high pointed arches created the impression of great distances. Kodi was enamored of the building itself, for this was a form of architecture that appealed to his senses, and Lyndz remarked often on the art everywhere.

Finally, Liddeus approached a smaller set of double doors half-way down another long hall. Guards stood here too and saluted the Sage and opened the doors for them to enter.

Inside was a room, not too large, yet with two enormous fireplaces roaring away and providing strong heat. The walls were paneled in dark walnut, and heavily upholstered chairs sat near to the fires. There were several library tables containing books and candelabra, and yet there was plenty of light too from high windows.

In one chair sat an old but lordly individual listening intently to a middle-aged woman in smart attire who seemed to be discussing with him treasury matters. To the old man's right sat a lovely young woman with fair northern features listening to the conversation.

When they saw the visitors, the old man and the young woman stood and smiled graciously. The other woman nodded, then took her ledgers and marched away.

"Lord Curdoz, my dear, dear friend!" called the king stepping forward.

Curdoz bowed and Kodi followed his lead instantly. Lyndz curtsied perfectly.

The king continued. "So good to see you! Your journey the last few weeks was a success I see. These must be the very twins you spoke of from your Vision!"

"Indeed they are, Your Majesty. And I think you will be quite interested to know who they are!"

"Tell me! Stand straight, young man, young lady! Let me get a good look at you!"

"Your Majesty, may I present the Lady Lyndz Fothemry and Master Kodi, heir to the Fothemry estate."

The king paused for a moment, then radiated cheer. "Really! These two are the children of the Lord Hess? Well, I think I see the resemblance now! I haven't seen your father in three years, but I remember him very well! Very well indeed! He is a cousin to Duke Amerro, if I recall?"

"Yes, Your Majesty," they both answered.

"And the Escarantine heritage is there. Such handsome specimens, I say! You two are as pleasant to look at as...as my daughter here!" He turned to the young woman. "This is my daughter, Isatura!"

"It is a pleasure!" said the Princess, in a kind voice, deeper than what might be expected for a woman. She was truly lovely, with long blond locks and clear face. She was probably not five years older than the twins.

Lyndz took her hand and curtsied again, "Your Highness!" she said.

Kodi had never been introduced to a high-born woman in his life, yet he had at least seen other important men present themselves to his mother. Quite properly, he therefore bowed again and kissed the princess's hand, repeating his sister's greeting.

"They are indeed handsome, Father! Lord Curdoz, it is good to see you again!"

"As it is to see you, Your Highness!"

It was all very pleasant, and Kodi and Lyndz felt as though they were being treated as the most important people who had ever stepped foot in the palace. Perhaps they expected kings to be aloof and stern, yet they found Carlomen a kind old patriarch. They sat to refreshing iced drinks and cakes, and then the princess took the twins under wing for a half hour while Curdoz remained to speak privately with the king.

Isatura endeared Lyndz to her by taking them on a brisk walk through the walled gardens.

"Lord Curdoz told us some time ago that twins appeared in his Vision from the High Guardian! It is good to see that he found you! It has all been a great mystery, of course, but my father and I believe you must be of great value to the High Lord Meical. The Guardian must have important plans for you? We understand the Sage must take you on a journey. We certainly offer you our most hearty blessings! Anything the Lord Curdoz has ever done is a blessing to this country. You must know he is held in the highest regard by my father."

Lyndz and Kodi were as sincere and polite as they were capable of being, drawing upon all the advice and guidance their mother had given them over the years on how to communicate with high lords and ladies. The twins were easily drawn into the princess's sphere, yet with sufficient grace resisted telling her anymore of Curdoz' plans, and they made no mention that Kodi too had experienced a Vision.

They did, however, speak of their home and family. Isatura was well-versed on the happenings in other parts of the country. She wanted to know whether the manor house had been completed, was perfectly familiar with Felto's location, the name of the Wolf River, and the ambernut trade originating from there. From the garden she led the twins to a large study where on one wall was displayed the most enormous map the twins had ever seen. It was perhaps twelve feet square and showed every village, baronial estate, river and road throughout the whole of the Kingdom of Solanto and the Principality of Hesk.

"...and I do hope you will see Guardian's Gate! If Lord Curdoz should take you on his ship, you will certainly have an impressive view of it!" She pointed to the spot on the map where the Duchy of Duranti dipped southward, nearly touching the former Domain of Lorinth, now the Republic of Tirilorin, though the map did not show much beyond Solanto's boundaries. Guardian Lake took up most of the space on the bottom of the map, and Island Saundry, the home of the Sage of Solanto was shown just offshore from the Grand Duchy of Escarant. "If you go to Lord Curdoz' estate, you will take the road through the grand duke's estates. He too is a great friend of my fathers. I hope you will get the chance to meet him! You know, I am familiar with many of the connections among the great families. Since you are Amerro's cousins, you are connected with the grand duke, did you know? You have common ancestry, and of course it shows in your dark olive complexion. If you travel through Escarant you'll find it very common there. Most Solantines descend from Elenite ancestry, on the other side of the Imperial Mountains, but the Escarantine lines come from Nant. Of course, these lines are very ancient, dating to the time of the Emperor Terianh and the Conquest."

She went on talking about families and kingdoms and connections and history, and Kodi and Lyndz found it all fascinating. Much of the information was new to them. They certainly knew their father Hess had Escarantine blood, and though Curdoz had mentioned it to Kodi, Lyndz had no idea that the Escarantines had centuries ago come from faraway Nant, the great island kingdom. Of course, none of these places existed under those names prior to Terianh the Great, but they had been populated by their ancestral peoples far back into the days of the Ralsheen and before.

She asked about their mother. "Your mother's name is Elisa, is it not?" She inquired as to their mother's health. "And it is my understanding that your father is again in the wilds of the Tolosian Peninsula. What a fearless adventurer! Kodi, I can see an eagerness in your face that I suspect comes from him. Do you plan to follow in your father's footsteps?"

"It was my plan to train under Duke Amerro and to become a knight in his service. However, now that Lord Curdoz is taking us out of the country, I will learn elsewhere."

"You have the makings of a great leader, Kodi! I wish you well! And dear Lyndz! What is your great wish for yourself?"

Lyndz was rather shocked by this question, for since the Sage and Mother Idamé had come into her life, her earlier ideas of what she anticipated for her own future appeared in flux. "I will, for the time being, follow where I am led, Your Highness."

"Oh, that will never do, dear one! You have the same blood as your brother here and all the great ones in your family! Your potential is just as great, I know it! You shall be a strong leader, too!"

The princess was such a generous spirit, and yet she was keenly aware that the twins could not give her too much information. She readily admitted that she presumed Curdoz had warned them to be wary of offering too much information, and was wise enough to understand that the future was elusive. She did not, therefore, press them too much and returned to talking about the map, the importance of the various places they had traveled through already, and connections. Kodi noted, however, she never once mentioned the Principality of Hesk or its princes, ignoring that section of the map altogether.

She escorted them back to the Hall of Fire where the Sage and the king had just concluded their conversation. The king's face seemed to show a bit of concern now, perhaps from the news the Sage had imparted. However, the instant he saw the others his cheer returned and he stood.

"You shall all be at dinner tonight with us! I regret it that the Lord Curdoz must leave our country, and he intends to leave here tomorrow noon." He then looked directly at Kodi. "Lord Curdoz has just mentioned to me, Master Kodi, of a bow of ambernut heartwood that your grandfather crafted for you, is that right?"

"Yes, Your Majesty!" said Kodi, surprised.

"I would very much like to see it! You bring it with you just before dinner!"

"Certainly, Your Majesty!"

They parted the company of the king and the princess, and Curdoz himself led them to his set of rooms in a tower attached to the west wing of the palace. It consisted of several resplendent chambers with a parlor centered upon a grand marble fireplace and containing high-arched windows behind a large desk, and overlooking the gardens with the blue lake in the distance beyond the city's walls. Three bedrooms adjoined it, one being Curdoz' own, and two guest rooms, each with two large tester beds. Brother and sister did not mind in the least sharing a bedroom for a night, leaving a room for Idamé.

The Matrimonial Mother was lying down on a large divan in front of the parlor fireplace when they arrived, but she promptly rose and patted Kodi on the cheek in greeting. The four of them sat and talked, eager to catch up with one another and to consider their forthcoming travels. Occasionally, they would veer away from sensitive matters when servants would enter in order to tend the fires and bring them refreshments. Kodi and Lyndz eventually became aware that the apartment contained another room, an enormous bathroom with two large white marble tubs and a tap of running water which the servants were now using to fill several smaller kettles that they heated in another fireplace in the same room. There was even a plumbed water closet off to the side, eliminating the need for chamber pots.

The twins had never known such luxury. For Kodi it was even more splendid than the bath at the Asterian Monastery. The two women and then the two men took their turns, and Kodi was flabbergasted as manservants dressed him afterwards in a complete set of fine new clothes, dyed in a dark blue, which had been purchased by the Sage, he having ordered Linnaeus to send for them.

"How did you know my sizes, Curdoz?" he asked after offering his thanks. "And they made them so fast!"

"It's much different in Ferostro than in other cities. There are tailors and dressmakers here that compete by actually stocking the fashions in various sizes. You're an inch taller than me; that was easy, and all Linnaeus had to do was tell them you are large and fit! If they had not fit, we could have returned them for another size. Your wool and leather clothes are excellent for traveling, but you could use other. Your boots are still good." In fact, Kodi found that his boots had been cleaned and polished while he had taken his bath. "Your sister had a dress made after Idamé brought her here, and frankly, you may find good use for it all in Tirilorin."

Later, Lyndz emerged from Idamé's room in her new fine linen dress of a rich cream and sporting her emerald necklace that her father had had made for her. The servants had braided her dark hair. Kodi looking at her proclaimed his sister the most beautiful lady in all of Solanto, to which Curdoz and Idamé readily agreed. "As beautiful as a princess!" added Idamé.

Lyndz beamed.

Curdoz had shaved and put on his best clothes which had been carefully ironed, along with a more elaborately embroidered, though still mostly green stole, and Idamé too was lovely in a plain blue dress and her colorful Matrimonial shawl. She wore no jewelry as was the typical practice of Order Members.

The servants left them, and the foursome had another hour before they were to present themselves for dinner with the royal family, so they continued to talk about their adventures so far.

"And what about the Mother Superior, Curdoz?" asked Lyndz. "She obviously didn't see you this afternoon."

Curdoz laughed. "I decided on a slightly different tack. The least I could do was to offer to lead the morning meditation at the chapel. So, I will meet with her after that tomorrow."

Idamé looked over at him. "You don't expect me to go there with you, I hope? She has made me feel guilty enough!"

"No. I need you to get everyone packed to leave. And if you all need to shop for anymore traveling gear before we leave the country, Ferostro is the place to do it. We will leave after the lunch hour. We're taking a carriage the rest of the journey to the Lake. A large coach. Father Marco is traveling with us to Grand Duke Mannago's palace in Escarant where they and I need to have a very long conversation. I am putting Marco in charge of the Orders when we leave the country, and he will speak for me in Council."

"I'm glad you're not putting the Mother Superior in charge!"

It was obvious to everyone Idamé was rather bitter about how the Mother Superior had treated her the last two weeks. Idamé hated confrontation.

"She'll be at dinner tonight, I'm afraid," said Curdoz.

"Oh no!" said Idamé gloomily.

"You will sit next to me. I already have that part arranged with Liddeus. She will be at the other end by the king. You won't even have to talk with her."

"I will, too. You know I will." Idamé frowned.

A servant came to them again at the proper time and led them all through many doors and hallways. Kodi was so glad to be reunited finally with his bow, and he gladly carried it with him as the king requested.

However, they were not at first taken to the dining hall, but rather to a small audience chamber where the king and princess stood to greet the Sage and his companions. The pair greeted everyone again cordially.

The Princess spoke to Lyndz, "Lady Lyndz! My dear, what a lovely jewel! How stunning you are tonight!"

Stunning and stunned. Lyndz was beside herself when Isatura presented her a lovely green sash interwoven with beautifully embroidered floral patterns which the princess promptly wrapped around Lyndz' waist, looping it through a rather large, but beautifully worked, solid gold buckle. "It is perfect with that jewel!" Isatura exclaimed. "The silk comes from Essemar. I will write a letter to your mother and tell her about our visit together! You shall sit beside me at dinner!"

Lyndz thanked her most graciously.

The king took Kodi's bow and examined it. "Magnificent, young Kodi! Your grandfather is inspired! A golden ambernut bow; I'm sure I've never seen such a thing in all my time!"

He then signaled to a servant who stepped forward holding a gorgeously tooled, large leather quiver with brass rivets and displaying a stag's head in silver, it being the symbol of Solanto. It contained perhaps four dozen well-wrought arrows. The king took it from the servant and presented it to Kodi.

Kodi was assuredly as overawed by the gift as Lyndz had been with hers. He took it and bowed with proper thanks. The king spoke again. "May it serve you well! You have rendered good service to Lord Curdoz already, I hear. And he tells me you are a superior marksmen!"

"Indeed he is the best, Your Majesty," added Curdoz.

"Unfortunate we don't have time before you leave to call an archery tournament! But you have my blessings, Master Kodi." He then spoke to both of the twins. "Your father has done great service for this country opening Tolos to exploration and settlement, and it would be remiss for us not to offer his son and daughter tokens of our gratitude when they visit us!"

They bowed again at the kind words of the king.

The same servant who brought the quiver took it and Kodi's bow with the promise to return them to Curdoz' rooms. They all followed the royal pair to another hallway where, in a line, stood a dozen or so additional guests that the king had invited with the purpose of honoring the Sage of Solanto before he left the country for what was to be an unknown length of time.

There were a great many greetings and introductions that seemed to occupy some ten minutes before a bell rang calling them all to dinner.

The dining hall was massive and could easily have seated a hundred guests, so the table contracted and set for twenty persons seemed rather small in its setting, and yet it was surely the biggest, most splendidly set table Kodi had ever seen. He hoped his table manners would be adequate. Lyndz was also impressed, though she was probably less self-conscious, more used to dinners in palaces having been presented at Duke Amerro's court in Cumpero the previous summer.

Servants by the dozen presented glorious foods one course at a time, and the conversation around the dinner table was reasonably light-hearted and pleasant. A number of toasts were offered to the Sage, wishing him well on his upcoming journey.

The king was at one end of the table in a high-backed, throne-like chair, and at his right-hand sat Isatura. Both wore gold circlets in their hair and were dressed handsomely. Next to the princess sat Lyndz, and the two young women laughed and talked happily about books and gardens. Kodi sat on the other side of his sister, and next to him was another man who was perhaps taller even than Xeno, far less massive, though of fit frame.

To Kodi's eyes, Father Marco was more sagely than Curdoz. Kodi had become rather used to Curdoz' usually scruffy face that he only shaved for important meetings, in addition to the man's traveling clothes which were rather common. Kodi could not imagine Father Marco ever allowing himself to appear scruffy. He had a black beard neatly trimmed and waxed; he sat as erect as a towering statue, and his mouth was thus so far away from his dinner plate Kodi was amazed he never spilled a drop from his soup considering how far it had to travel on the spoon. The dark hair on his head was short and combed perfectly, in contrast to Curdoz' shaggier pate, and his clothes were of a finer make even than Curdoz' best.

The man had such a severe expression that though Kodi had been introduced to him already in the hall, it took him awhile to work up the nerve to engage him in conversation.

His voice was quiet and deep, rather like Xeno's, but he actually smiled at Kodi's greeting, and then a warm twinkle appeared in his eyes.

"Lord Curdoz speaks very highly of you, Master Kodi. He says the two of you have had some, er, adventures together the last couple of weeks!" He then leaned in close to Kodi and whispered, "His Highness Filiddor is in cahoots with Tribesmen, is he? I can hardly wait to hear the full tale." He winked.

Kodi realized he was going to like the man better than he at first thought he might.

To the king's left sat the remarkable Mother Superior, whom Kodi had been inclined to dislike based on all the stories he had heard about her. She was tall for a woman, big-boned, with iron-gray hair in a tight bun. She wore a black dress but instead of a colorful shawl like Idamé's, the Mother Superior donned a gold and white lacy thing which trailed her broad shoulders. Perhaps she could be dower and mean sometimes, but at the moment she was engaging the king himself and another guest to her other side in light-hearted conversation, twittering pleasantly enough.

Lyndz noticed Kodi looking at her and leaned in to him rather like Marco had done a few minutes before. "Don't let that smile fool you, Ko. She's just putting on an act for the king. She has a foul temper like you've never seen!"

Kodi chuckled quietly. Other guests included the Lord High Mayor of Ferostro, a general of the Kingsmen army, several royal officials including the treasury woman they had seen earlier that afternoon, and two lords with two ladies who were currently visiting the city and whom Curdoz and the King apparently liked very much. These two couples were on the other end of the table engaged in conversation with Curdoz, who sat opposite to the king in the place of honor and with Mother Idamé at his right side.

Idamé was cheerful enough, but occasionally she would glance down the end of the table in the direction of the Mother Superior, and then her face would falter momentarily. At those times, Curdoz would distract her by referring to her in the conversations going on down at his end of the table.

Kodi asked Father Marco to tell him more about the various Orders of the Guardian.

"There are the several Orders, Kodi. However, the Order of Moment-masters, as you now know, has only one known, though very secret member, and therefore he poses as a Monastic. Then there are the three that most are familiar with, of course, those of the Monastics, the Matrimonials, and the Healers. The Order of the Sages includes those active among the kingdoms and Tirilorin, and those who have retired and have returned to the Valley. There are only twelve living."

"Are they the ones who choose the High Priest?"

"Yes. The High Priest usually, but not always, comes from the Order of Sages, and sometimes he is one currently serving in a kingdom and at other times it is one of those who has retired to the Valley. But if he has been serving somewhere, he must then be replaced, for he must remove to the Valley."

"Are there other Orders?"

"Yes. There is the Order of Seers, but the few Seers and Seeresses of that Order usually, though not always, live in the Valley. Most people are under the misguided impression that they fill volumes with their predictions of the future, but for the most part their Meicalian Prophecies are very rare. Mostly they become great scholars and write books. Sometimes they travel to the library in Aster to research, and even to the old imperial library in Tirilorin."

"Are any of the Sages ever women?"

"Oh, yes. There have been a few over the centuries."

"And what about the other races, sir?"

"Long ago, both the Qeteral and the Etoppsi sent some of their own to study in the Valley. But there have been none from the other two races since the last emperor abdicated in Tirilorin a hundred years ago, and they do not have Sages among them as far as I know. If they do, they have not received proper education in the Valley."

Kodi found it curious. "Are there any other Orders than those you've mentioned? What about the Scribes?"

"Well, the Scribes operate as a branch of the Monastic Order, although they tend to be more scholarly and often work in the estates of the noblemen. They handle letters and communications and act as tutors to their children. Then there is the Order of War Wizards."

Kodi raised an eyebrow. "Like Terianh? I didn't know War Wizards were an Order of the Guardian."

"There has only been the one, Terianh, since the founding of the Orders by the Sages during his day. However, there were two other War Wizards, back to the time of the Great War, that are numbered in the lists: Modelo of the Mold, Father of All, and Berug the Magnificent, of the Etoppsi, who continued the Great War of the Rebellion of the Gods after Modelo was killed. Only three, then, and so they are even rarer than Moment-masters. They are only Called when the world is in great danger. They have a very special relationship with the Guardian. I'm surprised the Lord Curdoz..." he paused and looked at Kodi. "Er...never mind. My mind is wandering."

He then launched into what the seven year study in the Valley was like, the differences in the daily lives of the three main orders, and then also how Sages are usually chosen. "...and so you see the fact that the Lord Curdoz was sent back to Solanto was out of the ordinary. Almost never does a Sage return to his home country, and Curdoz was very, very young. But it was a wise choice on the High Priest's part, it was. Lord Curdoz has brought much good to this country through the Reforms. Except, as I think you saw for yourself, in the Principality of Hesk."

"Right."

Marco leaned in again to Kodi and whispered. "I fear that whatever the prince is up to, it will not be a good thing for the Kingdom of Solanto. This Council of the Kingdom he has called for has everyone concerned. I fear some conflict is brewing. Filiddor is perhaps more willing to act on his ambition than some of his predecessors. I hope not. I will try to keep an open mind and not judge without more information."

"Lord Curdoz is very sorry to leave the country, sir. He is worried, too."

"Yes, and it is a shame. Nevertheless—and I expect he will tell me more—this journey the four of you are to take must be of great importance, Kodi. Meical the Guardian is at work!" He paused. "I wish to ask you something, if you know the answer. When your parents Bonded, was there an Aura?"

"Yes, sir! And my grandparents on both sides of our family from what I understand. It seems to be rather common in my family."

"I am not surprised."

Kodi found this curious. Neither Curdoz nor Idamé had ever really said much to him about Auras. Of course, he had never asked.

He had never before considered Auras to be of particular significance. There were anecdotes, though he had never paid them much mind. "Er, why, sir?"

Father Marco smiled. "Most lay people understand that it is an especial Blessing upon a couple when an Aura appears. And it is, certainly. However, in the Valley it is believed by some that Aura pairings are the way by which Meical the Guardian Plants His Seeds. Maybe you don't know what I mean by that."

Kodi suddenly remembered something. "You mean like He says in the Book of Histories?"

"Ah, so Lord Curdoz has enlarged that passage to you. He must see what I see."

Kodi pondered carefully what Father Marco was saying. "You're saying that Lyndz and I are...Seeds."

"It is important to note that perhaps not every child of an Aura pairing achieves fame, of course, yet it is likely that even the most seemingly insignificant of them hold within their natures some special traits that Meical wishes to emphasize, even if in later generations. Yes, I believe, based on what Lord Curdoz has told me of his Vision, you and Lyndz are Seeds. Your father for one has achieved a level of greatness."

"But it isn't my father you're thinking about just now, is it?"

"I'm talking of the Gift."

"Do all those who have the Gift come from these Aura pairings?"

"A great many of them do. But I refer, rather, to more unique Gifts. And so the reason I asked you, Kodi, is that I look into your face, and that of your sister's, and I see something that stirs me. The theory behind Auras is not proven, and Meical Himself said next to nothing about it. That passage from the Book of Histories is the only place He mentions Planting Seeds. It is all speculation, but speculation based on some evidence. No doubt you and Lyndz are Gifted."

"Maybe so, sir, but..."

"They will be discerned eventually."

Kodi nodded, uncertain what to make of all this. It was as if Marco was trying to tell him that he, Kodi, and perhaps Lyndz, too, were a part of some great scheme of the Guardian's, a plan that had been engineered long ago.

"So that's what Curdoz is trying to tell me with that passage from the Histories. You've taught me a lot, Father Marco."

"Your Calling appears at least to be different, Kodi. Your sister's likewise. Yet, I hope I didn't overstep. Lord Curdoz has his own methods perhaps for teaching and training you."

"Of course you didn't, sir. You've been a big help!"

"I wish you all the best. For my part, it will be difficult to take the Lord Curdoz' place while he is gone."

"Lord Curdoz says you are highly respected."

"Perhaps." He looked down at Curdoz talking at the other end of the table, then back to Kodi. "But he will be greatly missed."

When the dinner ended, the party moved to the Chamber of Fire, where a number of chairs were brought in for everyone to sit. A small group of musicians presented them with entertainment. After the instrumentalists played for perhaps a half hour, to the surprise of the twins, the princess herself stood forward. In her strong voice she sang.

In a valley where the greens show eternal
Take my hand and run with me. Time shall cease in a kiss.

Through emerald towers and ruby flowers,
When we walk through the veil of diamond showers
Two hearts find bliss.

Then to the mountains where the snows kiss the sky
We will soar, we will fly, we shall come, you and I!

O'er the seas of the night, past the stars all alight.
We will soar, we will fly, we shall come...

You and I!

The tune of the piece was startlingly beautiful, haunting even, and Isatura's deep contralto perfectly musical. Kodi and Lyndz came out of stunned reverie with the realization that everyone else around them was applauding. They joined in, of course, and the king stood and took his daughter's hands and kissed her sweetly on both cheeks.

Kodi and Lyndz took advantage of their time alone in their shared bedroom and lay back together on Lyndz' bed long into the night conversing about their time apart from one another. A palace servant had just left the room having stoked the fire and added wood. Lyndz had not participated in any real adventures, so it was mostly Kodi telling all about his, and Lyndz listening, interjecting, asking questions and commenting.

Kodi then had a thought not really related to his adventures, but nevertheless one that he'd been pondering. "Lyndz, do you reckon the Gifted are lonely? I mean the Order Members who never Bond?"

Lyndz thought for a moment. "They have many friends. And the Matrimonials, at least in Solanto anyway, are in Troupes. They seem to enjoy each other's company. You saw Mother Idamé's Troupe in Felto. And I saw how the Sisters are who live here in the city at the Convent. They're always cheerful and laughing all the time. Even the Healers travel in pairs like Danly and Xeno. They are very close friends, I could tell. But I know what you mean. Order Members give up a lot. You know, if it weren't for the Vow, I'd think that Curdoz and Mother Idamé would make a happy couple. Don't you think?"

"I think it's the two of them that I'm really thinking about. I sometimes wonder if they love each other, more than friends."

"I thought I saw Curdoz looking at Idamé tonight with a special look on his face, particularly when the princess sang that song. It is kind of sad. Some of the Gifted do Bond, but not many. Mother Idamé said something to me about what's called a Dispensation, when the High Priest in the Valley gives permission to Order Members to Bond. It's very rare. It's usually only when an Aura is seen. But I think I know what you mean. I don't want to be alone, either, Ko. I don't want you to be alone like that. Someday, I'd like to Bond a good man, yet be close to Mother and Father. You'll inherit Father's estate someday, Ko. You'll be the Count Fothemry."

"Father's still young, Lyndz. Hopefully he'll be the count for many long years, and Mom beside him." It wasn't that Kodi was in any way opposed to such speculation. It was simply that he had strong doubts that returning to Felto to live out his life was what he was being Called to.

"You're right. I hadn't really thought of it like that. It could be forty, fifty years. I certainly wish they'd live forever."

"And who knows what our Gifts are and where they will lead us?" continued Kodi, putting into a few words those thoughts. "I don't think I can be a baron and a member of the Order at the same time anyway. But Curdoz seems to believe my Calling is different and told me already that he doesn't think I'll have to take the Vow. Er, he kind of got angry with me when he overheard me say something rather rude about it—which I deserved. I was being judgmental. What I really want to do, Lyndz, is learn to fight. I want to be a warrior and go fight in the wars in the east. I want to make a difference. This book Theneri gave me about Terianh the Great—it's amazing what all he did."

Lyndz looked at her brother. He had expressed these sentiments in the past on their walks to and from the manor worksite back home in Felto, especially when their father was gone to Tolos. She had not encouraged him, and neither had their mother, for it was simply their way as women to discourage him from seeking out what they perceived to be unnecessary danger, for the country was not at war.

But it was different now since Curdoz came to find them. There were troubles brewing in other parts of the world, and since they had left home she had begun to understand her brother better than before. She sensed a destiny in him beyond what they had ever conceived of while living in Felto. There was no point in pretending anymore. She took hold of his hand, looked him in his brown eyes and said for the first time, "I know, Ko. I know you want to fight. You would make a great warrior, you know. You will be a great man and leader!"

"That means a lot coming from you."

"You need to start training. You're already excellent with a bow. You've got good boxing moves and wrestling moves. You're good on your feet and really fast. You win all the contests back home. You're large and strong enough to wear heavy armor now, if that's the style of fighting you want to do. I think you're a bigger man than Father, now. And Curdoz mentioned back in Thorune that he'll have you begin training when we get to Tirilorin."

Kodi was surprised by his sister's comments. She always seemed to dislike those rough and tumble contests between the boys and the men at the festivals. But now it seemed that all along she was actually watching him and even rooting for him. His appreciation for his sister, always strong, increased.

"You know, Lyndz, I think I know the direction your Gift is in. It's how you look at people and understand things that they never even say. You watch what they do, how they behave. I guess maybe you see it in their eyes, even. Am I right?"

She looked at him again, surprised. "Is…is that a Gift? I hadn't really thought of that. You mean like the Matrimonials see Auras over couples and know that they're meant for each other? I don't know, Ko. I don't want to be a Matrimonial. I absolutely refuse to take the Vow. And why would I as a Matrimonial be important to this quest? It's very strange. I can't see why the Guardian would choose Idamé, for that matter. Of course, she's been like a mother to me, and I'm very glad she's going with us."

"I'm not talking about Matrimonials; there's others like that. There's the Seeresses like Grandpa's mother, and there's the Moment Masters. I wish you could have seen Theneri back in Aster. Eerie, you know, but a useful gift. But you descend from Kalemna, so maybe…"

She pondered this. "Maybe. But Curdoz and Idamé both said that even though the Gift can run in families it doesn't always manifest as the same Gift. Of course it's not very common for Gifted to even have families."

Kodi had always been 'ready' for it, whatever *it* was, for that was his nature. Always moving forward, never looking back, ready to see and do and be and conquer his fears and 'beat the foe,' whoever it was. Lyndz had never pondered any such thing, for she had presumed she was meant to be a home body, a devoted daughter, and useful Bond-mate and companion to some good man from Tulesk or Ascanti. At most she envisioned herself a lady Bonded into one of the other baronial families. She'd never expected to be far from her mother, and was reluctant to accept Curdoz and Idamé's insistence that she was Gifted and meant to be a member of this adventure or quest—all based on Visions which she had never experienced and which appeared dubious in the manner in which they referred to her. Yet she couldn't cast the idea aside. She remembered what the princess had said to her, too.

As if Kodi was reading her mind he asked, "Could you hear tonight what Father Marco was telling me about Auras?"

"His voice was too quiet for me to hear, and Princess Isatura and I had so much to talk of."

Kodi then told his sister everything Father Marco had said.

"Well, that's fascinating! He thinks you and I...at least you've had a Vision. Ko, really. What do you think that Vision meant for me? You know, when you saw my face in a 'frame' next to the Alkhaness? Surely you have some idea. You've had more time to think about these Visions, and you've had all these conversations with Curdoz the last few weeks."

Kodi was hesitant to answer at first. Indeed he had thought about this one element as related to his sister often. But then he considered their current conversation and how they had complemented one another. It had cost his sister a bit to encourage Kodi, for he knew she never really wanted him to face any life-threatening dangers, and yet that was the way of a warrior. So he decided he was going to have to give up something, too. He had wanted to protect her from it, of course.

Looking into her own brown eyes which largely mirrored his, he said, "Yeah, I've thought about it a lot. I think it means one of two things. For all I know, though, it could be both, or neither." He sighed. "I think it means that in some way you are meant to be the opposite of *her* in some great way. She is evil through and through, I felt sick being close to her, and you're as good as gold. Like your goodness is to oppose her somehow. But I don't know how."

Lyndz frowned. She really didn't know what to think about that idea, and yet maybe in the very back of her mind as she had waited in the Convent and had time to think on it, she'd touched on that possibility. "And what's the other?"

Kodi swallowed hard and looked down. This was difficult. "That maybe you actually have to face her someday. And I think I might have to face the Alkhan."

For a minute or two she said nothing. Finally, "Do you think I can do that?"

Kodi didn't know what to answer that would make her feel happier about it, so he decided to just be honest. "Not yet, anyway. I'm not quite ready, either."

"So what you're saying is that I need to start training, too."

He nodded. "I guess, though, that it's hard for me to think of *you* becoming a warrior, you know, with a sword and wearing armor and all. That's just not who you are. I hear that the eastern kingdoms have women warriors. You just don't find it in the western countries."

"No. No, I don't think I want that at all. Of course, I'm not sure what I want. I think you're surer about what you want, though."

Kodi went to retrieve the parchment that he used to mark his Terianh book and handed it over to Lyndz. "This is the passage Marco was talking about. Curdoz had this copied for me at the Monastery. What do you think?"

While she was reading, and having never in his life cared a whit whether his sibling saw him naked, Kodi ripped off his new clothes in front of the fireplace and pulled out a lightweight linen pant he liked to sleep in. He put it on and crawled back into Lyndz' bed.

After rereading the passage a couple more times, Lyndz said, "Curdoz is trying to tell you something with this, Ko."

"It's about the purpose of war, is what he told me. Then of course Marco talked all about that Planting Seeds idea, which I admit stood out for me the first time I heard Curdoz read it out loud."

"Yes, and maybe more, too, I think. I think he's telling you that war is coming, and that you had better prepare for it. And maybe in a different sort of way than perhaps you've been thinking of what war is about."

"You think I've been too...I don't know. Keen?"

"He's already given you enough assurances that you are meant to train as a warrior, Ko. I think he's telling you that when you do, you need to understand what you're fighting for. War is about bringing peace and freedom more than it is to dominate and defeat the enemy."

"But you have to defeat the enemy to do these things."

"Yes, you do, but it's a matter of your attitude when you fight. You mentioned how much anger and hatred welled up in you when you saw the Alkhan in your Vision. Emotions can interfere. I think Curdoz is reminding you to be wary of your feelings and motives when you fight your enemies. Your Calling could be…" she hesitated for only a moment. "Well, like Terianh's."

"Why doesn't he just say so? Terianh was a War Wizard. He used powerful magic in his battles with the Ralsheen Emperor and carried a magical Eagle Staff. I've been reading all about him in this book Theneri gave me. You think Curdoz is saying I'm meant to be a War Wizard?"

And is this what he, Kodi, really wanted and yet until now had been unwilling to speak the words?

"Maybe." Lyndz said. "Curdoz isn't telling us everything, you know. And there is no reason for him to tell us everything he suspects, because he probably doesn't know it all. He hesitates because he doesn't want to give the information to us in case he's wrong."

"So you think he's guessing?"

"You said Marco said all that about Auras is a theory. The Visions tell us a lot, but they don't tell us everything. But I suppose I want to trust Curdoz, don't you?"

"Sure, I trust him," said Kodi, "I love the man. He's helped me learn. He's not holding me back…"

He almost added *like Father did*, but he held his tongue. He was learning to put those thoughts out of his mind, for they didn't matter anymore. He loved his father, and Curdoz helped him to understand things from his father's point of view.

Lyndz didn't notice. "I also think he avoids talking too much about the dangers, because he thinks we're young. But it's hardly any different than me or mother not wanting you to train as a warrior and knight for fear that something might happen to you someday, or for you to want to protect me from whatever I might be facing."

They discussed for a short while longer, but finally Kodi yawned and sat up in order to move over to the other bed. Lyndz grabbed his hand.

"I hope we won't be separating again for a long time, Ko. You're my brother and I need you to help me get through this. Leaving home and leaving Solanto is hard for me, but I don't mind that as much as not knowing what to expect."

Kodi very much wished his sister had experienced a Vision like his own. If she had felt the Guardian's presence and urging, and had heard His Voice speaking words of confidence, then he believed Lyndz would be less fearful. On the other hand, considering the fact that she had not, that she was following along based on the direction and guidance and faith of others, she was adapting quite well. And most of the time she was fine. It made perfect sense that on occasion she should feel anxious. Curdoz believed it was only a matter of time until Meical spoke to Lyndz. Until then, Kodi intended to be a rock for his twin.

"I expect we'll be together for weeks, Lyndz. Maybe even months. At some point I will have to fight my battles, but for the time being I'm sticking close." He bent over his sister and kissed her on the forehead. "I love you, you know."

Reassured, she let go of his hand and quite soon fell into a peaceful sleep.

Kodi moved to his own bed and read his book for perhaps another half hour. The fire burned low. With the exploits and heroism of Terianh the Great raising up a new flame in his soul, he too fell into slumber.

Chapter 16—Farewell to Solanto

A band of hills, now clothed in the brightest spring green, separated King's Valley, the Domain of Carlomen, from the Grand Duchy of Escarant. The road wound lazily through these hills, and the scenery lifted the spirits of the two women especially. Idamé was her usual cheerful self again having left the dour presence of the Mother Superior far behind. Lyndz, whose favorite season anyway was springtime, had momentarily cast aside her concerns for the future and delighted in the good weather and being surrounded by people she cared about and who cared about her. She would point out to Kodi and Idamé the various estates they passed, the green and blooming things close to the road, and she would listen to Father Marco and Curdoz elaborate on the geography and the various peoples who lived in these more southerly parts of the kingdom as if they were on a tour of the countryside.

They passed through many towns, and assuredly almost as soon as they had passed the borders of the Grand Duchy, the twins did note the difference in the looks of the people. The lighter complexions and brighter eye colors so common elsewhere in Solanto became the exception, as they now encountered those who looked much more like they themselves with their olive skin tone and dark eyes and hair.

Indeed, when they arrived at sunset on the fourth evening out from Ferostro, Grand Duke Mannago's estate in the central part of his domain, spectacular with its backdrop of hills and surrounded by green fields, dotted with sheep, he welcomed the twins in particular, not as the distant cousins they were, but as if they were his very own family.

Which was large. As a matter of fact the proliferous grand duke and his wife Merelda boasted some seven equally handsome children, two sons and five daughters, the two oldest being older than the twins by a couple of years, and the youngest being nine years old. The oldest son Matteo was actually not present, off to the south on errands for his father, but the others were there, and they treated Kodi and Lyndz as if they were their own siblings.

They remained there three nights, and while Curdoz was closeted long with Mannago and Marco discussing the Prince of Hesk and plans for dealing with problems after Curdoz was to leave the country, Mannago's older children took Kodi and Lyndz on a long horseback ride and picnic into the surrounding countryside. Musca followed along, running with renewed vigor. Today was the twins' nineteenth birthday, and they were in a celebratory mood. At one point their cousins took them to the top of a green hill that surveyed the lands about and where they held their picnic. It was a gorgeous country which Lyndz rapidly fell in love with, far more open than the forested southern Tulesk. After their lunch, Kodi and the second son, Olaron, a strapping youth of fifteen, engaged in a spirited round of target shooting, and afterwards the two raced down the hill on horseback and went on a long ride together. Olaron had been training under his father for knighthood for two years already, and was a masterly rider, but Kodi held his own. They were each very intrigued by the fact they were related as distant cousins and hit it off like brothers. Olaron, like a sneaky young buck, had a hidden flask of brandy he readily shared with his new-found friend. The two shared very similar experiences growing up as privileged boys of rank and laughed at each other's stories pertaining to their masculine escapades. The friendship between these two would prove long-lasting.

In the meantime, Mother Idamé was engaged near the stables in horseback riding lessons with the stablemaster. Lady Merelda stood near with her two youngest children and offered wonderful encouragement to the Matrimonial who had heretofore been fearful of beasts any larger than the baggage ponies the Troupes engaged on their travels. Idamé exhibited her latent bravery and put down her fear in order to try her best. It was a reasonable success, though of course the stablemaster had chosen a very docile mare for Idamé. Yet she was pleased with herself, and when the young people returned from their ride in the country, they found her on an outing with Merelda, riding around the palace grounds. The twins congratulated her for her efforts and quick progress.

The grand duke was, not counting Prince Filiddor of Hesk, the wealthiest man in the kingdom. In comparison to Filiddor whose wealth was supplied by the fur trade and rich mineral mines, Mannago's holdings were both massive and very diverse. They included several large farms spread throughout his domain, and other operations. There were dairies for milk, butter and cheese production, a winery supported by hundreds of acres of vines—indeed they drank fine wine by gallons at every meal—a lumber mill, grist mills, several bakeries, iron-ore and smelting operations, an armory to provide Mannago's share of military supplies to the king, smoking houses for preserving meats, weavers and clothing industries supplied by thousands of sheep and innumerable acres of flax, leather tanning facilities, horse-breeding farms, every variety of crop, blacksmithing forges, and more. Countless villagers and servants worked these operations and were paid fair wages, and those who wished for it received good acreage upon which to grow additional food, and there was common property in numerous locations for the domesticated animals belonging to the common folk. Kingsmen trained under the supervision of Mannago's chosen officers and were sent out to monitor and keep safe the highways. And outside his personal estate, yet still within the lands he ruled, were numerous towns, baronial estates and the important port city of Karuna. Along the shores of Guardian Lake were a number of prosperous fishing villages, and a large part of the Solantine naval fleet called Karuna home. Mannago's estate was perhaps twenty miles from the city of Tiango, where he maintained a second palace.

The three older men sat in Mannago's elaborate study, recently paneled floor to ceiling in expensive ambernut from Tulesk. All the furnishings were ambernut, too. Tall, glass-paned doors were cast wide, the weather superb.

A variety of topics made their way into the conversation, but most were related in some way to the news Curdoz had brought. The grand duke was infuriated by Filiddor's move to secretly embrace the Ice Tribes, dismissing any notion that it was related to the fur trade. Mannago assured Curdoz he would do everything in his power to deal firmly with any conflict that Prince Filiddor might try to stir up.

"I will personally send my own people, Curdoz. I can play the same game he does. I'll have spies all over the north within a month, and if Filiddor's intentions are not made clear in this Council he has called, I will get to the bottom of it. Your own network is working well, and you have uncovered critical information, but you need more than a handful of Monastics and Healers sneaking into Filiddor's palace. I can get people into his towns and cities, to monitor his barons, and even into his armies. If Father Marco agrees to share what information your people discover, then we should be able to thwart any unsavory plans he may have."

"It is the king I worry about the most," said Curdoz. "If demands are made, then I fear Carlomen may yield in order to forestall any conflict."

"I know what you mean," admitted Mannago. "He is old, and the fire that made him great once upon a time has burned low. Our dear queen is no longer among the living to inspire him as she once did. He will shun conflict, as you say, and none of the lords will desire to go against his wishes. Be that as it may, I will not sit idle, and I can assure you that Amerro will not. His father and mine were very close. If there are demands made, I will bet you a thousand of my finest horses it will have something to do with the Tolosian Peninsula. And if that is the case, Amerro will fight a war before he gives away a trice. The twins' father, my word! If it were not for Hess's daring, no one would have ventured there for many years to come, and Amerro has worked hard these last years to establish a fortified post in Tolos in case the Ice Tribes should attempt some incursion in the future. Sacrifices have been made. Some of my own people have gone to Tolos to seek their fortune. Filiddor will regret it if he presses his father's old demands."

"It has occurred to me that Tolos is at issue, based on the Prophecy we discovered. Do not speak your thoughts to the twins, though," said Curdoz. "Kodi was there when we discussed the Prophecy, but I do not want them leaving the country with heightened concern for their father. There is nothing they can do. We are Called to other tasks."

"Let us hope," said Father Marco, "That whatever comes out in this Council, it will not be as bad as we fear. Perhaps it has nothing to do with Tolos. However, Lord Curdoz and I are not blind to Filiddor's history and his ambition. Our eyes are open. Princess Isatura is a friend of mine, and if the fire has burned low in her father, it is rekindled in his daughter. She will be a great queen."

"She will indeed," agreed Curdoz. "Someday. However, though Solanto has had ruling queens, history shows our country's people to be very conservative, especially the barons. Queens are more greatly respected by the lords when they have strong husbands at their sides. Isatura is betrothed to no one, and it concerns me some."

Father Marco laughed. "It is because she doesn't know what she seeks in a Bond-mate, and so far her father has given her free rein over her own personal affairs. He might have insisted upon a betrothal long ago. She and I have had some good talks, and I can assure you she has her eye open. That young Kodi caught her eye, I can tell you that. Slightly young for her, perhaps. He is a handsome fellow, and my old heart is stirred at the sight of his sister. She is the most beautiful young lady I have ever laid my eyes upon in all my days."

Curdoz laughed in his turn. "Why, Father Marco, one would begin to doubt your Vow! You're old enough to be her grandfather!"

"Do not doubt my Vow, Lord Curdoz, but 'twould be a shame should those twins follow into common Orders and take it themselves. They are not meant for it, I know it. They deserve strong Bond-mates. But, considering what you've told me of your Vision, I think it is safe to presume their Calling will not be *common*. You are not taking them to the Valley, are you?"

"Definitely not. Although everyone thinks I am. We are traveling to Tirilorin, and then to Nant, but beyond that I am not certain."

"What do you suspect is their Calling, Curdoz?" asked Mannago. "Nant is aiding Hralindi and Essemar in the war with the Alkhan, and there is news from the south that the eastern kingdoms are requesting more aid, though they have yet to ask us. The south, beyond Tirilorin anyway, is dangerous."

Curdoz was silent for a moment. "I hesitate to say very much, for much of what I guess is simply that—a guess. For now I will only say this to you, for you are my closest confidantes. Although I suspect Marco too has made some calculations in his mind?"

"Twos are easy to calculate," Marco replied knowingly.

Mannago caught on and raised both his eyebrows. "Curdoz! You mean young Kodi and dear Lyndz are to counter the Alkhan and the Alkhaness? At their age? That is a fearsome thought! Does Count Fothemry know what you suspect?"

"No, and neither does his wife, the Lady Elisa. Hess is on Tolos, of course, and cannot know. And I would have had a difficult time getting Elisa's parental Blessing for them to leave home if I had been plainer, particularly where Lyndz is concerned."

"You haven't been so plain with the twins, either, have you?" asked Marco. "Kodi suspects."

"Kodi is eager. Of course he does. I'm not hiding it from him, but I prefer he figure it out on his own, for his own interpretation of his Vision and his sense of Calling is likely to prove more valuable than mine. But if Lyndz suspects it's only because of her conversations with her brother. The Guardian has yet to speak to her."

Mannago looked at him. "If that is the case, my friend, I can tell you this. Though I do not wish for them to face such dangers, the siblings have great strength of will from their father's side of the family; it's obvious in their speech and bearing. Kodi has the markings of greatness, but I say Lyndz does as well, no less so than her brother. Marco is correct. She is the epitome of feminine beauty, but she also has a daring spirit. I showed them this morning on my pedigree where they connect to my line. It was my great-grandfather, Bagarro. He is our common ancestor. The twins and my own children are third cousins."

"Bagarro!" exclaimed Curdoz. "I had no idea their connection to you was that close! Bagarro!" He repeated. "That's…why that's extraordinary, Mannago!"

Father Marco appeared at a loss. "My studies have been geared towards Meicalian Order history. Am I missing something? Who is Bagarro? Was he grand duke?"

"My father's father's father, yes indeed," said Mannago. "The twins' father Hess, and also Duke Amerro, descend from his daughter."

"I am still missing something. Why is he important?"

"Bagarro," said Curdoz, "was the general chosen by the last emperor to lead the war to dislodge the armies of the Alkhan and Alkhaness when they overran Lintiri a hundred years ago. It was brilliant, for Bagarro was a superior strategist and overcame them without the use of any sort of magical Gift. He was not a War Wizard like Terianh the Great, who was the last. However, at the last, the enemy's armies were defeated and what few survived had boarded a handful of remaining ships in order to sail back to Khestadon. The Alkhan was infuriated by his losses and challenged Bagarro to single combat…"

"And he accepted," said Mannago grimly. "He should not have, and there was no reason for him to, but he had hopes of eliminating at least one of our enemies once and for all."

"But the Alkhan employed dark magic and tricked Bagarro when he rode to confront him. Behind a veil of invisibility were some dozen great monsters he had bred from mountain bears, though they were twice as large and fierce, and under His control. The Alkhan lowered the veil and Bagarro found himself surrounded by the beasts. The Alkhan laughed and rode away to his ship, and the beasts set upon and killed Bagarro. He had no chance against so many. Bagarro was not a War Wizard, like I said. He carried no Staff and was not Gifted. The Alkhan would likely have destroyed him in any event, considering how proximate he was. He simply wanted to watch as the beasts tore him apart."

"The Imperial army was incensed," added Mannago, "for they had been watching. They charged forth and nearly destroyed the remnant of the enemy's forces as they boarded their ships. In fact, they destroyed several of the remaining ships, but the Alkhaness apparently used her own magic to conceal her cohort before he could be overtaken. Those two escaped back to Khestadon.

"It was a bitter war, though we won it…that is, we expelled the enemy from our continent. When the emperor abdicated the Nantians took control of naval duties in the southern seas and have kept the enemy at bay. At least in the west. The east is at war again, and the Enemy have regained their strength, now with two realms since the Alkhan moved across the Strait to establish Eastrealm Khestadon. But, back to my history: Lintiri was largely abandoned as we all know, and most of its inhabitants who survived removed to Tirilorin where they were welcomed by the last emperor, Zarelio, not long before he abdicated."

"Yes," said Curdoz. "But Bagarro is considered a great hero, the last great hero of the Anterianhi Empire. And this connection between him and the twins gives me great hope!"

"If what you've said is true, then Meical is giving the twins a chance to avenge the death of our ancestor, the result of the Alkhan's treachery!"

Marco looked down, and Curdoz shook his head. "Not quite, friend. Such a motive would be atypical of the Guardian. Revenge is not Meical's way. But some of what you imply is perhaps true: Meical has chosen descendants of Bagarro to confront the enemies. They are, in fact, the same enemies, and that is where the hope lies. Bagarro did not have what it took, ultimately, to eliminate the enemy, only his armies. Bagarro's strength and daring and bravery, however, likely have come down to his descendants."

"But we are *presuming* they are Gifted, unlike Bagarro," added Marco. "Are you going to tell them about this? Lord Mannago, did you tell them more about Bagarro other than regarding your familial ties?"

"No," said Mannago. "Not at that time. We should tell them. It could inspire them."

Curdoz shook his head. "For now I'm glad you did not tell them. They do not need to know. Kodi especially. Not quite yet! I do not think I want the motive of revenge added to the mix of his emotions if he truly is to face the Alkhan."

"Curdoz is right, Mannago," added Marco. "Revenge has no place in the Order of the Guardian. Kodi has been Called. Lyndz has been Called, though indirectly through the Visions of others. They are for Meical."

"Yes," said Curdoz. "Mannago, listen. It is good, perhaps, that we three know the truth, and it may help me to help the twins in future. The inspiration you speak of could be of value later. I may tell them at some point. But for now let us drop the subject of Bagarro. But I'm very glad you told me. To know that they carry the blood of one who has already faced the same enemy and had the bravery to do so eases my mind somewhat. It tells me they have what it takes to face the terror ahead. It makes me a tad less anxious, frankly. In Lyndz' case, especially. The two are so interesting to watch, for Lyndz has wisdom and Kodi has courage. My effort will be to help Lyndz find her courage and Kodi to find his wisdom. And they do gain, day by day. I've been fearful of moving forward. Danger is coming, perhaps on more than one front. But it has been a burden on my soul to think that I have been given the responsibility of leading the twins to some unknown doom. My greatest concern has been, do they have what it takes? Do *I* have what it takes?"

"You believe you can answer such questions in a more favorable light, now?" asked Marco.

Curdoz nodded. "I've told myself a hundred times that the Guardian knows what He's doing in choosing us, but always have I had doubts. And I of course have been reluctant to leave Solanto, particularly now because of Filiddor. But I feel better, now. Better than I have felt in a while. I believe now the reason the prince appeared in my Vision was in order to tweak me to gather information and pass it on…to you two. And because of the effort, we've gained that Prophecy and that cipher. I've given you warning, my friends. It's up to you to deal with Filiddor and things here at home. It's time for me, for us, to leave. I think I can say 'goodbye' to Solanto now, with a reasonably clear conscience."

The morning they were to leave, it began to rain. Mother Idamé was tender from her riding. Though the woman had strong legs from walking she was otherwise plump and it did not help. However, Father Marco laid his hands on her and healed her of the soreness. Indeed she was feeling good again when the party—minus the Healer, who was to return to Ferostro—boarded the coach again for the ride to the coastal city of Karuna.

Curdoz spoke one last time to Mannago and Marco. "My good friends, I will miss you. I leave you a burden, but you are clever enough to handle things. When the Council has concluded, though, I want you to send me a coded missive telling me everything."

"And where do you want it sent to, Curdoz?" asked Marco.

"Send it to Tirilorin to Sage Enric. If I have gone, he will forward it to me."

"Safe journeys, Lord Curdoz!" said Mannago. "And safe journeys to all of you!" he added more loudly to the rest of them as they, and Musca too, got into the carriage.

As they rode along, the rain came down harder, and it was a good thing the roads were reinforced with stone. Curdoz spoke with the others of his upcoming plans. "My ship is in Karuna. It will take us to Tirilorin and perhaps to Nant, but it is a coastal ship and is not meant to carry us into the open sea. The Vision suggests we will engage a fleet of Nantian vessels to carry us in search of the land of the Qeteral."

"Will we stop at your estate, Curdoz, on Island Saundry?"

The Sage appeared sad all of a sudden. The twins had never before seen him thus and were surprised. "I fear my dear uncle will depart this world before our return. Yes, I feel a powerful need to see him one last time. He was more a father to me than my own father, you understand. I owe him every good thing, and I am all the family he has left, for he never Bonded and had his own family. So, yes, we will stop there, and I must write a letter and have it sent to the High Priest in the Valley telling him somewhat of my plans and of Father Marco substituting as the Order's representative."

For the remainder of their journey to the coast, Curdoz told them what he could of the history of Tirilorin since the abdication of the last emperor. He admitted that there was much he did not know, particularly about how its republican government actually functioned, but he was apparently in communication with its Sage, Enric. The twins were surprised to learn that the Meicalian Orders were not held as high in regard there, due to a rather cynical attitude toward the Guardian. "Tirilorines are good people, don't get me wrong. Very generous people. But their whole focus is on trade and prosperity. They have with great deliberation cast aside imperial history in favor of the present and in the accumulation of wealth. And in the casting aside, they have, unfortunately, discarded much of their belief in Meical. Most see Him only as a historical figure. He is not real to them despite the Order's work."

They also discussed the elements in Kodi's Vision and Curdoz' Vision that pertained to Tirilorin.

"Do you have an idea who the 'friend' is in my Dream, Curdoz?"

"No. No more than I knew who you two were until I beheld your faces in Felto. You mentioned he was dressed in very fine clothing, but the city is full of wealthy aristocrats and merchants. The curly blonde hair and fair complexion is as common in Tirilorin as it is in most of Solanto and Eleni. But we will find him. Or rather, you will. Finding him, getting to know him, and gaining his trust and willingness to go with us will be your main task." He leaned back and continued. "Now, my Vision implied that I would find answers to questions in the Imperial Library. Oh, they don't call anything *imperial* now, of course. It is simply the Great Library. It is much, much larger than the one in Aster. It was built by the Etoppsi, as were the walls of the inner city and the Grand Palace. Anyway, though I have questions, yes, I hardly know what I'm looking for. Lyndz, I expect you to help me. Idamé may, too, unless I find another task for her.

"Also, I saw myself in conversation with Genehbro, the grandson of the last emperor, who I mentioned to you is one of the Masters on their Assembly. I saw myself in conversation with him in what I presume is his study. As a matter of fact, he dwells in a portion of his ancestors' Palace, though the Imperial Audience Chamber has been converted into the Assembly Hall of the Masters. So, hopefully, I will gain useful information from him."

"Or you will help him," offered Lyndz quietly.

"Hmm?"

"Well, the logic of your Vision doesn't *assume* you're getting information from him. It could be that he needs *your* help. Right?"

The Sage looked at her. "I see more and more your value, Lady Lyndz. You have a very keen, logical intellect for one so young. You're right. I haven't thought of it in that way. I do tend to assume, don't I? I have another task for you, by the way. When we get to my estate, I want you to begin decoding your great-grandmother's book using the cipher Kodi discovered."

"Oh, sure! " she said with obvious enthusiasm.

"And it is possible that the cipher does not work precisely the same way with all that is in that little book. It may prove we were simply lucky on the first one, and that the symbols or order in the cipher may need to shift, or even to be subjected to formulas in order to work each one out. Promise me you won't read too much into her writings before we have time to discuss them together. Prophecy and poetry can be tricky. And let us all agree that it is quite possible we will not be able to understand much of it. It is often the case that Prophecy is only understood after the fact. It is likely to prove the same with Deroge's writings. I think, though, it is safe to presume it will be useful to us in some way. And you won't likely finish it during our short stay at Villa Saundry, but you can work on it more in Tirilorin."

By the time the weather had cleared again and after two days and two nights traveling they had arrived at their destination. Karuna on Guardian Lake was a busy port, not only because of trade with the grand duchy and the southern parts of the Kingdom of Solanto in addition to a major pass through the Imperial Mountains to Eleni which brought much merchandise to the city, but also due to its location on the main route to the Valley of the Gifted. The very lake in the center of the Valley that Kodi dove into in his Vision, Curdoz explained, was the source of a river that cut its way through the mountains to sea-like Guardian Lake. There was another large monastery located in Karuna where the Gifted and Monastics would stay on route to the Valley or from the Valley on their way to Solanto, Nant, and Tirilorin. Solanto's navy was not remotely comparable in size to that of Nant or even Tirilorin, for the kingdom was many hundreds of miles away from the Southern Continent and the threat of the Alkhan and Alkhaness. Nevertheless, they did set out on patrol in late spring when the icebergs in the northern ocean thawed, allowing the Ice Tribes to send forth their fishing fleets. They ensured that the Tribesmen remained far away from the Solantine coasts and their own fishing fleets. The Lake was ice free, whereas the currents on the western coast could carry large icebergs until mid-spring. Therefore much of the fleet was stationed in Karuna in winter.

Now that the weather was good, most had set sail through the Meicalian Strait and beyond Guardian's Gate on their way up the coast. However, merchant ships from Tirilorin were already plying the waters for the season, and Curdoz and company found the city with its many warehouses bustling with activity.

Being in a coach was of benefit, otherwise Curdoz would have been hard-pressed to greet all the Gifted and Monastics who walked the streets of the city. They drove straight to the wharves and disembarked. Musca was glad to get out and move around. Curdoz found his ship and its captain ready, for a messenger had been sent already by swift horse by Mannago.

Shortly after noon they boarded for what was typically, depending on the winds, a half-day excursion from Karuna to the wharves on Island Saundry. It was a small ship with only a dozen crewmen, but with two large sails, and overhead the green banner containing the golden sun-like symbol of the Orders of Meical floating in the wind. Gulls by the hundreds flew overhead. The Lake reflected a blue sky.

The twins and Idamé found that even though the ship was small it was solidly built and well-apportioned having been constructed under Mannago's father as a gift to the Sage many years ago to assist him in his travels. In fact, the Captain and the ship's mates were under the employ of the grand duke.

"Mannago is very good to me, and his father before him," explained Curdoz. "Since I live on an island, of course, it is very useful. I usually only travel to the ports of Solanto. In fact, had it been late spring or summer I might have taken it to Ross instead of walking to Tulesk. Though, of course, the extra time ended up proving useful, or I would not have run into Idamé."

"It's a lovely ship!" said Lyndz. Curdoz' cabin was small but contained four cushioned hammocks, two bunked on each side, a small writing table, two hanging brass lanterns, built-in storage compartments, and two small windows of thick glass.

"Why not Cumpero instead of Ross?" asked Kodi. "Especially since all you knew was that we lived in Tulesk."

"Too risky, in my opinion. Captain Shond hardly agrees with me on that. Usually, only large naval and merchant vessels will travel around the Tolosian Peninsula to reach the northern Tulescian cities. You see, our route to Tirilorin and to Nant is somewhat protected. I'll have to show you on a map to explain, but there is what is called the Inner Route, and it's protected by barrier islands off the coast. I took my ship once to Tirilorin long ago. It will take us about twelve or thirteen days once we leave Island Saundry."

They were soon underway. Lyndz may have liked the looks of the ship and the comfort and accoutrements of the cabin, but Kodi was more intrigued by the very notion of sailing. Not happy standing by as the ship's crew worked at something he considered fun and fascinating, and since the women had chosen to rest in Curdoz' cabin, he was determined to involve himself.

Stepping over to the captain who was in the middle of shouting orders, he waited for him to pause and said, "I'm willing to learn, Captain, sir! Give me something to do!"

Captain Shond, who Curdoz had warned always smelled strongly of rum, and whose speech was rather colorful, looked at Kodi doubtfully, and said, "How old're ye, anyways?"

"Nineteen now, sir."

"Healthy bastard. Pretty face. Lords don't sail—Meical's Chickens!" He shouted a few more orders to some of the crewmen, pretending to ignore Kodi, though with a grin on his face that showed several teeth missing.

Kodi knew he was being complimented and ridiculed at the same time. He also knew he was being tested. "I can do what you tell me, sir, with a bit of help from the mates."

"Ye hadn't e'en been on a fishin' boat on a pond, have ye? Them muscles come from pluckin' daisies all day for pretty girls, I reckon."

"No, sir, though I've never minded hard work, and I've studied ships and sailing in my grandfather's books."

"Books! Aw, me pap's a donkey! Young lord reads, he does?"

Kodi laughed. "Yessir."

"Wha' kind o' ship ye standin' on then, Master *Bookman!*"

"Small caravel. Two-masted, lateen sails, though I suppose you could use square if you rigged it so."

"Master Bookman ken both read *and* see! 'Mazin' tha' is. Thank the Guardian, young lord ain't as stupid as he is pretty! And I'm a guessin' His High Lordship over there told ye me ship ain't good enough for the open seas?"

"Er, yessir. Afraid he did say something along those lines."

"First job, Master Bookman, ye don't listen to no barnacled old Sages on me ship." Shond spat this with an accompanying friendly wink at Curdoz who stood nearby chuckling quietly, admiring Kodi's willingness to fit in whatever set and situation he found himself a part of, whether it be royals in palaces or half-drunk sailors on ships. "They don't know what they're talkin' 'bout, them Gifted folks, see?" the captain continued. "Especially the men, like His High Lordship—jes' anxious *stiffrods*, 'cuz they don't ha' no titty mates to soften 'em at night when the lamps burn low."

Kodi laughed. "You're absolutely right, Captain. I agree with you. But I swore not to tell His Lordship that to his face again," he said with a sidelong glance and grin at Curdoz who could easily hear every word.

"Smartest thing ye said, so far, Master Bookman! By the ways, how many titty mates has that pretty face o' yours charmed up? We's all curious, ye see, cuz none o' us be quite so *charming* as ye."

"Couple or three in every port, can't count that high, sir," Kodi stated with a broader grin. "I pluck women, not daisies." He was glad the women were in Curdoz' cabin. Particularly Idamé, whom he knew would not appreciate such boastful jocularity even if it was utter nonsense.

"Ye got the Guardian's Nuts, eh? Maybe so. Ye even got all yer teeth, I see, and His High Lordship keeps company wi' such scoundrels as ye?" Shond queried, continuing to test Kodi's humor. It was clear he was beginning to like him very much.

"I like to learn from you; he likes to learn from me. He's got a pair waiting in his cabin, doesn't he? Or *four*, if he drops his eyes a bit from their faces."

The crewmen close by who had been chuckling all during this exchange, laughed uproariously at this, and Captain Shond burst out gleefully. "Well, blows us overboard, I reckon he does at that!" He whacked Kodi on the back, as Curdoz shook his head and rolled his eyes. "Ye'll do, Bookman, I reckon! Help yonder mates at the sails, they'll teach ye a thing or two quick enough. Here, matey," he added, pulling out a flask—every man on board seemed to have one, and every time Captain Shond pulled his out, they did, too. "A swig or two'll help ye keep your sea legs. 'Course this ain't the *open sea!*" he added loudly in Curdoz' direction. "Jes' a big fat wet lake! No great, scaly sea monsters, no mad scary waves and naughty currents, but the Grandified Duke pays well, eh?"

Kodi winked at Curdoz as he accepted the flask.

He hadn't had so much masculine fun since he'd parted company with the manor house builders a month ago. As long as the women remained out of earshot and Curdoz retained his deaf ear, Kodi readily took part in the captain's and the seamen's chauvinistic banter, shared their flasks, and learned something about the operation of the little ship. As he worked with the crewmen, who all took the captain's lead and referred to him continually as 'Bookman,' he would occasionally glimpse the Sage standing near the rails with Musca, watching the water and listening to the gulls, apparently lost in thought, as the ship cut its way through the blue water, the shores of a large, green island growing ever closer.

By late afternoon they had come quite close, and though Idamé remained secluded in the cabin, Lyndz came out and stood with Curdoz, and began pointing at various landmarks on the island and asking questions of the Sage.

"Crab snap off yer tongue, Bookman?" inquired Captain Shond noticing that Kodi had mostly gone silent as soon as Lyndz came on deck. "She's prettier than a pearl, that one. 'Bout your age, too."

"Yeah. I mean, yessir, Captain. Er, she's my twin."

"Your *sister*, is she? Well, ain't that jes' your bad luck! Puts a mighty squeeze on the Guardian's Nuts, that does!" He laughed, slapping Kodi on the back again. "I reckon she and you do favor. Well, Bookman, hope she ain't for the Vow-ly o' the Gifted. Know what I mean, matey? *Vow*-ly? Waste o' good breedin' that'd be, I say! Um, um, um. Pretty brown skin. Curves, nice ones, yip. My wife's a right witch—craggly, prune-face walrus. 'Course they don't know much about 'breedin' anyways, in the Vow-ly, do them Gifted? Bunch o' singin' daffydils and nutless…" He trailed off when Lyndz turned around and came towards them. He took another swig from his flask and with a rather melodramatic "M'lady" and a nod at Lyndz, he walked away, grumbling, "And the prune-face walrus turns out wild boar fer yungins, and then them goes and turns out a passel o' pug-face piglets." Kodi and the other men close by were chuckling uncontrollably at Shond's hilarity.

"What?" said Lyndz, stepping up, oblivious to the exchange among the men. "What's funny?"

"Can't say, Sister. Best keep my lips sealed on that. Is Idamé all right?" he added quickly to change the subject.

"Yes, she's fine. She's lying down." She unexpectedly leaned in close to Kodi's face and breathed in deeply through her nose. "Ko!"

"Er, what?"

"Have you been drinking?"

"A bit."

"Nasty brandy."

"It's rum, actually, bit watered down, though I suspect Captain Shond does that for good reason. Acquire some for you if you like," he said with resolute sincerity.

Though the men would not dare directly flirt with a woman who was a guest of the Sage, one of the men reached out in order to hand Kodi his own flask and said, "If ye give it to the pearl girl and she a'swigs it, and then I does after, it'd be 'bout as good as a kiss, I'm thinkin'."

Lyndz laughed. "That's very thoughtful of you, kind sir, but perhaps not just now, thanks. Ko, are you drunk? Are you learning about the ship?"

"That'd be a 'yes' on your second question, and a 'only very slightly' on your first one. But Curdoz asked me to watch myself around Mother Idamé, so no need to worry; I'm not having any more...just now."

"I'm not our mother, or Ansy. I'm glad you're all enjoying yourself. But yes, Curdoz' is probably right about Idamé. In *your* case anyway."

"Ar, the *Shawl Lady* keepin' her eye on ye, Bookman?" hollered one of the mates. "Better you than me, I reckon!" The man took a very deliberate swallow from his flask. Several of the others brayed like donkeys and took up on his cue.

"Tha's right! Watch out fer the Shawl Lady," said another. "She'll put one o' them 'Horrors' over your head, Bookman, and yer charmer days be over. Be a walrus and piglets for ye, like Cap'n Shond!"

Lyndz, Kodi thought thankfully, was as innocent as a spring flower where it mattered, but she was not a prude and tended to give men a lot of leeway when it came to joking about and around women and having a good time. She was of the mind that men, particularly in groups such as this, were engaging in a form of odd competition, albeit with audacious humor and drinking being important to the game. Men teased openly—especially when they were drinking—more so than women, who preferred talking about their men folk in secretive, more civilized settings. Usually, it was all in fun. Men and women were just different, and Kodi was lucky to have a sister who acknowledged it, for it made it even easier for him to love her so devotedly. She never interfered and she never judged him. Obviously, there were limits to what she'd take from other men, but Lyndz clearly felt no sense of danger around the ship's crew, hired by Curdoz and Mannago as they had been, and befriended already by her brother. There was no danger from this set, Kodi knew. They knew instinctively there were lines they should never cross.

It was just as well, considering they were all going to be sharing very close quarters for the better part of the next two weeks. What was not clear, yet, to Kodi, was the subtle influence his twin— and Idamé, too, for that matter—would have upon Captain Shond and the crew in the days ahead, as they subconsciously began to cut back on their rum consumption and vulgarities without Curdoz ever feeling the need to say a word in reprimand. In fact, as the women began to feel more comfortable spending more of their time on deck, the men's protective and chivalric instincts tended to show through. Idamé would then pat their grizzled cheeks, call them 'dear' to their faces, and thank them readily for every dashing display of politeness they displayed towards her. And by the time they reached Tirilorin they were washing their clothes and taking baths when they'd anchor in the mouths of rivers at night and treating "Her Ladyship Lyndz" like a queen and demonstrating a self-discipline—at least in her presence—comparable to the world-famous sailors of the Nantian Royal Navy.

They landed on a wharf on the northwestern shore of Island Saundry shortly before sunset. Some three other ships not unlike theirs were currently docked here, too, for there was much coming and going between the Island and Karuna.

Their cheerful moods did not last, however, as a very dignified Monastic, clearly Curdoz' entrusted chamberlain, met them on the dock. All noticed he wore a grim expression.

"Brother Tommas!" said Curdoz. "Why the long face?"

"Lord Curdoz! You have arrived just in time! Your uncle!"

"Normene?" replied the Sage with sudden foreboding. Idamé rushed to Curdoz' side and put her hand on his arm.

"He does not have much longer, Your Grace. I am so sorry to bring you such news. Healers are with him, of course, and he does not suffer, but do come!"

It was somewhat of a climb, as the group, with Musca pattering alongside, meandered their way to the top of the cliff, where a hilly landscape lit by a pink sunset met their eyes. The Palace of the Sages stood near at hand, surrounded by deep green lawns and magnificent, well-spaced clumps of trees in a park-like setting. It was as pretty as Mannago's place, but with a magnificent view of the Lake on three sides. Around the palace were tall, tight, yew hedges planted long ago to block the winds. If the moment was not so desperate, Lyndz in particular would have ventured forth to explore the gardens contained within the hedge walls. As it was, they were all marching as rapidly as they could to reach the front doors.

Monastics by the dozens who operated the household bowed to their lord in the entryway, their silence telling, as Curdoz entered and followed Tommas up a flight of marble stairs and down a long hall. Lyndz noted that though the palace was indeed comfortable, there was nothing elaborate in the decoration; tapestries bore simple patterns, carpets were plain, and there was not a hint of gold anywhere. Wood paneling was so common, that the place felt more like a huge grand lodge rather than a palace.

They came to a set of doors at the end of the hall, and the twins and Idamé made to hold back, but Curdoz said, "No! You will all come with me!" He grabbed Idamé's hand, and looked her in her eyes.

Though Kodi had always known Curdoz to be of fairly reserved demeanor, often stoic, stern when necessary, cheerful enough when the situation called for it, he had never known the Sage to be anxious or uncertain. But the look he bore Idamé seemed to speak of some deep, ancient fear.

Idamé said, "You knew this day was coming. You are not alone!"

The doors opened into a room of dark paneling lit by a warm fireplace and soft lanterns. A pair of Healers, the first female pair the twins had ever seen, stood next to a large, four-poster bed, each with a hand on the forehead of a very old man, who did indeed resemble Curdoz somewhat, though older and grayer. Green light emanated from the hands of the Healers, sinking with slow, rhythmic pulsations into the man's skull.

Curdoz and Idamé together strode forward. The Healers backed away, allowing them room, their magical light vanishing.

Curdoz let go of Idamé and bent over the bed. The old man's eyes were closed. He appeared to be sleeping peacefully. Curdoz slipped his hands under the covers, found his uncle's and held them.

"Uncle Normene!" Curdoz called out. "Uncle! It's me...Curdoz. Can you hear me?"

There was silence for a moment, but after a time the man's eyes opened, and a smile, very faint, appeared.

"Uncle Normene!" For the first time in the twins' recollection a number of sad tears fell from the Sage's eyes.

The old man spoke in a voice barely above a whisper. "Did you find them, Son? The twins from your Vision?"

"Yes, Uncle. How do you remember about that? Yes, they are here with me."

"I seem to recall much that slept in the back of my mind." He spoke slowly. "Much is clearer, now. Let me see them. I want to know them before I go."

Curdoz paused, then turned and beckoned Kodi and Lyndz. Lyndz in her sweet way came forward readily. Kodi was decidedly uncomfortable, wondering if the rum he had drunk on board ship with the mates was interfering with the emotions he knew he ought to be experiencing. Perhaps at the surface they were, but deep down he actually felt more emotion than he had felt since saying farewell to his grandfather in Felto those weeks ago. With resolve he squelched his hesitation and stood forward with his sister, the two of them now looking down at the old man on the bed.

"Uncle Normene. This is Lyndz, and this is Kodi. Their father is the explorer, Hess Fothemry. You and I have talked much about Hess, and Duke Amerro and the land of Tolos."

Normene looked up at the twins with the same blue-gray eyes as his nephew, both twins leaning far over the bed in order for the weak man not to have to turn his head. "Wisdom, hmm...and Warrior. Handsome lot. The World Gods have returned to This Side of the World?"

The compliment caused Lyndz to smile sweetly, reach out and touch the man's face. "That is very kind of you, dear sir," she said softly.

"If all goes well, you shall rule the world, sweet child," he said to her with odd certainty. He then looked into Kodi's face. "And you. Meical has claimed you as His Brother. Do you talk to Him?"

Kodi was very confused. Did this dying man have any idea what he was talking about? "Er, no sir. I have heard His Voice in a Vision, though."

"Soon, you will hear Him, and you will not have to sleep."

Kodi turned and looked at Curdoz curiously.

"What do you mean, Uncle?" asked Curdoz with a nervous chuckle. "What do you know of such things?"

Normene's smile did not falter. "There are those who see, and those of us who...See. Death is new life. What we know here are clouds and mists, with glimpses of sunshine and double moonlight, moments of Joy. But afterwards, the sun and the moons and the stars shine on all, and the mists depart forevermore." He turned his head slightly and looked past them. "Who is the lovely lady with the shawl? Is that your friend?"

"Yes. You met Ida before. Years ago. You remember her, Uncle?"

"Ida, yes! She was spoken of many a time though you did not always speak her name. Come close, dear one. Whisper something in your ear. Keep my secret!"

Idamé came close. "What do you want to tell me, Uncle Normene?"

"For your ears only, dear one."

Idamé looked at Curdoz with a raised eyebrow, but she did as she was told and put her ear close to Normene's lips.

There were mumblings and whispers upon the flickering light of the fire, but no one else heard what Normene said. When Idamé stood back, her face was as purple as cooked beets, and both her eyebrows hit the ceiling.

Before anyone could call forth the nerve to question her, however, Normene spoke again. "Come close, Son." The rest backed away from the bed, and Curdoz knelt close to his uncle. "Doubts still, Son?"

Curdoz looked around at the others. He appeared rather embarrassed. Kodi felt he had entered into a private world, a conversation begun perhaps decades ago, that was not meant for his ears. He felt like he ought to tiptoe backward and out the door where Musca waited. And yet something in the very back of his mind told him he ought to listen carefully. The Sage answered his uncle in a manner not unlike Kodi's in a youthful, respectful way. Hiding behind the pretense of aloof strength was no longer an option. "Er, yessir. I know it is wrong, though."

Normene breathed a little deeper, speaking very slightly stronger. "Yes, my son. Your doubts come from a mother who loved you fiercely but passed on to the stars when you were too young, and a father who could not comprehend your greatness."

"But I am not great."

Normene smiled again. "Solanto is a good place to live because of you. How many people does it take, Son, hundreds? Thousands? To tell you that you are great, for you to believe them?"

To Kodi's shock, Curdoz' tears began to flow like a river. "I...I don't know. Maybe just one, sir, but...but the one I need to hear it from is gone."

With his last strength, Normene reached out and touched Curdoz' wet face. "His love for you was thrice mine. He just did not know how to show it, Son."

"You are easy to love. Why was he so difficult?"

"His self-doubts dwarfed yours. Listen. I sleep soon, and I will not awaken in this world again. I will soon dance among the stars. Keep your heart wide open, for there are those in this room who will thrive on what you did not receive. Knowing how to love should not become your failure like it was your father's. Though you may doubt yourself, these here should not doubt themselves."

"Yessir."

"I love you, Son. To have been your family was my greatest joy in life, and you have been well-worth my love. Meical has given you a new family. Now…allow them to love you. They already do, you see."

The old man slept.

The burial took place the following afternoon, and Normene's body was laid to rest in a sheltered garden. All work at the estate stopped in order for the servants to attend, for each and all had enormous respect for the old man who had lived among them these many years. Though Curdoz shed no more tears and spoke clearly during the rites, he was nevertheless contemplative the next couple days and said little otherwise. Yet Idamé rarely left his side, and whenever Kodi returned to the house from archery practice, or Lyndz returned from walking the gardens or came out of her room from working on Deroge's book, Curdoz would look warmly at them, touch them on their shoulders often, and otherwise make them aware that their presence was greatly appreciated.

After Curdoz had placed a lengthy letter to the High Priest in the Valley of the Gifted in Tommas' hands with his final instructions, the foursome with Musca made their way back down the cliff side to the wharf. The ship had been stocked with plenty of food and provisions for the journey.

The crew was relatively reserved compared to their boisterousness during the trip from Karuna to the island, attuned as they were to the Sage's recent loss.

Curdoz had Captain Shond swing southward towards the southern shore of the Lake. Having had time at the Villa to study the maps, Kodi asked him, "I would think it would add time, sir. Coursing straight west would be faster."

"I want you and Lyndz to see something. Idamé saw it once long ago, but I know she would like to see it again. And it was Normene's favorite view. It is worth the detour."

They had been sailing since their departure shortly after breakfast, and by late afternoon they had approached the place Curdoz wanted them all to see. The southern shore of Guardian Lake, though claimed by Tirilorin, was the northern end of an unpeopled and mountainous land that stepped ever higher into white peaks southwards. This wild region ended at the Lake's edge in great, jagged cliffs. It was not possible to navigate close to this shore due to the dangers of vast boulders having been broken off and tossed into the blue waters like so many pebbles by the vast hands of mountain giants. All was very rugged indeed, and many violent rivers ended here, pouring their waters in hundreds of torrents, most falling from elevations ten or twenty times higher than the Great Falls on the North River. As these magnificent white curtains met the surface of the Lake, mists rose in great clouds, rolling outward a mile or so from the lake's edge. The four travelers stood on deck together and took in the magnificent view.

"It is called the Fountains of Noromoray."

"I am so glad to see them again, Curdoz," said Idamé. "How wonderful for you to bring us here!"

"Noromoray was one of the World Gods, wasn't she?" asked Lyndz.

"Yes," replied Curdoz. "In the Ancient Book, Noromoray was the Goddess of Rains and Rivers. She was a sister of Vanaratu, he having departed the Other Side of the World with his other sister, the beautiful but evil Siriné."

"Grandpa used to read us stories about the World Gods. What do they teach in the Valley?"

"According to the legends, all three of those gods along with many others assisted Meical in the first Great War, when many of the World Gods rebelled. Many thousands of the Three Peoples— Humans, Etoppsi, and Qeteral—were slaughtered by the jealous gods until Meical appeared in what you may know is referred to as the Second Appearance, His First Appearance being at the time the Three Peoples were birthed in the depths of time. Meical gathered all the gods who loved the Three Peoples and with their help overthrew the rebels. The rebels were forever after Imprisoned beyond the Guardian's Teeth at the southern end of the world, far beyond the Infested Jungle on the Southern Continent. The painting that Kodi saw on the domed ceiling in the Library in Aster depicts the Condemnation. Despite the help of many of them, Meical deemed it wise for the remaining gods and the Three Peoples to live apart, fearful that the Three Peoples would come to worship the gods as they were prone to do. And so the Favored gods received The Other Side of the World as their everlasting abode, and the Three Peoples were given This Side of the World. The gods were forbidden to cross the Great Barrier which separated the two domains. Siriné, however, convinced her brother, Vanaratu, to cross the Barrier, for they loved the Three Peoples and did not wish to be apart from them. However, as it turned out, Siriné was lustful and desired a Human male to fulfill her lustful nature, and it was she who after many long years corrupted the Ralsheen emperors. Vanaratu, according to old Qeteral stories, lived among their race in peace for a time. When Meical came the

Third time, He called Terianh to fight against the Emperor, and He Himself went after Siriné. Siriné was afterwards imprisoned in the Great Serpent Sea, but Vanaratu disappeared. Some say he returned to the Other Side of the World, but Meical told no one what happened to him."

"How much of the legend do you think is true?"

"I think most of it is more than legend, and there are many more stories of the World Gods, many that you heard as children. But even if you discount the Ancient Book and the early tales as fiction, as some are prone to do, there are records of Siriné living among the Ralsheen. She was a powerful, magical temptress, took Human-like form and became the consort of the last Ralsheen Emperor. And the Qeteral definitely hold that Vanaratu took Qeteral form and lived among them."

"I have always wondered," said Kodi, "if you can travel to the Other Side of the World and see the World Gods."

"The Great Barrier cannot be breached by the Three Peoples, but it is probably the dream of many an adventurer who seeks to Know, to be able to behold the gods in all their splendor. The Fountains, if indeed they were crafted by Noromoray in the depths of time, are a reflection of her wild beauty. Though the gods no longer dwell here, there are Qeteral tales that remnant spirits of the gods, apparitions if you will, both of the Favored and of the Condemned, haunt those far mountains." He pointed to the far off peaks beyond the falls. "They are called the Corellyan Mountains. It is a dangerous and treacherous land, though some say very beautiful, and no people live there. The Qeteral land of Ulakel is beyond them. But to get to the Qeteral, we will of course take the long sea route, south and around."

In two days they were following along the narrows where the Lake emptied into the Western Sea. They moved through rapidly, the sails being used mostly for ensuring that the ship remained in the center of the channel. Three times they passed other ships sailing eastward, but these would hug the northern coast in order to avoid the central current.

Finally, before them rose in the distance the magnificent multiple arches of Guardian's Gate, known throughout the world as one its greatest engineering wonders. Built four hundred years ago by the great winged Etoppsi, it was the largest bridge in all Dumhoni, and was unique in that it consisted of three arms, connecting three lands. Its northern terminus ended at the cliff-top city of Lodicio on the southern tip of Duchy Duranti, whereas a southwestern arm reached to the large island of Donesk, the southernmost duchy of the Kingdom of Solanto, and finally its southeastern arm connected to lands claimed by the Republic of Tirilorin, old Lorinth. The old road that connected the Bridge to the city of Tirilorin far away was rarely used anymore and was in disrepair, for there were no towns for a hundred miles southwards on its length. However, before the kingdoms had built up large merchant marines, the road was a much-used highway between Solanto and Lorinth. Nowadays, only sporadic messengers would use it, and only in winter when ships from the south would avoid the shipping lanes due to winter storms and of course ice even further north. Therefore, most travelers used only the arms of the Bridge that connected Duranti and Donesk.

Besides travelers, however, the Bridge was the home to some two hundred Monastics who maintained a large monastery here, tending to its many-tiered gardens and towered abodes. Ships could indeed dock on the bridge underneath its vast arches on stone wharfs at its base, and travelers and crewmen were given good hot meals, baths, and rest. There was even a hospital where they could be housed and tended to by Meicalian Healer pairs. It was virtually a city unto itself, although it was connected quite closely to the ducal capital of Lodicio whence it received many of its supplies.

Lyndz thought the Bridge the most remarkable thing she'd ever seen, and though Kodi did as well, being attuned to engineering and how things worked, he was overwhelmed trying to understand how such a monstrous structure could be conceived and put together.

"I really want to meet the Etoppsi someday. They must be extraordinary."

"I hope you get to, Kodi, but it is not likely, unless they find themselves drawn into the eastern wars," said Curdoz. "There is some slim chance we will see them, I suppose. Once per year a few of them will fly to Nant at that king's invitation to celebrate the old Feast at the autumnal equinox, like I mentioned to you back in Felto, and it is said they will on occasion fly to Tirilorin. Who knows? Maybe by chance they will show up while we are in those places."

Though it was only mid-afternoon, Curdoz chose to stay at the Bridge for one night, so he had Captain Shond dock under one of its structural arches. The twins and Idamé were delighted at the chance to spend the rest of the day exploring such a grand place, and of course Musca, who as it turned out could be quite restless on board ship, was glad for any opportunity to disembark.

The Sage had special rooms reserved for him here just as he did at the monastery in Aster, and he and Kodi shared the space. Idamé and Lyndz were housed nearby in rooms just as pleasant. Pipes brought in water from an aqueduct system from nearby hills in Duranti, and these supplied all the needs of the Monastics including baths and cooking facilities, in addition to filling reservoirs for the watering of the terraced gardens. Kodi had studied these sorts of gravity-supplied systems in his grandfather's books, but generally, they were considered advanced, and few commoners ever experienced such amenities, although he knew that most fountains in the cities operated with them.

Located in the very center of the bridge was the tallest of its several towers, and though Idamé was not happy to climb so high and chose to remain exploring the lower gardens with Musca, Curdoz and the twins took the climb.

Many hundreds of stairs led around the tower, opening occasionally upon balconies. Each view was stunning, but at the top, which contained a small grassy courtyard surrounded by a low wall, the world was wide open all around them. It was as if they were at the peak of a flat-topped mountain. There were the three waterways which met at the Bridge, and too the lands they bordered: mountains southeastwards in old Lorinth, green hills to the north and northeast, and the flat, plateau-like Donesk, beyond which the sun was now slowly falling. On the waters far below could be seen perhaps twenty ships of sundry size, traveling in various directions.

"Look, Ko!" said Lyndz suddenly. "Is it a Blue-tail?"

Circling the airs around the tower was a large bird. "Yes! Someday I'd like to capture a youngling and train it."

"They are intelligent birds," said Curdoz thoughtfully. "As large as some eagles."

As they watched the raptor, it fell into a magnificent dive, and as it neared the water far below it caught itself and flew a hundred feet or more, skimming the surface. Finally, it broke the water, and then regained altitude rapidly and flew in the direction of the onlookers.

"It got a fish!" exclaimed Kodi.

As it passed by them, they could all see the small fish dangling from its talons. It then flew on in the direction of Donesk.

"Do the Qeteral really speak to all the birds, Curdoz?" asked Lyndz.

"They speak to many species of birds, yes. The Qeteral are deeply attuned to the natural order. They are capable of communication with many beasts, for it is a part of their magic, but birds are most favored by them, and they use them to send messages long distances across their lands. It is to be hoped that when we find the Qeteral, we may see how they communicate with the birds. They say it is by magical singing."

They were silent for a time as they continued to watch the sun fall and the shadow of the land of Donesk creep across the waters below. Finally, Lyndz spoke again.

"I ought to feel sad leaving Solanto. But for the first time, I feel really good about having come on the journey."

Curdoz looked at her, smiling.

Kodi asked, "What makes you say that now, Sis?"

"All the wonderful places we have seen. My heart is opened, I guess. Does that make sense? I'm keen to see more."

"Perhaps your father the explorer is coming through in you, Lyndz," offered the Sage. "I am glad. The opportunity to experience the new may help sustain you should our journey turn dark someday."

"Yes, it may," she replied. "It may."

At the top of the world and enjoying one another's company, the three stood there long, pondering the past, considering the present, and anticipating the future.

Chapter 17—Conflict in the South

"A contingent of the Khestadone attacked us on the Great Wall, oh King! Eye-tower Fifty-five is taken, and Eleven Feathers from Cloud 109 were slain!"

The messenger, a Wing-sergeant from the Wall Cyclone with silver wings folded behind his charcoal body, nodded with respect to Eagleron, Lord of the Etoppsi, King of Berug and High Marshall of the Southern Skies. To the king's left, his Bond-mate and queen, Silverwing, Lady of the Sunrise, turned to her partner. The chiseled, tight-furred face of the king was grim upon hearing the news.

"This is an unforeseen event," replied the king slowly. His voice boomed across the huge audience chamber. "That is the southernmost tower! We have always presumed the Humans feared entering the Infested Jungle!"

"The Alkhaness has grown bold," offered Silverwing, whose voice was at a pitch much lower than a typical female Human's. "She wields powerful compelling magic over the minds of her soldiers if now they can enter the Jungle without fear of the Dragons and the dangers there." Silverwing herself showed little emotion in her deep voice, nor did she act as surprised by the news. The queen was more practical and less intense than her husband. "Sergeant Bluewing, how did they manage to enter the Eye-tower? The entrances of every tower are from above, are they not?"

"There is a door at the base of Eye-tower Fifty-five, my Queen. It is the only such door along the Wall as far as I know. It is used so we can access the ground easily with our equipment to keep the Jungle trees and vines cut back from the tower. It is on the western side. It has hidden mechanisms so it can be opened by us from the outside, but no Jungle creature would know how to open it, and too small for Wingless Dragons to force it. As a rule, it was not kept locked, and the Humans were able to release the mechanisms. All of us were on patrol above, and before we were aware, the Humans had infiltrated the complex in large numbers and overwhelmed us. Bow and spear are at a disadvantage in such a confined space. A few of us made use of long knives, and killed many of them, but it wasn't enough. Five Feathers were injured, but we were able to carry them away along with the bodies of five of the dead. We could not retrieve the other six, but we know they did indeed die. None were taken alive by the enemy." Bluewing looked down. He had lost good friends in the attack.

The king looked at the Wing-sergeant with sympathy. Yet he needed more information. "Have our forces made an attempt to retake the Eye-tower?"

Bluewing looked up again. "No, oh King. The rest of the Cloud has withdrawn to Eye-tower Fifty-four, and await further instructions, although we are now patrolling above Fifty-five continuously from the safety of the skies. I was sent to inform you, of course, but to also ask for reinforcements. Even with the sixty Feathers of Clouds 107 and 108 stationed at Eye-tower Fifty-four, it may not be sufficient to take a sealed tower. Pulling Clouds from other sections seemed unwise until more is known of the enemy's movements."

Queen Silverwing was chewing on the information. "Was there only one Cloud stationed at Eye-tower Fifty-five?"

"Yes, my Queen. Until now it was always deemed sufficient because of the Jungle."

"Most of the Feathers in Cloud 109 are young recruits, Mated One. It was really a small training base." Eagleron explained to his queen. And it seemed likely that those who died were quite young, barely beyond their topling years. He sighed and turned again to Bluewing. "What of the Dragon Hunters?"

"We have not heard from them in many days, although that is not unusual. The last we heard was that the greater part of the River Legion was headed to the Western Coast on an expedition to assist the Coast Legion on Serpent patrol. It is the spawning season. We did send word and request help because of their skill in the Jungle, but it may be a week before any can come."

"Too far away, yes. And how many Humans do you believe are in the enemy contingent, Captain?"

"It is not possible to know because of the jungle cover and because they are now holed up in the tower. But because of the nature of the attack, Cloud-captain Allflight believes there to be at least five hundreds of the Humans, oh King."

"Five hundreds! But what kept the Dragons from discovering..." Eagleron began, looking at his mate. Her face was stoic. She had voiced her fears on this matter before, but no one, himself included, had done anything to act upon her insight. He looked back at the messenger. "We need more information, of course. And no sign of the Alkhaness of Westrealm?"

"No, oh King. We do not believe she is there. No one saw sign of her, and no magic was used against us, but their swords overcame us in the confines of the tower. The Jungle would give them advantage in a counterattack. There is precious little room to fly in and land on the ground by the door, at least not in great force. Cloud-captain Allflight is of the opinion that they will block the roof entrance, and it will be nearly impossible for us to storm them from above, and without reinforcements we do not have the numbers needed to enter the area on foot and challenge them the Human way."

After a quarter-minute of silence while they pondered the information, the queen asked, "I am gravely concerned by this, Mated One. We have been caught off-guard despite the good work of the Eyes. I believe they must be right that the Alkhaness was not there. When she is near, her presence is felt. The enemy could not achieve a surprise attack with her among them. And yet she could be in the area directing the attack."

"Of course she directed the attack, even if she remained in her castle."

"Maybe, Mated One."

"What are you thinking, my love?" Such endearing communication was common between Etoppsi couples, even by the king and queen.

"Unless it were someone else. A rogue commander perhaps? Mated One, this an act of war upon our territory, not a common skirmish in the plains beyond the Wall. The Alkhaness is devious but not a fool. She has wisely shunned open war for many years, so this would be unusual for her. Nevertheless, it is only speculation on my part in consideration of all possibilities. We should assume the attack was ordered by the Alkhaness. What should we do?"

Eagleron considered for a minute before responding. He knew his Mate was correct. It was an odd move for The Alkhaness. Even so, a firm response to the aggression was needed. "I will issue a high alert order to the Sky Front. It could be a diversion for some greater attack, and so the Cyclones need to prepare. I will go myself to the south and take a Storm of King's Guards. Three hundred Feathers should be more than sufficient." He then turned to the messenger. "Eye-tower Fifty-four is well-secured in your opinion, Sergeant Bluewing?"

"We believe so, oh King. It is two miles from the edge of the Jungle and so any approach by an enemy would be seen, unlike at

Fifty-five. I was sent to you almost immediately, but the Eyes will be patrolling the skies heavily now to watch for movement in the area. If the enemy proceeds to march atop the Wall from Eye-tower Fifty-five, they would easily be spotted. It is likely they are still holed up in the Eye-tower. Cloud-captain Allflight does not foresee them approaching from atop the Wall; it would prove suicidal."

It had never occurred to the Skyfront Command that Eye-tower Fifty-five was vulnerable. Most believed it was perhaps the most secure. Only a small area around the Eye-tower itself was clear cut in order to keep vines and creatures from climbing into the high windows. Otherwise, it was the dangers of the Infested Jungle itself that provided protection. It was the primary reason why the Wall extended three miles into the Jungle, as it was a logical endpoint. It was presumed the Humans would never dare skirt the end of it without disturbing the Dragons and other vicious and venomous creatures, not to mention the poisonous and snaring plants, alive in themselves. It was highly dangerous even for the Etoppsi. The Jungle could not under typical circumstances be penetrated very far in any regard, not even by an army. It seemed as secure a boundary as did the Wall itself. Eagleron considered all this.

As did his queen. In some ways, Silverwing was more attuned to tactics and the cunning ways of the Alkhaness than her mate, for she had studied more of the histories.

"If the Jungle is no longer a barrier, then we must consider extending the Great Wall to the Western River. I have recommended this before," offered the queen. "You say this is unexpected, but I have counseled otherwise. The Alkhaness has evolved over her long years into a crafty sorceress."

"Yes, you have so counseled, Mated One, and it is clear your thinking was prescient. I am sorry we did not act upon it long ago, but the Jungle has always stopped Humans. It would be many years before even a low wall could be constructed. That land is soft and yielding; there are no hills of stone to quarry, and so blocks would have to be carried far. But yes, I agree that a permanent solution must be found, but for the moment we must go and eliminate the invaders."

"You must capture some, Mated One, if we want answers. Send them to me."

"It will be done, my love."

"Will we enter on foot, oh King?" asked Bluewing.

"I believe we will have to. Engaging them from above will have to be a part of the plan, but we will have to access that ground door if we are to dislodge them. They surely would not block it. It is their only way in or out."

The queen spoke again. "We Berugians have not trained in Human-like combat in centuries. It will be difficult. The Feathers are adept at spear and bow, but we have no swordsmen, for that is typically a Human method of fighting. And I am concerned there may be more to it than Human soldiers. I worry what you will find when you go, Mated One."

"What are you thinking, Lady?"

"The Wing-sergeant here and Cloud-captain Allflight may believe that no magic is being used, but how then do we explain their penetration of the Jungle if not with some form of magic? Hidden and dark. Only Dragons are immune to the poisons of the Jungle, and the Khestadone have nothing like our Dragon Legion. But apparently Human ingenuity has achieved what they have done? It may be possible but I suspect there must be more to it. Indeed they have attacked us at Eye-tower Fifty-five, but I suspect there is more that we do not see. If it is not some rogue commander, then there has to be a larger plan on the part of the Alkhaness."

The king considered for a moment. "It is curious, Mated One, and I cannot answer your suspicions without more information. But at the least we must act now before they send more. If it is an advance force, then they must be destroyed in order to deter those who would dare come next. I do see your point. It may be wise to send many Clouds to the Jungle eaves on the south border."

"They could roost in the outlying trees, oh King," offered Bluewing. "There are many small groves that the Dragon Hunters themselves use for espying the Jungle border. It is true they are Jungle trees, but the outliers are not in themselves dangerous to us. There are platforms built in many of them; easy to take off and land."

"Yes, they could very well use those. That would perhaps serve almost as well as a Wall, at least for the time being. Excellent thinking, Wing-sergeant Bluewing!"

The queen had more to add. "Mated One, I know it will be unpopular among the Feathers, but I am telling you that you should open the old armories from the Ralsheen wars and find shields and other devices to assist you. You can use maces, for less skill is needed than for swords, and you need to protect your bodies if you are to fight at ground level as the Humans do."

The messenger was shocked. "My Queen, do you mean body armor? But only the Dragon Hunters use…"

"You are forgetting your place, Wing-sergeant! She is your Queen. She knows who uses it and who does not."

"I apologize, oh King." Then he turned to Silverwing and bowed. "My apologies, my Queen. I suppose I was indeed expressing what you said about how the Feathers dislike it."

Silverwing had a forbidding dimension to her personality and few dared cross her, but she was genuinely empathetic and patient.

"Be at ease, Wing-sergeant. I am glad you speak your mind. But it is not just for fighting. The armor will help protect those that march on the ground through the Jungle to that tower door."

Centuries ago thousands among the Berugian Sky Front, the army of the Etoppsi, wore armor made for them by the Anterianhi, and yielded maces and long scimitars, but that was due to the nature of those ancient wars which were far more dangerous than those of recent times against the Khestadone. They could easily espy Human soldiers in the Barrens, the forty mile strip of land on the far side of the Great Wall that the Eyes patrolled, and where nearly all the skirmishes took place. The Etoppsi used massive bows and also great spears which they could throw with uncanny speed and accuracy, and they had the advantage of flight and height, but it was an advantage they did not have in the Jungle, nor in close combat. In fact, it was the Wall that made such combat seem obsolete. So, of body armor, it was not used anymore by the Feathers, the flying soldiers of the Berugian Sky Front, but only by the Dragonhunter Legion as a necessity. It was partly a cultural issue: the Etoppsi had great pride in their bodies, for they were indeed a magnificent race, furred, sleek and muscular, and so they almost never covered them, even in war.

"The queen is right. Indeed she has been correct about many things." Eagleron reached and took his mate's hand and kissed it tenderly. "This is a very serious situation and body armor is required." He looked at the Wing-sergeant, and though it was clear Bluewing thought the idea distasteful, he did not say more. "Mated One, send word to General Heavywing to come before you in person and dictate our orders. He can cull each of the Clouds from the Cyclone on the Great Wall to create a force of two Storms, promoting officers as needed. He should concentrate them in a westward line from the Wall perhaps thirty miles. He can determine the details, but he needs to seek advice from the Legion as well, for they will have knowledge of the land."

"Six-hundred Feathers. That will weaken the forces upon the Wall, Mated One," she replied and thought for a moment. "But it is nevertheless the wisest choice. Except for Eye-tower Fifty-five the rest of the Wall is likely as safe as it has ever been, at least for now. And by doing that we will not need to use forces from the Coast Isles. The Island Cyclone should remain in place."

"Exactly. If this is a diversion, then the most logical attack by a greater force would be by Sea. With determination they might slip by the Nantian navy in that region. This will have to do for now until we know more of the Alkhaness' intentions. And for that purpose have Heavywing triple Eyefeather patrols. Let us find precisely where on the Jungle borders their forces may be entering, but also any other gatherings of their forces. Have him send reports to me at Eye-tower Fifty-four, and…" He unclasped a wide, elaborately engraved and ancient gold bracelet from his lower right arm. "You may make further decisions on our part in my absence."

"Yes, Mated One. It will be done." She then held out her own, and the king clasped it upon her.

Bluewing shifted, as did all the—entirely male—attendants in the audience chamber.

The queen knew why. The Feathers were deeply prejudiced against females serving in the Sky Front, and it was not allowed by the Generals. With the bracelet she had authority over the Generals.

"But I can no longer wait. I will go now to the south," said the king. "They will rue the day they entered into Berug. Unless The Alkhaness is there herself, five hundred cannot stand against a full Storm of my King's Guard, and if the Wing-sergeant here and Allflight say she is not there, then you should not worry, my love."

"Do me one favor, my King and Mated One."

"Yes, my love, what is that?"

"Take Two Storms." She smiled then for the first time.

As did King Eagleron. He looked lovingly into his mate's eyes and touched her chin. Most present on the audience platform were familiar with the couple's affectionate interplay, yet the Wing-sergeant turned away unwilling to intrude upon such a personal exchange. "All right, my Lady of the Sunrise. I will do as you command," said the king.

When he stood, Eagleron was fully nine feet in height. With trim chestnut fur that covered his body and the broad black Feathers on his mighty wings he was a magnificent specimen. Even as king he wore no garments, in order to fully display his superb physicality, though he wore a wide golden collar around his neck and heavy matching bracelets on his lower arms, ancient symbols of his military authority, although one of these was now on his mate's arm. Sometimes he wore also a treasured crown of gold and emeralds, a relic presented centuries ago to the Berugian Royal House by the Anterianhi Emperors in the happy years following the Conquest when there was much contact between the new Empire and the Land of Berug. It was presented as a symbol of everlasting alliance between the Kingdom and the Empire. The face of the king was proud with his high cheek bones and broad brow.

Queen Silverwing also stood, and she too was resplendent, donning a rich, tight gray fur with matching feathered wings, white-tipped and preened with oil to their highest gloss. She wore a silver circlet upon her head, and instead of a collar she wore a magnificent necklace with woven strands of silver and gold, polished, and sporting pearls and rubies of magnificent size.

Together Eagleron and Silverwing were the epitome of their exotic race. Etoppsi were mesmerizing to Human eyes. Like the rest of their bodies their faces too were covered in fine but dense hair like that on a young northern pony, and indeed all their fur was as glossy as that of the finest well-kept steeds in Human lands. But like Humans, each Etoppsis was different from the next, with different features. Though they were all members of the same race, their coloring was of great variety. The rich chestnut fur and black feathered wings of the king and the silver gray of the queen were wonderful to see. But all natural earthy colors were represented among the Etoppsi, browns of all shades, a rare rich red, golden yellows like the wild cats of the grasslands, and among some of the island tribes there were many who were white as the seals in the seas. There could also be found those of solid, shiny black—shadows of the skies. The fur of the Etoppsi sometimes contrasted with their great feathered wings which were as often as not of a different color. Some of their wing feathers were sleek and solid in shade like that of the king, but others might have elaborate spotted patterns or be tipped in white like that of the queen.

The females were typically smaller than the males. Whereas it was common for the males to stand at heights of eight or nine feet, a female Etoppsis rarely reached eight feet, seven being more common, and yet even they seemed giant to Humans for they were much more massive and muscular than any Human. Some might say that because of their fur and feathers the Etoppsi were more like beasts, but despite this, their whole body shapes, sans wings of course, and their faces, were much more like that of Humans, giant furry Humans to be sure, than to any beast. It was said by the Guardian Meical—the one the Berugians referred to as The Taxiarch—in the Ancient Book, that the Etoppsi were formed of the same Mold fashioned by the Creator in the Early Times as were all the Three Races. They were a race as important to this World as that of the Humans and of the secretive Qeteral, and the Mold was the same.

Though they were held in awe by Humans, they nevertheless unnerved many of them, for since the Etoppsi wore no garments, their physique could be disconcerting, for their fur did not camouflage by any means, but if possible its glossiness defined their shapeliness more intensely. The males were always perfectly muscled, though if such a physique could be scaled down and placed upon a Human man, the upper body in particular would have seemed overly exaggerated. Their chest and back muscles were massive, not only to give them super strength in their arms but even more so for the maneuvering of their vast wings. The females too, though smaller and lighter, were muscular as well and very shapely with large breasts and wide hips. As a race the adults were universally sleek and sensuous, and to Human noses, musky.

These physical features of the Berugian people were a sight to behold among the few northern Humans who could ever say they had seen or communicated with them. But this was nothing to how they appeared when they unfolded their vast wings and flew high among the clouds. From tip to tip their wings stretched from twenty feet in the smallest females to thirty or more among the largest males. They were as gods in the skies, and magnificent to see among their northern friends. But they were feared by the Human soldiers and slaves of the Alkhaness, for all in all, the Etoppsi could be fearsome enemies.

Strong beyond measure of any Human, the Etoppsi were famous throughout the known world as the Great Builders. They were responsible for many of the great Wonders of the Anterianhi Human world. Guardian's Gate, the Palace and the Library of the Emperors, and the Temple of Peace in the Valley of the Gifted were universally admired. But these were few and widely scattered in the Northern World. Here in the Land of Berug were many great structures and towers of astounding size to accommodate the needs of their race, and of course there was the Great Wall built on the eastern border to keep out the soldiers of the Alkhaness. Over a hundred years it took them to build this vast expanse and every six miles was a watchtower from where the Feathers could watch for movement in the east. Eastwards the land was not favored by the Etoppsi, for just beyond the Barrens it was more forested: the Etoppsi preferred the open savannah lands on the western side of the Southern Continent.

They were a good and great people, and very proud. They could often appear serious in demeanor in their relations with one another and with the other races, though this could to some degree be attributed to the formal language style among the high-born, but they were nevertheless generous-hearted and intensely loyal friends. Occasionally their formality gave way to displays of humor and affection, and their airborne mating rituals were both curious and fascinating. To Humans they could seem aloof, but the Berugians did not disdain all Humans, and were friends, even in these post-imperial days, with the Nantians and others in the north who were once a part of the Anterianhi Empire. However, they did not understand the complexities of Humans and their apparent eagerness for conflict and division, for the Etoppsi were a fully united people under their king and queen, direct descendants of Berug the Magnificent, placed on his throne by Meical the Taxiarch in the deeps of time.

The differences in the races made it easier to remain separate, but once per year, a delegation would fly to the island Kingdom of Nant to celebrate the Meicalian Feast. And it was not unheard of for them to be seen in Tirilorin, for they had the highest regard for the Emperors all the way until the abdication of the last one and the establishment of a republican city state. However, the descendants of the last emperor still lived in the city, and their friendship with the Berugian people was not forgotten. But, to many who lived in other portions of the old empire, it was presumed by the unlearned that they were no more than legend. In the far north, in the Kingdoms of Solanto and Eleni, and in the far eastern kingdoms, they had not been seen since the high days of the Anterianhi Empire.

But legend they were not.

Berug was a very great kingdom here on the Southern Continent, and an important power for a thousand years. It was a great and wide land with much wild game and there were pastures in the hills for sheep and goats, and many areas, too, planted in fruit trees. Meats, fruits, nuts and root vegetables provided the diet of the Etoppsi race. The mainland stretched southwards to the Western River and the Infested Jungle. Separating the savannah from the Jungle was a wide land of fen and river where Dragons would sometimes roam, but the Legion, the widely admired Dragon Hunters, dwelt near and protected the southern flank from the encroachment of wild beasts. In addition to the mainland with its rocky hills and grassy savannahs, many inhabited islands extended off its northern coast towards Nant, and also off its western coast into the tropics.

With the Khestadone kingdom they had at times been in conflict. Precisely when the Alkhaness and the Alkhan first came to the Southern Continent the Berugian Royalty was not certain, for the enemy remained far to the east on the shores of the Khestadone and Serpent Seas and were slow to build up their kingdom and their armies, and secretive, and for long years were not a threat to the Berugian people. However, as time went on there were skirmishes as the Khestadone expanded westward, and so the Etoppsi decided to build their Great Wall. It stretched many hundreds of miles from the Sea in the north to the Jungle in the south, and was fully sixty feet high interspersed every six miles with an even taller Eye-tower, and the Eyes patrolled the lands forty miles into the Barrens east of the Wall to forestall any advance upon it, and all the cities of their great kingdom were well-protected behind it. Though the Alkhan had left long ago to begin his own kingdom east of the Khestadone Sea, the Alkhaness remained and expanded her domain to within a few miles of the no-man lands that the Etoppsi patrolled. The enemy rarely entered that borderland, and to date they feared the Infested Jungle with good reason.

The Berugian peoples had always believed themselves safe. Yet it was clear to those with eyes to see that in the last few decades the power eastwards had grown immensely. It was believed by some that the Alkhaness had developed magic that could be felt in the airs above her realm even by the Feathers and Eyes who spied upon her territory. It created anxiety among some, and King Eagleron, and to a stronger extent, Queen Silverwing, could sense its antagonism. The queen had often counseled improved defenses, but as there had been no direct threats or major skirmishes for long years, the Etoppsi had concluded that their Wall, the Jungle, and the courage of the Feathers was sufficient, and till now Silverwing had demurred.

But not any longer.

Donning the golden bracelet, Silverwing now had the authority that was required to issue any military orders necessary in the king's absence. He expected her to need it when Cyclone-general Heavywing appeared at her summons, for he would presume the orders had come from the king himself. In reality it gave her full control of military matters while the king was absent, and though she had not had time to discuss it with her mate, Silverwing had other ideas to implement under her newly acquired authority. The situation was certainly urgent and time was of the essence, and it had taken a full day to outfit the king's armor-reluctant Feathers in the old Anterianhi gear from the Museum at the Institute. Eagleron departed in haste sometime in the night.

When Cyclone-general Heavywing arrived from his station at the center of the Great Wall that following afternoon, he had already been informed of the breach at Fifty-five, so he was not unaware of the king's plans, and the first of the queen's orders did not seem out of place to him.

"Yes, my Queen," he said, glancing at the bracelet on her arm. He had never taken orders from a female in his entire military career. He hoped his annoyance was sufficiently suppressed. "I will return immediately and begin a culling of the Eye-tower Clouds. I assure you it will not weaken the Wall defenses."

"You are partly correct in that, General Heavywing, for the Wall remains strong, but it does weaken its forces from what they currently are, and under a high alert at that. It is far from ideal. But I only say that to you so that you do not make the mistake of believing that the security of the Wall to date guarantees its impregnability."

"But two Storms is less than a fifth of the total defenses, my Queen. I have always believed, and have made it clear in council that the current defense is far greater than needed…"

"And yet Eye-tower Fifty-five is now taken and the southern end has been skirted by the enemy, is that not the way you see it, General?" Her fur bristled, and that forbidding element of her countenance exerted itself.

Heavywing almost swallowed but bit his tongue. "I see your point, my Queen. You are correct. What are you suggesting I do differently? What else did the king order?"

She lifted her right arm with its bracelet and stared fully into the general's face with her penetrating black eyes.

It worked.

Heavywing wished now he had not said that about the 'king's order'. It was too obvious. He had better be more careful. "I beg your pardon, my Queen. What are *your* orders?" He was not happy to think what she might suggest. But he was bound to her dictates as long as she wore that bracelet.

"I want you to immediately begin a recruitment campaign. Coordinate with Cyclone-general Gullfeather of the Island Cyclone, and within one month I want you to have recruited two full Thunderstorms, eighteen-hundred young Feathers, and to have begun intensive training for them."

With shock, Heavywing replied, "My Queen, are you sure that is necessary?"

"I am telling you, General Heavywing, that the Alkhaness is a vicious and fearless adversary. At some point soon she will feel strong enough to engage us. We are at great risk, and the breaching of the Infested Jungle and the taking of Eye-tower Fifty-five signals a greater war to come. Hopefully, it is not immediate."

"I am your loyal servant, of course, my Queen, but how do you know this for certain? I know you have counseled greater precautions, but we have always agreed…"

"No, General Heavywing. The rest of you have agreed. I, on the other hand, have often argued otherwise. I am telling you that the evidence is pointing towards an escalation. We have been attacked, General! A piece of our territory, *Berugian* territory!" she emphasized, "has been invaded! And for the first time since the Ralsheen Wars, occupied by an enemy! The Alkhan maintains war in the far east, and I believe it is only a matter of time before the Alkhaness more openly assists her cohort. We know she sends him much rice and other foodstuffs and supplies for his armies. The Nantian navy keeps her hemmed into the Khestadone Sea, yet what if someday she uses her magic and breaks through? I want you to understand, General, that though I have the greatest admiration for the Sky Front, your male-only thinking is based too much on pride and you consider little these threats that seem distant to us in Berug. It is now time, in fact it is past time, that we do more."

General Heavywing was silent for several moments. On the one hand he resisted the idea that the breach at the southern border was more than a skirmish, and at the very most a testing of the waters by the forces of the Alkhaness, that once put down by the king, would end the whole affair. The Alkhaness would realize her error, back off, and not threaten them again. It made sense of course that a new force should be established on the southern border now to protect from further incursion, but that was only wisdom, and again probably temporary. What he could not see was the limitations of which the queen spoke, of male pride, magnified among the tradition of the Skyfront Command, which disavowed any acknowledgement of a serious weakness on the part of the Kingdom of Berug. The threats she outlined were indeed distant. Berug had never in a thousand years, not even during the time of the Ralsheen Empire, been conquered by an invasive force. Human empires came and went, but the Kingdom of Berug of the Etoppsi was secure.

Yet as he pondered the words of Queen Silverwing and the facts as she so resolutely expressed them, he could perhaps make himself see that something essentially new was indeed developing. No doubt Westrealm was a threat, for the Great Wall was built for a purpose. Humans were terrified, with good reason, of the Infested Jungle and under normal circumstances could not penetrate its dangers. Perhaps, he began to think, it actually was powerful magic that allowed that force of five hundred to traverse it however many miles and capture the southernmost Eye-tower. The Alkhaness had never demonstrated such magic before now. Even for the Etoppsi the Jungle was dangerous. The Dragonhunter Legionnaires were the only ones to regularly enter it, and yet only its first few miles, in order to destroy Dragon nests or to give chase to an adult. Nor were Dragons the only danger in the Jungle.

No, he concluded, it really was unusual that five-hundred Human soldiers could penetrate that far. If the Khestadone navy should indeed someday break through the Nantian blockade, it would increase the threat enormously. Reluctantly, he agreed. Silverwing was known to have instincts beyond what was typical.

He looked up again at his queen. Most Etoppsi were enamored of her great beauty, and she was admired far and wide. She was formidable in Council and held great sway over it and over her mate the king, on many matters. Although less so with the military. The Sky Front was, by law and tradition, dominated by male Etoppsi.

However, the king always insisted that she be listened to and accorded the fullest courtesy, and on occasion, such as the move to increase the Wall forces ten years previously, the queen's recommendation was pursued by Eagleron despite objections from the Cyclone's commanders, including himself. Maybe she was right on more matters? Heavywing realized he must set aside his prejudice towards her being female. *Queens tend to be of that sex, do they not?*

He buried deep his joke.

"I will carry out your orders, my Queen." He bowed his head to her to show that he respected her view and acknowledged the order. "Eh, is there more?"

"Yes. Yes there is," she replied, dashing his hopeful presumption. "One of those new Thunderstorms can be trained by traditional methods, and I expect them to replace those culled from the Wall. The other, however, I want to be trained for ground combat against Humans. With full armor."

"I…" he started to protest, and his wings even loosened themselves unbidden, outward a foot or two, but the words would not come. He drew his wings tight again and stood resolute. If he had come around to her views, then he could not see good reason for arguing against this point either. "Yes, my Queen. However, that could make it more difficult to recruit, but I can see how it would prove useful. I must admit, however, there are almost none of us who have such training ourselves."

"For some young males, yes. The need to cover themselves as do the other races is not understood by them. However, there are those who admire the Dragonhunter Legion despite their heavy protective garb, and yet due to less skill have not been allowed to join it, and there will be even more, particularly when the word spreads that our borders have been violated, that will be willing to learn Human-like combat. There have been times in our own history in which armored battle gear was more common than not. And upon your point that the Cyclone Command is not adept at the training, I am well aware, and it brings me around to my final order—at least for now. I want you to send a delegation of officers that you yourself choose, and subjects that I myself choose, to fly directly to Nant and request from King Monticu a group of one hundred Human males to come to Berug and conduct the training. And also for them to send skilled armorers to assist our own in outfitting the new Thunderstorm. If the King, my husband, keeps two thirds of his Guard in the Anterianhi armor, then that leaves us with only four hundred useful suits remaining at the Museum. And yet those are old and in poor condition and must be refurbished. You will need hundreds more, and replacements, and it will take time."

To the proud Heavywing, this was a bizarre twist. "My Queen, does King Eagleron know of your plan?"

The pause was telling. Heavywing hoped he had not just made another error. He dug deep, but he realized his response had nothing to do with her being female. He would have been flabbergasted had it been the king himself.

Finally, "No, General. We have not discussed it. Frankly, there was not time, and it is only since he flew south that this particular idea has manifested itself in my mind. I know it is, shall we say, a unique idea for this day and age, however it was quite common during the era of the Downfall of the Ralsheen in the days of the Alliance and Third Appearance of The Taxiarch. I believe it is a necessary step in improving our defenses."

"Pardon me, my Queen, but Human-like ground combat for us is not a defensive strategy except on a minor scale. It is an...oh!"

She nodded. "Yes, General. And trust me, I have no immediate desire for an offensive war. But again, I am telling you that times have changed, and such a thing is now among the possibilities. The King and I have discussed that possibility, and we do see eye to eye on it...if that makes you feel more at ease about the order, General."

This last could have been taken as an insult, and that more than anything caused Heavywing some discomfort. He was running the risk of getting on the queen's bad side, and considering her reputation, that was very unwise. He stood straight and tall. He would confront his prejudice head on.

"I will follow the order because you are my Queen. You wear the Bracelet of Command that the Taxiarch Himself gave to Berug the Magnificent, and there can be no doubt that the King gave it to you with good cause. I will admit that I have not always seen things quite the way you do, but I will say this. You have convinced me fully." He bowed deeply to demonstrate his respect. Thinking it might ease any discord he decided to address her with her official military title. "Yes, Queen-marshal, I will carry out your orders willingly."

She nodded.

Apparently the subtle apology was accepted, for she smiled.

Thank The Taxiarch. "Now, do you have the civilians in mind for the delegation to Nant, Queen-marshal?"

He suspected she did.

"The King's uncle Hawking I believe will gladly go."

"He is aging, my Queen. How old is he now? Over a hundred, is he not?"

"He is now a hundred and two. But the flight should not task him. He is familiar with the Nantians and has attended the Meicalian Feast there for decades. He will represent the Royal family and will speak for us. I sent for him this morning and expect him to arrive here anytime. When he does I will explain everything."

Of all those on the Sky Council, Royal Hawking was one of those who fully supported all of Queen Silverwing's proposals, even the military ones. She was sending a strong ally, Heavywing realized, and someone that the king too, trusted. "He is a good choice, my Queen, if you deem him hardy. Who else?"

"I will let Hawking choose two whom he believes best. I will also send Rainwing of the House of Green Isle."

Despite his strong desire never to allow emotion to show on his face, Heavywing puckered his eyes at this. "I know of her, my Queen. She is the professor of geography now at the Institute, is she not? And teaches some military history classes. She came after my time as Sky-colonel in charge of officer education. If you don't mind me saying, the Feathers do not like her. She has a reputation as a Meicalian Zealot."

"I know how the Feathers view her. You only call her a zealot because she refuses to mate."

"Yes, my Queen. It isn't natural, that. She must be in her fourth decade! She should have mated and Bonded twenty years ago."

"She is an old-school traditionalist, no doubt. It was more common long ago in the days of the Anterianhi emperors that those few Etoppsi who studied with the northern Sages chose to be what they call 'celibate.' They believed at the time that to have a mate interfered with the Gift. I admit that I doubt that that aspect of things is true based on what I have studied over the years. Among those with the Gift the Humans make exceptions to the celibacy requirement. Nevertheless, there are those few females like Rainwing who hold to the old view."

"Does she have a Gift? Only Bond Matrons and Physicians are known to have a Gift." He watched the queen closely to see if some body language might add to his suspicions. He was disappointed, however. Not even a twitch in her facial muscles revealed itself.

"You will have to ask her yourself, General. I do not know."

"But you have suspicions."

"She and I talk, General, and I feel I know her quite well, which is why I'm choosing her for this task. But if she has a Gift, she has not revealed it to me. I think rather she is latching onto the old Monastic disciplines for personal reasons. Human Monastics have no other Gift besides occasional Taxiarchan Visions. I do not know if she has experienced one. In any regard, her knowledge in her subject is unsurpassed as far as I am concerned. She will likely be able to answer many questions that the Nantians might choose to ask. Geography may be her specialty, but I know for a fact that she has studied military history in far greater detail than most. She teaches some of those classes, just as you said. And though the Sky Front may dislike her, Rainwing was a Dragon Hunter, and despite her choice to be celibate is considered a heroine by her kin in Green Isle."

"I do not deny her bravery, and I can see how her areas of expertise would be helpful. Be aware, though, Queen-marshal, that no matter what Skyfront officers I choose, they will be hotly prejudiced against an adult female who chooses not to mate. I will directly order them, however, to refrain from antagonizing her and to treat her as an equal in all other regards. They will do as I say."

"Thank you, General. Try reminding them that there are other by-choice life rules that comply with the Taxiarchan Disciplines besides those of Skyfront Feathers, even if they do seem archaic to some of us. Choose wisely four officers. I want the delegation to leave here in three days, and I am sending a message today by swift flyer to Nant to expect them. If all goes well and the Nantians agree, which I believe they will, they could be here in less than a month."

"We could bring some of them with us on the return flight."

"Perhaps, yes. Excellent idea. I will suggest that to Royal Hawking, and I will leave that up to him and the others, based on the talks. They say Humans dream of but fear flight."

"Fear flight, my Queen? I had never thought of that. I suppose they might. I rather fear their compelling desire to ride on little rafts upon the Great Ocean, their *ships,* and also to ride the horse beasts."

The queen smiled, in a friendly sort of way this time. "Humans must do what they can to help them travel faster and to cross the seas. We need not these things, of course, so we can sometimes think their ways silly. Those Nantian ships assist in protecting our northern waters, as you know. You need to read more history of the Northern Continent. You have not studied enough."

"I know our kingdom's history thoroughly, my Queen!" he replied, withholding his annoyance with great effort.

"And of the time of the Alliance?"

"Enough for strategy. I have never cared for *Human* history."

"We are one world, General."

"Yes, my Queen. Some Humans are worthy of our attention, true. The Nantians are certainly great friends."

"And yet you know little of their ways, it seems. If peace is retained, General, I will recommend that you be sent to Nant for the next celebration of the Meicalian Feast."

Heavywing was unimpressed by this possibility and simply nodded, unwilling for his words to be misconstrued in any way as encouraging such a ridiculous idea. He had no desire to attend what he and many others among the Skyfront Command considered a silly festival of the northern Humans, friends or not. The work of the Taxiarch was to be continued through the watchfulness and the Disciplines of the Sky Front. As far as he was concerned it was disastrous that the Anterianhi Empire, established by the Taxiarch Himself, was allowed to fall apart a century ago, and the Berugian people, particularly those of the Front, blamed the lack of discipline that was all too common among Human rulers. He was wise enough to give credit to the Nantians for trying to maintain something of the old order, but he saw no reason for them to celebrate as if they were adhering to the Taxiarchan Disciplines. Folly, he thought it. And as to the continuation of the old annual feast? Scandalous.

The queen, thankfully, did not press it.

"I am grateful, General Heavywing, for your work on all these matters."

"Yes, Queen-marshal. It is an honor to serve. I will need to go to the Institute and have them suspend officer studies for some. We will need them for the new southern force and for recruiting. If I hear news from the south, I will send word immediately."

"You can trust me to do the same. Keep alert, General. I know that you will, but what I am especially concerned about is the enemy's magic. We believe it to be gaining rapidly in strength, and we do not know exactly how the Alkhaness will use it. It is right for us to fear it and to prepare."

"Yes, my Queen." He nodded to her one last time, then turned and walked to the edge of the great platform as sentries saluted him. He spread his vast black wings and launched himself skyward.

He realized that his opinions of the queen had changed with this encounter. He finally understood that Eagleron chose her for far more than her famed beauty. He wondered that they had no toplings as yet. The Royal pair had mated dozens of times, for he admired their mid-air couplings high above the city in past years when he once served in the capital. They were the handsomest of pairs. There was still plenty of time for her to bear the king's toplings, of course, and she surely bore within her by now some seeded eggs. Perhaps soon she would choose to gestate one. If times were to become more dangerous, perhaps the time was ripe to produce an heir. As he made his way towards the Institute, he thought upon his own son,

Ravenfeather, a noted leader in the Dragonhunter Legion, and also his new-born grandtopling, Springwind. He had a sudden notion how interesting it would be if the queen should choose to bear a topling male soon, for the right timing might just possibly put such a prince and Springwind at the Institute together. She had the proper heritage of a noble house. *You never know,* he said to himself, catching a westerly breeze and doubling his speed; he skirted the tall towers of the city. For now, he suppressed this elusive wish and considered instead how he would carry out his queen's orders.

There was much to be done.

Chapter 18—Battle at Eye-Tower Fifty-Five

Two Storms, six-hundred strong, all in ancient Anterianhi-made armor began landing on the Great Wall and on the western ground by Eye-tower Fifty-four. This gear the king and his officers had to cull in order to find what was serviceable, but at least it had been reasonably well-preserved in the Museum at the Institute. Suits with shields had been preserved from the Conquest when the Etoppsi allied with the Anterianhi Humans in the overthrow of the Ralsheen. Its use was unnecessary afterwards for hundreds of years, and even when the Khestadone began to harass the eastern border, the Skyfront Feathers, with their proud warrior-body image, resisted making use of it again. And when the Great Wall was built it seemed to be obsolete.

There was some banter therefore on the part of the Eye-tower Guard towards individual Feathers whom some of them knew as friends among the King's Guard, teasing them for covering their bodies, yet when they saw Eagleron their own king fitted with the heavy, bronze-plated steel, they demurred. The Wall Cyclone's officers understood the need for the armor, and it only underscored the seriousness of the situation: Humans had captured a piece of Berugian territory and occupied one of its watch towers. It was a thing unknown since the Ralsheen War, and extraordinary measures had to be taken. To enter the Jungle on foot in order to engage the Witch-queen's force in face-to-face Human-like combat inside the tower, would be a test of resolve. If anything, Humans, since they were smaller, could be quick, and were undoubtedly superior with swords, so whatever advantage the armor could give them was appreciated.

However, the ancient scimitars remained at the Museum, for the Etoppsi hadn't trained with any sort of sword in over four-hundred years, and they needed to be sharpened and there wasn't time. Instead, each of the King's Feathers carried a heavy mace. These were also preserved from the Ralsheen War and were so huge that only the strongest Human man might have been able to pick one up, and yet he would not be able to swing it. It promised to be a useful weapon in the close quarters of Eye-tower Fifty-five where the typical weapons used by Skyfront Feathers—bow and spear—would be useless.

The king found already many Feathers ready for action, the sixty from the two Clouds that were stationed at Eye-tower Fifty-four, although many of them were momentarily absent on Eye patrol, and nine strapping young male survivors still fit from Cloud 109 of Eye-tower Fifty-five. The remaining survivors had been flown to Intuk, a city about twenty miles north, to have their injuries treated.

The king then received the information he needed to formulate a plan. A number of Eyefeathers, the specialty spies of the Sky Front, under the cover of the previous black night, had finally, after inspired effort, pinpointed where the enemy had entered into the Jungle, a spot twenty-five miles east. With their hawk-like vision it was discovered that around a hundred Human soldiers were stationed there as an apparent rear guard. It was a small area of land that consisted of rocky hills jutting up from the plain and extending southwestward into the Jungle for some miles. It was perhaps the only such landform around and made it unique. It was not all that far from some of the outlying forest-lands in the western part of the region under the control of the Alkhaness. Humans could very well have covered the short distance on the open plain on the blackest of nights without being seen by the Eyes, and this was apparently what had taken place. Close to the Jungle edge was a cave-like cliff overhang with its opening facing east. Because of this, the Humans had been well hidden till now from the Eyes.

Unfortunately for the Humans, however, the Eyes had been scouring the area with four times the usual numbers and with far greater urgency, and they were discovered. King Eagleron was determined to destroy this force first. A few of the officers pressed him for an immediate assault upon the main force at Eye-tower Fifty-five almost as soon as his two Storms arrived. Eagleron, however, was not High Marshall and King without reason. Over the years, through his study of strategy and from experience, he had learned patience. He had his reasons therefore for his order to eliminate the smaller force. Once eliminated it would not be able to assist the troop at Eye-tower Fifty-five. Secondly, by making use of a contingent of his newly armored ground troops with cover from flyers at this more open position on the edge of the Jungle, it would give those Feathers a bit of training with their maces and shields before the assault on the main force at Eye-tower Fifty-five. Finally, it would minimize the potential for escape.

Therefore, approximately four hours before dawn, the king launched this assault. Two hundred Feathers flew off, three-quarters of which were Anterianhi-armored King's Guard with spears and maces, the other quarter consisting of bow and spear-carrying, Wall-trained Feathers, and all were led by a highly capable Thunderstorm-colonel Highflight, one of Eagleron's Guard commanders.

Before long they had arrived at a point above the Jungle border where the enemy rear-guard was encamped under the cliff. However, the Humans were not entirely taken by surprise, for despite the earlier setting of Solvermoon, Orohmoon still hung in the sky with its dim yellow light, and the seeming flicker and dimming of the stars by the Berugian force was easily seen and interpreted correctly by the enemy commander and the lookout. Quickly they aroused the entire contingent, but even as they gathered their weapons the arrows of the Berugians fell. Etoppsi were blessed with eyesight greater than perhaps all other living creatures, and the darkness was little hindrance, and Orohmoon was quite sufficient to allow them to pursue the foe with deadly accuracy. Within a minute or two at least a quarter of the enemy force was slain, while the rest retreated within the edge of the Jungle presuming the unclothed Etoppsi would not dare follow them under the perilous trees. They were shocked when at that point Berugian troops in full body armor actually landed on the ground and advanced. Never had they expected such a tactic and never had they heard that Etoppsi ever wore protective gear.

Injured enemy soldiers were immediately dispatched by spear and mace, for the Berugian Sky Front was well-known for showing no mercy to the Khestadone. Though a number of enemy arrows from the Jungle edge did indeed find a mark, for a number of the Etoppsi still had difficulty making full use of their weighty shields, the rest of the Feathers swiftly reached them and made quick work with their maces.

With the horrid prospect of venturing the deep Jungle in the dark or facing the menacing winged giants, a number of the enemy attempted to flee across the plain. These were quickly downed by the arrows of some fifty Feathers who remained aloft. Within twenty minutes it was over. The Humans were mortified at the approach of eight and nine foot tall Etoppsi males in full battle armor, and in their panic they were slaughtered. The last remaining was the commander. He was the only one who was spared, although he suffered an arrow wound in his left shoulder. He was quickly bound. A force of three Clouds—one air and two ground—remained to secure the site, while the rest, with the enemy commander in tow, along with the bodies of five dead and fifteen wounded Etoppsi ground troops, returned to the king at Eye-tower Fifty-four.

The king first paid his respects to the dead Feathers, and these were soon afterwards buried on Berugian soil, alongside those who had been buried earlier from Eye-tower Fifty-five and whose bodies had been recovered. In time a monument would be placed here. Within an hour, the enemy commander was brought to the king. His wound had been attended to, but sheer terror of the giant winged creatures kept him from remaining on his feet. He cringed and shook before the king.

"Why has your witch-queen the Alkhaness broken the peace and taken our Eye-tower!"

To a Human, the deep booming voice of the giant Etoppsis was more than intimidating. Coming from an angry king, however, only intensified the commander's dread.

"I… I do not know their reasons!" the man replied, terrorized. "I only do as I am commanded!"

"They? What do you mean by *their* reasons? Is this some band of rebels acting on the orders of some renegade officers? Don't tell me the Alkhaness is not behind this!"

"I…I do not know. We have been acting under *his* orders. Her Majesty loaned us to *him*."

King Eagleron paused. He did not at all like what he was hearing. "Who…is *he!* Who are you talking about?" He was afraid to put words in the Human's mouth. Let him say it himself.

"His Majesty from the Eastern Realm!"

"The Alkhan! The Alkhan of Eastrealm?" exclaimed Eagleron.

The Human gasped at his own admission and looked around in terror as if lightning might strike him down.

The king continued his questioning. "Why would he come here? What purpose does he have? The Khestadone have declared open war with us by taking our Eye-tower!"

"I do not know their reasons! I swear! I only do what I am commanded!"

"Then what precisely were you commanded to do? Speak, Human! Tell me everything you know, or I will have your eyes clawed out and have you flown into the deep Jungle where you will be devoured by giant snakes!"

The man hesitated, looking all around as if determining if there were any sort of escape, but he was surrounded by at least two dozen gigantic Feathers and several officers. His predicament was impossible. He swallowed hard, his mouth dry from panic.

"We... we were given instructions to build a trail through the Jungle along the line of cliffs east of the tower. Afterwards, we were told to take the tower."

Eagleron considered. "What other orders have you been given? What advantage is it for you to gain control of *one* of our towers? Surely you don't expect us to let you keep it!"

"I... I don't know any of that! All I know is that Major G'lud and two strangers—I don't think they're Human—that came with His Majesty from the east are searching for something in those hills, but I swear I don't know what it is."

Cloud-captain Allflight spoke hurriedly in the king's ear.

The king then asked the enemy commander. "How have you penetrated the Jungle? Humans have not penetrated it so far before! How have you managed it; I must know this!"

"Don't make me tell you! They will kill me!"

"You will die in any event. You can die rapidly and painlessly when I have your head removed from your body, or you can be cast deep into the jungle naked and blind!" The man began to sob hysterically. "Speak, Human!"

It took almost a minute before he could do so. "He...," he began weakly.

"What is it? What has the Alkhan done, Human!"

"He has trained them, m'Lord! He has trained them...some of the Wingless...the Dragons that is." He broke down, fell fully on the floor, and couldn't speak again for several minutes.

At this revelation there was a general clamor in the Eye-tower room. "But! How can that be?" asked Captain Allflight. "Dragons cannot be trained! Only The Taxiarch and the ancient gods could even communicate with them according to old tales. They are vicious, wild creatures!"

The king was quiet for a long while. He stared at the trembling Human before him, attempting to decide whether what he was saying was true or not. It seemed impossible that such a thing could be. He and Silverwing had sensed that the power of the Alkhaness had grown. If she were working more closely with her cohort the Alkhan of Eastrealm, it might explain it. It was well-known that in Westrealm, though their slaves and armies were all Human, the Alkhan was known in the east for the use of monstrous beasts and other strange creatures in his ongoing attempt to conquer the eastern Human kingdoms. Clearly he had learned to control such creatures, but could he now control the wild Dragons of the Infested Jungle? The king realized the Human before him could probably not easily lie in his obvious fright, and also, such a fact would explain a great many things about the assault on Eye-tower Fifty-five. It was risking open war, but if the Alkhaness was now more fully aligned with the Alkhan, she might feel secure enough in taking that risk. Silverwing had predicted that it was only a matter of time before the Alkhaness leant open support to the Alkhan's eastern war effort. The question was what did Eye-tower Fifty-five have to do with it? It was many hundreds of miles away from the eastern front.

He looked at Allflight. "Captain Allflight, were any Dragons sighted during the assault on Eye-tower Fifty-five?"

"The day before, oh King. One was sighted from the tower as it stretched itself in the top of a giant tree. Wingless of course. But it is not unusual; we see them from time to time. We thought no more on it, for the Wingless are not a threat to the Eye-tower, not even with fire."

The king was glad it was Wingless. It was bad enough to think on that idea. If the warlock-king had somehow learned to train the Winged ones, they would prove even a match for the Sky Front. The Winged ones were seldom seen, and were quite rare. They were also more than four times as large as their Wingless cousins. If *they* could be trained, it might take only a few to neutralize the air advantage that the Berugians had claimed for a thousand years.

He then looked at the Human and said, "Do you know how he has accomplished this? By what methods has the Alkhan been able to train them, do you know?"

Allflight in his skepticism was about to interrupt, but Eagleron held up a hand to stay him. Finally, the Human spoke again, although by now nearly all his courage had drained and he could barely be heard.

"It is certainly by magic that he has done this. The men say Their Majesties are more powerful than ever before, and I believe it. She controls our minds from afar, and he controls all beasts, they say. But I don't know the answer to your question beyond that."

"Are they near? –in the area?—Your witch-queen and the Alkhan?"

The man looked at Eagleron. "She led us here three months ago. After we began building the trail through the Jungle, Her Majesty returned to her citadel. She returned several weeks later with His Majesty. By then our trail had advanced only a short ways and many died in the building of it, but when they came, he brought with him two Wingless Dragons and the two strangers who made quick progress on the trail. They continued their search in the hills, but eventually Her Majesty left again. His Majesty then ordered the extension of the trail in the direction of the tower and the attack, but he left just before our assault took place. I don't know why."

"And you say they are looking for something, but you have no idea what it is?"

"No. I have answered well! Spare my life! Take me to your king and let me beg before him!"

"He is the king, you worthless Human worm!" exclaimed Captain Allflight, unable to contain himself.

"Y...YOU are the King of Berug?" And though he was already on his knees, he proceeded to prostrate himself before the giant in front of him.

"Get up, Human! Obeisance from Khestadone slaves is worthless to me! How dare you attempt it!"

But as the man began to lift himself from his prostrate position, something seemed to snap in his mind. He sneered insanely. Then, quicker than a flash he produced a hidden throwing knife with his still good right hand and launched it at the king. If the king had not been wearing his antique battle gear, it would have penetrated his heart. Most likely he wanted to aim for Eagleron's unprotected head, but he could hardly be expected at this stage to be that accurate. As it was, it glanced off the king's breastplate and clattered to the floor.

The Human then screamed in the face of the king. "You hideous beasts! Fur and feathers! Foul-smelling pigs! I hate you and your filthy race! My great queen will knock down your Wall and overrun your land, and you will become a memory!"

By the time he had finished this tirade he had been restrained by two massive Etoppsi guards, one pulling his left arm and leg and the other pulling his right limbs, so that the man was sprawled feet above the ground and stretched painfully to where he could only move his head. They were awaiting the word of the king to rip his limbs from his body. Instead, however, the king whispered to Allflight who then stepped over to the prisoner. In a move that would have sickened most, with his right hand he grabbed the man by his hair and held his head perfectly still, and then thrust forward with his left. The man screamed in agony. Blood dripped from the now empty eye sockets as he was removed from the presence of the king. Two Feathers began to clean up the mess, and a third came forward with a towel and basin and offered it to his captain to clean his bloodied hands.

The king spoke again. "Thank you for administering the penalty, Cloud-captain Allflight!"

"I will gladly fly him to the deep jungle myself, oh King."

"No, a different judgement has come to mind for my would-be assassin."

"Yes, oh King?"

"This Human talks. It could prove a lucky thing. I hope we can capture that major or those two strangers he spoke of when we retake Fifty-five, but if not, it may be that we can get more information out of this one. Have his wounds attended to by Gifted Physicians and then have him taken to the queen. If he does have more information, or if he was lying about any of it, she will be able to determine it. She is, ah, good at that sort of thing."

"As you wish, oh King."

Eagleron then turned to the others present, pausing for a moment before continuing. "Now, as it is, I think I am forced to act on the Human's information as if it were true. Have another Cloud take to the air above tonight's battle site as a precaution, and have the ground troops withdraw from the Jungle's edge, until day. I don't even want them inside that overhang. If there are trained Dragons on the enemy's side, then our forces are in danger in the dark that close to the Jungle. They will be far safer waiting in the outlying grasslands, with space to maneuver and to take flight if necessary, but they must keep a coordinated watch to ensure no enemy escapes from or enters the Jungle. As soon as the sun is high, they can return to the Jungle's edge and secure the head of the trail the enemy has made. Only armored King's Guards are to enter under the trees. Unclad Feathers are not safe even if there is a trail.

"Send Wing-sergeant Glidelow and his Wing together in swift flight west to find the Dragonhunter Legion. They need to be told what has happened if they don't know already. But I want two-hundred of them to report here to me as soon as possible. That may be far more than needed for two Wingless Dragons, but the situation I deem is unpredictable. We will not engage the enemy at Eye-tower Fifty-five until those Legionnaires have come. I want to utterly wipe them out. Dragons or no, the Khestadone must be taught a lesson."

All was done according to the will of the king. Though he was yet unwilling to engage the enemy at Eye-tower Fifty-five until the Dragon Hunters came, Eyes continued to patrol the skies at great height to observe what movement they could of the enemy. No additional forces could be seen eastwards for many miles, so reinforcement by the Alkhaness at this point was unlikely. Though movement by Humans could indeed be seen at the enemy-occupied tower and atop the Wall stemming from there for a couple hundred feet or so, anything going on below the tree canopy of the Jungle, such as the presence of Dragons, or a search in the hills, could not of course be made out. No Dragons made an appearance above the tree canopy, either.

It was a puzzle to the king and his commanders. If the Human was speaking the truth then the Alkhan and Alkhaness were present in the area only a short time ago, and the warlock-king withdrew after he ordered the assault on Eye-tower Fifty-five. It appeared as though the two Khestadone rulers were looking for something and didn't find it, and yet they had left a force at the Eye-tower. Surely they would expect the Berugians to respond in force? Yet, if the search had ended, then why would they stay? Staying was potential suicide. The enemy force was not sufficient to suggest a trap, nor large enough for further incursion. It was more as if they didn't care what happened to their own troops, not entirely shocking perhaps for the ruthless Khestadone rulers, but curious nonetheless.

All the king could conclude on that front was that they had deemed the search for whatever it was worth the risk. But there was much more to the puzzle, however, about which he couldn't even make a guess. If the search did continue, then by what method would the Khestadone be able to hear news of success, now that the road back was blocked by his Feathers? It would take some time even for trained Dragons to build a new and necessarily longer trail through the Jungle to try to outmaneuver the Eyes.

And finally and most importantly, what was it that the Alkhan and Alkhaness were actually searching for? What could exist in that line of cliffs and hills of such supreme interest to them that they would risk such proximity to Berugian territory? The king could not possibly imagine. He sent messages to his queen with all this information, along with the hapless Human prisoner. Hopefully within a day or two he would hear news from her and indeed her own advice on the matter, particularly if she deemed it prudent for the upcoming assault to retake Eye-tower Fifty-five.

The following day, some five Feathers who had been lightly wounded in the battle returned to duty from being treated at Intuk. The erection of the stone monument began at the grounds where the slain Berugians were buried. Eyes ceaselessly patrolled the skies for many miles around.

On the morning two days after the first attack, Eagleron began to receive some intelligence. Queen Silverwing sent a secret missive that she had compiled for him which he read thoroughly and in private.

She told him several things. She had determined that the Human prisoner had told the truth as he knew it. None of it was implanted in his mind by magical means. However, she was not able to determine other information except for the fact that the Human force in control of Eye-tower Fifty-five numbered roughly five hundred. On the possibility of the presence of trained Dragons at Eye-tower Fifty-five the prisoner suggested it was possible, but had not himself seen the beasts for many days. He believed that they had been used solely in the building of the trail through the forest and were involved in the secretive search. He was, however, adamant that only Wingless Dragons had been trained, and he had never heard that any of the rare Winged had been also.

There was, however, dark magic at work. The Human had no memory of attacking Eagleron, which suggested that an assassination response was triggered when the man discovered his questioner was the king. ...*and I believe you to be in danger, Mated One. It is possible that this assassination trigger has been fixed by dark magic into all their soldiers should any ever come into your presence and discover who you are.*

Silverwing fully concurred with her mate's decision to wait for the Dragonhunter Legion before retaking the Eye-tower. She had also another piece of information to offer. On the question of how the Alkhaness could communicate with the presumably stranded legion at Eye-tower Fifty-five, Silverwing reminded her mate that in the past the witch had used black crows and red vultures to send messages. It was likely that they continued to use them in this manner.

Her final piece of advice was regarding the search. ...*If there is something to be found in that set of cliffs, it must be immensely important and otherwise unique. I have ordered a search for old maps that include that region. However, the attack on Eye-tower Fifty-five is odd to me. Based on your information, it would seem to me that the search could have continued unnoticed by us indefinitely. The fact that it was the Alkhan of Eastrealm who ordered the attack is curious. There is assuredly a scheme behind this. He could have been acting under a common plan with his cohort the Alkhaness. Yet even if the Alkhan alone ordered the attack, the Alkhaness bears responsibility, for the Human attackers are clearly from her own forces. She is the one who led them there in the first place. The two must be considered a common enemy whether they maintain separate realms or not. I have warned often the two would soon act more conjointly.*

"Yes, you have." Eagleron said quietly to himself. He carefully refolded the letter and put it away.

Sergeant Glidelow returned sooner than expected with word that a contingent of a hundred and fifty Dragon Hunters was already on the way and should arrive within two days additional time. It was indeed a very long way to the coastlands where most of the Hunters of both the River Legion and the Coast Legion had recently gathered to scout the rivers for Serpent spawn. They were now fully informed of the situation, and indeed had heard of the conflict at Eye-tower Fifty-five from the scouts that had been sent out previously. They had already acted on the earlier request for assistance and had spread the word. Though the king had wished for two hundreds, he realized it might take an additional week for more to arrive from the coastlands. He would make do with the hundred and fifty that were now on the way. It should be far more than enough. If anything, his total force should easily overwhelm the enemy at Eye-tower Fifty-five, even with the possibility of Wingless Dragons present. The Legion was superbly skilled.

Finally, there was information that had been gathered at the site of the recent battle. As suspected there was a trail through the forest that began at that point and followed the baseline of the cliffs. It was wide enough for the purposes of Human men but was not of course so wide that it had resulted in the removal of large trees, something that might have been marked by the patrolling Eyes. Dragon fire had apparently not been used, perhaps deliberately, for the fires and smokes would likely have been espied from the Eye-towers. All was done under the cover of the dense jungle canopy to approach as secretly as possible. There was, however, a great trampling and ripping out of understory growth. Vines were severed and ripped aside. All was done in such a way that the Humans would not have had to come into contact with the poisonous thorns and deadly choke vines as they traveled along the trail. There were claw marks upon many trees that could have been made by Dragons. Birds and beasts could be heard in the distance, but interestingly, the typical Jungle creatures like the great predators and snakes had disappeared in the adjacent area of the trail. Armored King's Guards walked this trail for a mile or so to determine the nature of the trail, but they saw no other Humans and returned to the Jungle's edge. They dared not go further without experienced Dragon Hunters. Plus, it was unwise to approach the enemy from the east, for it was presumed the trail or at least an offshoot of it must at some point head in the direction of Eye-tower Fifty-five.

The bodies of the Humans slain in the battle had been cast into a pile and burned with wood cut from outlying trees. In another time and place the Berugians would have allowed them to rot, but it was decided that it was unwise to deliberately draw out carrion beasts from the forests or to attract crows and other scavenger birds. It made the king wonder if Storm-major Flamefur, who was in charge there, had the same thoughts about such birds as the queen.

The Dragon Hunters came. The Legion was famous far and wide throughout Berug for their exploits in controlling the Jungle borderlands. Without them, incursions of beasts would have been common far into the Berugian heartland. As it was, the Etoppsi felt confident in maintaining pasturelands and orchards all the way to the Western River that bordered the Jungle on most of its length. In addition, there were cities established in the far west near the mouth of the River that would have been hard pressed by Dragons without the work of the Legion. Not only did they hunt beasts that would leave the Jungle in pursuit of game on the southern grasslands, they also worked hard to discover nesting sites and eggs of the creatures several miles into the Jungle itself in order to destroy them. Legionnaires did not function alone, but rather in units of ten or more, and because of this it was rare for them to be killed by Wingless Dragons. Once every few years, a rare Winged Dragon could be a cause of great concern, for their fire was hotter, their bodies far bigger, and they could do much damage. Always, however, they were eventually overcome by large contingents of the more agile Legionnaires or chased away far over the deep Jungle.

The Legion was also responsible for ridding the Western River of Sea Serpent hatchlings. On occasion some years seemed to produce them whereas other years did not. This year apparently there was greater need for diligent, what they called 'fishing,' and the western Coast Legion had requested assistance from the River Legion in the east. This was why none were available nearby when Eye-tower Fifty-five was attacked.

But now at last a large contingent had arrived.

Despite the no-attire standard among the Feathers, the Legionnaires, who worked proudly and independently of the Sky Front, wore layers of protective clothing designed not only to counter the fires of the Dragons, but also to allow them to move more safely through the Jungle. Their gear and their shields were fashioned from actual Dragon scales and skin. Over the years they had created many trails in the Jungle by which they could travel with more ease to reach nesting sites, and open glades, too, into which they could fly without having to attempt landings atop the dangerous trees.

There was also another important difference between the Legion and the Sky Front. Whereas the Feathers that made up the Skyfront armies were by law and tradition all male, the Legion attracted a sizeable contingent of female Etoppsi. A quarter of the Legion was female, and a number of their Unit-leaders and Dragon-captains were, too. Though most Etoppsi females chose lives traditional for their gender, the Legion provided an outlet for those who desired risk and danger, and they were an elite caste in Berugian society. They were looked upon as heroes almost more so than even the males.

Of the force that now arrived at Eye-tower Fifty-four, fully one-half of these were female, and they were led by a well-known female Dragon-captain by the name of Greengull. Taller than most females, indeed as tall as many males, she was a formidable presence, and though she showed appropriate concern at the king's explanation at the possibility of trained enemy Dragons, Greengull nevertheless exuded extraordinary confidence and ingenuity.

"Even if they are trained, oh King, Dragonfire is only so hot," she said with metaphorical emphasis. "I would think that the greater threat would be the one or ones who actually control them. It seems unlikely to me that trained Wingless would be any more intelligent or skilled than untrained. At the most I would think that the controller would have little more power over the beasts than to encourage them to 'go here' or 'go there,' 'breathe fire now,' or 'climb this rock'. Their fighting tactics, if you can call them 'tactics' are not likely to be any different. It is even possible that they would be less uncontrollably vicious than they would otherwise be naturally."

"Then the greater threat would be the use of them in tandem as a group," suggested Cloud-captain Allflight. Being the Lieutenant-in-charge of Eye-towers Fifty-four and Fifty-five, he was one of several Skyfront officers present with the king and offering counsel. "They may not be more dangerous individually than they would be in their natural state, but it seems to me that they could do great harm against us if there were several of them used together."

"True, that thought has crossed my mind, to be sure," replied Greengull. She appeared even larger than she was considering the layers of leather and Dragon-skin armor that covered her. Even the thicker sections of her wings were capped in Dragon-scale mail. Only her flight feathers seemed vulnerable. "However, if two is the likely number based on your intelligence, they will pose minimal threat to the Legion. We can manage them easily if the Feathers cover us from enemy Human arrows. Half of us should be many times more than enough, and the other half can be held in reserve. You can retake the Eye-tower, oh King, although it may involve brute force once the lower door is opened. In any regard, we can approach from the ground secretly enough if you are distracting them with your attack from above. A contingent of your armored Feathers should accompany us whose job it will be to open that door. Once the signal is given, and the door is opened, more armored feathers can swoop in the narrow space by the tower and force their way from below. I must admit, oh King, it pleases me to see that you have fitted your Guard in armor!"

"We haven't needed it since the days of the Ralsheen menace. However, times change, and so must we." But as an aside to Captain Allflight, Eagleron added, "But tradition will suffice for those that man the Wall or attack from above."

Plans were finalized and the battle was to take place that night. It was determined that darkness was the best protection against enemy arrows from the Eye-tower, and as far as Greengull was concerned, it made no difference when it came to fighting Dragons. Solvermoon was only beginning his cycle and would be a minute sliver, and though Orohmoon was at her full, He would long set before She rose.

Later in the afternoon, the Dragon-captain crossed paths with the Cloud-captain once again. Each complimented the other on the contingents they led.

"Fine specimens, for sure," said Greengull to Captain Allflight. "Your males show fine fitness. You know, Captain, some of my females are mated, but there are many who have yet to find their bond-mates! We could arrange a Star Revel at the next male cycle."

"Not this round of the moon, though let me think on it. Your females do, shall I say, inspire? And in more ways than the calling of the, er, Solvermoon rounds. I definitely admire them. I am not as narrow-minded as some of the other officers. You are heroines, all of you."

"It's not a bad calling, you know, for females like myself who wish to serve our country. Most of our males, though, are already mated and Bonded, unlike the youngest of your Feathers. There aren't enough, shall I say, to go around? You should encourage your Feathers to seek us out more. The River Legion comes this way often, you know."

"Perhaps so, Captain. And yet, ha! You keep your bodies *covered*, I would think the mating dances would be rather…difficult, if you know what I mean."

It was her turn to laugh. "Only while on duty, Captain Allflight. It's a vicious rumor that our females remain covered all the time. One would think we never take time to prune a feather!"

"And yet you are always on call, are you not?"

"True. True, I must admit. We are busy. But the infestation these days is under control, although I confess more recruits would make life easier."

"You may get them."

She raised her furry eyebrow. "So you're thinking what I'm thinking?"

"That a bigger war is coming?"

"Is that what the king thinks, too?"

"I heard from Major Flamefur that…"

"That meaty, red-furred giant in King's Guard? I know they don't wear collars on duty, but I know a Stag when I see one. And that other one with him, too, though I didn't catch the name."

"Windsdown, yep, he's a Cloud Captain like me. They have the Stag reputation."

"Actually, I think I have heard rumor of those two! They are mating beasts!"

"They are the definitive mating beasts!" laughed Allflight. "Braggarts since they were teens! Every Feather on the Wall I think has heard of their mating feats! But trust me, they are of superior Discipline in the Guard from everything I have heard. Anyway, Flamefur is close to the queen who is certain war is coming."

"Ah, Silverwing!" said Greengull, "Our queen is a remarkable person! I have always admired her."

"I agree with you. Eagleron and Silverwing. The two of them together are brilliant. I do not know the greater picture of what the Khestadone twosome are plotting, but I believe we would be in a worse position if it were not for the forward-thinking of our king and queen. But yes. I think the Sky Front will grow, and with the threat of trained Dragons, whether it's true or not, the Legion is bound to grow as well if your Legion-masters allow it. But you realize that you might become more military than you have been?"

"The king speaks rightly. We will change as the times change."

"It could be that the Jungle border proves the best means for the enemy to attempt an infiltration. If they can train Dragons and use them…"

"They can try," interrupted Greengull. "What I mean is that maybe it is possible, and maybe they have trained a few Dragons, but it would surely require a form of mind-magic, and it seems only likely to me to be possessed by a very few, some sorcerers that the Alkhan has trained. The idea of an army of Dragons is preposterous."

"Wingless, though, is what you're thinking of, Captain Greengull. And what if they can control Winged Dragons? They would only need a few."

"Umm… yes. Not beyond the realm of possibilities, that. We will manage. I won't be opposed to recruitment of a bigger force, for sure."

"Frankly, I think the recruits will come to both the Sky Front and the Legion in droves with this threat."

"I can believe it." She then chose to test him, though she laughed as she did so. "You think the Sky Front will allow females if there is a war?"

"Speaking of vicious rumors, no!" Allflight replied with mirrored reaction. "Never! Not as long as there are any males in Berug left with even one feather on one wing! It would never work.

But if you ask me, if the threat is Dragons and the Jungle border, the Legion would have plenty of room for all females that wish to serve."

"I hadn't thought of it like that, Captain Allflight. I suppose it is…sufficient. It certainly worked for me."

"I've often wanted to ask you, Greengull, why you chose it for yourself. Don't get me wrong; you know I think of you as a superior leader. I'm just curious, that's all."

"I'll take your compliment. Thank you. I don't know," she said, as she reached into her memories. "As a topling I always liked the physical challenge. I'm bigger than most females—always have been, even when I was a young topling. I think I wanted to prove that I could do what all you males could do, you know. Raising sheep is what the females in my family have done for centuries, and I like it, that life is beautiful, but I wanted more. My father and grandfather are both in the Sky Front and serve in the Island Cyclone. They're still there. Grandfather never advanced to an officer's position, never wanted it. His name is Galemaster. House of Blue Isle. He plans to give it up this year. But you might know my father, Major Twinwing?"

"I've heard of him, but I've never met him. He was the one who assisted the Nantians when that pathetic fleet of the Alkhaness attempted an infiltration ten years ago. He's quite famous! Yet, I know hardly any of the other officers that serve on the Isles except for ones I met at the Institute."

"Yes, he was the one. So very proud of him! And I guess their stories appealed to me more than those of the females in my family. When I told them I wanted to train for the Legion, my father was all for it. Said he was proud of me. Meant a lot. Still means a lot."

"You've advance rapidly from what I hear."

"Luck, Captain."

"I don't believe it," he laughed. "You have led many a hunt and are excellent at it by all reports. And you have the record on nest discoveries."

"Ah, so they do talk about us in the Cyclone, do they?"

"All feats of skill are looked on highly by the Feathers as Taxiarchan Disciplines. You would make a great Cyclone-general of the Legion."

"We don't have such a rank in the Legion," she said. Then she raised that furry eyebrow again. "Ah! You mean if there is a war, you think there will be a need for a stronger hierarchy like in the Front. Perhaps so. Thank you, Captain. You are full of compliments today! I hope you are as sweet to your Bond-mate!"

"I try to be, when I see her. Thankfully, she lives in Malipinth. It is only three hours flight northwest from here, so I see her often. Who is your Bond-mate, may I ask?"

"His name is Bronzemight. He is House of Blue Isle, too."

"That is far away…"

"Oh, no, Captain, he isn't so far. He moved with me, you see, when I joined the Legion."

"Is he in the Legion as well?"

"Ah, he would be the sheepherder in my family, Captain!"

They both laughed at the grand joke and looked at each other with appreciation which turned quickly to warmth and affability.

Allflight with a knowing gleam, yet with proper humility, asked, "You do remember me, do you not?"

Greengull grinned hugely. If it weren't for her fur-covered face, one might think she was blushing. "Of course I do! You and I mated in my very first Star Revel. How could I forget it! Oh, Allflight! It was an overwhelming night, I must admit. *Both* moons were bright, and it was a grand reverie!"

"That is good! If you had not remembered, er, that would be rather disappointing!"

"It was a wild romp! Bronzemight won my heart, though. After several more Star Revel nights. But had he not been around…" She winked.

"You never know!" Allflight completed the statement with a bit of amatory charm and a return wink. The two reached out with their hands, and each with their five fingertips touched that of the other, a common expression of goodwill between close Etoppsi friends.

Greengull for her part smiled again as happy memories encompassed her of a time long ago. "May Berug's spirit inspire you this night, friend."

As Allflight waved, Greengull took flight from the Wall and soared in an arc toward the western plain where her Legionnaires were now assembling for the battle.

There were far too many of them to have crowded into Eye-tower Fifty-four, and to assemble upon the Wall might have been too conspicuous if there were indeed spies watching from the east. As the sun set in low clouds, the sky's colors blasted forth in brilliant crimsons. High above, fifty Eyes could be counted throughout the skies in all directions, keeping watch upon the lands about.

There had been no new movement observed by the Eyes espying Eye-tower Fifty-five. The king sent word that as soon as it was fully dark the movement would take place.

The signal was given. It was deep dark. From the plain, eighty Legionnaires and four Clouds consisting of some one-hundred, twenty armored Feathers from the King's Guard took low flight and followed closely along the western side of the Wall so as to minimize any shadows. Within a few minutes they had all reformed on the ground at the edge of the Jungle beside the Wall. Though the tallest, most massive Jungle trees had been removed long ago, lower growth continued all the way to the Wall itself. It was very dense and it was slow-going for the huge Etoppsi. It was understood that it might take up to two hours to make their way the three miles to the small cleared area around Eye-tower Fifty-five, for they were to approach as quietly as possible, slashing away as little of the jungle growth as needed so as not to cause a disturbance. The Legionnaires were used to this with their high boots, and Captain Greengull and her command led the way, watching and listening for any sign of Dragons. The armored Guardfeathers, too, had become used to their gear by now and followed behind. Only occasionally did live vines reach out snake-like in order to ensnare a victim, but they were quickly slashed away with the great brush knives the Legionnaires used. They had loaned some of these to the Guardfeathers for their use as well.

There were snakes, too, some quite large, and they would lash out at the legs of the Etoppsi. Nevertheless, the steel armor of the Guardfeathers and the Dragon scale and leather boots of the Legionnaires turned aside their fangs, and the snakes' heads were slashed off in lightning retaliation. In the trees were other creatures whose eyes shone in the darkness, but though they would hiss and snarl, they must have considered the Etoppsi much too big for prey, for they would retreat at the approach of the giant winged creatures.

There were, however, a few casualties, for on occasion one of the Guardfeathers would lose his footing and fall, and if he were unlucky great poisonous spines of low bushes would work their way through connections in the armor or catch an unprotected wing. Their wings were always the most vulnerable part of the Etoppsi, even when armored, for the armor on the rump of their wings themselves had to be light and flexible so as to be able to fold their wings behind them when not flying. Though it was still quite difficult to slash, it was nevertheless quite easy to pierce. When this happened the Guardfeather had to be carried with care back to the edge of the forest by two others and flown directly to the Physicians at Intuk. So it was, when they finally came within sight of the clearing at Eye-tower Fifty-five, there were twelve Guardfeathers fewer than when they started.

Greengull waited in silence until the full contingent had caught up. She had ordered the Legionnaires to disperse in a semicircle while still in the thick of the Jungle, although the Guardfeathers split into two cohesive units, one prepared to attack and the other to remain in reserve. She was pleased they had made it so far, with far less noise than all the whistles and calls of the night-time Jungle creatures. Before her she could easily see the clearing around the Eye-tower, and here were some four dozen Human soldiers caught in the light of a bonfire near to the entrance door. They were chattering and laughing among themselves, and most of them had set their weapons aside.

Greengull pondered this, for typically it wasn't safe to build a fire, for it often attracted Dragons. On the rare occasions in which she had been required to stay in the Jungle at night, it was always in one of the Legionnaire clearings, and she would have to lie quietly so as not to attract creatures, and building a fire was forbidden. So to see these mere Humans at their ease with most of their weapons cast aside made her uneasy. Could they indeed have a trained Wingless nearby, and could it be trained to keep predators and other Dragons away?

Immediately she signaled a shift in her plan to the commander in charge of the Guardfeathers. She indicated that the Guardfeathers were to rush forward when the attack from the air began. They would charge the soldiers at the bonfire and at the door, and if a Wingless appeared, then the Legionnaires would rush in and surround it and dispatch it. Within a few minutes she received word that her orders had been received by everyone.

They all stood silently while the Jungle creatures carried out their night-time catcalls and the Humans continued to chatter heedlessly. There was movement in and out of the door, but as yet none of them seemed especially cautious, nor did they appear to be issuing any warnings that might cause the Humans to increase their alert. Ten more minutes passed. It wouldn't be long now.

Finally, from far above there was sound, Human voices yelling commands and the clatter of weapons and armor. The king had launched his air assault upon the top of the tower. As the Humans by the door began to snatch up their weapons, the Guardfeathers crashed through the remaining Jungle growth and rushed forward. Terror struck the Humans as many of them fell in the onslaught; one blow from a Feather with his massive mace was easily enough to crush even an armored Human body. Others began to flee through the door, but as they converged upon it in a crush, they became easy targets for the Feathers. Greengull hoped that the crush would keep the Humans from closing the door. So far, she was correct, for it remained open while more Humans slipped within.

Just then a great roar was heard from the far end of the tower. A blast of bright orange flames shot from behind it. Greengull and all her Legionnaires recognized it immediately and rushed forward as a Wingless Dragon, glittering yellow-green in the firelight, rounded the end of the Wall casting more flames here and there from its maw. When it saw the struggle at the lower door and the presence of Etoppsi engaging the Humans in close quarters it stamped angrily. It breathed another blast straight into the melee and seemed not to care whether any Humans were also engulfed, but strode forward. Immediately, the Feathers retreated to the relative safety of the Jungle growth while the Legionnaires, protected by their Dragon armor strode forward, Dragon-scale shields held aloft.

But as the Dragon turned in their direction to meet the onslaught, Greengull beheld a shocking sight. A Human-like figure sat upon the very back of the Wingless, and a harness with reins attached was cast around the head of the great beast. The figure wore a helm and its face could not be seen. Its armor consisted entirely of steel plating. It carried no other weapon, but it seemed not to need one. With great deftness it moved the beast hither and thither, and with a strange song-like voice it seemed to order it to advance upon the Legion.

Greengull could not believe her eyes, but she did not have time to think upon it, instead calling out to her Hunters to encircle and advance. They did this quickly, and the scaled, serpent-like creature, the length of four large horses standing nose to tail, was soon surrounded by a triple-layered wall of Etoppsi.

The Dragon and its rider-commander continued to tear, slash and burn, but it could not break out of a circle of eighty fearless Etoppsi Legionnaires. Behind Greengull the Berugian Feathers had returned now that they were no longer the object of the Dragon's fire and just as the last of the surviving Human soldiers had ducked inside the door. But before they knew it, the Feathers had charged forward and blocked the movement of the door before it slammed shut. Greengull noticed this and was pleased, but she was too intent on the beast in front of her to call out a congratulation.

"Bring it down, but capture the one who rides it!" shouted Greengull.

"You will not capture me!" the rider screamed, though in a very odd high-pitched dialect, and it advanced directly upon Greengull herself. The strange rider sang again its eerie song urging on the creature. But with massive maces in hand, at least five Legionnaires gathered next to their Captain and burst upon the creature with great ferocity, and even as it blasted orange fire upon Greengull, it fell, stunned. With skill, the female Etoppsis had put up her shield just in time, blocking the worst of the flame. She plunged forward and smashed the eyes of the beast, killing it instantly.

Just to be sure, other Hunters stabbed the beast point blank with heavy spears designed for this purpose, but before they could lay hands upon the now silent rider it shockingly disappeared!

"Where'd he go?" yelled one of the Hunters.

All appeared lost for a moment. "A shadow, there!"

"It's magic!" screamed Greengull. "Surround and capture!"

Suddenly the rider in his black armor reappeared, for invisible or not there was indeed no way it could have broken the tight ring of Legionnaires. Unlike them he didn't have wings.

Before anyone could react however, the rider had in his hand a short-bladed knife that it had pulled from its side. It then slashed itself brutally across the throat. Blood shot outward and it fell forward across the neck of the dead Dragon.

"Guardian's Teeth!" shrieked Greengull. "I wanted him!"

She turned away from the carnage, however, to see what was happening at the door.

Allflight was quickly there, having flown down from above. "That was a near thing! Our Feathers are in the Eye-tower now, but it would have been far more difficult if the Humans had been able to shut the door."

Feathers continued to drop one by one from the skies into the small clearing and hurried through the lower door. All of these were armored, of course, and carried maces. Wall Feathers filled the skies shooting arrows nearly as long as Human spears through the great guard windows at the top of the tower.

"And the door atop the Wall?" asked Greengull.

"Still blocked, but it shouldn't be long now with so many of our Feathers inside. The Humans were prepared for an attack from above. But what you did down here was a complete surprise to them."

"I think you're right. They didn't expect us to attack through the Jungle. Idiots."

Yells from within and distant noises continued. Allflight had gone with a dozen more Feathers inside the lower door. All was relatively quiet in the clearing now with the death of the Wingless and its rider. Some of the Legionnaires were examining the beast and its harness and gear. Two others were standing guard over the body of the rider per Greengull's orders. She knew the king would want to see it for himself once the battle was over.

Greengull looked over the gear of the rider. It was clearly Khestadone in origin with the symbol of the Wolf emblazoned in gold.

"It's not very practical, though, is it, Captain?" asked one of Greengull's Unit-leaders, pointing out the black metal armor common to a Khestadone knight. "I mean I would think that being around them they would use Dragon scale armor to deflect heat. He would roast alive if it accidentally received a blast of fire from that Dragon."

"Truly. I suspect they're new at this…this 'taming' of Dragons, if you ask me," Greengull replied.

Shortly, there were great yells and Human screams from high above, and a half-dozen bodies fell from on high. The Khestadone soldiers were jumping to their deaths.

"They have no way of escaping," stated Greengull, casually.

She was right. A dozen more jumped soon afterward, but the height of the tower windows was perhaps seventy feet, and all died upon impact. No attempt was made to try to save any of them. They were not capable of abandoning their vow to the Witch-queen, imposed by magic spells, and so they would always pose a threat. And under typical conditions, Berugians did not take Khestadone prisoners anyway.

Soon it was over. There were no more screams, no more Humans casting themselves out windows in their terror of so many giant Etoppsi who had overrun the tower.

"What of their commander, Captain Allflight?" she asked her friend as he now landed for a second time beside her.

"Dead. The great coward jumped out on the eastern side. You haven't been around there, have you?"

"Just waiting for the all clear. Humans are not our specialty," grinned Greengull.

Allflight laughed. "But who killed the rider?"

"He slit his own throat. It was horrifying, really. One moment he was singing, which must have been how he was controlling the beast, but as soon as the Dragon was killed, he disappeared for a moment. Obviously he possessed some strange magic! Then suddenly he reappeared and killed himself before we could lay our hands on him. He clearly didn't want to be caught."

"Strange. Very strange. The king will be here momentarily. Has the Legion had enough time to scour the area for more Dragons?"

"Yes. There are none nearby. We should be safe for a while."

"Good. But as soon as the king sees this, we should retreat inside and seal this door. The Legion can return to the plain if they wish, to camp."

"Fair enough. But in the morning I'm coming back. I want more clues."

"I'm sure the king will want a thorough search."

Looking up, they saw King Eagleron followed by his escort swooping down into the small clearing at the base of the tower. He had not taken part in the fight, for risk of a trap was too great, and the commanders had pleaded with him to remain until they could capture the Eye-tower. Now that it was secure, the risk had lessened.

"Oh King!" saluted the two friends at the same time.

"Captains." The king nodded. "Major Flamefur told me you needed me to see something down here. There is certainly a dead Dragon. Very good. I'm glad to see you dispatched the beast, Captain Greengull."

"There is more, oh King." The Legion captain then pointed to the harness. "You will see that it was harnessed like the horse beasts Humans use and what they call a 'saddle' I think."

The king lifted his brows at Greengull's statement and proceeded to take a closer look. He called for torches and these were brought from near the door. The bonfire had mostly burnt out. "This is unbelievable, to be sure! How could this be? It was being ridden?"

"And controlled." Then Greengull indicated the figure lying apart, over which stood her two guards. They stood away so the king and the torchbearers could approach. The king drew near and looked carefully. He frowned.

"How did he die? Who slit the Human's throat, Captain Greengull? Surely you have better control over your Legionnaires! You should have held this one!"

"With respect, oh King, he slit his own throat before we could reach him. And just before that he disappeared for a few moments. Vanished! It was strange. I am most sorry, but he reacted that fast after we killed the beast. He was infuriated by the death of his Dragon."

"I am sorry to have jumped to conclusions, Captain. But that is an unfortunate thing! He could have told us how it was done—how they trained a Dragon and what they are up to!"

"He was riding it and apparently controlling the beast with singing."

"Singing! That is strange indeed! The Forgotten Folk of the land of Ulakel sing and can communicate with the birds of the air. It is a form of innate magic..." He paused as he considered. "And there are other forms of magic they possess according to the legends. Remove the helm, Allflight. Let's see what he looks like."

The Cloud-captain complied with the request. He reached down and pulled the helm off the rider's head, but as he did so, all gasped in astonishment as a brown, though bloodied face was uncovered, and on top of the head was a shortened crop of shiny, jet-black hair.

"Upon my oath to the Taxiarch!" exclaimed Allflight.

The group stood in a semicircle about the rider, and all, including the king, had their mouths open in disbelief.

"She...! Is that what I think it is, oh King?" asked Captain Greengull.

"Hand me something to wipe the blood!" King Eagleron knelt and looked intently at the dead face, rubbing away some of the bright red blood on its cheek and chin. Its features, though very much like a Human's, were otherwise flawless and unblemished. Dark eyebrows traced out and slightly upward. Indeed the face was quite beautiful. "Her hair has been cropped, but yes. If you had reported this to me and I had not seen it with my own eyes I would never have believed you. But the magical singing, and the ability to vanish at will...yes, indeed, Captain Greengull. She is as you suspect."

Allflight looked at Greengull and mouthed the word.

Qeteral!

THIS ENDS BOOK ONE

Continue with

Companions in Prophecy

Book 2 of

Heirs to the Taxiarch

Enjoy a preview chapter of

Book 2

Companions in Prophecy

Companions in Prophecy

Chapter 1—Fateful Bliss

A midnight breeze drifted silently across the lake. Bright stars and a young Solvermoon cast soft shadows on the wall. Through an open balcony, owls called and crickets played fiddles.

The cadence of this chamber music did much to soothe Nikal. He had grown more accustomed to other melodies. The sea performed a ballad dramatic and melancholy. The battles he fought in the east conducted a dissonance of glory and duty on the one hand, pain and loss on the other.

He breathed in her lavender scent, her face resting on his shoulder. Dira had drifted off following their bliss earlier in the night.

Oh, how he had missed her. He would Bond her tomorrow morning if he were allowed. He would have done so long ago.

Without permission, and in spite of the peaceful nighttime tunes, Nikal's mind wandered upon the reasons that prevented this one happiness. Crown Prince Lekktor must choose his life-mate first, a ridiculous decree passed down by their jealous grandfather when their great uncle, as the result of an Aura, Bonded the very woman their grandfather had wanted for himself. It should not have been an issue, yet it turned into a tortuous struggle, and since that time the legalities of Aura Bondings had been set aside among the royals and nobility of Nant. Among the great families, Matrimonials were only summoned now to perform the actual Rites, and the Gifted were forbidden to interfere with the powerful men who chose and contracted their Bond-mates for reasons usually not related to love.

Other Disciplines too had slackened amongst the highest classes over the last fifty years or so. Women had few rights in this kingdom dominated by men. Nikal was ashamed to recall a loathsome side of himself as a teen: heartless sexual indulgence and drunken orgies, alongside his brother, with young women the servants would bring to their bedchambers. The unfortunate circumstances of these poor girls eventually broke through to Nikal's conscience, and he came to despise his actions, chastening himself in order to someday be made worthy of something higher and better. His view of women was transformed.

He credited the old Sage for his turn-around. Sage Antonin was a very good man and understood his struggles. Antonin said he had had a Vision from the Guardian concerning Nikal—that through him there was hope for a brighter future for the Kingdom of Nant. He provided a repentant Nikal with Absolution and more than anyone taught him about the Principles and true manliness. Together they outlined an appropriate Discipline to which Nikal could adhere and live up to.

It was many years, however, before Nikal had the occasion to encounter that higher love he longed for in the person of the daughter of Duke Rothee. Nikal had come to the port of Noess after fighting in the east for two months. He'd returned to persuade the nobles to send more ships and men, for the Easterners needed better expertise in those early days against the Alkhan. The Duke invited him to rest a few days at his estate. So for the first time Nikal met Dira, with her dark hair of long ringlets and perfect oval face, and when he heard her musical voice of welcome, he was smitten to the core.

And quite obviously, so was she. They grew to know one another over a peace-filled week. Near the end of his visit, he rode out on a pleasure jaunt through her father's estate. Indeed he had quite deliberately followed her out secretly, and in a romantic fantasy come true, she led him to this same quiet hunting lodge on tiny Lake Winnett.

That was now ten months ago.

Two more times the prince returned from the eastern war, and he would come to Noess first. It was convenient, for the city was on the common route from Tirilorin to the Nantian capital, Sevarr. He would sit offshore and wait for his trusted General Aron to make arrangements, and when all was dark and quiet, Nikal would row secretly to shore, mount the horse Aron had provided, and make his way to Lake Winnett. There she would be, at her father's hunting lodge, waiting for him.

Just like tonight. The wars and other responsibilities occupied the greater portion of Nikal's life, but those few times together were pure joy in an otherwise hard year. She made him feel human—helped him heal, body and soul, and allowed him to experience true love and peace and contentment.

His desire to legally Bond her would just have to wait. Lekktor must choose first. And the moment he did so, Nikal would declare for Dira.

As his confidante, Aron in his funny manner would warn him every time of the possible *consequences*, but being a prince had some advantage in the law. The rules in Nant were strange, and though Nikal did not care for them, he would take advantage of them if he had to. In the unlikely event he should become ruler of Nant, he would change them back to the way they were when Meicalian

Principles and a common Discipline held full sway. In other countries the rules were looser, for women had as much choice in the matter of mating and Bonding as men. Not in Nant. In Nant, among the upper echelon, men held all power. Nikal was considered the great warrior and general of his age, but he could only hold his authority by playing the games of the powerful noblemen of Nant. In the meantime, Nikal would treat Dira as well as he could.

Someday, he thought, all would be well for them. He could wait, and she was committed. *Damn, Lekktor,* he said to himself. *Hurry, you fool of a brother.*

Perhaps in her sleep his lover detected his silent expletive. She stirred and opened her eyes. "Slumber evades you, dearest?" She asked sleepily, reaching up with her fingers to caress his short black beard.

He drew her close. Her smooth skin against his own nakedness felt glorious. Though it was warm with windows open, a low flame in the fireplace cast a flickering glow upon her tender face. "Yes. Wishing."

She observed him through sleepy dark eyes. "I know what you wish for. The same as I."

"Yes." He looked at her steadily. Was there anyone more beautiful in all the world? More understanding? More loving? He kissed her and circled his fingers around and over her breasts, charming her out of her sleepiness. "But this moment is a good one, love. You never told me whether it was difficult to get away here tonight."

For a minute she lay back allowing him to perform his magic, now with his tongue and the tickling hair of his face. Her nipples hardened, and she sensed an eager relaxation in her groin. Sleepiness was exchanged for anticipation. "Father has gone to Sevarr. Mother likes you. She always has."

Nikal paused in his administrations and leaned up on his arm. "Your mother knows about us?" That would be news.

Dira giggled as she pushed him back down. She began kissing him lightly in his own key places, encouraging a body she knew needed what she could give. "She caught sight of you last time. She will keep our secret. In fact, she knows we are here, tonight. She says you are different than most men. She maintains that those who truly love one another should...love one another."

He reached behind her and traced his fingers down her spine and to the curves of her hips. He was happy, knowing what their bodies were about to repeat from earlier. "It is that way still among most. The Matrimonials move freely among the common folk, outside of Sevarr anyway, and I hope that never changes. I am often sorry for being born a royal. And for you as a high lady. It would be much easier if I were a shopkeeper, say, and you a farmer's daughter."

"Ah, yes," she said. "A Matrimonial could have Bonded us long ago. On the other hand, you would not be my prince, and you would not be the great hero and general of Nant. You could set it all aside and I would still love you, but it all makes you into the man you are. I would not want you to be any less than that. I tell you, dear, Meical the Guardian walks with you."

Nikal was enchanted by her words, for they spoke to his heart. He kissed her fervently.

"You are still willing to go into seclusion...should it become, eh, necessary?" He placed a palm on her belly.

"How sweet of you to ask, considering all." She said, teasingly. And in order to reassure him, she leaned over, caressing his groin, and applied her tongue and lips upon his stiffening virility. She knew he needed this, ached for it, and she needed him just as much.

Nikal leaned back with his hands behind his head in order to allow her gift. "I often fear."

"I do not. I am quite content should I bear a child. We risk this every time you come here, of course. Should I go into seclusion, it will only be until your brother finally chooses his life-mate. And while in seclusion, I would be raising our child. I would not be lonely. Mother will be pleased, and Father will take the news in stride. He is not a fool. He has often wished that our family would connect to yours. He practically gave you his permission when he invited you here that first time. He tends to shade his eyes. In all ways I am freer than other women of my station. Have no fear, my dear. Cast it aside." She returned to pleasuring him, listening happily to his soft groans.

After a time, he reached up, beckoning. She cast the blanket off the bed and leaned up astride him, kissing him again and running her cool hands over the muscles of his chest and down the hair of his abdomen.

He sighed in perfect satisfaction as she lowered her warm body onto his. Her seductive curves captured all his senses. "Oh, my love!" he softly exclaimed.

"You like this?" she asked teasingly, as she raised and then lowered herself in slow rhythm.

"Ah...ah! D...d...don't speak! Y...y...you n...n...know the answer!" He stuttered as his body dampened the unnecessaries of speech in favor of that pleasure designed in the Molding of the sexes at the dawn of history.

"You're beginning to sound like Aron!" She said, giggling. But then her own voice faltered as he reached with a large thumb to apply extra pressure to her most sensitive spot. "Oh...oh!"

"Shh...sh...shh. Th...th...at's what you g...get for th...that quip!" He was as happy as he had ever been, and he wished it could go on forever.

Morning came, and with it came General Aron, alone on horseback.

"Y..yyour Highness!" he called out. Aron drew out his words in a rather inconsistent stammer. As a boy he was teased for it, but all in all it had no effect on his leadership skills. Those who knew him well, such as the prince, barely noticed it anymore.

Nikal and Dira had already participated together in a quick swim at dawn, and he now stood alone, bare-chested on the verandah. He was listening to the sounds of an unconcerned morning, looking out over the lake with its light mists rising, and drinking the hot herb tea Dira had made for him.

"Why, Aron! Eh, the lady inside is not presentable. Not to you, anyway. Keep your distance."

The man chuckled. "I'm sure."

"And why are you here? I sent a message. Her father is away. I intend to stay three nights more."

"Y..yyour hawk, er, your hawk is not lost, sir, and I...I...I got the message. And of all people y...you should know that I have no desire to interfere with...ah...yourrr pleasures. Ah, you deserve them." He looked around. A loon called across the lake. "Grr...rand place. Lovely."

"Yes, and quite private. That is until you rode up. Now why did you not take the message seriously?" It was at that moment that Letti, the Common Grayhawk the prince and Aron used to send messages to one another, called out shrilly and landed on the balustrade. Nikal looked at it. "Hunting, were you?"

The bird looked at its trainer with no visible emotion in its sharp eyes.

"I...I say I did take the mmm...message seriously, Your Highness!" Aron replied in slightly aggrieved tone. His speech difficulty was more noticeable when he was nervous. Yet in the heat of battle, it oddly disappeared, never a detriment. In this case, however, he did feel a bit anxious in this unannounced interruption. "But odd nn...news has been heard in Noess, and I deemed it ah...imperative you hear it from me. A...ah...Berugian messenger has flown to the capital with the nnn...news to expect a delegation.

And considering the distance and timing for the mm...messages, I should say they will arrive in three more days."

Nikal set his cup on the balustrade, stepped down the stairs and approached the rider.

"Etoppsi are coming to Nant? The Meicalian Feast is months away! Whatever for?"

"The ah...news isn't plain, Yy...your Highness, but it would mm...imply something regarding the war."

"Westrealm has made a move? The Alkhaness?"

Dira emerged through the door in a long dressing gown. With chivalric instincts Aron dismounted and bowed. "Mmm...my lady! It is ah...pp...pleasurable to see you again. Do you know this scalawag? If not, I shall gladly throw down a challl...lenge to him."

Dira laughed as she stroked Letti. "And he shall beat you."

"As usual," added Nikal.

"Nnn...nonsense!" intoned Aron with pretended indignation. "He lll...loses to me all the time, my lady."

"At Fifty-twos," said the prince knowingly.

"Indeed, yes! His Hiiigh...ness has forked over unquantifiable amounts of gold to me over long years." They all laughed. "Ah...ah...actually, I don't think this lll...little...that this little conversation is progressing in my favor, is it? I sh...shall, however," he added with a second bow in Dira's direction, "acknowledge that upon the challenge of ah...wooing lll...lovely ladies, His Highness has left me wallowing in mud."

She laughed. "Would that be because His Highness tells me you have vowed a temporary celibacy, General Aron?"

Aron, swordmaster, famed general, and Nikal's right-hand, flattened his lips and drew his eyebrows in close. Turning from the lady to the prince, he said, "I told you that in the strictest confidence, Your Highness, some years ago." His impediment disappeared not only in the heat of battle but also when he was annoyed or angry.

"You told it to me and at least a dozen others in a very drunken state, my friend. Everyone in the navy and the army knows your little 'secret,'" Nikal teased. "Forgive me for speaking of it to the Lady Dira."

"I will not," Aron replied with a pout.

"He speaks of you often, Aron, for he loves and trusts you, of course," said Dira consolingly. "You are his great friend. He likes to share these things with me. Besides, I think it's very honorable! A man who as a boy had a little Vision from the Guardian, who told him to retain his passion until a promised Aura?"

Because he did feel a dash of guilt, Prince Nikal added, "It would be a better world if all were so inclined to honor a Discipline, as the General here does."

Aron was still annoyed. "He made it plain to me men should restrain their desires in favor of their true love, or when Auras occur."

"And you are very right!" said Nikal, with a sense of finality. "Would that that particular Discipline held sway among all."

"Yes," said Dira. "You have no skeptics here, Aron. There is no need to justify yourself to those present! Children should be born to happy parents. It is best that way. Your children are to be of great value to the Guardian! I'm sorry for teasing you. Now, General, are you going to come inside and have a bit of breakfast with us...your friends?"

An hour later, a full-bellied General Aron and Prince Nikal took their leave of one another.

"I will return tomorrow evening after sunset, Aron," said Nikal in a quiet voice. "My heart tells me to...how shall I put it? The war. It grows. The enemy pushes and has grown stronger despite all we have done. I...I do not know when I shall see her again."

"The Guardian Affirm you, Y...your Highness. You are not the only one who searches for words! I have pestered yyy...you many a time about the Lady Dira, and I realize I have, er, erred. Forgive me. Her ll...love for you is pure gold, Nikal." Aron was one of the few in all Nant who addressed the prince on such familiar terms. He mounted his horse. "Truly. Mm...may your extra day be...blessed. However, I *should* warn..."

"General, tomorrow evening we will set sail, so for now can you please dispense with the *howevers?* I know what I'm doing."

"I have my doubts. Birds and those, er, lovely buzzing bees. *Royal* bees, no less. Tsk, tsk. Even for the common man, *th...thumping thumpers make three,* you know, sir."

"Depart, you scoundrel," said Nikal, though he couldn't stop the grin on his face.

"Yes, *sir!*" Aron offered up his most cheeky wink, and rode away.

When Nikal returned to the bedroom, to his great delight he found Dira standing at the side balcony looking over the lake. Banishing his concerns of Aron's news, he quickly removed his own garb in order to mimic her own state of undress. From behind he reached around her, and she melted back into his embrace.

"You were expecting me?" he questioned.

"Whatever gave you that impression?" she responded, beaming.

He then picked her up lightly and carried her to the bed. They had most of two days remaining and a night between to make up for many lost months.

Would that life concentered on the joys of two lovers loving. Unfortunately, in the Imperfect Worlds, duties and sorrows too often interfere. Some are lucky, and for them such intrusions are fewer, though never absent even among the luckiest. Yet for many, what few joys they have are dampened by the demands of the world, or by the evil choices of others who in their jealousy cannot allow them to experience what they themselves can never know. For their sake, it was good that these two did not know what the following weeks were to bring, for if they had, the enchantment—and the blessing—associated with these all too short days together may, out of fear, never have taken place. And the Kingdom of Nant—indeed all of Dumhoni—would have suffered from the denial of those delight-filled hours. But also, at the individual level, joys, no matter how few or how short, can help sustain one through the worst depression. This would prove the case for Nikal and Dira.

Works by Terry Lee Martin

Fiction:

HEIRS TO THE TAXIARCH

Book 1: *Seeds of the Guardian*   (2021 Silver Goblet Press)
Book 2: *Companions in Prophecy*   (Forthcoming in 2021)
Book 3: *Brothers of Myghal*   (Forthcoming in 2021)
Book 4: *Daughters of Vanayema*   (Forthcoming in 2022)
Book 5: *Champions of Dumhoni*   (Forthcoming in 2023)

Non-fiction:

"Love's Young Dream," The Letters of Dr. Edward Noel Franklin to Miss Nannie Hillman—1871   (2018 Silver Goblet Press)

About the author:

Terry Lee Martin is a native Tennessean, an alumnus of the University of Tennessee at Martin with majors in Psychology and History. Having received teacher's certification through Tennessee Technological University, Martin taught high school history, psychology, government, economics, and geography. Martin lives in Tennessee with his wife and two sons. His first book, the non-fiction work, *"Love's Young Dream," The Letters of Dr. Edward Noel Franklin to Miss Nannie Hillman—1871*, explores two prominent Middle Tennessee families of the antebellum and postbellum South. The book received positive reviews by professors and historians. Martin has presented his research at various historical societies. Martin's venture into fiction began with his fantasy world-building in the early 2000s, coming to fruition in his *Heirs to the Taxiarch* book series. The first volume, *Seeds of the Guardian*, was published in 2021 by Silver Goblet Press. All rights to these works, their content, art, symbols, and maps are reserved. Contact Martin at the following email address: tmartin@silvergobletpress.com

Visit the *Silver Goblet Press* website to find Martin's blog along with details and updates on his publications: *www.silvergobletpress.com*

CPSIA information can be obtained
at www.ICGtesting.com
Printed in the USA
LVHW081508220121
677206LV00026B/557/J